THE
GOOD
WIFE

BOOKS BY ELLERY KANE

The House Sitter

ROCKWELL AND DECKER SERIES

Watch Her Vanish

Her Perfect Bones

One Child Alive

THE
GOOD
WIFE

ELLERY KANE

bookouture

Published by Bookouture in 2022

An imprint of Storyfire Ltd.
Carmelite House
50 Victoria Embankment
London EC4Y 0DZ

www.bookouture.com

ISBN: 978-1-80314-849-6
eBook ISBN: 978-1-80314-848-9

"There is no client as scary as an innocent man."

–Michael Connelly

PROLOGUE

Tonight would change everything. She felt it deep in her bones. It reverberated in the solid thump of her heart and thrummed through her veins while she dressed in the dark. She moved quickly and took only what she needed.

Outside, the wind cut right through her, daring her to turn back. But she only picked up her pace. He would be waiting. And that made her quiver with anticipation. Just the thought of him. The thought of winning. She felt triumphant. Nothing could stop her now.

When she finally spotted her destination, she smiled to herself. Soft yellow light glowed from within, and she imagined him inside. Tonight would most certainly change everything. It would make up for all that had gone wrong before him. It would make her whole again. It would bring her back to life.

She approached the entrance, exhilarated when the door opened to her touch.

AFTER

CASSIE

ONE

I straddled my still-sleeping husband. I felt powerful up there, with my legs squeezing against him, his body already responding to my touch. I traced the familiar tattoos on the curve of his bicep, watched his lashes flutter. Right then, he belonged to me and no one else. The way it should be.

As I leaned in to kiss his neck, I eyed the baby monitor on the nightstand. Seventeen-month-old Abby nestled in her crib, mercifully silent. Her little arms stretched above her head, just like her father's. Already, she had his features. Sometimes, I lay awake and watched her sleep, marveling at her perfection.

"Hello there." Theo squinted up at me. His hands roamed my thighs, the guitar calluses on his fingers rough against my skin. He sounded groggy. He still smelled of alcohol, and he'd shown up late and rain-soaked to our anniversary dinner at Serafina. But I lowered my mouth to his anyway, hopeful that he still wanted me in spite of it all. The unexpected pregnancy that gave us Abby. The road map of stretch marks on my once-flat stomach. The corporate law firm job that demanded too much of me, too much of both of us.

"This is your wake-up call," I whispered into his ear, inhaling the familiar scent of him.

"I slept like a log." He groaned and closed his eyes again. "I blame the champagne. I haven't felt this hungover since college."

"Oh." His rejection always hurt but it stung worse this morning. "If you're not feeling well..."

He grabbed my wrists, holding me in place, and glanced over at the monitor. "Is Abby still out?"

"For now. But it's almost seven." I didn't need to explain. Theo knew Abby's schedule better than anyone. Better than me.

"So, you're telling me I better work fast then."

My heart swelled with relief, but I didn't let on. Instead, I pressed my lips to his jaw, teasing him. "Mr. Stone is always saying, 'Work smarter, not harder.'"

"Oh, *does* he? Well, you tell your boss I can be efficient when I have to be."

I giggled as he flipped me on the bed. It had been a while since we'd laughed like this. Come to think of it, Theo seemed different this morning. Lighter. Like a weight had been lifted. Reading his moods came easily to me. I could sense the change in his weather by his eyes. Like now, for instance. The way he gazed down at me like no one else existed. Maybe I hadn't messed things up, hadn't driven him away.

"I love you, Cass. You know that, right? No matter what."

I answered by tugging him closer, his bare chest warm and heavy on mine. I liked him right there, with no space between us, knowing he could crush me if he wanted but never would. And that's love boiled down, isn't it? Giving him a loaded gun and trusting him not to pull the trigger.

The knock on the front door startled me. The sound seemed so foreign, so out of place for an early morning in quiet Noe Valley, especially the Sunday after Christmas, that I thought I'd imagined it. I concentrated on Theo's mouth nipping at my shoulder, but it came again, louder this time.

"Do you hear that?" I asked.

Theo whispered into my hair, "Ignore it. Whoever it is will go away."

The knocking grew more insistent, almost threatening, setting off a pounding in my chest. Then Abby began to cry, her fraught whining building quickly to a desperate wail. I stiffened beneath him.

With a frustrated huff, Theo pushed himself off of me, leaving me cold, and padded down the hallway toward the nursery. After he disappeared from view, I heard him call out, "Will you get the door, hon?"

I thrust off the covers and tugged back on the T-shirt Theo had discarded at the foot of the bed. While I searched for my sweatpants, I watched him on the monitor, clutching Abby to him and swaying to their own rhythm. Already, her crying had slowed.

Downstairs, the knocking came once more. "San Francisco Police. Anybody home?"

When I peered through the peephole, my mouth went dry. A uniformed officer waited on the stoop. His badge loomed impossibly large through the concave lens, conjuring my father's ghost, and my lungs pinched shut. I flung open the door before the memory overwhelmed me.

At least it had finally stopped raining. I inhaled a gulp of damp air. "Good morning, Officer. Is everything alright?"

I sized him up with a glance. He looked harried, apologetic. The name, Pettigrew, embroidered with gold thread on his breast.

"Does Theo Copeland live here?" he asked.

"That's my husband. He's—"

"I'm here. I'm right here." Theo stopped halfway down the staircase with Abby in his arms. A hard sleeper like her daddy, her blonde hair stuck out adorably in all directions. "What's the problem, Officer?"

"Do you lease the building at 865 Church Street?"

"Actually, we own it. I use it as a rehearsal space. But it's more of a fun thing these days. Gotta grow up some time, you know?"

I marveled at the casual way he said it. Not a trace of bitterness. Not a hint of fear.

The officer nodded glumly. "There's been an incident, and we need access to the property. Would you mind coming with me?"

"What kind of incident?" I asked, before my husband could answer. I couldn't help the clipped tone of my voice. As the youngest senior partner in the history of Stone and Faber, my inner lawyer wouldn't be silenced. I needed details. I needed an explanation. And I didn't trust cops. Which was exactly why I'd chosen corporate, not criminal, law.

"A homeless man discovered a dead body in the dumpster behind your husband's studio."

Stricken, I turned to Theo, only to find him right behind me, with a rare frown darkening his face. Abby clung to his neck, her head buried in the crook. I wished I could do the same.

"And it's a good thing he did, since it's garbage day. She would be well on her way to the landfill by now."

"*She?*" Theo repeated, looking horrified. "How did she die?"

The officer made a face that told me all I needed to know. "From what we've gathered, it looks like a homicide. A body doesn't just turn up in a dumpster on accident. Anyway, we're asking all the tenants to come down and make sure there's nothing out of the ordinary."

"Of course. Just give me a few minutes to get dressed and..." Abby squirmed in Theo's arms before he shifted her to his other hip, absentmindedly pressing his lips to her forehead. Watching them together, I felt a rush of gratitude. I understood why the other mothers in "Stroller Valley" envied me. Being a stay-at-home dad came naturally to Theo. But then, everything came naturally to him.

"I'll go with you," I said. "Your mom can watch her for a bit."

"No, you should stay. I'm sure it'll be a quick trip." Theo glanced at the table in the hall. "Hey, have you seen my phone?"

I evaluated the officer's noncommittal expression, the way his gaze roamed over my shoulder and into the living room and beyond. I shook my head at Theo and reached for Abby. "It's probably still in your jeans pocket. Or your leather jacket from last night."

As Theo headed back up the stairs, I called after him, "Phone your mom. I'm sure she'll be thrilled to spend the morning with her granddaughter."

The officer waited in the foyer with me, making silly faces at Abby. She wriggled until I set her down, then toddled to the corner, where she plopped in front of the coat rack, babbling and smacking her fingers on the floor with glee. *"Wawa wawa..."*

"Cute kid," he said. "I've got my first on the way. Any advice?"

But I barely heard him. I understood Abby's gibberish now, and a cold sensation gripped me like a hand to the back of my neck. A small puddle of rainwater had formed on the hardwood directly beneath Theo's black raincoat. It was wet. All wet.

My mother-in-law, Gloria, swooped in ten minutes later in a full face of makeup and a garish Christmas sweater, the standard grandmother holiday uniform. Her silver bob perfectly coiffed, like she'd been waiting for the call.

"Come to Grandma." Abby willingly surrendered to her arms, content there.

"Has she eaten?" Gloria directed the question to Theo, though I stood directly in front of her. She had a way of making me feel unseen, even in my own home. But I supposed I had myself to blame for that. Gloria had quit her job as a dental assistant one week after she'd given birth to Theo and never returned to the office. *I don't know how you do it*, she'd told me more than once. *I could never have left my baby at home with Tom.*

"We just got up." I maintained the practiced neutrality it had taken years of law school to cultivate. On a typical workday, I managed multimillion-dollar mergers. I could certainly handle a disapproving mother-in-law. "But I can heat up some oatmeal."

"No need, dear. I'll sort it out." She set Abby in her high chair, smoothing her wild tufts of hair into submission. "I know what she likes. She always eats for me."

It felt like a dig—I knew it was—but I ignored it even when Theo bristled on my behalf, flashing me an apologetic smile. Gloria wouldn't get the best of me. Not today.

"Thanks for watching her."

"It's no trouble at all. I just hope everything is okay."

I planted a kiss on Abby's forehead before I followed Theo to the door. I paused there, letting him go ahead with the officer, and turned my attention to his coat. My stomach curdled when I touched the sleeve, the hood, the back panel, soaked with rainwater.

When Theo popped his head back in—"Are you coming?" —my heart skipped like a pebble across a lake.

"Just grabbing my jacket."

"You don't need it," he said, pointing toward the dawning sky, the color of a grapefruit. "It's going to be a beautiful day."

TWO

In the back of the police cruiser, Theo reached for my hand, giving it a reassuring squeeze. He knew enough about my father to understand my rigid spine, my sweaty palms. All courtesy of Sergeant Mickey Maines, the ghoul I couldn't shake, no matter how many years had passed since my mother laid him in the ground in Buttonwillow Cemetery. Now, she lay next to him, joined to that asshole for all eternity. For worse or better, exactly how she'd wanted it.

The sight of the red-brick façade of Theo's rehearsal space came as a relief. Known simply as The Spot, it sat in the middle of a triplex, bookended by an artist's studio and a secondhand bookstore. Yellow crime scene tape stretched obscenely across the alleyway, and as the officer pulled to a stop, I craned my neck to see down the shadowy expanse of pavement that led to the dumpster and the chain-link fence beyond.

The slick concrete shimmered in the sunlight like a golden road. At its end, a dozen more officers just like the man who'd greeted us at our door thirty minutes ago. Nondescript but powerful still, they moved en masse. *Cops stick together*, my father always reminded me, which had terrified me more than anything else, because it meant my mother and I were trapped. No one would come to our rescue.

"Wait here," Officer Pettigrew told us. "I'll get the detectives."

I stepped out of the cruiser and into the cool, moist air, hugging my arms against my midsection. Theo joined me there, key in hand.

"This is surreal. And creepy." He gave voice to my thoughts, as I stared at the gray lump resting in front of the dumpster. A body bag, I realized.

"Yeah. Really creepy."

A few curious bystanders stood behind the tape, snapping pictures with their cells. The sight of them jogged my memory. "Did you ever find your phone?" I asked Theo.

"No. I must've been drunker than I thought. But I'm sure it'll turn up."

Before I could remind Theo that I'd helped him into bed last night, a heavyset woman emerged from the alleyway and flashed her badge. Unlike her male counterparts, she didn't puff out her chest or walk with a swagger. She smiled and offered her hand.

"Detective Henrietta Mason. How are you folks this morning?"

"Hungover," Theo said, with a laugh. Already, he'd succumbed to her charm. "Yesterday was our two-year wedding anniversary."

"Well, happy anniversary. I'm sorry we had to drag you down here. But my partner and I want to cover all bases. I'm sure Officer Pettigrew briefed you on the situation."

"A dead body in the dumpster." I cringed, as we trailed Detective Mason down the sidewalk toward the front entrance of The Spot.

"A young white female. Well dressed, well nourished. Somebody will be looking for her soon. You can bet on that."

"That sounds awful. How can we help?" I wished I could be as trusting as Theo. But the other shopfronts were dark, their tenants nowhere in sight. My insides twisted into a knot.

"Do you have any security cameras on your property?"

Theo shook his head. "Never thought we needed one."

Detective Mason gestured to the door. Through the reflection in the glass, I spotted a man approaching from behind us. He had the look. The one meant to remind anyone in shouting distance exactly who was in charge. Already, I knew he wouldn't like me. My father certainly never had. When he died, I felt like I'd finally managed to outrun my own shadow. Still, he kept reappearing, reincarnated, to remind me of my place.

"This is my partner, Frank Kincaid. Now, if we could just take a look inside and make sure that everything is as it should be, we'll get you two lovebirds on your way home to enjoy the rest of your anniversary weekend."

Theo inserted the key into the lock and pushed the door open, allowing Detective Kincaid to cross the threshold first.

He took a slow turn around the room, pausing to admire Theo's retro poster collection of rock icons that hung above the old leather sofa, along with his first guitar. Then, he made his way past the acoustic foam and speakers toward the heart of the place. The vintage drum set I'd given Theo for his thirty-first birthday. Before marriage, before Abby. Before real life set in. I wished I could get that girl back. The girl in the front row who'd sung until her throat hurt. Who'd caught the lead singer's eye and captured his heart. In the years since, I'd lost her somehow, buried her under a mountain of diapers and legal briefs.

"So, you're a musician then?"

"Used to be." Theo ran his hand along the smooth surface of the ride cymbal. "These days I'm a stay-at-home dad to our daughter, Abby, singing 'The Wheels on the Bus.'"

"*Go round and round.*" When Detective Kincaid chuckled, his belly shook beneath his starched button-down. His playfulness made me wonder if I'd misjudged him. I only ever heard my father laugh at my mother's expense. "I know that one," he said.

"Don't be so humble, babe." I jabbed Theo with a playful elbow. "He's an accomplished singer-songwriter. You might recognize him from—"

"*Starbound*!" Detective Mason smacked her hands together and gestured toward the shelves in the corner where Theo displayed his *Starbound* finalist statuette. It sat beside the stuffed bear one of Theo's young guitar students had gifted him months ago. "I knew you looked familiar. You were in that band... oh, what were they called?"

"The Sluggers." Theo shrugged off the attention like always, but I knew it mattered to him. Everyone wants to be seen, to be noticed. To be special. Maybe that's where I'd gone wrong. I'd stopped noticing him. I'd let my job consume me. "But that was years ago. These days, I just play for fun and teach guitar lessons here and there when I have the time."

"Did you come in yesterday?" Detective Kincaid fiddled with a drumstick as he lobbed the question. His casualness worried me.

"Uh, around four or so." Theo glanced at me, looking down when our eyes met. "I had a songwriting session for about an hour."

"With a student?"

"Yeah, I guess you could call her that. She's a friend of ours. She works as a nanny for the Hamiltons—a family down the street. I taught her to play guitar, and we wrote a few songs together. She's really talented."

"Elise Sterling," I offered. Someone had to save Theo from himself. He talked too much when he got nervous.

The detectives exchanged a pointed glance that Theo seemed not to notice. "And your daughter?"

"She came along."

"Abby can't get enough of the drums," I said.

"Can you blame her? You know, there's a place in Berkeley that offers drumming therapy. They say it's cathartic." Detective Mason grinned. Her warmth came as a welcome reprieve from her partner's no-nonsense interrogation. But he didn't miss a beat.

"And after? You locked up, I presume."

Theo nodded. "I locked up, dropped Abby with the sitter, and took a taxi to Serafina for dinner with my wife. Do you think someone broke in here?"

"We're not sure what happened, Mr. Copeland. But we've got a girl out there, bludgeoned to death and drag marks in the wet asphalt from your back door to the dumpster. We're still trying to figure it all out, same as you." Detective Kincaid shrugged. But I didn't buy it. Cops always know more than they let on. And he'd just dropped a couple of well-timed bombs on us. "Could we take a look at your cellphone?"

Theo absentmindedly patted the back pocket of his blue jeans. "It's missing. Or I misplaced it. I'm not sure which. I had a little too much to drink last night."

"Is Theo a suspect?" I asked.

"Of course I'm not a suspect, Cass. Why would I be a suspect?" The silence stretched too thin. Like a rubber band about to break. "*Am* I a suspect?"

"Let's sit down," Detective Mason suggested, indicating the sofa.

Only Theo sat. He sank into the butterscotch cushions like he wanted to disappear and waited for her to deliver his fate. I kept watch on Detective Kincaid, who'd begun to wander again. I wondered if they'd rehearsed this little act, which seemed to be headed for its climax.

"We were able to locate the victim's identification in her back pocket."

I steeled myself, resting my hand on Theo's shoulder.

"I believe you know her."

Theo swallowed hard. "I do?"

"You both do, apparently."

Suddenly, my knees felt weak. Detective Mason waited while I joined my husband on the sofa where we'd once made love. A relic from his bachelor pad, Theo had insisted on keeping it. I clung to the worn armrest like a life raft.

"Her name was Elise. Elise Sterling."

The sharp intake of Theo's breath matched my own. I couldn't look at him. I thought I might be sick.

Theo doubled over, wincing as if the detective had landed an elbow in his gut. "Elise? That's not possible. I just saw her. She was—"

"You *just* saw her? But you told us—"

"That's not what I meant. It was yesterday afternoon, exactly like I said. I'm telling the truth. I would never hurt her." He stared off for a beat too long. "Have you called the Hamiltons? Bryce and Caroline. They'll be... oh, God."

Theo stumbled over his words, unable to finish his sentence, so I coped the only way I knew. Somebody had to pull the ripcord and fast. "We're done here. He's not answering any more questions."

"But, Cass, I don't have anything to hide. It's fine. I want to help."

I turned to him, lowering my voice. "It's not up for debate. You need an attorney."

"You *are* an attorney."

"Exactly. And I'm telling you, *as an attorney*, to keep your mouth shut." I forced myself to stand, to face both detectives head-on, even as my legs trembled beneath me. When Elise's face swam across my eyes, I squeezed them shut for a moment. "I'm afraid we have to ask you both to leave unless you have a search warrant."

Detective Mason gave me a pitying look. As if she had a

clue what it felt like to be me. Right here, right now. In the middle of the firestorm. She had no fucking idea. The sense of peace I'd felt that morning had been blown to bits.

"We don't have a warrant, Mrs. Copeland. Not yet."

"But we will." Detective Kincaid waved his partner over, pointing solemnly to the wall. I forced myself to follow her, to look. Two specks of red dotted the brick. So small, they would have been easy to miss. But Kincaid had the same eagle eyes as my father, spotting a jelly stain on my shirt, a dish out of place in the china hutch. Any little mistake could set him off. And to him, no mistake was little.

"It looks like paint," I said.

"Blood spatter," he pronounced. "I have a feeling when we get the Bluestar in here, this place will light up like a Christmas tree."

Our own Douglas fir still stood in the den. We'd picked it out together from the lot on Market Street and decorated it with the help of Theo's mother. Belting out "Jingle Bells," Theo had lifted an awestruck Abby to place the angel on top. Thinking of our daughter, I searched Theo's panicked eyes for a sign. But behind his fear, he looked the same to me. He looked like my husband. I had to defend him.

"We'll see about that."

After I escorted the detectives out the front door, they didn't leave. I'd only made them more determined. Detective Mason quickly retrieved her cell, no doubt securing that warrant, while Kincaid waited like a dutiful soldier, standing guard at the window. His gaze fixed on the brick wall, on those two red spots.

I turned the lock and pointed Theo toward the room at the back, a small unfinished space where he kept all the unsold band merchandise. We had to hash this out here, not in front of

Abby. Certainly not in front of Gloria. My mother-in-law would find some way for this to be my fault. Me and my "corporate" job. She always made it sound like a dirty word. To her, a woman could only play one part.

"Is there anything you need to tell me?" I asked Theo, shutting us inside. The only light came from a bare bulb flickering from above. "We need to get out ahead of this. If you know something, tell me now so I can think about what to do."

"*Really*? That's how you want to start this conversation?" Theo's jaw clenched, as he ran a hand through his chestnut hair. His eyes welled. "*Elise is dead.* How about that?"

"I'm well aware. I saw the body bag." I choked back a sob before I started again, softer this time. One of us had to hold it together. "You're right. I'm sorry. There's no playbook for this kind of thing. I just want to be sure you and I are on the same page here."

"The same page?"

"Yeah. Those detectives aren't going away." My husband could be painfully naïve.

"I know that, Cass. But I didn't do anything wrong. You should've just let me talk to them." Theo flumped down on one of the old boxes, sending up a cloud of dust. Puzzled, he glanced around the space. "Is something missing?"

I frowned.

"That black tarp. The one we used to cover the gear when we painted the place. I swear I stuck it on top of... *what?*"

"You're worried about a piece of plastic?" I shook my head, disbelieving. "Focus. Those detectives mean business."

"Not all cops are like your dad. They seem perfectly reasonable. Besides, I was with you all night. I'll even take a polygraph if they ask."

I couldn't get Theo's raincoat out of my mind now. Abby's wet hands, the puddle on the floor. All the old doubts crept in, summoned from the dark basement where I'd banished them.

They wound their way around my brain, leaving a stain across my face.

"What's that look for?" Theo asked me. "You think I had something to do with this?"

I wanted to yell at him. I wanted to cry. To beg him to tell me the truth, to put me out of my misery. The cramped room suddenly felt too small for both of us, and a hot rash flamed up my neck. "Of course not. But can you blame me for wondering? You haven't been honest with me lately."

"Not this shit again."

Just like that I went right back there. To that first day, six months ago. The beginning and end of everything. It still ached like an open wound. And now, I could only wonder exactly what Theo had done.

THREE

Theo snorted in frustration. He pushed himself up from the dusty box and began to pace the small storage room like a caged animal. "How many times do I have to tell you? I did not have an affair with Elise."

"I saw you two together. I saw the way she looked at you. The way you looked back. I found her bra in the sofa cushions. I'm not stupid."

"You told me you trusted me. You told me you believed me about the bra. I thought we were good. I mean, last night was good, right?"

Good. The word clunked around in my head. Theo had no clue how adept I could be at pretending. At white-knuckling it. At saying what he needed to hear. But that wouldn't help him now. Brutal honesty. That's what he needed. "I was trying to trust you. *Trying.* That was before Elise turned up dead behind your studio. Before they found blood on the wall."

"Seriously, Cass? You remember what a mess this place was when I moved in. It's probably paint. You said it yourself."

The place *had* been a mess. But I'd found it for a steal, after we moved to the three-bedroom rowhouse in Noe Valley, and used a chunk of my savings to buy it outright. Because I knew how much Theo had given up to make me happy. We'd fixed it up together, slinging paint at each other like two kids.

"What about your jacket?" I asked.

Theo looked clueless. "What about it?"

"It was soaking wet. I felt it myself. You went somewhere after we got back from dinner last night." I replayed the entire scene. Slipping into the slinky dress I hadn't worn since my pre-baby days. It fit a little snug across the hips and belly. Theo's late arrival, his effusive apologies. The champagne. The filet. The chocolate sponge cake. A single malt Scotch or two for Theo. Coffee for me. We'd both been in bed by midnight. At least, I thought we had.

"Where would I have gone?"

"That's not an answer." I made one last try, pleading with him. "Why was your jacket wet?"

"Jesus Christ. You're acting *crazy*." I hated that word. It was classic Mickey Maines, directed at my mom to belittle her, to gain the upper hand. To leave her doubting herself, the same way I'd doubted myself for months now.

"I'm not crazy."

"I shouldn't have said that. But it pisses me off when you make me sound like a liar. A cheater. I can't stand it, Cass. And you know why."

I backed off a little. I *did* know. "If there's something you're hiding, just tell me. You can tell me anything. I can handle it."

That wasn't true. Not really. Some words can't be spoken aloud without shifting the entire world off its axis.

"Well?" I asked.

Finally, he'd had it with me. He threw up his hands, then retreated behind them, burying his face. I fixated on those hands. I loved those hands. Strumming his guitar, caressing my cheek, comforting our daughter. I tried to imagine them being something else, something rotten. Something evil.

"Look, I was pretty damn toasted last night. I lost my phone, for God's sake. I don't remember leaving the house, but if I did, I'm sure I had a good reason. With the storm picking up, I probably got worried about the patio furniture blowing around out there. You know that the wind will turn those chairs into projectiles."

I could've reminded him that I'd stacked the chairs and secured the umbrella weeks ago, when the first winter rainstorm hit San Francisco. But he seemed on the verge of collapse, and we still had to walk out of this place, past the detectives, and the three blocks home. For better or worse, I had to get him through it.

"Alright. That makes sense."

"Really? You believe me?"

I nodded, and Theo tugged me to him. When I started to pull away, he only gripped me tighter. I glanced up over his shoulder at the storage room, remembering the black tarp. I'd folded it myself and laid it on the stack of boxes furthest from the door. Over time, its color grayed with dust. Where it had gone, I could only guess.

FOUR

A block away from the studio and safely out of earshot of the detectives, I turned to Theo. "Before we head home, maybe we should swing by Serafina to see if your phone turned up. I'd rather us find it than the detectives."

Theo nodded, his hopes momentarily buoyed. "Good idea. I'd bet anything it's there."

We didn't speak on the walk to the restaurant, but I let Theo hold my hand, as if the morning had never happened. I forced a smile at the harried mother zipping her daughter's jacket, the old man on the bench. The young couple arm in arm while they crossed the street. They all seemed alien to me. Like actors in a play.

"It's packed." Theo pointed up ahead at the Sunday brunch crowd spilling from the restaurant. The smell of crepes and the sounds of laughter had already reached us, making me feel more alone even with Theo beside me. The world kept turning while Elise lay dead, zipped in a body bag a few blocks over. With the front door looming, a wave of nausea swept over me.

"Let me handle this," I said, breathing through it. "It's best if I'm the one asking the questions."

Theo followed me as I wove through the cramped entrance and approached the hostess stand. A pretty blonde blinked back at me, a toothy smile brightening her face. She reminded me of Elise.

"Did anyone turn in a cellphone last night? My husband's is missing."

She glanced at Theo behind me, her eyes stuck for a moment. When I cleared my throat, she snapped back to earth. "Uh, I'll check and see."

"It has a unique case," Theo added. "It looks like a guitar, with the sound hole and the strings."

The hostess disappeared into the coatroom. When she returned empty-handed, Theo groaned.

"I'm so sorry. Why don't you write down your contact information? My name is Haley. I'll be sure to call if it turns up."

"That won't be necessary," I said. But already, Theo had jotted his name and my cell number on the back of the restaurant manager's card. He slipped it to her with a grin.

"Haley, would you please ask around? I really need my phone back."

She peeked at the card, a flush reddening her cheeks, and looked past me to my husband. I'd suddenly become invisible.

"It *is* you. The gal who works nights told me you come in here sometimes, but I didn't believe her. You know, I saw your band in concert right after your season of *Starbound*. You were amazing. Do you think, maybe, if it's not too much trouble, I could get your autograph?"

I watched Theo in disbelief. The easy way he moved under the weight of her adoration unnerved me. "I'll do you one better. How 'bout a picture?"

The hostess squealed. She slipped her cell from her pocket and thrust it at me. "Would you mind?"

I did mind. Very much. But I took the phone anyway and aimed the lens at the two of them, counting them down until I snapped the photo. When Theo wrapped a muscled arm around her slim shoulders, I worried she might swoon. The sliver of space between them disappeared completely. "Big smiles, in three, two, one..."

After Theo waved goodbye, he tossed a smirk over his shoulder. "Keep an eye out for that phone, Haley."

She twittered. "Of course."

Outside the restaurant, I hissed at him, "What was that?"

"You catch more flies with honey, Cass. I guarantee she'll be on the lookout for my phone now. Hell, I bet it'll turn up by the end of the day."

"Yeah. And what if the cops stop by here in the meantime? It's not a good look, Theo. You cozying up to a female fan just after you've been questioned in a murder case."

His shoulders slumped. "You're right. I didn't even think about it. I don't get recognized that often these days. I figured I should make the most of it."

I walked ahead of him until we reached the corner, letting my frustration subside. I understood his motives. *Get the phone back.* That made sense.

"I'm really sorry." Theo reached for my hand again while we waited for the light to change. "I wasn't thinking."

"Don't worry about it." I managed a half-hearted smile. "I cropped you out of the photo anyway."

As we neared the house, Theo squeezed my hand tighter. "Can you deal with my mom?"

"What should I say?"

He shrugged. "Just get rid of her. Tell her I'll call her later."

"I'll try my best. But you know how she is." Gloria wasn't the kind of mother-in-law you sent away. Since Theo's dad died, she'd practically moved in with us, buying the first house with a FOR SALE sign on our block. I couldn't hold it against her.

With Freddie gone, she had no one left to care for, and the ghosts of an imperfect marriage to haunt her. I'd peeked in her medicine cabinet before and seen the orange bottles, evidence of her struggles.

When I opened the gate, I spotted Abby at the window, her little face pressed to the glass. She pointed at Theo and squealed. *Dada.*

"So much for slipping in unnoticed." Theo smiled back at her, waving like a goof. I tried to put on a cheery face but I couldn't really manage it.

By the time we reached the front porch, Gloria already waited at the door, holding Abby on her hip. "Is everything okay?"

Theo sighed, reaching for our daughter, and left me there in the foyer alone with his mother. To clean up his mess.

"Remember the Hamiltons' nanny, Elise?" I headed inside, making my way to the kitchen, and Gloria followed.

"Isn't Theo helping her with her music? He said she's a sweet girl, if I remember correctly. Good with Abby, too."

"Well, she's dead. Murdered." I'd planned to break it to her gently. But she never gave it a rest, and her little jabs hurt worse than I let on. Every late night at the office, every early morning, every first I missed, chipped away at my heart. I already felt like a terrible mother. I didn't need her constant reminders.

Mouth agape, Gloria stared at me. The last time I saw that face Theo had just told her we'd eloped to Vegas. That I was eight weeks pregnant. "Oh, dear. That's atrocious. Do the police know what happened?"

Theo appeared in the doorway, with Abby latched tight to his leg. When I reached my arms out to her, she shook her head willfully. Like a lightning rod, our daughter always sensed a change in the weather between us. Naturally, she took her father's side.

"Mom, it's been a long morning. Cass and I need to be alone for a while."

"Alright. I get it. I'm in the way." Gloria sulked while she made a show of putting on her coat, probably hoping one of us would stop her. But Theo had already disappeared again. "If you need me, I'll be at home. Alone. Worrying, like I always do."

"Wait." As Gloria opened the front door, I grabbed her shoulder.

"Did Abby eat okay?" I whispered, my cheeks already hot with shame. *Please say no. Please say no.*

"A whole cup of oatmeal. She gobbled it right up. And she used her spoon too."

"No problems?"

"Not a one." She smiled sweetly, before cutting me off at the knees. "Don't beat yourself up, dear. Mothering doesn't come naturally to everyone."

The sound of Theo's voice led me to Abby's room. I stood beyond the doorway and out of sight, peering in at them, until my boiling blood cooled to a simmer. "You're such a good mommy," he told her.

Abby cradled her baby doll in front of her.

"Mama," she parroted back to Theo. I still got a thrill every time she said it. With all the time she spent with her father, I couldn't believe "mama" had been her first word. It gave me hope that I hadn't done it all wrong. Take that, Gloria.

She carefully laid the doll on the floor, covering it with her favorite blanket. "Go night-night."

"What should we do while the baby sleeps?" Theo asked, joining her on the floor. He gave her his full attention. I felt jealous of that sometimes, the way they disappeared into their own world. Most days, Abby treated me like an interloper. I never expected how that would crush me. How I'd pad into the nursery, exhausted from another twelve-hour day, and beg her to forgive me. To love me.

"*Shh.*" Abby held a finger to her lips, then toddled over to her toybox, where she retrieved a pink bottle. "Baba eat."

"Oh, so *now* she's hungry?" He grinned at Abby. Like it was any other Sunday. "Better feed her before she starts to cry."

Abby crouched down, pressing the bottle to the doll's lips, and I watched her, rapt.

"You *are* a good mommy." I made a face at Theo. "What a good baby too, eating like that. She'll grow up big and strong like her daddy."

Theo chuckled. "Subtle, Cass. Real subtle."

Abby carted her doll into the corner and propped her up on the sleeper chair. I shrugged at Theo, lowering my voice. "Remember what the doctor said. She's working through something."

She's fine, Theo mouthed. Which made me feel like I wasn't. "Mom says I was a picky eater too."

"Speaking of, I got rid of her like you asked. Do you want to talk about it?"

Theo didn't answer.

"We should probably talk—"

"Baba sad." Abby rocked the doll in her arms, while she made her way back to Theo's side. She wobbled a bit, losing her footing when her bare foot tangled in the blanket, and went down hard on her knees. I beat Theo to her, scooping her up as she wailed. For a moment, she clung to me, wetting my shoulder with her tears. For a moment, she needed me. I savored it.

"It's okay," Theo told her, hurrying over to us. "You're okay."

When Abby heard his voice, she had to have him. I couldn't hold it against her. I'd done this to myself, cutting my maternity leave two weeks short at Mr. Stone's insistence. Even now, I worked too long and too hard. After you've sold your soul to make partner, you most certainly don't fuck it up.

Feeling like an outsider, I left them to listen to their sounds through the wall in the master bedroom. I searched for Theo's missing phone, first in the pockets of the dark-wash jeans he'd chucked on the floor last night and the leather jacket he'd slung over the ottoman. Then, in all the usual places. On the nightstand, on the bathroom counter, beneath the bed. I even wandered downstairs to check between the sofa cushions, trying not to think about what I'd found the last time I'd gone looking there.

Overcome with sudden exhaustion, I returned to the bedroom and crawled beneath the sheets, still unmade from the morning that seemed a lifetime ago. Theo found me there, staring at my own cellphone.

"I put *Peppa Pig* on for Abby. She's glued to the screen like a bug on a windshield."

I couldn't muster a laugh, even to please him.

"Look." I held out the screen, showing him a photograph I'd taken months ago. Elise, at our kitchen table, with Abby balanced on her knee. "I still can't believe she's gone. *Murdered.* Who would do something like this?"

Theo shook his head, as if he couldn't bear to look at Elise with her halo of bright blonde hair and her megawatt smile. I chastised myself for testing him. Of course he didn't want to be reminded. Neither did I. But Theo didn't know loss the way I did. How it could catch you off guard, like a sudden rain shower on a sunny day. How it changed you in ways you never expected. The best way to get through it? Keep your head down. Don't look it in the eyes.

"And why would they do it *there*? At The Spot?"

"Coincidence?" Theo suggested, hardly sounding like he believed it himself. "Maybe Elise forgot something at the studio and some creep followed her back. That makes sense, right?"

I agreed to make us both feel better. One coincidence might be bad luck. But two or more amounted to circumstantial evidence.

"It's already on the Noe Valley Neighbors Facebook page," I said, navigating to the site to show him the proof. "They don't know it was her yet, but it's only a matter of time."

Theo grimaced, reading the comments beneath the post: DEAD BODY FOUND IN DUMPSTER ON CHURCH STREET.

Crazy. I heard the sirens this morning during yoga.
Totally interrupted my flow.
This neighborhood isn't safe for our kids anymore.
So sad. Thoughts and prayers to the victim's family.
Anybody know who?
No, but I know where.

"What a prick." Theo tossed the phone onto the bed. "Shaun DeMarco. Do you see him stirring the pot? 'I know where.' Come to think of it..."

He started pacing. "That guy, *he* should be a suspect. He had a thing for Elise. Remember that night she hurt her ankle? It was probably him following her. And he was always hanging around the playground watching us."

"When was this?" Shaun stood out, and not in a good way, partly because no one understood him. As the owner of the tech company Generation Gamer, he worked from home most days as a video game developer, kept the hours of a vampire, and flew drones around the neighborhood for fun. I wondered if they felt the same about me. A mom who wore business suits instead of leggings and negotiated deals instead of play dates.

"I don't know. Off and on. You've said yourself that the guy is a weirdo."

"I think I called him 'eccentric'. That doesn't make him a murderer."

"Weird. Eccentric. Same difference." Theo paused, his nervous energy vibrating like a force field around him. Abby's gleeful attempt to sing along with the television sounded out of place in the background. "I'm going over there to talk to him."

"What? No, you're not." I grabbed his arm, as if I could hold him there. His skin burned hot beneath my fingers. "That's not a good idea."

"So, what am I supposed to do then? Just wait around here for the detectives to show up?"

"Yes. We wait together. We talk about it. We make a plan. This isn't a game, Theo. You can't charm your way out of it."

As soon as I spit the words at him, I regretted it. I hated myself for using the very thing I loved—his undeniable magnetism—against him.

"I'm not trying to charm my way out of anything. But I'm not going to sit by and—" He dropped his head, turned away from me, and made an awful noise. Guttural and desperate. I didn't understand, not at first.

"Are you okay?"

"She's dead," he said, simply, before he abandoned me again. With a bone-juddering slam of the front door, he silenced Abby's singing, storming out of the house without saying goodbye.

FIVE

I tried to steady my breathing as I retrieved a stray macaroni from my forehead. Seated in her high chair, Abby let out a warrior's cry before she chucked another handful of mac and cheese at me from her plate. I ducked this time, cringing when I heard the splat against the tile. The glob of food landed beside the plastic spoon she'd already hurled like a missile.

Theo had been gone for exactly two hours, leaving me to brave the lunch battlefield alone. Now, I felt defeated once again, completely outmaneuvered by the adorable tyrant I'd birthed myself. But at least it gave me a purpose, a distraction, a place to focus myself.

"C'mon, Abs. Just one bite. You love the star macaroni." I pointed to the fork on her tray, trying to maintain appropriate boundaries. Rule number one for toddlers with 'feeding difficulties,' which seemed a euphemism for the kind of brutal warfare Abby had been waging since day one, when she'd failed to latch. I shouldn't blame myself. I'd done nothing wrong. The nurse said so. But Theo had looked worried. Like maybe I wasn't cut out for this after all. Like my body knew something he didn't.

"No." Abby pounded the tray with her fist.

I held back, keeping a pleasant smile plastered on my face. Rule number two: Maintain a neutral attitude. Don't get anxious or angry.

"What about the banana?" I took an exaggerated bite from the plate I'd fixed for myself. "So good."

Abby selected a small piece of fruit and held it carefully between her fingers. My heart filled with the kind of reckless hope born of despair. Maybe today would be different. What kind of mother can't feed her own child?

When my cellphone rang, it shocked us both. Abby pushed out her lips and frowned at the banana, as if she'd just realized I'd laced it with poison. She dropped it down to the floor below and waited for my reaction.

"Hello?"

A robotic voice greeted me. "You have a collect call from an inmate at San Francisco County Jail. Do you accept the charges?"

Abby released a second banana slice to its doom, followed by another. She craned her neck to see the evidence. "Yes. Yes, I accept."

"Cass? It's me."

"*Theo?* I don't understand. Why are you—"

"Just let me talk, okay? I only have a few minutes." He sounded browbeaten. Like he'd already lost a battle. I could relate.

"Okay. I'm listening."

"I've been arrested. I need you to come down to the station."

Abby watched me with curiosity. She'd stopped crying but her plump cheeks remained flushed.

"Arrested for what? Is this about Elise? I told you not to—"

"Assault and battery. But the police want to talk to me about her too. I don't want to say any more on the phone. These calls are recorded, right?"

"I'm on my way. Don't breathe a word to them until I get there."

Numb, I hung up the phone and sat there, my thoughts racing. I had to tackle Abby's mess. I had to summon Gloria. I had to drive to the station. I had to do all those things, and still, I couldn't move. Theo, in jail for assault? The same Theo who'd once given me the silent treatment after I smushed a house spider beneath my sneaker? It made me wonder if I knew him at all. Or if he'd changed like I had—slowly, imperceptibly—into someone else.

Abby grabbed for the last slice of banana. Anticipating her next move, I reached out to stop her. I had enough to clean already. With one delicate chomp, the banana disappeared into her mouth.

The nondescript gray building in the Northern District of San Francisco smelled no different than the police station in my hometown of Buttonwillow. It reeked of the kind of stress sweat that dampens the armpits and leaves your shirt sticking to the small of your back. The odor had seeped into my father's uniform and clung to the ugly brown recliner where he got drunk every night. Fresh linen and sandalwood scented my corner office at Stone and Faber. Another reason I chose corporate law. It smells better. It smells nothing like my past.

I approached the desk, wishing I'd had time to change out of my sweats. But I'd been desperate to flee from Gloria, to dodge her endless stream of questions. The officer barely raised his eyes to me.

"Your name?" he asked, already bored.

"Cassandra Copeland. I'm here to see my husband, Theo. He's been arrested." I considered pinching myself. It sounded unreal. It sounded like a nightmare.

He hardly blinked. He'd heard it all before. Slothlike, he

gestured to the plastic chairs in the lobby. "Take a seat, ma'am. I'll be with you shortly."

I didn't sit down. I didn't so much as glance at the chairs. Mr. Stone always said, *Everything in life is a negotiation. Make your position known.* "I think you might have misunderstood. Let me reintroduce myself. Cassandra Copeland, attorney-at-law. I will see my client immediately. Unless you'd like to explain to the lieutenant why you violated my husband's due process rights."

"So he's your husband *and* your client? Sounds complicated." Now I had his attention.

If he only knew how simple it had been to fall in love with Theo. The complicated part came after. And it kept getting trickier. Like a knot in a chain that tightens every time you pull. "Are you letting me in, or not?"

Just then, the door buzzed open. When I spotted Detective Kincaid, I plowed right through. I had no choice. Theo didn't stand a chance against him.

"Hey! You can't go in there." The officer made a half-hearted move to stop me, backing down when Kincaid held up a hand.

"It's okay. I'll handle it." The detective glared at me with the intensity of a hawk, and I felt ten years old again. I could practically feel the sting of my father's hand against my cheek. The shame of it always hurt worse than the blow.

"I'm sorry to burst in. But I'm here representing my husband. I'd like to be present during questioning."

"I imagine so." The corner of his mouth ticked up, before he led me to the interrogation room. "I'd want to know if my husband was having an affair with a dead woman, too."

Detective Mason had already backed Theo into a literal corner. He sat there, gray-faced, barely raising his head when I entered the room. The two-way mirror on the wall revealed the black circles beneath my eyes, which looked more like bruises in the unforgiving fluorescent light. I stared directly into the glass, unafraid, knowing someone with a badge watched from the other side, passing judgment.

"Let me do the talking, okay?" I pulled my chair close to Theo's, hoping it would give him strength. I'd never seen him like this. My Theo had confidence in spades. At the very least, my Theo could look me in the eyes.

Detective Kincaid spoke first. "Your husband—uh, *client*—has been arrested for assaulting your neighbor, Shaun DeMarco. Mr. DeMarco alleged that your husband attacked him in his front yard, punching him in the face and destroying a drone in his possession. He was treated by the paramedics for a broken nose."

"No comment," I said, feeling Theo tense beside me.

"That's the least of your problems, Mr. Copeland. We got that warrant, like I told you we would. Those two spots tested presumptive positive for blood."

"That doesn't prove anything," I said. "That blood—if it *is* blood—could belong to anyone, including Theo."

"And he's sticking to his story? That he saw Elise late yesterday afternoon for *songwriting*? That his phone is conveniently missing?"

Kincaid made songwriting sound lascivious. But in the last few months, I'd done the same. I'd made myself sick wondering what went on in those lessons. Where his lips had been, his hands. "Theo already told you when he saw her last. His 'story,' as you put it, hasn't changed, because it's the truth."

Detective Mason finally spoke, addressing me with a curious tone. "You believe him, Mrs. Copeland? You don't have any doubts?"

The dripping jacket. The missing tarp. "No, I don't. Theo would never hurt anyone, much less murder a friend."

"A friend, huh?" Detective Kincaid smirked at me again before he turned his predatory gaze to my husband. "Is that all she was to you, Mr. Copeland? Just a friend? A buddy. She certainly was a knockout."

"Don't say anything." I'd wanted to shake the answer from him myself many times. I couldn't pinpoint when I stopped trusting my husband, only that once I had, it seemed impossible to start again. No matter how Theo tried to convince me, my doubt sprouted from a poison seed and spread its roots in silence until it choked out everything else.

"That's one thing a lot of murderers have in common," Detective Kincaid continued, obviously intent on getting a rise. "The nicest guys. Nobody thought they'd ever hurt a fly. Until they do. Maybe you don't know your husband as well as you think. Maybe, just maybe, he *was* having an affair with Ms. Sterling. Maybe they argued about you yesterday. She wanted to tell you, to confess everything. She wanted him to leave you, wanted to start a brand-new life together. But he was too much of a coward to do it, and she wouldn't take no for an answer. It's a tale as old as time."

A thick lump rose in my throat. I couldn't speak, and Theo followed my lead. Though I'd told him to keep quiet, a part of me wanted him to fight back. To tell the detective he had it all wrong. I wanted so badly to believe him.

"Did you argue with her, Mr. Copeland? Did you realize your charade couldn't last? That Elise Sterling was about to blow your whole world to bits, explode your little family? Hell, you were only trying to protect your wife from yourself."

I drew the line there. He made me sound like a hapless hausfrau. "It seems like you're just spouting theories, Detective. So, unless you have proof—"

"What about a statement from Alberta Knox, the elderly woman who manages the bookstore next door? She told us that she heard a couple arguing in your studio yesterday afternoon. Does that count as proof in your book, Mrs. Copeland?"

"She's eighty years old. And wears a hearing aid. It's hardly a smoking gun."

"Funny how you're the only one talking here. I haven't heard your husband deny my theory." Detective Kincaid moved closer to Theo, so close I could smell his aftershave. The heady scent of it as strong as my father's. "You set up the meeting so you could get rid of her. So you could continue on with your picture-perfect life."

When Theo finally spoke, I barely heard him. "No," he said again. "That's not what—"

I silenced him with a look. Now, I wished he'd said nothing. I needed a bang of a denial, not a whimper. I put my hands in my lap, squeezing the web of skin between my thumb and forefinger. The trick my mother taught me as a girl had always kept me from crying. There was nothing Mickey Maines despised more than the tears of a woman.

"Then how do you explain this?" Detective Mason opened the folder on her lap and slid a sheet of paper across the table toward us.

I didn't want to look. But what else could I do? I scanned the printout of Elise's cellphone records, reading the final text. I showed no emotion as I catalogued the facts.

It had arrived at one thirty this morning.

Meet me at The Spot ASAP. I want to talk about our future.

It came from my husband.

JUNE

SIX AND A HALF MONTHS BEFORE THE MURDER

Theo

SIX

A woman in a tailored suit never failed to turn me on. I watched my wife with awe, as she blotted her burgundy lipstick with a tissue. She tugged at her skirt, the navy fabric stretching against her curves, and made a face at me in the mirror.

"This thing used to fit."

"I'm pretty sure it still does. In fact, it fits better." I stepped behind her and ran my hands down her hips. "You look sexy as hell," I whispered against her hair, wound into a knot at the base of her neck. "*Bewitching.*"

"Ooh. Good word. But you have to say that. You're my husband."

"Lucky for me." I understood how she felt, though. Since Abby arrived eleven months ago, my six-pack had disappeared beneath a ten-pound layer of goldfish crackers and chocolate pudding. Sometimes, I wondered where the old Theo had gone. The cocky musician who'd stood center stage, shirtless, strumming a guitar and belting out his own rock songs on national television. That guy would've dropped dead at the thought of a dad bod. My fifteen minutes of fame crash-landed here in suburbia. But I didn't regret a damn thing. In fact, every time Cassie offered to hire a nanny, I flatly refused.

"Are you sure you have to work late again tonight?" I asked.

Cassie sighed as she buttoned up her blazer. "Unfortunately. Things are really heating up with the MetaTech acquisition, and Mr. Stone needs me to run point on the due diligence. This is the first time he's put me in charge of something so big. As the newest partner in the firm, I have to show him I deserve his confidence."

"I know, I know. It's just that you're bound to miss it. The way Abby's cruising around, she's gonna be walking on her own any day now."

Cassie turned to face me. Her eyes started to well. Not this again. "Do you think I made a mistake? Your mother says Abby's going to have issues. Mommy issues. What if she's right? I mean, look at my mom. She was always too busy keeping up with my dad's moods to pay me much attention. I was just in the way."

"And look how amazing you turned out." I laced my fingers through hers and hoped like hell she'd cut the waterworks. I knew how to comfort Abby when she cried. Feed her, change her, hold her, put her to bed. But Cassie's tears always came from nowhere and caught me off guard.

"You're sweet, Theo. But whatever I am, it's in spite of my parents, not because of them. That's not what I want for our daughter. Maybe I should—"

"Listen, we agreed on this plan. I love staying home with Abby, and I refuse to deprive Stone and Faber of the best damn lawyer they've ever seen. I'm talking Atticus Finch meets Harvey Specter meets Ally McBeal."

She laughed like I knew she would. No matter what, I could always make her laugh. That I could count on. "Wow. Ally McBeal. That's a good pull."

"Thirteen-year-old Theo had a massive crush on Calista Flockhart. Anyway, since you're a partner now, it'll ease up a bit."

"I hope you're right." She didn't sound convinced. And I was only blowing smoke. By now, I knew the drill. Corporate law firms billed by the hour to line their pockets, with their lawyers slaving like cogs in a wheel. Cassie got paid a shit ton of money but it didn't come free. "And you think the eating thing is…"

"Just a phase. I promise. Especially now that she's gobbling up finger foods." I glanced back over my shoulder at Abby in the baby swing. She brightened when she saw me wiggle my fingers at her. She had my chin. But those brown eyes, soaking up the world like a sponge, belonged to Cassie.

"Shit. I'm late." Cassie's body tensed against mine. She placed her palms on my chest, keeping her distance. "Mr. Stone likes to say, 'Early is on time and on time is late and—'"

"'And late is unacceptable.' I remember." I latched onto her wrists and held her there anyway, kissing her. Soft at first, then harder, until I'd worked myself into a frenzy. "But trust me, Cass, if Mr. Stone could see you right now, he'd totally understand. In fact, he'd give me the corporate stamp of approval."

"Raincheck?" She kissed me once more, then pulled away decidedly. You couldn't argue with my wife. She'd earned a degree in arguing. Literally.

"Absolutely."

Pushing the stroller, I jogged up the hill toward the playground. My lungs burned with the effort, but I could run the whole mile now without stopping. It felt good, pushing my body again, testing my limits. Abby seemed to enjoy it too. She squealed with delight each time we traversed a bump in the sidewalk. Already, I could see the usual crowd gathered near the benches between the seesaw and the swings. Cassie called them my fan club.

Alexandra Fairchild stood near the sandbox, keeping close watch on two-year-old Parker and addressing the other women with the snobbish authority of a head cheerleader. Alex and her cardiac surgeon husband owned the largest house on the block; their two oldest kids attended a "private boarding institution"; and Parker had apparently already been accepted into La Petite Academy, the ultra-competitive bilingual preschool downtown. Cassie and I used to make fun of highbrows like the Fairchilds, but last week I'd found a slick brochure in the kitchen drawer. Because preschools have brochures now. Apparently, Stone and Faber had an in at La Petite. No matter that Abby was still in diapers.

"Hi, Theo." Alex tossed her blonde hair over her shoulder and waved at me, as the other mothers swiveled their heads in my direction.

With a nod, I pushed the stroller to the dad bench, also known as *my* bench, and unclipped Abby from the harness. She pointed at the baby swing and shrieked with sheer joy. "Message received. One vote for the swing."

While the mothers fixed their eyes on my back, I carried her over, making airplane noises as I dipped her down and around. Once I secured her in the swing, I flashed the mothers one of my stage smiles. No bright lights, no flashy set, but I could still put on a show.

Usually, Alex would take the opportunity to compliment my stellar dad skills, and the other mothers would enthusiastically agree, all of them oohing and aahing as if I'd cured cancer or won a Grammy, and not simply performed the very tasks they'd been doing for years without notice or accolades. But that morning, Alex and her crew had their heads down, whispering and casting furtive glances. Which could only mean one thing.

I scanned the playground until I found her. The new face in

the crowd. No wonder Alex looked pissed. That face could only be described as Disney Princess flawless. She sat alone near the sandbox, while the Hamiltons' twins, Elliot and Xavier, scooped woodchips into a bucket with their plastic shovels.

I knew Alex's game. She could be as cutthroat as a gang lord. So, I caught the woman's eye and beckoned her closer to introduce myself. Xavier toddled behind her, bucket in tow.

"Theo Copeland. This is my daughter, Abby." She accepted my hand with suspicion. Clearly, she needed an ally. "I haven't seen you around the playground before."

When she smiled shyly and dropped her eyes to my wedding ring, I felt like a total perv. That sounded like the kind of skeevy pick-up line that I would've delivered five years ago.

"Elise Sterling." She leaned down to coo at Abby. "I just started working for Mr. and Mrs. Hamilton. I guess their last nanny didn't work out."

I raised my brows. Like I hadn't heard Alex recount the whole drama last week... several times. *Can you believe the Hamiltons' nanny let the boys drink apple juice? That stuff is pure sugar.* The horror. "I assume you're well acquainted with Caroline Hamilton's stance on sugar?"

"The white devil, you mean? Apparently, she'd sooner I filled their sippy cups with her husband's twenty-year Scotch."

"Or lace their steel-cut oatmeal with rat poison."

"You're horrible. Absolutely terrible." Elise grimaced, and I wondered if I'd gone too far. Though I'd expertly morphed into Theo the House Husband—changing diapers, pureeing carrots and singing lullabies—the old me showed his face sometimes. The kid who'd practiced headbanging in the mirror until he got dizzy had grown into an egomaniacal playboy who went through women like pairs of underwear. Thankfully, father-hood had flipped my good-guy switch. It might've been different if we'd had a boy. But I wanted to be the kind of dad Abby could be proud of.

"That was out of line."

"Totally out of line," she agreed. "I like it."

A sharp laugh burst out of me, drawing the attention of the mothers. I pretended not to notice. "You know, the Hamiltons threatened to sue Georgina for negligence."

"Yikes. I'll have to be extra careful then. I certainly can't afford a lawyer."

"Don't worry. My wife's a lawyer, and a damn good one. If it comes to it, she'll take your case."

"I can see the headline now. The Hamiltons versus the Neglectful Nanny and the Juice Box of Doom. That would be the trial of the century. Speaking of which..." Elise jerked her thumb toward little Elliot. "I better get back to my job. Before I really do screw up."

"Of course."

She walked a few steps before turning back. "Why do you look so familiar?"

I shrugged, half hoping she'd recognize me. It felt good to be recognized by a beautiful woman, especially now that my days of pseudo stardom seemed so far behind me. "Maybe you've seen me around the neighborhood. I stay home with Abby, so..."

"Wow. Your wife is lucky. But I'm sure she knows that."

I nodded, smiled, and gave Abby another push. I wasn't surprised when I spotted Alex advancing toward us. She never missed an opportunity to cause trouble.

"I see you've met our resident celebrity." Alex grabbed onto my bicep, her pointy pink nails digging into my skin possessively like she intended to cart me home in her designer stroller. To my horror, she began to sway next to me, singing, "You're a superstar... you're on center stage... the best singer by far... you'll be on the front page... because you're... *You're*..."

She pointed to Elise with expectation. "C'mon, surely you've seen it. You're not *that* young."

Ignoring the insult, Elise puzzled. Then, her eyes grew

wide. "*Starbound*! Oh my gosh. I feel so stupid. I loved that show. I can't believe they cancelled it."

"Yeah, well, that's what happens when the executive producer turns out to be a womanizer who's harassed half of the contestants. Right, Theo?"

I wouldn't give her the satisfaction of my agreement. Scandal hadn't sunk *Starbound*. A year after The Sluggers won the Gold Microphone, ratings tanked. The network went in a new direction with a reality show about couples in crisis. Apparently, nobody could look away from the train wreck of a failing marriage.

"You're Theo Copeland? I remember your season." Elise gave me that look. My drummer, Danny, and I used to call it the SEG—the starry-eyed gaze—and ten times out of ten, it led to a wild night I wouldn't remember in the morning. There's an exception to every rule, and mine had been Cassie. "I'm a bit of a musician myself. Well, I'm a songwriter mainly. It's just a hobby. But I've been hoping to—"

"Dear, I hate to interrupt but..." Alex clutched her chest. "Did someone steal your stroller?"

Elise whipped around in a panic. "Oh my God. It's gone. Shit, shit, shit. That thing is worth, like..."

"Two weeks' salary," Alex offered.

"More like five."

"Well, you really should be more careful. Strollers are expensive, but babies are priceless. And two babies... I can't imagine how Caroline would feel knowing that you were too busy socializing to keep a close watch on the boys."

Tears filled Elise's eyes before her face crumpled. She hurried over to the sandbox, where the twins sat side by side, making a sand pile. "I would never let them out of my sight."

Alex shrugged. As if she hadn't started this fire. "If you say so."

I slowed Abby to a stop, plucked her from the swing, and rested her on my hip. "C'mon, Alex. Play nice."

"What do you mean? I can't help it if the girl is in over her head. It takes a special sort of person to care for someone else's children. Selfless, attentive, mature. I can already tell you, she's not it."

Elise pretended not to hear her, busying herself with the boys. But the slump of her shoulders gave her away.

"Give the woman her stroller back."

"Or what?" Alex teased, leaning in so close I could smell the cloying scent of her perfume.

"Or I'll let the ladies in on your little secret that your Prada baby bag is a knockoff."

Alex scoffed. "You wouldn't dare. I told you that in confidence."

"Watch me."

"Thanks for your help today." Elise pushed her fancy double stroller alongside mine, as we headed back down the hill. After issuing my threat, Alex had scurried to retrieve the missing stroller from behind the fence, where one of her crew had hidden it. "I thought I'd graduated from high school fifteen years ago, but apparently I've re-enrolled with a whole new cast of mean girls."

"They're really not as bad as they seem."

Elise cocked her head at me.

"Alright, fair enough. But they prank all the new nannies. Actually, you got off easy. The last time they let the poor girl call the police to report her missing Bugaboo. The cops found it parked around the corner. With a couple of mushed bananas in the seat."

"Well, I'm just glad you had my back. Something tells me

they don't mess with you." The corner of her mouth turned up. "In fact, I think Ms. Fairchild might have herself a bit of a crush."

"That's what Cassie, my wife, says. But I'm convinced she's only nice to me because she thinks I know Adam Levine."

"*Do* you?" There it was again. That twinkly look. Like sunrays dancing on blue water.

"Not really. We opened for Maroon Five a few times though. And I might've let Alex believe we shared a tour bus."

I paused for a beat.

"And the same hairdresser."

Elise threw her head back, revealing a small freckle on the hollow of her neck. Instantly, I wanted to hear her laugh again. She didn't cackle like Alex.

"Hell, I had to do my own hair."

"Still, it must've been fun. Do you miss it?"

"It *was* fun, for a while. But the shine wears off quick. You can't tell who your real friends are, and you start to forget what you loved about music in the first place. I'll tell you though, there's something so pure about watching somebody else fall in love with it. I've been giving guitar lessons part-time, mostly to teenage boys who think it'll help them get laid. And it's more fun than playing a sold-out show." As we reached the crosswalk, I peered down at Abby, fast asleep and drooling. "Nobody beats this little groupie."

"She is pretty darn adorable." Elise pointed down Diamond Street toward the Hamiltons' place. Our house was a couple of blocks in the other direction. "I better get these boys home for a snack and a nap. You know the drill."

I gave her a wave and watched her start across the street. My feet felt so light beneath me, I figured I'd run the rest of the way home. Expel some of that old Theo energy that rushed straight to my head. Fame is as powerful as any drug. But before I stepped off the curb, Elise's voice pulled me back.

"Hey, Theo, I know it sounds silly, but would you ever consider teaching a nanny to play guitar?"

AFTER
CASSIE

SEVEN

"Could you give us a moment alone, Detectives?" I hardly recognized my own voice. It seemed to come from faraway, as if I'd fallen down a deep, dark well. I pried my eyes from the offending text, pretending to be unbothered, while Theo remained as rigid as a plank beside me.

Detective Mason offered a sympathetic smile. A winner's smile. She'd landed her blow right where it hurt, leaving us both reeling. "Of course. We'll wait outside. Take your time."

I glanced at the two-way mirror and back again. "As Theo's acting attorney, I expect this conversation will be confidential."

"Certainly. You won't be observed or recorded. You have my word."

They left the printout sitting on the table, where it demanded my attention like an unwanted guest. I flipped it over, grateful to have it out of my sight, and waited for Theo to fill the silence. But he just sat there, blank as the paper itself, his vacant gaze fixed on the wall. He looked small and weak. Breakable. Not at all like the man I married.

"Say something, Theo. *Anything*."

He took a shaky breath and raised his eyes to mine. "I don't regret it. I only wish I'd punched him harder. Do you know what he said about her? That she *deserved* it. What kind of asshole would say something like that?"

Theo answered his own question. "A guilty one. That's who."

"What about this?" I asked, tapping a finger to the page. A part of me wanted to snatch it up and shove it in his face.

"It proves I was right about the phone. Someone must've taken it at the restaurant. Or I suppose it could've fallen from my pocket on the walk over. All I know is I didn't send that text."

I clung to a frayed thread of hope. But I couldn't let myself become my mother. I'd already ignored so much.

"So, the killer just happened to find your lost phone?"

"It seems far-fetched, I admit."

"*Far-fetched?* It sounds like the plot of a Lifetime movie. The cops are never going to buy that story. Are you sure you didn't meet Elise last night? Maybe the killer saw the two of you together."

The violent shake of Theo's head didn't deter me. It felt satisfying to watch him deny it. It gave me a reason to hold on.

"The worst thing right now would be to get caught in a lie."

"I swear to you, I'm not lying."

"You're positive, then? There is zero chance this came from you?" I slid the paper in front of him and turned it back over. We both had no choice but to face the undeniable black print. Looking at it twisted my gut.

Theo rested his head in his hand and pinched the bridge of his nose. I wondered if he might be sick. Upchucking in the interview room certainly wouldn't help his chances. I rested my palm on his back, making slow circles, and his muscles relaxed beneath my fingers. I couldn't decide whether to hate him or pity him.

"I suppose it's *possible* that I don't remember. I mean, I felt like hell this morning. And back in my Sluggers days, I could forget a whole night like it never happened."

"I'm well aware." The evening we met, Theo brought me back to the Sluggers' tour bus, where he'd tossed back so many shots, I lost count. I'd been drunk myself. Drunk enough to throw myself at the hot lead singer, at the Stone and Faber end-of-year company retreat, no less. But not so drunk I'd forgotten his name the next morning. That should've been my first clue. Instead, I'd seen it as a challenge.

"I haven't done that sort of thing in years, Cass. I didn't even drink that much last night." He paused, then asked, "What reason would I have for texting her anyway? 'Talking about our future'? That makes no sense."

"You tell me." I returned my hands to the table, suppressing another surge of anger. "Even if somebody else sent that message from your phone, they must've believed Elise would buy it. That she'd come to meet you. At 2 a.m. in the pouring rain. What would make someone think that?"

Theo shook his head. He gave no answer. I sat back, resigned to his reticence. He would never admit it. At least not to me. "You need a lawyer. A proper defense attorney. I'll talk to Mr. Stone. I'm sure he knows someone."

"I don't want *someone*. I want you. It has to be you. Nobody else will defend me like you will. No one else will believe me."

He thought *I* believed him. "I'm a corporate lawyer. Not a criminal one. It wouldn't be right. Anyway, we're getting ahead of ourselves. They haven't charged you with..." I couldn't say it.

"What if they do?" I watched tears well in his eyes. He looked so much like Abby that my wrath never lasted. It blew in and out like a summer storm.

"Then we'll get you the best criminal defense attorney in the city. In the whole country, if you want."

His face brightened. "But you represented me before.

Remember Soul Patch Studios? You saved me from a lifetime of musical servitude."

"That was different. I only reviewed a contract." Right before Abby was born, Theo had almost gone solo. Soul Patch had offered him a bogus record deal—he'd have to pay the studio back for all their production costs and give them a hefty portion of his touring and merchandise revenue too—which I advised him to decline. There had been no other takers. By then, he'd devoted himself to the brand-new project we'd made together. "This is *your* life we're talking about, Theo—both our lives. Abby's too. We have to make a smart decision."

Theo grabbed my hand so suddenly it scared me. He clasped it in his lap. "You're right. It *is* my life. I *am* being smart. Who else would I trust with my life but you? Please, do this for me."

Now I felt nauseous, with that text swimming at the edges of my vision. A brew of fear and doubt sloshed in my gut. I wrested my hand from his grip. "I'll think about it."

The unfriendly face of Detective Kincaid greeted me on the other side of the door.

"Good talk?" he asked.

"What exactly has my husband been charged with?"

"I'm glad you asked." He held up one finger, then another. "One count of PC 240. One count of PC 242, and—"

"Assault and battery then." I hoped I'd called it right. Professor Masterson's Intro to Criminal Law class seemed ages ago, the thick textbook collecting dust in the corner of our garage. I'd been glad to pack it away. I liked the sterility of corporate law. Defending a man in a fight for his life had always struck me as too heavy a burden. What if I lost? Or worse, what if I helped a man like my father go free?

"I wasn't done yet."

I stood on legs of lead above a precipice, waiting for him to speak the rest of it. I understood the brutal force of gravity, the sudden drop below. Detective Kincaid had the power to push me over the edge, to send me hurtling toward doom. To change my life forever. Naturally, I pretended to be nonplussed. "Please continue."

"And one count of PC 187, first-degree. That's homicide, in case you were wondering. I imagine you don't have much reason to reference the penal code at your fancy law firm downtown."

Attorneys deal with facts, not feelings, so I walled off my devastation and focused on the acquisition of information. Information, I could manage. Information, I could control. "What happens now?"

"Your husband will be booked into county jail for the night. His arraignment will likely be scheduled for tomorrow. You can bet the DA will ask the judge to deny bail."

"Why would he do that? Theo has no prior criminal record. He's not a flight risk. He's been fully cooperative with your investigation."

Detective Kincaid shook his head at me like I just didn't get it. "The victim was bludgeoned to death, Mrs. Copeland. The back of her skull was crushed in like a tin can. And the minute you let him out of your sight, he punched your neighbor in the face. As far as I can tell, your husband is a dangerous man. The real question is, are you blind or complicit?"

The first time I saw my father hit my mother, I cowered behind the sofa. He stumbled through the door in his uniform, looking like an unmade bed. He smelled sour too. My mother pushed him away when he went in for a drunken grope. Without warning, he reared back and struck her, lashing his knuckles across her face. At six years old, the impact hit me like a shockwave, changing my landscape forever.

That's how it felt to watch my husband leave the room in handcuffs. Like a tsunami had swept away the life we'd built together, leaving me to wade alone through a waist-high pool of sludge.

I raced home, anxious to wrap my arms around our little girl. Already, I wondered how I would make her understand that Daddy wouldn't be home tonight. That she'd be stuck with me instead, his second-rate replacement. Detective Kincaid's question kept nagging at me, too, rising like a decomposing body in the muck. *Are you blind or complicit?* It didn't help that Gloria waited for me in the living room, wringing her hands on her lap. I'd only told her I needed to step out for a bit to pick up Theo.

"Where's my son?" she asked, peering around me. As if he might be hiding there like a scared little boy. "Is he alright?"

I didn't want to lie, so I delayed the inevitable, heading up the stairs instead and cracking the door open. I padded to the crib where Abby lay napping. I smoothed back the blonde tendril that curled across her forehead. She didn't stir. I found a glimmer of peace in the flutter of her eyelashes. The predictable rise and fall of her chest.

"Are you going to tell me what's going on?" Gloria stood in the doorway, her face pinched with worry.

I pressed a finger to my lips and left Abby there, sleeping peacefully. Gloria followed me back downstairs and into the kitchen. Taking a breath, I pointed to the barstool. "You should sit."

Ignoring my suggestion, she opened the dishwasher and began returning the glasses to the cabinet. Stress cleaning. We had that in common. "Has Theo been hurt?"

"No. Theo's fine. But, there's no easy way to say this. He's been arrested, Gloria. He's in jail."

Gloria kept moving. Even as her jaw slackened and she gaped at me like I'd sprouted horns. She'd always been oblivious to her husband's faults. To Theo's too, apparently. Even though he'd flunked out of USF in pursuit of his music career, she'd never questioned him. Which was probably why she hated me. She was the original Theo Copeland groupie. I'd dared to take her place.

"For what?" she asked, steadying herself against the counter.

"It's bad, Gloria. Really bad." No way to sugarcoat it, I had to rip off the Band-Aid. "He assaulted a neighbor, and the cops suspect he murdered Elise."

The news settled, graying her face. "Murder? That's impossible. Theo would never... He was with you all night."

"I know."

"Well, did you tell them?" Her sharp tone cut deep, though I'd been waiting for her to lay blame. To make Theo's mistakes about me.

"Obviously I told them. But they have evidence."

She waved her hand, swatting it all away. "They're just saying that. Because it happened at his place. They couldn't have any—"

"He sent Elise a text early this morning, asking her to meet him at the studio. I saw the message. It's real."

Gloria picked up steam again, carting a small stack of plates to the shelf. She spoke over her own clatter. "You actually think he's guilty. You think my son took a woman's life." I had no energy to argue with her. I couldn't tell her that I suspected her precious Theo of having an affair. She would turn it around on me, ask what I'd done wrong. And I had, of course, done wrong.

"I need to talk to him," she continued. "He needs a lawyer. A good lawyer. Freddie used to golf with a defense attorney. Maybe he can help."

My skin prickled with indignation. So hot and insistent, I

momentarily forgot my doubt. "I *am* a lawyer, Gloria. Theo's asked me to represent him."

Gloria stood still. I'd finally managed to stun her into immobility. "*You*? That's ridiculous. Is that even allowed?"

"Yes, it's allowed, so long as that's what Theo wants. Which he does." I'd oversimplified one issue to get to the other. To get to the word that really burned. "Why is it 'ridiculous'?"

"As far as I know, you've never even been in a courtroom. You deal with companies, not people."

"Companies are made up of people. I made it to the national finals of moot court representing USC. I graduated magna cum laude. I can handle myself in a courtroom."

"*Moot* court? That's rich." Before Gloria turned away, finding her legs again, I swear I caught an eyeroll. "When would you have time, anyway? You're always rushing here and there. Mergers, deals, negotiations. Too many late nights. You barely see your own daughter. It's no wonder you two haven't really bonded. Frankly, I'm not surprised my son started making new friends."

A part of me wished I could be more like my father. That I could rip the casserole dish from her hand and hurl it against the wall, screaming at her until she trembled. But deep down, I had my mother's wounds. I deserved Gloria's disapproval. She spoke to my weakest parts. Until I met Theo, I never expected to be a wife or a mother. It scared me too much—the thought of messing it up royally like my own parents had done.

"Fine. I won't do it."

"It's for the best, dear." Gloria calmly slid the dish into the cabinet and shrugged at me. "Let's face facts. If you can't handle your own mother-in-law, you could never defend Theo in a fight for his life."

I hung my head, declaring her the victor.

"Are you okay looking after Abby for a few minutes?" she asked, sticking in one last barb.

"She's my daughter, Gloria. Of course I am."

"I'll go home and pack an overnight bag so I can be back to help you with dinner." Gloria patted my shoulder, simpering at me, as if she hadn't just stabbed me in the heart. "Don't worry. I'll stay as long as you need me. You focus on holding yourself together, dear. Let me find an attorney for Theo."

That's when it hit me. A sickening flash of my future. If Theo went down for this, Gloria would never forgive me. She'd fight me tooth and nail for Abby. She'd petition for custody, telling the court about my corporate job and my long hours and my inability to make my daughter eat a goddamned strawberry. She would dig and dig and dig until she'd unearthed the one secret that could break me. Then she could feel justified trying to steal Abby from me.

I watched through the window for a moment until Gloria reached the sidewalk. Then I stalked back to the kitchen and flung open the cabinet, setting my sights on that casserole dish. It was part of the china set she and Freddie gifted us for our wedding. I raised it above my head, determined to end its life.

Abby's sudden wailing stopped me.

I abandoned the dish on the table and ran to comfort her, already sobbing myself.

THE SAN FRANCISCO CHRONICLE

"Former Sluggers' Frontman Arrested in Brutal Slaying of Noe
Valley Nanny"
by Elaine Yu

Theo Copeland, former lead singer and guitarist for
The Sluggers, was arrested on Sunday for the homicide
of Elise Sterling, a thirty-three-year-old nanny who
worked in the affluent Noe Valley neighborhood. Sterling's body was discovered in a dumpster early Sunday
morning by a homeless man who frequented the area.
Police have released few details about the crime but
have confirmed that the victim sustained blunt force
trauma to the head.

Copeland rose to fame in mid 2010s when he and
his band—whose name was chosen after Copeland
broke his high school home run record—were named
the winners of the reality singing competition, *Starbound*. After winning the competition, The Sluggers
performed on the *Starbound* tour and later opened for
such acts as Maroon Five and Train. Though Copeland

was rumored to have been offered a profitable solo contract with Soul Patch Studios a few years ago, he disappeared from the music scene entirely before releasing an album. The nature of his relationship with the victim remains unclear.

Copeland's arraignment has been set for Monday. He faces charges of first-degree murder.

EIGHT

I could've taken a holiday on Monday. I probably should have, with Theo's name and mug shot circulating online. Splashed across the headlines of the *San Francisco Chronicle*. But I took refuge in my routine. I woke early to steam my blouse and downed a few sips of scalding coffee to kill the usual guilt about leaving Abby—this time in Gloria's more-than-capable hands—and drive my car the five miles to my office in the Transamerica Pyramid, where Stone and Faber had set up shop for more than four decades.

"Don't look at the Internet," Gloria warned me before I left. Naturally, I spent the entire drive checking my cell at stoplights. With every story, the pit in my gut deepened.

I took a quick detour to pick up a new cellphone for Theo. Then I swiped my badge at the building entrance and headed for the elevator bay. In the stark quiet of the lobby, the *click-clack* of my heels against the marble tile counted down my arrival like the second hand of a clock. In exactly two hours, Theo would stand in front of a judge and enter his plea with Stanley Riggles, his father's old golfing buddy, by his side. I would be here, hiding in my hamster wheel of polished steel and shiny floors.

Corporate law was soulless work, requiring the kind of cutthroat control and painstaking precision my father had cultivated in me by proxy. Everything had to be just so—the house, the lawn, his dinner, my mother. I'd watched her devote her life to never quite meeting his exacting standards. And every failure came with a high price. The demands of Stone and Faber paled in comparison.

At least the office would be deserted this week. Even the lowly junior associates took vacation during the tiny sliver of time between Christmas and New Year's, gearing up to start fresh in Q1. Not me, though. Even if Theo hadn't been arrested, I would've turned up anyway. I felt confident here. Capable. I knew exactly what to do, what to say. I could predict the outcome of any deal and anticipate my clients' needs before they'd uttered them. In contrast, motherhood left me flying blind.

As I waited for the elevator to arrive, footsteps approached from behind, filling me with dread. I didn't want to see anyone I knew. "Good morning, Cassie."

Least of all, him.

"Mr. Stone." My brain glitched at the sight of my boss. His skin, tan, in the middle of winter. His thick white hair, sleek as a helmet. And those teeth, straight and white as Chiclets. The man took care of himself but paid dearly for the upkeep. Rumor had it he shelled out forty thousand for a set of dental implants to match his wife's veneers. "I thought you were planning to spend the holidays in St. Bart's."

"Shelly changed her mind. She wanted snow. So, we did Christmas at the chalet in Vail instead."

"How wonderful." I realized I'd been foolish to consider this place a safe harbor. Right now, it felt like a den of wolves. "You were lucky to get away. It rained here. For days."

"So I heard."

When the elevator dinged and the doors parted, I thought of turning tail. The prospect of that thirty-second ride loomed like a death drop.

"May I have a word in my office?" It only sounded like a question. Mr. Stone didn't ask, he commanded.

Like a good soldier, I stepped onto the elevator and nodded. "Of course."

The buttons lit up as we ascended in silence to the executive offices on the forty-seventh floor, just beneath the conference center and the crown jewel. The elevator opened to the Wall of Fame, where the framed photographs of the partners lined the hallway. I glanced down to the end at my own likeness, added only eight months prior. The largest of the portraits —Martin Stone, and the newly retired Alex Faber—were positioned front and center, unmissable.

Mr. Stone guided me toward his corner office with its breathtaking view of the bay. My own floor had the same view wasted on a series of meeting rooms. I suspected the choice was intentional, meant to send a subtle message. You had to earn an office with a view like this. You paid for it with your most precious resource. *Time.*

Mr. Stone pointed to the leather armchair, and I sat. "I must say I'm surprised to see you here today, Cassie."

"You saw the news, I presume."

"Hard to miss it." He lingered by the window, peering out at the tangerine sunrise. I leaned forward a bit and tried to read his face, the way I'd learned to do with my father. "I'm sorry to hear about your husband's situation. I always liked Theo, even if I couldn't quite picture the two of you together."

"Opposites attract," I said, stupidly. I felt entirely out of kilter. As if I was the one with a murder charge hanging over my head.

"I imagine you'll be requesting a leave of absence, then."

"I hadn't intended on it, sir. As you know, MetaTech is only a few months out from finalizing the Player One Gaming acquisition. No one else knows that transaction as well as I do. I need to see it through."

Mr. Stone continued to stare off into the distance. I kept talking. Rambling, really.

"Their CEO won't trust anyone else to close the deal with Player One. You know how finicky Alistair can be. Somehow, we've managed to build a strong working relationship. But I can guarantee he'll balk if we make any changes now. The last thing I want is to jeopardize the acquisition, so if it's all the same to you, I'd like to continue working."

"I see." Finally, Mr. Stone gave me his face. A sad smile softened his stony jaw. He could be kind when he wanted to be but I wished he wouldn't. It would be easier to hate him. "I won't tell you what to do. I only ask that you consider the impact to the firm's reputation. We don't need this kind of publicity. Scott can handle MetaTech."

Junior partner Scott Barker most certainly could not handle it. He had the personality of a golden retriever. This deal required shrewdness and tenacity. A take-the-bull-by-the-horns kind of approach. "Is this about the due diligence? Those emails I uncovered?"

A razor-thin crease split Mr. Stone's forehead. "I asked you not to bring that up again. It's a dead issue. You're a partner now, Cassandra. One of the boys. You can't be swayed by emotion."

"Understood." I quickly changed course, cursing myself for having mentioned it. "Have any of our clients expressed concern about Theo's charges?"

"Not yet. But the story's only just hit the news. Take a look at this." Mr. Stone sat beside me, displaying the screen of his cellphone, where Stone and Faber had been tagged in a tweet of the *Chronicle* article.

@stoneandfaber are you okay with employing a murderer's wife?

The number beside the retweet symbol grew by one, two, ten, and the spacious room closed in around me. Beads of sweat began to prickle beneath my hair. "A murderer? So, we're just assuming Theo's guilty?"

"I know. You're right. It's not fair. But if there's one thing I've learned in my career, it's that life *isn't* fair. And it's a damn good thing for most of us that it's not."

Mr. Stone had always been a pillar. My own personal Rock of Gibraltar, never swayed by a fickle wind. Sometimes, I'd even pretended that *he* was my father. But now, I saw he was no better than the gossips on the Noe Valley Neighbors page. "What happened to innocent until proven guilty? I thought we practiced law here. It seems like you're more concerned about the court of public opinion."

"And an unmerciful court it is. Whatever skeletons you and Theo have in the closet, they'll find them and make them dance."

"What skeletons?" I spit back at him. But already, I knew. I'd kept mine in the dark for so long its bones had returned to the earth. Dust to dust.

"C'mon. Everybody has at least one. What if your husband is convicted? What then? I have to think about the firm, Cassie. As much as I value you and your contributions—and believe me I do—I think it would be best for everyone if you took a few months off to get your affairs in order. Once the trial is over, we'll see if you still have a place here."

I pursed my lips together to keep the tears at bay. I'd never cried at work. I'd be damned if I started now. Mr. Stone would have a field day with that. Still, his words punched a hole clean through my chest. I could practically feel the wind whipping through the heart of me. Aside from Theo and Abby, this place was all I had.

"I understand, sir. But, with all due respect, I am a partner now. And I think you're making a big mistake. There's a reason why you voted in favor of my promotion. A reason why you trusted me with this account. You and I both know that Scott couldn't negotiate his way out of paper bag."

"I'm sorry." Mr. Stone returned his eyes to the window, ending the conversation. "I'll have my assistant draft up the paperwork for your leave of absence from the firm. She'll be in touch."

I made my way to the door, as limp and unsteady as Abby's baby doll. No matter how Mr. Stone put it, I felt like the one being left.

"Wait," he called, pulling me back from the brink. I clung to that word with everything I had.

"Yes?"

"I expect you'll maintain radio silence on the MetaTech merger, no matter the state of your employment with the firm." When I nodded numbly, he added, "Happy New Year, Cassie."

Panicked, I stabbed at the elevator button. As the doors sealed me inside, I tried to still my breathing. But it came in shallow gasps, like a fish out of water. I couldn't catch my thoughts either. Each worse than the last, they tumbled one after the other, leaving me buried in an avalanche of loss. Theo, guilty of murder. Abby, ripped away from me. My career, over. What would be left?

Nothing. *Nothing.* Nothing!

I braced myself against the wall and waited out the steady descent. When the doors parted, I knew exactly what I had to do.

. . .

I burst through the door and into the crowded room without catching my breath. I'd slipped off my heels and run the whole way there, inexplicably leaving my car parked at the office. In unison, heads swiveled to gape at me, like I'd just interrupted a royal wedding. Everyone stood at attention, which meant I'd arrived later than I thought. Maybe too late. At least the clerk had steered me to the right courtroom, with the Honorable Judge Katherine Macy presiding. Her name placard rested at the front of the bench.

I made no apologies while I hurried up the aisle toward my husband. A cascade of whispers and hushed voices followed me as I passed.

"...In count one, that you committed the crime of murder in violation of Penal Code, Section 187, in that you did willfully and unlawfully and with malice aforethought murder Elise Sterling..."

As Judge Macy read the charges, Theo didn't look away from me. He wore the same gray Zegna suit he'd donned at this year's Stone and Faber holiday party at the Fairmont Hotel. The irony threatened to knock me over.

"What are you doing here?" he hissed at me, more shocked than angry.

"...It is further alleged that you did use a deadly and dangerous weapon..."

"I'm here to represent you." I realized how crazy I sounded. But I needed this. My whole life depended on it.

"I thought you weren't coming."

"I changed my mind."

Judge Macy abruptly stopped speaking, shooting daggers in my direction. She resembled a queen, lording over us common folk. Her fiery red hair, her crown, drawn into a tight bun atop her head. "Counselor, is there a problem?" she asked, directing her question to the small, weaselly man at the defense table beside my husband.

Mr. Stone always said that he who speaks first, loses. Not this time. I had to get it out before I changed my mind. "I'm Cassandra Copeland, representing the defendant."

Her eyes darted between the two of us, and she sighed. "I thought we'd already covered that. Mr. Riggles, aren't you representing the defendant?"

"I thought so too, Your Honor." He sounded slick as oil. The kind of man who made his living standing up for snakes. It sickened me to think that Theo might be one of them. "I'm not sure who this woman is, but I'd like her removed from—"

"That's my wife." Theo said it like he hardly believed it. "*And* my attorney. You're fired, Stanley."

The woman beside me gasped, then hastily scribbled into a notebook on her lap. I recognized her SFTV news badge. I'd forgotten that half the room would be filled with reporters or bloggers or worse... fans. Apparently, watching the arraignment of a C-list celebrity qualified as newsworthy.

"Are you sure?" I asked Theo, even as I pushed my way to the table. Stanley stood his ground, refusing to budge. I breathed deep, trying not to wilt under the heat of a hundred pairs of eyes, or succumb to the frenzy of murmurs that sounded no friendlier than a swarm of bees buzzing behind me. As much as I blamed my husband for ending us up here, I wanted to shield him from these people who had come to witness his fall from grace. *Our* fall.

The judge cleared her throat, mercifully silencing the courtroom. "Mr. Copeland, before we can proceed, you need to pick an attorney. It seems you've got several contenders. Do you need a recess to make your decision?"

"No, Your Honor." Theo reached past Stanley, grabbing for my hand. "She's my attorney. There's no doubt about it."

"Well, then. Mr. Riggles, I'm afraid the defendant has dismissed you."

"Your mother is not going to like this." With a sneer, Stanley gathered his briefcase and stepped aside, pausing to issue his last pronouncement. "Good luck. You'll need it."

Once he'd brushed past me, bumping against me with his knobby shoulder, I joined Theo at the table and set my own briefcase beside me. I certainly looked the part of a big shot attorney but my palms felt as sweaty as my first day in law school.

"Thank you," he whispered.

"Alright. Now that the matter of your attorney is settled, Mr. Copeland, do you understand the charges against you? Shall I review them again?"

Theo pushed his shoulders back, head held high. He returned to center stage, a consummate performer. He couldn't fool me. I saw the tension in his face. "That won't be necessary."

"And how do you plead?"

I looked at my husband. I thought of our wedding day. The way he'd recited the vows he wrote himself without once dropping his eyes from mine. I thought of the day Abby was born. The tears that spilled over onto my cheeks as he kissed them. There was only one answer.

"Not guilty."

A breath rushed out of me. I wanted to throw my arms around him.

"Your Honor, if I may..." For the first time, I let myself glance across the aisle at my opposing counsel. With his chiseled jaw and his stiff suit, he reminded me of a department store mannequin. "...The State requests that the defendant be held without bail pending trial."

Or a robot. An infuriating robot.

"That's outrageous," I said. "Theo is not a flight risk. He's a long-standing member of the community. He grew up here in San Francisco. He owns a business in Noe Valley, a music studio. We have a daughter, who he cares for while I work. His mother lives down the street. Not to mention, he has no prior criminal history and certainly no history of violence."

The robot sputtered to life again. "I believe defense counsel is mistaken. According to the arresting officers, Mr. Copeland has a prior charge for domestic abuse. Furthermore, he recently assaulted his neighbor, Shaun DeMarco. The State asserts he is a danger to the community, and given the severity of the charges and his ample financial resources, potentially a risk to flee the jurisdiction."

"A charge for domestic abuse? You must be mistaken." Already, I heard the scribble of the SFTV reporter as her pen documented the revelation.

Theo touched my arm ever so gently. He shook his head at me, muttered, "It's true. It was a long time ago. I was only nineteen."

The courtroom spun like a tilt-a-whirl, Judge Macy's head coming in and out of focus. I steadied myself, gripping tight to the table in front of me. I did what I had to do. I pretended to be twenty-four again, back in moot court, defending the constitutional rights of a faceless appellant I'd never met. "Mr. Copeland was practically a juvenile at the time of the domestic... *incident*. And as for the assault of Mr. DeMarco, guilt is yet to be determined in that matter. I'm sure the prosecutor is familiar with the Sixth Amendment."

Judge Macy appeared to ignore us both as she issued her proclamation. "Bail is hereby set at one million dollars. Mr. Copeland, you will need to surrender your passport to the court immediately."

Robot-lawyer glared at me. I stared straight ahead, pretending not to notice, and willed myself to keep going. To power through. To forget about the secret my husband had kept from me. The secret that had just been unearthed in a courtroom and would be splashed across tomorrow's front-page news. Another betrayal.

"Your Honor," I began. "My husband hopes to clear his name as soon as possible, so the defense would like to move for a speedy trial, preferably the first date you have available on the docket."

Consulting her laptop, Judge Macy replied, "Well, Ms. Copeland, you're in luck. I recently granted a continuance in another matter. So, February 7, six weeks from today, is yours. Will you be ready?"

Six weeks. A bubble of fear rose in my throat. "Of course. If the prosecutor can be ready, so can I."

He cocked his head at me from across the aisle. "Oh, I'll be ready. But, Your Honor, are we going to address the proverbial elephant in the room?"

"Which is?" Judge Macy asked.

"A ruling on the permissibility of the defendant being represented by his spouse. It seems highly unorthodox."

"Is there a motion there, Mr. Callaghan?" So, he had a name. A lawyerly sounding one at that.

"Now that you mention it, yes. A motion to have defense counsel removed because of a conflict of interest."

Though just yesterday I'd tried to convince Theo of the same, I rolled my eyes. I wouldn't be upstaged by a man whose hair didn't move. "There is no prohibition against being represented by one's spouse. Besides, it should be up to the defendant. He's made his decision clear."

Judge Macy addressed Theo. "Mr. Copeland, do you understand that it's your wife serving as your attorney? If she gets mad at you for leaving your underwear on the floor, she might just blow your case."

The gallery erupted with laughter, breathing life back into the courtroom.

"I understand, Your Honor. I'll have to be on my best behavior."

"Ms. Copeland, I assume you've entered into this arrangement willingly and intend to argue in your client's best interest, no matter the state of your personal relationship."

Willingly. I pondered the gravity of that word. I had so much at stake, so much to lose. I wouldn't leave my husband's fate in the hands of Stanley Riggles. No matter how many snakes he'd set free. "Of course."

"Then, I pronounce you attorney and client. Happy, Mr. Callaghan?"

The prosecutor sized me up then. How out of place I was here. Perhaps he'd known it all along. A sneer slipped through his perfect smile. "Thrilled."

JUNE

SIX MONTHS BEFORE THE MURDER

Theo

NINE

I helped Abby shovel the last spoonful of spaghetti into her mouth. Half her dinner had landed on her bib. The other half on my favorite Nirvana T-shirt. She smacked her lips together, licking the sauce from her chin.

"Keep that up, Abs." I grinned at her and gave her a little tickle. "Less work for me. You won't even need a bath."

Abby babbled back at me while I checked my phone. Sure enough, Cassie had texted five minutes ago.

How did dinner go?

Mealtimes had been a challenge for Cassie from the beginning, when she couldn't breastfeed the way she wanted. Lately, she and Abby butted heads like two mules, one just as stubborn as the other. Inevitably, it ended in tears. Cassie's. After snapping a pic of Abby looking a mess, I typed a reply, hoping to distract my wife with a laugh.

Don't you mean where did dinner go?

Cassie didn't respond. Maybe she'd gotten busy. But more than likely she resented me for having it so easy with Abby. I whipped off my tee and held the stain under the hot water, blotting at it with a dishtowel.

When a knock came at the door, Abby squealed in delight.

"Who could that be, huh? Did you invite someone over?"

When I made a face at her, she flashed her first three teeth and giggled. The best sound ever—better than a Zeppelin guitar solo—I never tired of hearing it. I wondered what it would be like when she started talking, what word would come out first. It worried the hell out of me. Sometimes, I practiced with her. *Mama. Mama. Mama.* Please let it be that. I didn't know how Cassie would handle another blow. She'd always been perfect at everything. But with parenthood, there's no such thing.

Holding my wet shirt in my hand, I headed for the door. Probably the mailman with that toy keyboard-piano I'd ordered for Abby. Or Mom stopping by unannounced as usual. Sometimes her closeness felt smothering, passive-aggressive. Like she wanted to catch me in the act of screwing it all up, just like Dad, only so she could defend me.

"Elise?"

"Hey." She blinked back at me from the porch, somehow just as startled.

I had an instinct to shut the door. I suddenly felt naked, standing there shirtless in my gray sweats. Her face reddened, as she searched for a place to put her eyes. Finally, they landed safely over my shoulder on Abby. And *my* eyes? Well, I planted them anywhere but on her bright pink sports bra, her shoulders tan and freckled beneath it.

"I thought you were going to come by the studio *tomorrow*." I'd agreed to teach Elise the guitar, even though she couldn't afford my lessons. I liked her. She made me laugh, and she didn't go around with her nose in the air like the Fairchilds and

Hamiltons of the playground. She needed a friend. That much I could tell.

"I know. I'm sorry. Mrs. Hamilton took the twins for their checkup. So, I thought I'd go for a run to get to know the neighborhood better. Clumsy me, I tripped over the curb and..." She held up the sneakered foot at the end of her long, shapely leg. "I think I sprained my ankle. Anyway, I remember you saying that you lived here. And... I'm so sorry. I shouldn't have come."

"No, don't worry about it. I'll grab you something from the freezer for your ankle." I jerked my head toward the kitchen, trying to remember when I'd told Elise our address. I blamed my forgetfulness on Abby. Since she started teething, I'd been scraping by on less sleep than I'd gotten in my tour bus days. "As you can see, we're in the middle of dinner. Which ended up on my shirt. Would you mind keeping an eye on Abby while I make myself decent?"

"Of course." She peered around the corner while she made her way inside. "Is Cassie home?"

"At five thirty? We should be so lucky. Most days, she makes it back in time to put Abby to bed."

I found Elise a bag of frozen veggies and left her to it, hurrying to the bedroom to change. I tossed on a clean tee and swapped my sweats for a respectable pair of jeans. A quick pause in the mirror revealed my uncoolness. My hair stuck out in all directions. A stray spot of spaghetti sauce dotted my cheek. That settled it. Next time I fed Abby spaghetti, I'd don a goddamned hazmat suit.

Elise's voice carried up the stairs. *"The wheels on the bus go round and round, round and round, round and round..."* She didn't sound half bad. I hummed along with her, as I splashed my face and ran a wet hand through my hair. It's not like I cared to impress her, but I had a reputation to uphold, especially since she'd admitted to buying *Starbound*'s Greatest Hits album, which featured a song from each season's winner.

She'd seen me at my hunkiest. This version had to be a total letdown.

"*The horn on the bus goes beep-beep-beep... beep-beep-beep—*"

"*Beep-beep-beep...*" I started to sing the rest of the lyrics and padded down the staircase. "Why'd you stop?"

I stared at the open front door, trying to make sense of it.

"Elise? Are you still—*shit*, Cass? What are you doing here?" My wife stood in the kitchen next to Elise, as Abby happily pounded her little fists against her tray, making her own music. Elise rested on one of the island barstools, her injured left foot propped on the other.

"I live here. Remember?" They both shared a laugh at my expense.

"I just meant, we didn't expect you back so early." I gestured to our houseguest, making my way over to Abby. Grabbing the damp dishrag, I wiped at the sauce on her cheeks. Abby squeaked, turning her face away from me. "This is Elise Sterling. She works as a nanny for the Hamiltons."

I looked on, bewildered, while Cassie wrapped an arm around Elise's shoulders and gave her a squeeze. "I know who she is. But I still can't quite believe it. Elise Sterling in San Francisco. In *my* house."

"You know her?"

"We went to high school together." Elise shrugged at me. "It really is a small world, huh?"

"Wait. You lived in Buttonwillow too? According to Cassie, that town only had ten residents, and half of them were cows."

"That sounds about right," Elise said, with an awkward chuckle. "But yeah, I moved there in high school after my parents' divorce. Mom thought we needed a fresh start. In the absolute middle of nowhere. Cassie was a lifesaver. She took me under her wing. Her and Jessica. She even convinced me to try out for cheerleading. The three of us, we were... well..."

"Inseparable." Cassie finished Elise's sentence. Then, she busied herself with Abby, picking her up from the high chair and bouncing her onto her hip. I could only hope I'd gotten all the red sauce from Abby's fingers because right now they were Velcroed to her mother's designer blazer. "I must've mentioned Jess and Elise to you before. Those two girls were the best part of high school."

"Must have." I'd stopped probing Cassie about her past long ago. I knew the basics: an alcoholic cop dad, an emotionally absent mother, and an aversion to all things Buttonwillow.

"Theo tells me you're a high-powered attorney now." Elise made a silly face at Abby, who predictably giggled. "I always knew you'd make it big." Then to me, she added, "Cassie was the smartest girl in the whole school. The prettiest too. Everyone envied her."

I gave my wife a wink. "I don't doubt it."

"*And* you married a rock star. Not to mention this beautiful little girl you've got. Jeez, Cass. Way to make the rest of us feel like real losers. I don't even own a car."

Cassie replied with a tight smile. I took the hint, clearing my throat to draw the attention my way instead. "'Star' might be a bit of an exaggeration. I'm pretty sure I'm more of an asteroid."

That got another laugh, which I considered a victory. Cassie smirked at me, while she pried Abby's fingers from her gold necklace.

"Did Theo tell you he's going to teach me guitar?" Elise asked.

"Oh, really? No, he didn't mention it."

"I was going to, hon. I just—"

"It's fine." Cassie waved her hand, dismissing my concern. "He's a great teacher. But I thought you gave up on music after high school."

"I found my inspiration again, I suppose." Elise shrugged and removed the bag of frozen veggies from her ankle. When she dropped her foot from the stool and stood up, glancing at her watch, I felt relieved. "I've started writing my own songs. Remember how I used to jot down lyrics? Well, I've got a whole notebook full now."

"How interesting. Good for you." Cassie barely glanced at Elise, as she craned her neck to outmaneuver Abby.

"We were all so creative back then, weren't we?" Elise looked off wistfully.

"Cassie too?" I couldn't imagine my wife as anything but the left-brained badass that had clawed her way to the top of a man's world.

"Absolutely. After Jess and I bought her a camcorder for her birthday, we started making movies. Cassie was the director, of course."

"I'd forgotten all about that," Cassie replied. An uneasy silence passed between them, until Elise cracked a smile.

"You're right though, I'm no Joni Mitchell. That's why I asked Theo. I mean, who better to help me than the Sluggers' lead singer? As I recall, you wrote your own stuff too, didn't you, Theo?"

"Uh, yeah. I'm not sure how good I was though. I was kind of an idiot back then." I gave Cassie a look. "We were planning to start tomorrow at the studio. With the lessons. But then..."

"I took a bit of a tumble," Elise explained. "Luckily, Theo answered the door and saved me with his frozen produce. And then here you were. A blast from the past."

Thank God she didn't say *shirtless*.

"Luckily," Cassie echoed, distracted by our daughter's grabby hands. Suddenly, the chain snapped. The necklace broke free and fell to the floor. "Abby! No!"

Sensing her mother's disapproval, Abby melted into a puddle of tears. I rushed in, uncertain who to comfort first. "It's okay," I said, to both of them.

"What a shame," Elise said. She reached down and

retrieved the broken chain and locket. "This looks just like the one you had in high school."

"It's from Theo," Cassie told her, raising her voice over Abby's wailing. "Open it."

While I searched for Abby's baby doll to soothe her, Elise popped open the heart, gazing down at the small photos inside. She set the necklace on the counter, wiping at her cheek. Was she crying?

"I should probably go. But it was so great to see you, Cass. It feels like no time has passed at all. Jess would be so proud of you."

Cassie walked with her to the door, linking arms. "She would be proud of both of us."

Abby splashed in the bathtub, her tears a distant memory now that she had bubbles and a rubber duck. It didn't take much to make that kid happy.

"I still can't believe Elise lives here now. In our neighborhood." Cassie stood in the doorway, unbuttoning her work blouse, oblivious to my ogling. She seemed completely unaware of her own magnetism, which only drew me to her. "It's surreal."

"Yeah. What're the odds?" I kept my focus on Abby. I didn't want to spook my wife with questions about her past. Because I'd made up my mind. I had plans for her tonight. Grown-up plans. "It sounds like the two of you were pretty close. How'd you lose touch?"

"I suppose the usual way. We grew up, went away to college. Made new friends. It's sad, really, how that happens." She slipped off her blouse to reveal the lacy black bra beneath it. I felt dog-tired, but still my skin prickled with desire. It had been a while since we'd both managed to stay awake long enough for anything racier than a good night peck.

"So, Elise is nice, isn't she?" Cassie asked, unzipping the back of her skirt. "Pretty too."

I found Cassie's eyes in the mirror but I couldn't read her. She'd never been jealous, not like the women I'd dated in the past who demanded my passwords and got their hackles raised when I showered first thing after a gig. But under her business suit of armor, Cassie had an eggshell heart. It cracked a little every time my mom made a snide comment, every time Abby rejected her. "If you're into that type, I guess."

"Hmm... A tall, leggy blonde. Isn't that every guy's type?"

I wiggled my eyebrows at her. "I don't know about every guy. But I'm into you." I fished Abby out of the bathtub and wrapped her in a towel. As I carried her toward the nursery, I leaned over and kissed Cassie on the shoulder. "I'm glad you came home early. Once we get this girl to sleep, maybe we can have some alone time. You can tell me more about your cheerleading days. Do you still have your uniform?"

"Ha-ha. Very funny."

"Oh, I wasn't joking." I smacked her on the butt. "You never told me you were a cheerleader."

"Head cheerleader, if you must know." Cassie grinned at me. I missed flirting with her. But I missed settling down on the sofa, too, with a glass of wine, only to fall asleep in the middle of a movie. Between Abby and the law firm, we barely saw each other anymore.

"And a filmmaker too?"

"Elise might've exaggerated a bit. We just made these silly little movies, daring each other to..." Her voice trailed off. "You know, teenage girl stuff."

I wiggled my eyebrows at her until she groaned and disappeared into the bedroom to change.

By the time I diapered Abby and wrangled her into her favorite pajamas, Cassie returned, still smiling. She peeked over my shoulder, cooing at Abby in her crib. Every so often, it hit me, how miraculous it was that we'd made her together without even trying. The happiest little accident.

"Hey, where did you put your locket? I'll take it to the jeweler tomorrow to get a new chain."

Dismayed, Cassie pointed toward the bedroom. "It's on the dresser. I should've known better than to let Abs anywhere near it. She's got the hands of a circus strongman." On cue, Abby latched onto Cassie's finger.

"You're so right. I hope it comes in *handy*."

"She'll open our pickle jars."

"And crack our walnuts."

I put an arm around my wife and pulled her close to my chest, savoring the warmth of her. "Was I imagining that Elise got teary when she saw it break?"

"I didn't notice. But it wouldn't surprise me. She's sensitive. At least, she used to be. The three of us bought these cheap heart lockets at the mall and wore them until our necks turned green. Maybe she was just feeling sentimental."

"Maybe. I suppose it would be pretty overwhelming to randomly find yourself in the house of your childhood best friend." Lowering my mouth to her ear, I added, "Who's now a hotshot attorney and looks damn good in a power suit... and *out* of it."

"Don't forget the rock star husband." Cassie turned toward me, grazing her lips against mine. "Now, are you ready to put *me* to bed?"

THE DOWNTOWN STAR

"Sluggers' Frontman Had a History of Womanizing; Wife Agrees to Defend Him!"

Theo Copeland was once on his way to the top. With his movie star looks and his boyish smile, Copeland and his band charmed the nation, winning SFTV's *Starbound* in a landslide vote. The Sluggers' frontman seemed destined for fame and fortune. But like most rockers, Copeland had a wild side, and those closest to him suspected that his partying ways would lead to his downfall. Now, with rumors swirling that the fallen idol had a salacious affair with his wife's best friend, Copeland faces first-degree murder charges in the woman's death.

In a stunning interview obtained exclusively by *The Downtown Star*, an industry insider ("Jane Doe") confirmed that, like his famous father, Copeland had a wandering eye. She agreed to speak under the condition of anonymity, fearing the reprisal of Copeland's diehard fans. "Theo was a likable guy. He made everyone feel comfortable around him. That was part of his charm. But I saw the ugly side of that. Partying after the show. Bringing women back to the tour bus. He and his drummer joked about the power they had over women, power they could use to manipulate them into doing just about anything... 'starry-eyed gaze,' they called it. SEG. And it usually led to S-E-X."

According to Jane Doe, even Copeland's marriage began as a one-night stand. "He saw Cassandra as a challenge. She was different than the typical groupies he hooked up with. She had a future. She was going places." Copeland and his wife married in a hasty Las Vegas ceremony, leading to suspicion that she was already pregnant with their daughter at the time. In a strange turn of events at Copeland's arraignment, he fired his counsel and agreed to allow his wife to represent him, sparking debate about just how far one would go to defend one's spouse.

For the last few years, Copeland has largely avoided the spotlight but Jane Doe wondered what toll that took on his ego. "Theo was the kind of person who thrives under the spotlight. He needs attention to be happy. I wouldn't be surprised if he got bored with domestic life, especially with a beautiful woman noticing him again."

When asked if Copeland would be capable of violence, Jane Doe left room for doubt. "He could get mouthy when he'd been drinking. Once, he and his drummer got into a fistfight with a concert promoter over a woman. Guys like Theo are good at hiding parts of themselves. His father certainly was. And you know what they say about the apple and the tree. It doesn't fall far."

AFTER

CASSIE

TEN

Theo said nothing as we exited the jail and climbed into the Range Rover piloted by his mother. She'd insisted on coming with me to post bail, and after the "stunt" I'd pulled that morning—her word—dismissing Riggles mid-arraignment, I couldn't really argue. I'd obviously won the war. I hoped seeing Abby would make it all a bit more bearable for him. But she'd fallen asleep in her car seat, oblivious.

I slid in beside Abby, while Theo buckled himself into the passenger seat, wearing yesterday's rumpled clothes.

"Have you told him yet?" Gloria jammed the accelerator, and the vehicle screeched away from the curb.

"Jesus, Mom. Slow down." Then, turning to me, he added, "Told me *what*?"

"Well..." I tried to think of the right way to say it. So it wouldn't sound that bad.

Gloria let out an exasperated breath. "There are at least fifty reporters camped out on the sidewalk outside the house. There are Sluggers fans too, holding posters and begging us for your autograph. It's a three-ring circus."

"Fifty is a stretch," I said, annoyed with her for making it worse. "It's more like ten or so. Just the major networks and a few crazy fans. The cops told them to disperse. They were blocking traffic." I didn't mention that SFTV's lead reporter had the audacity to ring the bell and stick a microphone in my face. Or that I'd advised her of another place she could stick it. "And there's an article in that gossip rag about you. *The Downtown Star*. They interviewed an 'insider,' and she called you a womanizer."

Theo winced. "It's probably that stylist. The one who had a thing for me."

I nodded just to keep the peace. In the weeks before we met, Theo had slept with her a few times and flown her to Miami for one of their shows. Though he assured me that she took the whole thing as lightly as him, her sudden resignation had suggested otherwise.

"Why did you bring Abby?"

"I thought it would make you feel better to see her." Abby's head lolled to one side, the ridiculous bow Gloria had affixed in her hair discarded on the seat. What I didn't tell Theo was that I'd hoped the reporters would have pity on our little family and back off.

Glancing down at his watch, Theo sighed. "It's the middle of her nap time, Cass."

"And that's exactly what she's doing. *Napping*."

Next to me, Abby began to stir, even as I willed her to keep her eyes shut. Half awake, she searched her seat, repeating, "Baba. Baba." I realized then my grave mistake. A mistake Theo would've never made. I'd left her doll behind in the nursery.

"Your baby's at home," I told her, a hot rash of shame spreading across my cheeks. "We'll be there soon."

With the timing of a dramatic actress, Abby's whine built to a full-on cry. I wanted desperately to soothe her, to redeem myself after my stupid screw-up. I offered her the housekeys from my purse. Usually, she loved to jangle them, but today, she flung them onto the floorboard.

Gloria met my eyes in the rearview. "I told you it was a bad idea. That he wouldn't like it. You exposing his daughter to all this."

It took everything in me to bite my tongue, especially after this morning's revelation in the courtroom. Her perfect Theo wasn't so perfect.

"It's fine, Mom. Don't pile on. She meant well." He looked over his shoulder again and wiggled his fingers at Abby. Then he began humming to her softly, a melody I recognized. *"You're like sunshine on a rainy day. You take all my cares away..."*

Abby hiccuped, as her crying slowed. I should've been grateful. Instead, my stomach curdled. Because I knew that song. Elise wrote it. "Stop," I said. "Why would you sing that?"

"Because Abby likes it."

"Well, I don't."

When I caught Gloria frowning at me, I averted my eyes. Let her think whatever she wanted. I didn't want to hear that song. *Her* song. Not now. Not ever. Especially not out of Theo's mouth. And just like that, Abby started up again.

By the time we pulled onto our street, greeted by the waiting SFTV van, I'd gone numb to Abby's inconsolable crying. A dull ache throbbed like a heartbeat behind my eyes. No matter what I tried, she wouldn't be soothed. I'd almost given in and begged Theo to sing that wretched song again.

As we neared the house, the group of weary reporters came to life, stumbling over each other to get the best angle, the closest position. They followed on either side of the vehicle, clinging to the windows like barnacles, and shouted their questions into the void.

"Did you do it? Did you murder Elise Sterling?"

"No comment," I told Theo. "No matter what they say, no matter what they ask you. It's always 'no comment.' Better yet, total silence. We all wait till the garage door closes before we get out. Got it?"

Theo's jaw twitched as he stared straight ahead. Gloria grimaced at her hands white-knuckling the steering wheel. At least Abby seemed to enjoy the attention, turning her teary face to the window and waving.

"*Were you having an affair with Elise? Is that why you killed her?*"

Gloria pushed the key fob, and the garage door began its painfully slow ascent. The car lurched forward, as a fist thumped against the window. That reporter and her lipsticked mouth appeared in my face. Again. Her eyes eager, she signaled to her cameraman, who approached from Abby's side.

"*Is that even your baby, Cassandra? Or are you raising Theo's love child?*"

As a girl, my mother once read me the legend of an Eskimo woman who wrestled with a polar bear to protect her children. I never understood why she couldn't stand up to my father, who had no fangs or claws but could bear down on me like a wild animal, spitting his vitriol in my face. Now, with my own daughter, I'd wondered about that primal instinct. Whether I had it at all. Or whether, like my mother before me, it had somehow passed me by, leaving Abby to fend for herself while I looked on, unwilling and unable to rescue her.

My teeth gritted, I shoved the car door open hard and fast while we moved, scaring myself with my own ferocity. The woman let out a squeal, falling back and landing on the hedge that bordered our lawn.

"Leave us alone!" I shrieked at her, punctuating my outburst with the slam of the door.

After Gloria eased the vehicle into the garage, I sat there, fixated on my shaky hands. Neither Theo nor Gloria dared breathe a word, but they exchanged a wary glance that told me I'd crossed the line.

Abby looked at me and shook her finger. "Bad Mama."

Theo shut the bedroom door, leaving us alone. As alone as it gets with your mother-in-law downstairs and a throng of reporters and onlookers outside your door. I dropped my briefcase on the dresser and pulled the drapes tight, shutting out the dwindling sunlight. I positioned myself on the bed, facing away from the window. Even so, I felt on display, like an insect in a jar.

"Before you yell at me, just let me explain," Theo began.

"I wasn't going to yell. I'm way past yelling." Which sounded ridiculous in light of the downed news reporter I'd left in my wake. I wondered how long it would take for the footage to go viral. How long before Mr. Stone called to tell me how disappointed he was that I'd tarnished the firm's reputation for remaining calm under pressure.

"You *are?*" Theo didn't believe it either. "Is that a good thing or a bad thing?"

"Neither. I'm your attorney now. You need to start thinking of me as your lawyer and not your wife. You got arrested for domestic violence. I need to know what happened. And keep in mind, I'm going to see the police report eventually."

"It's not what it looks like, I swear. I'm sorry I didn't tell you. I just figured that you'd judge me. That you wouldn't believe me. That you'd hate me. Especially after what you went through with your parents."

I gave him a weary look. "Just the facts, please."

"Alright, alright." Theo slumped onto the bed, propping a pillow behind him. "It happened during sophomore year at USF. I'd gone out on a few dates with this girl, Amelia Ford, and she asked me and the guys to play at her birthday party. *Big mistake.* That night, she got hammered and started acting crazy jealous. Way over the top. I mean, we weren't even a thing. The shit really hit the fan when one of her friends started dirty dancing right in front of the stage. A catfight broke out in the middle of our set. They're going at it, pulling hair, screaming at each other. When I tried to break them up, Amelia grabbed my guitar and wouldn't let go."

"The Fender?" I knew how much that guitar meant to him. It hung in a place of honor at The Spot. "Wow."

"Exactly. You understand." I didn't correct him, didn't tell him that I couldn't understand anything anymore. Least of all him. He looked like my husband, but he felt like a stranger. "So, I jerked the guitar as hard as I could. Danny even tried to help. Eventually, my hands slipped, and the body popped up and got her on the lip. She needed three stitches. When the cops showed up, she told them I did it on purpose. She just wanted to punish me."

I studied him for the telltale signs of deception. Fidgeting, stammering, shifting. All the reasons my father had pronounced my mother a liar, which he used to justify what came next. Really, she was only terrified. "And the charges were dropped?"

"When she sobered up, she confessed the truth, and they dismissed everything."

"What happened to Amelia?"

Theo squinted at me in confusion. The DA would eat him up and spit him out, putting his skeletons on display for the whole world to see, exactly as Mr. Stone had warned. "Are they really going to bring that up?"

"Any attorney worth their salt will try. But I doubt the judge will allow them to introduce your criminal history during trial. It's way too prejudicial. Still, at the very least, I'm sure they'll leak the police report to the media."

Theo groaned. "Well, we ended on good terms. But I think she dropped out of USF before I did." Reading my face, he added, "Nothing to do with me."

"Alright. We should probably try to find her anyway. Get

her on our side before they do." I stood up and reached for my briefcase, snapping the clasp open and retrieving my Moleskine notebook and a stack of file folders. "Now, let's talk about Shaun DeMarco."

"That's it? That's all you have to say?"

"Do you *want* me to yell at you? Because I can." Honestly, I felt all yelled out. Exhausted from my outburst with the reporter. "I'm trying to stay calm for Abby's sake. It won't do her any good with us at each other's throats. But it hurts, Theo. Just when I get used to one lie, it turns out there's another. And another. And—"

"Alright, I get it. You think I'm a habitual liar." He hung his head. "And an idiot. I should've listened to you," he said. "I don't know what I was thinking going over there. It just made everything worse. Now, I look..."

Ignoring the shame splashed across Theo's face, I opened the notebook containing the evidentiary discovery from the prosecutor—blood evidence, fingerprints, interview transcripts. The only bright spot I'd found was mention of the bathroom window's broken latch. A possible entry point for an alternate suspect.

"Like a repeat violent offender?" I suggested, finally.

Theo looked disgusted with himself. But he had to hear the truth.

"The police report says you broke into Shaun's garage and confronted him there."

"Bullshit. I told him I wanted to talk. He invited me in."

"The report also says you called him a pervert and a murderer. That you seemed jealous of his friendship with Elise."

"His *friendship*? That's ridiculous. She felt sorry for him." The words Theo didn't say crushed me under their weight. Had he been jealous? I worked the web of skin between my fingers, refocusing myself.

"So you didn't call Shaun a murderer?"

"What I said was that Elise told me he made her feel uncomfortable. That I'd seen his post online. I asked him how he knew where the murder took place. Since that's something only the killer would know." The killer and anyone with access to the Internet. But I humored him. He would find out soon enough exactly what we were up against. DA Callaghan would take no pity on him. He would be out for blood.

"How did he respond?"

"He told me that he was at the park flying his drone that morning and saw a few cop cars drive past. He followed them. With the drone, of course. So, I asked to see the footage. I thought it might be helpful."

I waited for Theo to continue.

"He flipped out. He said the drone was his property and I had no right to ask him that."

Holding up the police report, I gave him a sad smile. "Well, the report says you punched him in the face, causing him to briefly lose consciousness. And that you stomped on a drone valued at $3,500. Is that accurate?"

"That part is true. I can't deny I hit him. But the guy had it coming."

"'Had it coming'? You mean you were justified to knock him out? To break his nose? Is that what you're saying, Mr. Copeland?"

Theo's eyes widened with understanding. "Oh, okay. I get it. You're playing devil's advocate here. Like a role play."

I cocked my head at him. This was no role play. I tried to wrap my mind around the idea that my husband, the father of my child, could so easily rationalize the vicious, purposeful throw of his fist at another man's face—in defense of *her*, no less. It made me wonder what other signs I'd missed. What else I didn't know about the man who shared my bed.

"You're right. I probably shouldn't have said that. I felt provoked by him. Threatened, even. But I handled it poorly."

"You felt threatened? What did he say?"

Theo glanced up at me with fear in his eyes. The eyes of a man with no way out.

"Just tell me. Remember, I'm your attorney." I faced him head-on and slipped my wedding band from my finger, placing it on the bed. The simple diamond ring had once belonged to Theo's mother. I hadn't had the heart to tell him it felt cursed. We both stared at it. My bare finger felt strangely naked with only a tan line around it.

"C'mon. Don't do that."

"If this is going to work, you have to think of me as—"

"I know. Attorney, not wife, I get it. Still, I don't want you to be upset. And I certainly don't want you to take your ring off." The way he sighed softly filled me with an unshakable sense of dread.

It took all my strength to say, "I won't be upset. I promise."

"He said he had drone footage of me and Elise together. That he would show it to you, if I didn't leave him alone." Theo reached for me as I pulled away. "I swear it's not what you think. It couldn't be. But we did spend a lot of time talking at the park, sitting on the bench together. He probably figured you'd read into it."

His words pricked my skin like acid rain.

"I told Shaun that Elise and I were just friends. But he wouldn't hear it. He said that if she'd been stupid enough to get involved with a punk like me, she deserved whatever happened to her. That's when I hauled off and hit him."

I kept my mouth shut. Because I only wanted to scream at him and I'd promised I wouldn't get upset.

"But Cass, there's something else." Theo reached into his pants pocket, conjuring a flash of the past, of him dropping to one knee less than twenty-four hours after I'd shown him the test with two pink lines. "When I socked Shaun in the face, he went down hard. I spotted this in the grass. He doesn't know I have it. It's a flash drive—"

"I know what it is." I looked at the small silver rectangle in his palm. *Stealth Drone 1, October–December*, penned in black marker down the length of it.

"With drone footage."

"Clearly. I *can* read." I sounded like a bitter shrew. Typical for me lately. No matter how hard I tried to soften my edges, to be the self-assured woman Theo had fallen in love with.

"Don't you think we should look at it?" Theo chose his words carefully, as if any one of them might set me off.

"If you want to."

"I told you. I don't have anything to hide." I let him take my hand, but it stayed limp—and ringless—in his. "If I did, I wouldn't have shown it to you. Right?"

I left his question unanswered without the reassurance he wanted. Let him see how it felt to be left hanging.

"Stay here." I set my wedding band on the dresser—best to leave it there so Theo would know I meant business when I said I was his attorney now—and hurried across the hall, closing the door to my office behind me. Standing there knee-deep in the rubble of my life, I felt like the screaming man in that expressionist Munch painting. Fixed to the spot, mouth gaping in agony.

The distant sound of Abby's laughter moved me. As I unplugged my laptop from the docking station, I wished I could be downstairs with her and Gloria, baking chocolate chip cookies, instead of here, preparing to defend my husband in a murder trial. My *unfaithful* husband. I'd been naïve to believe anything else. And now it seemed he had a violent streak he'd kept carefully hidden behind his playful blue eyes and soulful guitar strumming.

Moving like a zombie bride, I trudged back to Theo, back to

my marriage bed, carting the laptop with me. Together, we took our usual places beside each other. Though I kept my distance, I couldn't help but remember all the nights we'd spent pressed together, spooning so close our heartbeats synchronized.

"Alright. Let's see what Shaun's been up to," I said, inserting the flash drive into the port.

The screen populated with rows of video file icons, each of them named with a set of initials and a number.

"ES #1." I pointed to the first icon. "For Elise Sterling? Could it be that easy?"

Before I could rethink it, I double-clicked and a list of dates appeared. I selected a random file, transfixed as the video began. Down below the drone, a woman traversed the sidewalk, pushing a double stroller. She headed to the end of the block and turned right, and the drone followed. It must've been an unseasonably warm day, the way she'd dressed. Shorts and a tank top, her flowing hair tied back in a ponytail. I knew the route she travelled. Theo and I walked it most weekends, ending up at the children's playground. Once she arrived, she spread a blanket on the grass and unclipped the twins from their seats. As they played next to her, she lay back and tucked her tank under her bra, exposing her midsection to the sun.

Theo cursed under his breath. "This guy is worse than I thought."

The drone circled the park and returned several times. Each trip brought the bird's eye camera closer to Elise, until her face came into clear view. Her body, too. I saw her through Theo's eyes. Not as my childhood friend—with gangly limbs and braces—but as a woman. Once, she seemed to look directly at the drone, and I held my breath, waiting for her to cry out. But instead, she lazily rolled onto her stomach, propping herself on her elbows and reading a magazine, while the twins stacked a set of oversized blocks.

"Do you think she knew?" I asked.

"Hell no. She'd never let him get away with that."

"And she never said anything?" I closed the file, anxious to be rid of her taut stomach. The kind of slim, unmarred abdominals that hadn't been ravaged by growing a human being. No wonder Theo couldn't keep his hands off her.

"Just that he had a thing for her. That he made her uncomfortable, like I told you. But she never treated him poorly. She was so... *nice*."

I wanted to vomit. Instead, I agreed because he wasn't wrong. "Elise had a kind heart. She got along with everyone."

Theo leaned into my space, tapping the screen with his finger, and I tensed. I wanted him away from me, far away, and yet, I still wanted to be near him. I hated that about myself. It reminded me of my mother, icing my father's knuckles after he'd slugged her in the face.

"There's an AF too," he said. "Alexandra Fairchild. And a CH for Caroline Hamilton."

But I'd already scrolled past those files, my eyes falling fast to the bottom of the screen like a skydiver without a parachute.

"Look." I dragged the cursor to the folder marked CC and opened the icon. "He has one for me too."

"What an asshole." When Theo stiffened beside me, I felt a strange sense of relief. He still cared. He didn't want anyone else gawking at me. He pointed to the most recent file, and I opened it without question. The date read December 22.

"Is that you?" Theo asked, squinting at the figure on the screen. "Running?"

I nodded, studying myself in black leggings and a long-sleeve tee. A far cry from my usual buttoned-up attire. "I took off work that day. Your mom watched Abby, while I went for a jog downtown."

"I guess I was at the studio, huh?"

"You met up with Elise," I offered, trying not to sound

resentful. But the memory of that day left a bitter taste. "She gave you that Christmas gift for Abby."

"Oh. Yeah. 'The gift.'" The way he said those two words told me all I needed to know. He remembered the argument. It had been one of our worst. But looking back, I'd only been afraid of losing him. Afraid I already had.

The drone followed me at a safe distance, past the children's playground and the corner coffee shop. It paused when I stopped to stretch my cramping calf, zooming in as I bent over, my sore leg extended.

Theo growled, then hammered his finger against the screen to disappear the window. "Alright. That's enough. We have to give this to the police."

Frowning, I eased the laptop away from him. "We need to think carefully about that."

"What's there to think about? The guy is obviously a predator. He's the one they should be looking at. Not me."

"I agree. Nothing would make me happier than exposing him. But..." I had to ask it, no matter how much I didn't want to know the answer. "Is there anything on here that might make you look bad? I mean, worse than you already do."

Theo winced. "Damn. Are you this honest with all your clients?"

"You said yourself that Shaun had footage of you and Elise together. If the cops get their hands on that, it will only strengthen their claims about the two of you. It'll help prove their motive. We can't afford that, Theo."

"There's nothing. *Nothing*. I promise. I'll prove it to you." Theo grabbed the computer from my lap and reopened the ES folder. His eyes pleaded with me. "We can go through every single one of them together."

Just then, Abby let out a shriek of delight that carried up the stairs and into the bedroom. It jolted me back to the reality of our lives. No matter how bad it got, we still had Abby. The best part of both of us. "Let's take a break. After spending the night in jail, I'm sure you could use a hot shower."

"Is that a hint?" He nuzzled my neck, hoping I'd surrender to his touch the way I always did. I wanted to give in. But I kept hearing him say it. *We did spend a lot of time talking at the park.* I kept replaying that argument, the way he'd cradled Elise's perfectly wrapped gift. How could I be jealous of a dead girl?

"More of a strongly worded suggestion."

Theo didn't look away while he shed his clothes. Watching him move—the impressive curves of his biceps, the broad plane of his back—I had to admit he could drive a hard bargain, using my weakness for him against me.

Once he'd disappeared into the bathroom, I waited for the steady drum of the shower before I reopened my own file folder and scrolled back to the video of my mid-afternoon run. I pressed DELETE. I didn't want Theo to know how desperate I'd been.

Then, I padded to the office, cellphone in tow, shutting the door softly behind me. I dialed the number, kept my voice low. The man answered, as he always did, day or night. Mr. Stone paid him well for his special services. *Dirt excavation*, he called it, tongue in cheek.

"It's Cassandra Copeland with Stone and Faber. I need a favor, off the books."

In the dark kitchen, the laptop glowed. My eyes burned, dry as sandpaper. I squeezed them tight until they teared, giving me a bit of relief. I couldn't stop now. I'd nearly made it through Shaun's drone footage, fast-forwarding to the only parts that gripped me. The parts I couldn't look away from. My husband with *her* on that same stupid bench in the children's playground. I wanted to drive there right now and set it on fire.

October 23: She touched his leg, right where his shorts ended and his skin began. He didn't pull away.

November 1: He nudged his elbow against her ribs. She threw back her head, laughing.

November 17: She lifted the sleeve of his T-shirt and traced the lines of his tattoo. His first guitar—the infamous Fender—gifted to him by his father on his thirteenth birthday and preserved in ink on his right bicep.

November 20: He bounced Abby on his knee, while she played peekaboo with my daughter. Now you see me, now you don't. Did Abby look at me like that? Like her cup spilled over with joy?

November 23: No space between their thighs, they sat side by side, her notebook between them. I replayed it again and again and again, transfixed. She gazed up at him. He smiled back. I should've grown numb to it. Instead, each time it hurt worse, like ripping off a scab. And yet, I kept scrolling back, kept pressing play. It felt necessary for me to see the evidence of all my failures.

"You're still up?" A sleepy, bare-chested Theo shuffled in the doorway, his hair mussed.

I shut the laptop, casting us into darkness, and brushed away a tear. "Couldn't sleep."

"Were you...?" His eyes volleyed between my face and the computer until he realized. "I told you I would look at it with you."

"Why? So you could convince me I'm crazy? So you could tell me there was nothing going on between you two? I needed to see it for myself without you looking over my shoulder."

"And? What's the verdict?" How could he be so calm, so cavalier?

"It's just like I suspected. We can't show this to the police. And for our daughter's sake, I hope like hell the jury never sees it."

Theo moved closer to me and reached for my hand. Frowning, he grazed my bare ring finger with the pad of his thumb. "But what did *you* think?"

"I think it's best if I focus on just being your attorney right now."

JULY

FIVE AND A HALF MONTHS BEFORE THE MURDER

Theo

ELEVEN

I sat bolt upright, shaken awake by the wailing from the baby monitor. My girl had the lungs of a heavy metal frontman.

"My turn. Go back to sleep." Cassie lay next to me with a book in one hand, a highlighter in the other. Half asleep, I squinted to read the title. *Raising a Healthy, Happy Eater*. Abby's pediatrician had recommended it.

"Aren't you late for work?" A ray of soft light snuck in through the space between the drapes. Cassie usually disappeared before sunrise, a Stone and Faber vampire.

"It's the weekend, dork." She set the book on the nightstand and slipped out from under the covers. "I take care of Abs. You sleep in. Remember?"

"Roger that." I rolled over, eager for a few more minutes of shut-eye. Since Abby arrived, the days bled into one long stupor, broken by moments of sheer joy and abject terror more intense than any drug I'd tried. And guilt. That too. It buoyed me to the surface now, treating me to a flash of last weekend's oatmeal breakfast disaster when I'd slept late and left Cassie to fend for herself.

I dragged my guilt-ridden ass out of bed and trailed toward

Abby's room. Cassie already had her splayed on the changing table. When she frowned at me, I gave her a shrug.

"Couldn't sleep. I'll get her breakfast started."

By the time I got midway down the stairs, Cassie stopped me. She stood in the doorway, with a half-dressed Abby on her hip. "You can't keep rescuing me, you know. I have to figure this out with her. That's why I'm reading the book."

"I wasn't coming to your rescue, Rapunzel. But if you keep making a big deal out of it, it's not gonna get any better. She likes the attention, Cass. *Your* attention." I couldn't think straight this early in the morning. Which had to be the reason I'd allowed something stupid like that to leave my mouth.

"What is that supposed to mean?"

With no good answer, I fled into the kitchen, Cassie's bare feet padding behind me. She plonked Abby in the high chair. "You don't think I give her enough attention. You think I work too much. You think I'm a lousy mom."

"No, I don't."

"Just admit it, Theo."

I flung open the pantry to retrieve the carton of oatmeal, cursing under my breath. Nothing I said would convince her otherwise now. So, I focused on Abby instead.

"Are you hungry?" I asked, ruffling her hair.

"Not the oatmeal," Cassie huffed at me, brushing past to the refrigerator. "It'll remind her of last time. The pediatrician said—"

"Fine. Do it your way. Let's not argue in front of her." I kissed Abby's head and retreated toward the stairs. "If you don't need me, I'm gonna shower and head to the studio a little early. I promised Elise her second guitar lesson."

"On the weekend?" Cassie avoided my eyes, busying herself with a container of whole milk yogurt. She spooned a large dollop into a bowl. "Why didn't you tell me?"

"I thought I mentioned it last night at dinner. Anyway, she

has the day off. I won't be long. Two hours, tops." Abby preferred her yogurt blended with strawberries, but I kept that to myself since Cassie obviously thought she knew best. "Unless you want me to stay and help with—"

"Nope. We're all good here. Aren't we, sweetie?" Cassie still hadn't looked at me, as she loaded up a bite and aimed it straight at Abby's closed mouth.

I'd left my wife in the middle of a cold war, with Abby staunchly refusing to eat anything Cassie served her. Cassie had waved me away, mouthing *I'm fine*, when all signs pointed to an impending disaster. I should've insisted on staying. I should've told her about the strawberries. Instead, I'd yelled "See ya later" and headed out the door to teach guitar to her friend from high school, who just happened to be smokin' hot, objectively speaking. Now, I felt like a world-class asshole.

"What's wrong?" Elise stopped strumming the G-Em-C-D chord progression I'd taught her and rested her guitar on her lap. A quick learner, she could already play the first progression without relying on the beginners' handout. "You seem distracted."

"Is it that obvious?" I slumped back against the sofa cushion, running a hand through my hair. "To be honest, I'm feeling like a jerk. I left Cass alone with Abby."

Elise laughed. "Well, she *is* her mother. I'm sure Cassie can handle it."

"It's not that. She's the most capable person I know. She's a great mom. But lately, Abby's been fussy with her at mealtimes. Cassie thinks it's her fault for not being around more." I took the guitar from her and played a few chords myself, instantly feeling better with the strings beneath my fingers.

"You make it look so easy," Elise said.

"Well, I've been playing since I was thirteen. You'll get

there. Like anything else, it takes practice. You'll do most of your learning between lessons." I started to pick out an old Sluggers tune, and Elise's eyes brightened with recognition. "Please don't tell Cassie I told you about Abby. She hates being bad at anything."

"Don't I know it."

I passed the guitar back to her to stifle my curiosity. "Now, let's mix it up a little. Play the C-D first, then the E-G. Next time, we'll work on adding in an eight count."

While Elise played each new chord with painstaking precision, my mind drifted back to Cassie. How little of her past she shared with me. The moment Elise rested her fingers, I blurted, "So, what was my wife really like in high school?"

Elise pressed her lips together in thought. "If I had to sum up Cassie in a word... *perfect*."

"Oh, c'mon. You can do better than that. I need some dirt. Something juicy to tease her about. She hasn't told me much about that time in her life. I didn't even know she was a cheerleader."

"I'm surprised. I can't imagine why she wouldn't want to brag. Perfect family. Perfect grades. Perfect looks. The guys all wanted to date her, and the girls all wanted to be her best friend. Like I said—"

"'Perfect family?'" I made the same flummoxed face Abby gave me whenever we played a game of peekaboo. Elise didn't seem to notice my confusion.

"Her dad worked as the Chief of Police. He was so handsome that all our mothers had crushes on him. Her mom made the best homemade pizza. She was a real sweetheart. They spoiled Cassie rotten. Even her house was the nicest in town. It had these adorable blue shutters and a huge wraparound porch."

My head spinning, I replayed every conversation, re-examined every bone I'd carefully exhumed. Cassie's best friend had no clue what she'd been through behind closed doors. And it wasn't my place to tell her.

Elise plucked out a few more chords, as I sat there quietly reeling.

"Well?" she asked.

"It sounds like my wife had a charmed life."

"She did. But I meant my playing, silly."

"Oh, of course." My cheeks burned. Another reason I should stick to teaching tween boys. I can half-ass their lessons without feeling like a chump. "You did great for your second go-round. You're a natural. But I'm gonna need you to come up with something I can hassle Cassie about. Did she flunk gym? Blow up a Bunsen burner? Have a bad hair day? It couldn't have been all rainbows and lollipops."

In the silence, I listened to the gentle music of Elise's breath. She raised her eyes to mine, blinking back tears. "Has Cassie told you anything about Jessica Sanders?"

I didn't want to admit the truth. That I hadn't heard the name until last week. "She mentioned the three of you were close."

"The closest. My mom called us Triple Trouble." Elise wiped her cheeks with the back of her hand. "You can't say anything to Cassie. She took it really hard. We all did. I wouldn't want to upset her."

"Of course. I won't say a word."

"A month before our high school graduation, Jessica killed herself."

I opened the front door of our house with the caution of a cat burglar, peering down the hall and listening for signs of trouble. It seemed impossible I'd only been gone for two hours. I tiptoed in like a stranger, armed with the knowledge of what my wife hadn't told me.

"Hey." Cassie appeared at the top of the steps, wearing my sweats and carrying the baby monitor. I could tell she'd been crying. "I just put Abby down for a nap."

I glanced toward the kitchen and took in the scene. The bowl of yogurt lay upended on the floor. Beside it, a wet dishtowel. On the counter, I spotted Cassie's failed attempts—banana slices, a carton of cottage cheese. Even the forbidden oatmeal. I swallowed the questions I wanted to ask and settled on, "I'll clean up."

Cassie followed behind. "She hates me."

"Oh, hon." I let her collapse against my chest. "She's a toddler. She doesn't hate you."

"After thirty minutes of trying and trying and trying, she ate one bite of banana and spit it up. And I..." She peeked up at me, then hid her face again. "I threw the bowl of yogurt on the floor. I probably scarred her for life."

I laughed before I could stop myself. "So, you're saying she'll cross the street when she spots a Yogurtland. That she'll shudder in horror when she passes the dairy section. That she—"

"It's not funny. There's something wrong with me, Theo. Why can't I just be a normal mom?"

"What's a normal mom? Because I'll tell you, none of the women in Stroller Valley are normal. They're all fucked up in one way or another. Everybody is, babe. You're just doing your best."

She released her grip on me and spun away, giving me her back. I'd blown it. I never knew what to say when she got like this. She steadied herself against the sink, her shoulders shaking, and turned on the water to drown out her sounds. I let her have a moment while I stooped down to collect the bowl and mop up the glob of yogurt.

Disgusted with myself for failing her, I tossed the rag on the table. I should have told her about the goddamned strawberries.

Though I doubted the ordeal would've ended any better, at least I wouldn't feel the crushing weight of my remorse like a boulder on my chest.

"How was Elise?" Cassie asked finally, after she'd regained her composure. "Did the lesson go okay?"

I came up behind her, settling my chin into the nook between her neck and shoulder. I didn't want to lie. "Why didn't you tell her that your dad was an alcoholic? She thinks you had a perfect family."

"Are we really talking about this now?"

"I felt stupid, Cass. Like I don't know my own wife."

She gave her answer to the running spout. Her voice sounded like a child's. "'What happens in this house, stays in this house.' That's what my mom used to say. She desperately wanted the whole world to think she had it all. The house, the husband, the perfect child."

"So no one knew the truth? Not even your best friends? That must've been lonely."

"Jess did. But not because I told her. She lived next door, so I'm sure she heard the screaming matches. Once, in the second grade, I ran to her house, after my dad gave my mom a bloody nose. It was the first and last time I talked about it. I guess Jessica's mom told my mom who made it crystal clear to me what would happen if I ever did that again. Everyone in Buttonwillow would know our business, and nobody would want to be my friend."

Cassie turned to face me. "You didn't say anything to Elise, did you? I would hate for her to know that I hid something like that."

"Of course not." I squeezed her arms. For comfort, for reassurance. My own, more than hers. Then, I plowed forward, unable to stop myself. "What happened to your friend, Jessica?"

Stricken, Cassie slipped away from me to retrieve the wet

dishtowel, rinsing and wringing it out in the sink. "Did Elise say something about it?"

In truth, I'd pried it out of her after she'd sworn me to secrecy. Then, she'd shown me a photo, clipped from the Buttonwillow *Gazette*, that she kept folded in her wallet. The three of them, Triple Trouble, at the county fair. So worn at the crease, the paper had nearly torn in two. "She told me Jessica hung herself. That the janitor found her unconscious in the bathroom after school. Is that true?"

As Cassie scrubbed at the high chair tray, her head barely moved. *Yes.*

"Damn, Cass. Why didn't you tell me?"

"Because it happened almost sixteen years ago. Because it messed me up. Because it's not something I think about. Not until Elise showed up in our kitchen."

"But still." I walked toward her, quieting her hands with my own. I wrapped my arms around her even as she stiffened. "I'm your husband. You could've told me. You don't have to shoulder your past alone. That's what you've got me for."

"I know that." Yet, she freed herself again, as if to prove otherwise, and returned to her vigorous cleaning. "But I'm not like you. I grew up having to fend for myself. A leopard can't change her spots."

"Can't or won't?" I wondered aloud. Cassie didn't answer. Which told me all I needed to know. To be fair, she'd warned me about expecting too much from her. After that first night we spent together—when I'd asked if I could see her again—Cassie told me she sucked at relationships. Hell, so did I. Unless the passionate love affair between me and my Fender counted as a long-term commitment. I'd always been afraid of turning into my father, inheriting the roving eye and free spirit that kept him on the road for most of my childhood. Dad had worked as journeyman guitar player for some of the most popular seventies rock bands.

"Is that why you and Elise lost touch?" I asked.

"It's part of the reason, I'm sure. Being around her was just too painful. I imagine she felt the same." Cassie finally stopped moving. The floor glistened beneath her bare feet, the high chair tray polished white as bone. "Don't be mad at me, but can we change the subject? It's been a rough morning."

"Yeah. I get it." I reached for her, pulling her to me, giving her no choice this time. "As long as you promise me you won't shut me out. No more secrets."

"I promise." She pecked my lips, already glancing over my shoulder at the baby monitor on the counter. Abby would be waking up soon. I wouldn't have another chance to say it, and I'd told Elise I would ask.

"Hey, maybe you and Elise should get together for lunch or something. She mentioned that it would be nice to catch up. To have a friend in the neighborhood. It might be good for you too."

"Sure. Maybe." Cassie backpedaled toward the stairs. "I'm so busy at work. I barely have time for you and Abby. I'm not sure I need another responsibility right now."

I nodded, pretending it didn't sting to be reduced to a line item on her to-do list. I decided right then, petty as it sounded, to let her figure out the strawberries for herself.

AFTER

CASSIE

TWELVE

"This is ridiculous," Gloria said, peering out the side of the living room curtains. Two long days had passed since Theo made bail. Yesterday, Detectives Kincaid and Mason had dispatched their crew to search the house, leaving with Theo's laptop, his raincoat, and the last shreds of our privacy. The reporters had dwindled in number, but a few stubborn holdouts remained, waiting outside their vans to fire off their questions. A couple of diehard fans holed up there too, waving homemade signs that professed Theo's innocence. "We're not on house arrest. I'm taking my granddaughter to the park."

"I don't think that's a good idea, Mom. What if they follow you?" Theo sat on the floor, entertaining Abby. He ran a pink plastic brush through her doll's hair and started braiding it.

"Then I'll call the police. But I won't be held prisoner here. Neither should you. You did nothing wrong."

"I'm going with you," I said. Without work to distract me and the Christmas tree dismantled this morning, I felt useless, restless. Bored. A run—burning lungs, aching quads—sounded like a slice of heaven, and I had a destination, a plan to set in motion. Theo's plan, to be honest. I'd told him no, but the more

I combed through the evidence against him, the faster our options dwindled. The blood spot on the wall belonged to Elise. Alberta Knox, the elderly bookstore owner, felt certain she heard Theo arguing with a woman during children's story hour at four o'clock. Then there was the *Starbound* statuette, apparently covered in Elise's DNA. The only discernible set of fingerprints on it belonged to Theo. With the investigation ongoing, I feared what else the prosecution might uncover. I feared the prosecutor himself. District Attorney Edward Callaghan had the longest win streak in the history of San Francisco County.

"Really, Cass? After what happened last time?" The video of my little tirade had gone viral, with the hashtag *mamabear* trending on Twitter. Truthfully, I liked it. Finally, I'd done right by my daughter. Theo couldn't fault me for that. "I think we should lay low."

"And what do you think?" Gloria stooped down next to Abby, stroking her cheek. "Do you want to go to the park with Grandma?"

"Really, Mom? That's not fair."

"Go," Abby chirped, flashing an eager smile. She pushed herself up on her hands and stood, before toddling toward her father and waving her little hand in his face. "Go bye-bye."

I shrugged at him. "Looks like you're overruled."

Twenty minutes later, Gloria backed the Range Rover out of the garage, while I hunkered down in the backseat with Abby.

"*Where is he? Where's Theo?*" I heard one reporter call after us. "*Why is he hiding?*"

Once we'd cleared the block, Gloria gave me the okay, and I lifted my head to take in our neighborhood, which looked both familiar and strange. The sun felt too bright, the sky too blue. Like I'd been trapped underground and had only just emerged into the land of the living, where in spite of everything, a new year would soon dawn.

"Maybe Theo should give a statement." Gloria found my eyes in the rearview. "It might help. An innocent man doesn't need to hide his face."

"An innocent man doesn't need to say so either. Let the evidence speak for itself." I looked away, hoping she would take a hint. Gloria didn't know the ugly truth. If the evidence *could* speak, it would utter only one name. Her son's. "Besides, he didn't have to stay behind. That was his decision."

As Gloria steered the SUV into an open spot across the street from the park, Abby reached for my arm and pointed out the window toward the swings, squealing, "Go!"

My heart swelled at her joy. I felt better than I had in days. Until. "Oh, God."

"What is it?"

"Not 'what', 'who'. Alexandra Fairchild." She stood near the sandbox with her son. Peter? Porter? *Parker.* That was it. "I don't trust her. She's such a gossip. Please don't mention anything about the case."

"Of course. I wouldn't dream of it."

"She can be persuasive. And sneaky." But what I hated most about Alexandra was her effortless mothering. She made it look easy. Easy and fashionable. Little Parker had probably latched right onto her perky breast. Had never refused the delicious baby food she pureed herself. That kid worshipped her. I'd put money on it. Not to mention her shameless flirtation with Theo.

I stepped out of the vehicle and walked to Abby's side. After unclipping her car seat, I handed her off to my mother-in-law. "I'll meet you back here in thirty minutes."

"You're leaving?" Her mouth tugged downward, matching Abby's pout. Leaving my daughter never got easier.

"Just for a quick run. I have to clear my head." To Abby, I

added, "I'll be back to push you on the swing, I promise. Be good for Grandma."

Before either of them could mount a protest, I took off in the opposite direction, fueled by a familiar combination of guilt and relief. When I reached the corner, I stopped for a moment and glanced back over my shoulder just as Abby threw a fistful of leaves in the air. Gloria and Alexandra stood side by side, members of a club to which I would never belong. I couldn't quite make out their faces but I imagined them laughing, possibly at me. I wondered, not for the first time, if I would ever feel like a good mother.

I almost changed my mind for a million reasons. I could be disbarred, humiliated. Lose my job at Stone and Faber. I could even face criminal charges. But if I didn't follow through, Theo would lose faith in me. That wouldn't do either of us any good. In the last few days, "for better or worse" had taken on a whole new meaning. So I ran as fast as I ever had, taking the back streets to avoid being recognized.

Shaun backpedaled into his garage as soon as he saw my approach, nearly tripping over the cardboard cutout behind him. I recognized it as a character from *Battle of the Drones*, the multiplayer video game that had launched his programming career. I bit back a laugh and raised my hands in surrender.

"I come in peace. I just want to talk."

"Yeah, that's what your husband said..." He retreated to the corner. The way his eyes darted to the cardboard cutout, I wondered if he planned to use it as a weapon. "Before he gave me the nose job I never asked for. Your man's out of control."

I tried not to stare at the bruise or the misshapen bump. Though the injury overwhelmed his delicate features, it lent an air of mystery. Like a real-life Clark Kent. "Theo wants to apologize. In person. To see if the two of you can settle this without going to court."

"Yeah, right. I think it's a little late for that. It's not the first—"

"Oh, c'mon," I interrupted before he flat out refused. "You have something in common. You both cared about Elise."

Hearing her name startled him. Shaun blinked at me from behind his glasses, like he'd stared too long at the sun. "That's what I told the cops. Elise was special. I don't know why anyone would want to hurt her. She had a way of making me feel seen. Nobody's ever looked at me like that. Usually, I'm invisible."

I understood what he meant. Elise had a way with people. An ease I never had. Theo would've found her easy to talk to, easy to fall for. "Is that why you filmed her?"

"Uh, what?"

"The drone footage. I saw it, Shaun." I almost felt bad for the guy. The way the color of his face betrayed him. "Did you know there are over twenty hours of footage of Elise on that flash drive?"

"How did you—" He swallowed hard, a fleshy ripple coursing down his throat, before he began again. "Elise knew. She didn't mind. It was for a project at work. A new game design."

"A game design, huh? What about the other women? Did they know? Because I certainly didn't."

Shaun shoved his hands in the pockets of his jeans and shuffled from one foot to the other. No matter the smattering of gray around his hairline, he reminded me of a kid caught with his hand in the cookie jar.

"You're not a good liar, Shaun. The cops will see right through you."

"Are you threatening me?"

Though I'd done just that, I shook my head vigorously. There's a razor wire between one side of the law and the other. From my father, I'd learned how to walk it. "Of course not. I'm an attorney, not a goon. I don't break kneecaps. I negotiate. You come to the studio tomorrow morning at ten o'clock and let Theo say his piece, and I'll be sure that flash drive finds its way down the nearest garbage disposal."

I didn't wait for him to mull it over. I turned around and headed back the way I'd come, with no regrets and no apologies. I moved even faster than before, until the push and pull of my breath had blown my brain clean. One thing my dad taught me —a threat can be as powerful as a grenade. It can force people to listen to you, to do what you want, to never, ever leave you. But you have to watch out for the blowback. Once you throw it, stand clear. Better yet, run.

Following the sound of Abby's contagious laughter, I found her on the swing set. Gloria stood at her back, giving her a push. As I approached, Alexandra appeared from behind the play structure, holding Parker's hand. I froze like a rabbit in the grass, but I had no place to hide. I'd been spotted.

Alexandra called out to me and waved me over. I'd forgotten how striking she looked up close. Her forehead didn't move beneath her contoured makeup. Her eyelash extensions gave her a permanent look of surprise. And no one would call her a natural blonde. But the fearsome way she carried herself left me awestruck and a little afraid.

"How's Theo?" She stage-whispered his name, while she boosted Parker onto the top of the slide. "Your mother-in-law said it's been hard on him. I can't imagine what you're going through. You poor thing. You look exhausted."

"He's fine. We both are."

Parker zipped down the slide and into her waiting arms. "Well, have you heard that Elise's mother is in town? She's staying in the Hamiltons' guesthouse. Do you think they'll have the funeral in San Francisco?"

I would have preferred Alexandra kick me in the stomach.

Elise's mom, June, had always been sweet to me. She'd coined the three of us Triple Trouble and driven us to the mall in Bakersfield to buy matching lockets. Three friends, thick as thieves, with our lives stretching out before us as limitless as a long ribbon of highway. Now, only I remained.

"I doubt it. Elise grew up in Buttonwillow. It's a small town about four hours south of here. I imagine she'll be buried there."

"Oh, then I presume she's here to collect Elise's belongings and..." She turned away from her son and mouthed, *the body*. I could hardly look at her. "You know, I can't say I'm surprised about what happened to her. The girl was a flirt. She probably gave some pervert the wrong idea. But I'm sure I don't need to tell *you* that."

"What do you mean?" I asked, though I would rather not hear the answer. I wished I could run from her too, but what good would it do me? There's no escaping the truth.

"I don't want to stir up trouble, but she spent a lot of time batting her lashes at Theo. Men can be so simple. So obvious." When her eyes flicked to my left hand, I cursed myself for leaving my ring in the dresser drawer. Now that Alexandra had seen my bare finger, the news would spread faster than a fire.

"Elise and Theo were just friends. She was my friend too. A good friend. We knew each other since high school. There's nothing more to it than that."

Alexandra's deep sigh conveyed how pathetic she found my defense. I suddenly wished Elise and I hadn't lost touch after high school, that we hadn't become strangers. Maybe everything would've turned out differently, and I wouldn't be here with Alexandra, lonelier than ever.

"I really should get going," I told her.

"SFTV contacted me yesterday." Clearly, the conversation wasn't over until she ended it. "They're asking all the neighbors about Theo. Trying to dig up dirt. I thought you'd want to know."

I nodded.

"Of course, I told them what a standup guy he is. He's Mr. Mom, right? He wouldn't hurt a woman. In fact..." Her voice trailed off, and I pretended I didn't care what came next.

Alexandra reached into her Prada baby bag and produced a toy dump truck. Parker's eyes widened, as if she'd just performed a miracle. Abby never looked at me that way. "Why don't you take this over to the sandbox, sweetie? Show Abby your new toy."

After Parker toddled away, she refocused her attention on me. I felt hot under her spotlight. "Like I was saying, Theo's a sweetheart. A gentle soul. I only ever saw him get upset that one time."

"Which time was that?"

"Oh, you know. The bird incident."

Theo lived a whole second life without me. A life populated by others. Other parents, other children. Other beautiful women. I knew that. I'd always known that. I'd made it that way by pouring myself into my work. But I'd never been smacked in the face with it quite so often. The last few days served as a grim reminder. I couldn't trust him.

"He didn't tell you?" she asked, reading my face. "I just assumed with what happened between him and Shaun that he'd mentioned it. I'm not sure it's my place to—"

I rested my hand on her arm and fought the urge to squeeze her bony shoulder. "Just spit it out. I know you want to. Isn't that why you called me over here?"

Her pinched smile served as confirmation. "All I'll say is that it's not the first time those two have tussled over your so-called good friend Elise."

A sudden yelp of distress came from behind me. Abby sat in the sandbox, wailing and pointing her finger at Parker. Gloria tried to lift her but she shook her head and cried harder. I rushed over, with Alexandra following.

"What happened?" I asked my stricken mother-in-law.

"I turned my back for one second." She hung her head, no doubt feeling as guilty as I did. I should've been watching more closely. "And I think Parker snatched her doll away and..."

That's when I saw it. In the back of Parker's dump truck. The head of Abby's precious baby doll. The other half lay half-buried in the sand. I snatched both parts up, Abby too. Cradling her trembling body against me, I headed for the car.

"It's just a doll," Alexandra called out. But I didn't bother to turn around.

I could barely stomach the sight of my husband. Even as he doted on Abby, fixing her doll with a squirt of Super Glue. Preparing her dinner with the care of a gourmet prep cook. Giggling with her during her favorite show. Dutifully reassuring his mother, the same way he always reassured me. *Abby's fine. You've done nothing wrong.* Sweet, sickening Theo, always saying the right things.

I quietly seethed, saving up my anger like found pennies, all the while forcing myself to act like a normal wife. A good wife. A wife whose husband hadn't lied to her repeatedly. A wife whose husband didn't have criminal charges looming over his head.

After I laid Abby in her crib, I wandered down the hall to the guest bedroom, pressing my ear to the door. For the last few nights, Gloria retreated there after dinner, watching the Home Shopping Network and drifting off to sleep before eight. Satisfied by the soft drone of the television, I went downstairs to find Theo.

He sat at the kitchen island, nursing a bottle of beer and looking the opposite of a man accused of murder. I waited in the doorway at a safe distance. I didn't trust myself not to hurl a banana from the fruit bowl on the counter.

"Is Abby asleep?" he asked.

I could only nod.

"That kid, Parker. *Sheesh.*" Theo shook his head with a chuckle. "He's a budding psychopath."

"It's a doll," I said flatly, immediately annoyed with myself for parroting Alexandra's words. "And you're one to talk."

The muscles in his back tensed. He took another swig and clanked the bottle down too hard. "What's that supposed to mean?"

I stalked toward him and snatched the beer from his hand.

"Hey. What are you—"

"Do you really think you should be drinking right now? After what happened? You don't remember where you lost your phone. You don't remember why your jacket was wet. You don't remember if you texted Elise. You probably don't even remember if you killed her."

Theo's mouth hung open. It only egged me on. "Alexandra told me about your run-in with Shaun at the playground. She said that the two of you tussled over Elise. When were you going to mention that tidbit? When the DA has you cornered on the stand?"

"Am I allowed to speak? Or would you rather I just sit here and let you yell at me?"

"I'm not yelling." I chugged the last swallow of his beer, wishing for something stronger. Something to cure the ache in my chest, the tender spot between my ribs where all the tears I'd been holding back waited, gathering strength. "Okay, I'm yelling a little. But only because I don't know what else to do. Here I am, putting my career on the line to defend you. For all I know, there's a murderer sleeping in my bed."

"Bullshit. If you really thought I did it, you never would've shown up in that courtroom." Theo looked me dead in the eye, daring me to argue with that. "I didn't remember the disagreement with Shaun. Not until right now, when you mentioned it.

It was a non-event. Alex is just doing what she does best, riling someone up for no reason. Don't let her get the best of you."

I took a seat on the stool beside him, exhausted. Somehow, I'd turned into a bigger fool than my mother. Every time I doubted him, he made me believe. He had an answer for every question, a salve for every wound he inflicted. I could never manage to stay mad at him for long, no matter how much he deserved it. He wore me down simply by being himself. A doting dad. An attentive husband. A loving son. The kind of man Abby needed in her life. I wouldn't let her grow up like me, with a tin man for a father.

"So, what happened then? Was Elise involved?"

"Only tangentially. It was a couple of months ago, I think. Shaun showed up at the playground with one of his ridiculous drones that looked like a bird. All the kids were totally into it. But, he's not a parent. He doesn't have a clue about toddlers, and he's got zero patience. Parker broke the tail, and Shaun flipped out. It scared Abby, so I asked him to leave. He pushed me. I pushed him back. Elise tried to play peacekeeper. End of story."

"Alexandra made it sound like more than that. Like the two of you were fighting over her."

"She's a drama queen, Cass. What do you expect?" He put his hand on my knee and gave it a squeeze. "She never liked Elise anyway."

"Yeah. Because she wants you all to herself. She can't stand being out-fangirled." I peeked up at Theo. "What if she's behind this?"

"*Alex*? Really?" He paused, his brows knitting together in thought. "Though I suppose she's as good a suspect as any. She certainly couldn't stand Elise, especially after Parker got kicked out of that fancy preschool. Still, I can't imagine her bludgeoning anyone to death. That would require getting her hands dirty, possibly breaking a nail."

"You're right." One corner of my mouth lifted. "Alex would've laced her coffee with arsenic. Or hired a hitman."

Theo rose and stood beside me, grinning as he opened his arms. Somehow, he'd managed to win me over again.

I slipped my fingers beneath his T-shirt and around his waist, resting my head against the warmth of his midsection. But I kept hearing Elise's mom, *Triple Trouble*. And my mother, *Three is the loneliest number*. I kept wondering about the perpetual third person in my marriage. First, Elise. Now Alexandra. Even Abby made me feel like the odd one out. Always grappling for position. Always one step behind. The triangle seemed the only shape I knew.

"I did what you asked," I told him. "I spoke to Shaun. He'll be at the studio tomorrow. I'm sure of it. Now, we just have to get him to talk. Preferably to implicate himself."

He pulled me up to my feet and leaned in, his lips close to mine. I wanted to kiss him so hard that our teeth gnashed together. Wanted to push him away too, hard enough to knock him off his feet. "How did you swing that?"

"You're not the only one who can turn on the charm. I can flirt too, you know."

Just before he kissed me, Theo looked worried. Jealous, even. It gave me hope.

JULY

FIVE MONTHS BEFORE THE MURDER

Theo

THIRTEEN

I kicked back in a booth in the corner of Clipper's Café, the trendy little coffee shop where all of Noe Valley went to see and be seen, parking their Bugaboos out front along the sidewalk like a stroller brigade. I sort of detested the place, but they made a mean Americano.

I spotted Danny in the doorway and called out to him. Part-time drummer and full-time ladies' man, we'd been friends since little league baseball. After my relocation to suburbia, we'd managed to meet up a few times. No small feat, since he had to take the BART from Oakland over to my side of the bridge and hop a ten-minute bus ride the rest of the way. He didn't trust his run-down Camaro to muscle up San Francisco's infamous hills.

"Hey, man. Long time no see." Giving me a once-over, Danny let out a long whistle before he sat down at the table. "You look so..."

"Exhausted? I'm running on fumes and strong coffee." I took another scalding sip to wash down the harsh truth. In his beat-up jeans and black leather jacket that half covered the wolf tattoo on his neck, Danny looked a helluva lot cooler than me. Younger, too. Though he only had me beat by a month.

"I was gonna say domesticated. You wear it well." He leaned back, taking in the vibe of the café. Urban family chic. "How's the kid?"

I always swore I wouldn't do it. I wouldn't be *that* guy. But I found myself with a stupid grin, scrolling through my phone and subjecting my friend to every adorable snapshot of Abby. "See for yourself. She turned one on the fifteenth."

"I can't believe you have a one-year-old."

"You and me both. Sometimes *Starbound* feels like it happened yesterday. Other days, I feel like a different man. Like the whole thing was a dream that happened to somebody else."

Danny slapped me on the arm. "Damn, dude. Don't get deep on me."

I laughed but it unsettled me, saying it out loud. Being here with Danny reminded me just how much I'd changed.

"And what about Yoko?"

That joke got old a long time ago. But Danny kept telling it. He never liked Cassie. Mostly because she wouldn't give him the time of day. She picked me. And then, I picked her, leaving Danny and the rest of the Sluggers without the glue to hold them together. "Cassie's great. She was just named partner at the firm. The youngest woman ever. And for the last time, she didn't—"

"Yeah, yeah. I know. She didn't break up the band. But she convinced you not to take that solo deal with Soul Patch. She killed your dreams, man." Grimacing, he ran a hand across his throat. "Dead on arrival."

"It's a good thing, too. Soul Patch offered me a shitty deal."

"*Said Cassie.* You know, they just signed Saint Stallion. That guy is supposed to be the next Freddie Mercury. It could've been you. Hell, it could've been us."

I rolled my eyes, hoping he'd take a hint. The rest of the guys had moved on. "Good for him. But I'm telling you, man, I'm happy where I'm at. I don't need all that glitz and glam anymore. It's too much pressure. The biggest decision I'll make today is whether to take Abby to the park *before* or *after* lunch. Nobody's telling me how to dress, how to talk, what to sing. I'm my own boss."

"Well, I'm pretty sure you still have a boss. You have to answer to Cassie, right?"

"It's called marriage, Danny. You should try it."

Danny looked horrified. "No, thank you. Remember when we said we'd never get hitched? And the first guy to do it had to run naked through Union Square."

We both laughed at the memory. Danny had a way of taking me back. I recognized my former self, but I couldn't quite get back there. It felt like staring at a picture on the wall.

"*Theo?* Hey!" Elise waved at me from across the café.

Danny choked on his espresso. "Whoa," he whispered. "Who's that stunner?"

I pretended I hadn't heard him and beckoned her over. The crowd parted for the double stroller, leaving Elise a wide runway. I watched Danny watch her. I knew what he saw. The mile-long legs in her denim shorts, the curve of her tight ass. The outline of her perfect breasts beneath her tank top. The parts, rather than the sum. I used to think that way too. Before my daughter.

"Where's Abby?" Elise asked, giving Danny a polite smile. "I'm not used to seeing you with another dad."

A laugh burst from Danny's mouth. "Definitely *not* a dad."

"She's at home with my mom." I raised my voice to cover Danny's whispered vulgarity.

"But you can call me Daddy." He ran a hand through his shaggy hair and cleared his throat. He thought he had a chance. He wanted me to be his wingman.

"Danny, this is Elise Sterling. She's the hardest-working nanny I've ever met. Elise, this is my buddy, Danny Hendrix. One of my former bandmates. He was—"

"A whiz on the drums." She shook his hand with vigor. "I remember you. From *Starbound*. The Sluggers were one of my all-time favorites."

"Oh, so you're a fan." Danny grinned at me. "Tell me, who did you like better, the hot drummer or this guy?" He thrust his thumb in my direction. "The boring frontman."

"Danny." I sounded like the school principal. "Don't make the girl uncomfortable."

"It's okay, Theo." Elise winked at me. "I suppose now is as good a time as any to admit I saw your spread in *Hard Rocker* magazine."

That hit me like an amp, the heat travelling straight from my face to my groin and back again.

"The one where you're only wearing your guitar and—"

"Please say no more." I held up my hand, practically begging for mercy. I'd all but forgotten about that shoot. It had been my idea to drop trou. I'd been cocky as hell back then. "I know the one."

Thank God the twins heard my silent prayer. Just then, one of them tossed a shoe on the floor and started bawling. Elise sighed. "Duty calls. But we're still on for this afternoon, right? I have a free hour while the twins are at their play date."

I nodded, suddenly incapable of speech.

"Then, I'll see you later. Nice to meet you, Danny."

As Elise made her way out of the café, neither of us spoke. But at least I pried my eyes off her backside. Danny turned to me, jaw hanging.

"Damn, bro. Do all the nannies look like that?"

"Not exactly." I couldn't wipe off my stupid grin. Like a rubber ball, it kept bouncing right back, stretching my face obscenely.

"No wonder you like being a house husband. Hell, I might have a kid after all. You think they'd let me adopt? Maybe I could borrow your kid part-time. Take a stroll around the neighborhood."

I shook my head and focused on my Americano. I didn't even care that it had gone cold. "You're shameless, dude."

"You know it. No shame in this game." Danny puffed his chest like I'd awarded him a gold medal. "But that one is clearly spoken for."

Taking another sip, I feigned total confusion. I'd never seen that side of Elise—flirty and bold—and frankly, as much as I enjoyed the attention, it scared the hell out of me.

"Oh c'mon, Copeland. Don't be dense. She's into you. Major SEG going on there."

"I don't think so." Then, mostly to remind myself, I added, "Cassie knows her from high school. They were best friends back in the day."

"*Dude.*" Danny sat back, smug. For a moment, I envied him. "You are so fucked. And not the good kind."

"I hope it's okay that I brought Abby," I told Elise, when she arrived at The Spot with her guitar. "My mom made plans to go to yoga with a friend from the neighborhood. Bikram yoga, if you can believe it. She says it makes her joints feel twenty years younger."

I shut my mouth before I started rambling and told on myself. That I'd insisted on bringing Abby. That I'd sent my mom away. That I felt safer with my daughter here, playing in her bouncer. Because there's no mood-killer like a rambunctious toddler. Just ask my wife. Not that I expected a mood. After the meet-up at Clipper's, I didn't know *what* to expect from Elise. But it seemed silly to cancel, especially since horndog Danny had probably misinterpreted her whole vibe.

Elise made a face. "I never understood the appeal of hot yoga. Though Mrs. Hamilton swears by it." She removed her guitar from its case and started strumming the chords she'd learned the week prior. I could tell she'd been practicing.

"Me either. If I wanted to get sweaty with a group of strangers, I'd just start touring again. Those concerts were a real workout. I swear I dropped five pounds during every show." I made my way over to the sofa and perched beside her, careful not to sit too close. I couldn't get Danny's warning out of my head.

"I'll bet." Elise rested the guitar on her lap and looked up at me. "Your friend Danny seemed nice."

"Nice, huh? He'd drop dead if he heard you say that. Seriously, his ego would never recover."

"What's wrong with being nice?"

"Well, you know the old saying. Nice guys—"

"Don't get laid?"

Her humor always caught me off guard. But this time, I didn't laugh. Because laughing felt like flirting. And flirting felt like a step into dangerous territory. A step backward toward the old me. "Is that how it goes?"

She smiled, shrugged. I couldn't read her at all. "I hope I didn't embarrass you, bringing up the *Hard Rocker* piece. I must've read that article a hundred times."

"Um..."

"Not like that, silly. Your story inspired me. The way you talked about Bob Dylan's Nobel Prize for literature. You said that song lyrics can be just as powerful as a poem or a novel, maybe even more so, because they stick with you. Just hearing a simple melody can bring the words and the feeling right back."

I sat back against the sofa, relieved. "Wow. You did read the article. I'm not sure anybody has ever quoted me to me before. I'm flattered. But I was pretty full of myself back then. I'm no Bob Dylan. Not even a cheap knockoff."

"Don't sell yourself short. The lyrics you wrote for the *Starbound* finale were epic." Elise retrieved her guitar and resumed her playing. I checked on Abby—still babbling happily to herself in her bouncer—then sat back and listened, giving Elise a few minor corrections.

"Are you sure you haven't played before?" I asked. "You're a fast learner."

"Well, I have an excellent teacher." She strummed E major, followed by A major, her fingers perfectly placed. "Cassie must've been stoked when she saw that article."

"Honestly, I don't think she's ever seen it. We hadn't met yet. I'm not sure she'd be thrilled with the, uh... strategically placed guitar. And the questioning about the underwear throwing. Yikes."

The *Hard Rocker* reporter had finished the interview with a speed round. A few questions submitted by fans. *You get a lot of panties thrown on stage. Any special requests?* he'd asked. Me, the wannabe Casanova, had answered, *Two words. Lacy and red.*

"Are you kidding? As competitive as Cass was, I can't imagine her not wanting to show you off. Guitar and all."

"I'll think about it." But maybe she had a point. Cassie had been the one to push her way to the front. To make eyes at me during the goddamned whole set, while she shamelessly belted out my lyrics. To sneak backstage and flash major SEG.

"Trust me," Elise said, playing another flawless chord. "I know she'd dig it."

Abby interrupted, whimpering while she searched out the toy rattle that had tumbled out of her reach. I lifted my daughter from the bouncer and set her back down on her bare feet, holding her hands to help her balance. She grabbed the rattle and with my help, toddled toward the blanket I'd laid out for her.

"I learned one of the riffs you suggested. That Nirvana song."

"'Come As You Are'? Let's hear it." I pointed my thumb back at Abby. "She loves that one. Don't you, Abs?"

Elise started playing, and Abby's face brightened. She wiggled on the floor, shaking the rattle and squealing with delight. I watched in astonishment while she propped herself up to a squat, then rose to a precarious stand. She took one shaky step forward and then another.

"Holy shit," I muttered.

Elise stopped playing. "Was it *that* bad? I knew I should've practiced—"

"No. Look. She's walking." As Abby tottered toward us, reality smacked me across the face, and I panicked. For one horrible second, I thought about giving her a little push. "Cass is going to miss her first steps."

I patted my pocket in desperation, searching for my cell. Realizing I'd left it on the drum set, I groaned. "She'll be so bummed."

Bummed. The understatement of the century. Cassie would be crushed. She'd already missed so many firsts.

"I got it." Elise aimed her phone at my daughter and cheered, "Look at her go!"

Abby advanced three more wobbly steps before she took a tumble at Elise's feet. I scooped her up and planted a kiss on her cheek. "You're such a big girl. That was what, eight whole steps?"

As Abby wrapped her arms around my neck, I peered over her head to the sofa. Elise grinned up at me, nearly as proud as Cassie would have been. "That's amazing. I can't believe I witnessed it. I'm so glad I was here."

"Me too." I ignored a stab of guilt. "Me too."

. . .

Twenty minutes later, Elise tucked her guitar inside its case and ruffled Abby's hair on her way to the door. "Hey, did you ask Cassie about lunch? It would be nice to spend some time catching up. It's been so long."

"She said she'd love to. When she's not so busy. She's knee-deep in a big corporate merger right now, so..."

Elise waved it off. But I knew how it felt to be slighted by Cassie, wilting like a flower neglected by the sun. "I get it. She can be too driven for her own good. I might just show up outside that fancy law firm and kidnap her. Force her to have fun, for once."

"Give her a heads-up though. Cassie likes plans. And work comes first." I followed Elise to the front door, hoping she'd let it go. "But I'm sure you know that."

"Of course. Some people never change. They don't have to."

I pondered that. Maybe I'd been too easy on Cass. Maybe I hadn't required enough of her.

"You know, the three of us planned to go to college together at Stanford. It was Cassie's idea. She even made an Operation Cardinal folder for me and Jess to keep track of our extracurriculars. We filled out our applications together. We read each other's essays. We took the SAT on the same Saturday. Cassie architected the whole thing. Such a planner, that girl."

Elise put her hand on the doorknob.

"Wait." I grabbed her forearm to stop her leaving with another chapter of Cassie's life I'd never read. "But what happened? Cass went to UC Santa Cruz for undergrad, not Stanford."

"That's right. And I went nowhere. The best-laid plans, huh?" I detected a hint of bitterness that dissolved into a sad smile. "I'm not entirely sure what went wrong. But Cassie didn't get in. And then, Jess died. My whole landscape shifted. My grades dropped. I started skipping classes. Eventually, Stanford rescinded my offer. And here I am. A nanny with unful-filled potential. Pretty lame."

"Well, it's never too late to be what you might've been. At least, that's what they say."

Elise nodded, finally opening the door. "But they also say nice guys finish last, right?"

"I thought it was 'nice guys don't get laid.'"

At least she laughed. I felt better. Like I'd righted a wrong.

"I'll send you Abby's video," she said, almost as an afterthought before she waved goodbye. "Cassie will be so excited."

Abby lay sleeping upstairs. The kitchen clock chimed eight. I sat alone at the counter, scrolling through my phone, sipping a glass of red wine, and avoiding the pile of laundry that needed folding. A typical Tuesday night for Theo the House Husband.

When I heard the front door open, I downed the rest of my second glass and poured another. A little buzz felt necessary. I listened to the familiar sounds of Cassie's arrival. The turn of the deadbolt. The clatter of heels kicked off at the end of a long day. The thud of her briefcase against the hardwood.

"I got you the spring rolls from Laksa," I called out to her. "They're still warm."

Cassie didn't reply. She walked right past the kitchen and the takeout boxes I'd laid out for us.

"Bad day?" I asked, already uneasy. No matter how shitty a day she'd had at work, Cassie never passed up the spring rolls. She'd texted me her request—*That little Vietnamese place on Guerrero Street*—that morning for our usual Takeout Tuesday. Still, I felt like I'd done something wrong. Like I'd missed a crit-ical memo.

No answer came, so I went after her. Up the stairs and into Abby's bedroom, where I found her, leaning over the crib.

"C'mon, cheer up. They're your favorite."

That's when I heard the sniffling. She turned to me, wiping a streak of mascara from her cheek. I opened my arms to her, but she only glared at me. Her brown eyes, cold as the first frost of winter.

"What's wrong, Cass? Talk to me."

She held out her cellphone. "*This*. This is what's wrong."

I frowned at the video on the screen, utterly lost. When I pressed play, Abby took her first steps across the studio floor. "How did you get this?"

"So, you weren't going to tell me?"

"Of course I was. I couldn't wait to tell you. I was going to show you the video myself over dinner." I saw, then, the name at the top of the text thread, and groaned audibly. I'd definitely missed a memo. The one that said I'd royally screwed up. "I had no idea Elise sent it to you."

"Yeah, well, apparently, she did it by mistake. See."

As I scrolled down, I read Elise's panicked message. *NOOO! So sorry!!! I meant to send that to Theo.*

"Why does Elise Sterling have a video of my daughter's first steps? Why did she get to be there?"

I winced, as Abby stirred in her crib. It had taken me an hour to get her to fall asleep.

"Let's go talk about this downstairs, so we don't wake Abby. I can explain everything."

Cassie brushed past me, out of the nursery and into the hall. She stopped so fast, I almost ran into her. "It's not fair. I wanted to be there when it happened."

"I'm sorry you missed it, Cass. I hate that you missed it." I hugged her tight, pulling her back flush against my chest. "But I'm grateful Elise had the good sense to pull out her phone when she did. Otherwise, we wouldn't be able to watch it together."

She sighed, but her body stayed tense against mine. "It's not the same. I should've been the one filming her. Not a complete stranger."

"I know." I didn't dare say that, for a stranger, Elise seemed to know her pretty damn well. Maybe even better than me.

After a solid twenty minutes of sulking, I convinced Cassie to come downstairs with me, luring her with the promise of spring rolls and red wine. I reheated a plate for both of us and topped off two full glasses. While we ate at the counter in our pajamas, I propped my cell against the wine bottle so we could watch Abby's video, which I'd set to New Kids on the Block's 'Step By Step'.

"I don't know how you do it," Cassie said, after she drained her glass. "You always manage to make me feel better. I'm sorry I overreacted."

I leaned over and kissed the side of her forehead. "You didn't overreact, babe. You have every right to feel disappointed. Elise should have been more careful."

"I didn't even realize she had my phone number." Cassie frowned at me. "I wish you hadn't given it to her. Now, she'll be bugging me about lunch. She didn't mention it, did she?"

I stuffed the last bite into my mouth to avoid the question. Avoid, deflect, counterattack. Forget the art of war. This was the art of marriage. "I didn't give her your number." Then, quickly, "Hey, did you apply to any other colleges for under-grad? Besides UC Santa Cruz?"

"That's a random question."

"Just curious. Some of the moms were talking, and—"

"Elise said something, didn't she? About Stanford." I tried to keep a neutral face but I knew I'd been found out. That's what I got for trying to outsmart a lawyer. "Jesus Christ. She can't keep her mouth shut."

"Why should she? She cares about you, Cass. She misses

your friendship. And honestly, I'm glad she's talking about you. God knows, you aren't."

Predictably, Cassie hopped off her stool and gathered our plates, moving toward the sink. She'd always been a pro at stress cleaning. When she palmed the scrubber, I braced myself for impact.

"What do you want to know? That I got rejected by my dream school. That I showed up an hour late to the interview because my shit-faced dad couldn't drive me there. That the admissions officer refused to see me. That she flat out told me I'd disrespected her time. That both my friends got in, and I didn't. Is that what you want to hear?"

"I'm sorry. Elise doesn't know any of that."

The first plate clean, she attacked the second. "Of course she doesn't. Because I never told anybody. I was so embarrassed, so disgusted with myself. Jess and I had always planned to go to college together. That was our escape from school, Buttonwillow. Our families. My dad ruined it, like everything else."

"They wouldn't give you a second chance? Let you schedule another interview? You were only, what, seventeen?"

The scrubber hit the stainless steel, splashing up at Cassie's face. Though I couldn't see her tears, I heard them thicken her voice. "I tried. But the damage was done. It probably didn't help that I lied about why I was late. I was so stupid back then. No better than my mom, trying to protect him."

"You weren't stupid. You could never be stupid, even if you tried. You didn't do anything wrong."

Watching my wife unravel left an unbearable ache in my chest. She worked so hard at playing all the right notes. Sooner or later, fingers get tired and slip. A wrong note squeaks out. But it's the wrong notes that make the music. The more I saw Cassie's flaws, the more I loved her. The less she seemed to like herself.

"Don't say that. You don't know that. You don't know what I've—"

A scream cut through the suburban quiet of Noe Valley and sliced her thought in two. Cassie stood there, still and open-mouthed, until the sound came again, closer this time.

"Out back," she said finally, in a puff of breath. But I was already running.

FOURTEEN

I grabbed the umbrella from the corner as a makeshift weapon and headed down the hallway, flinging open the back door to the patio.

Like a smooth black ribbon, the night sky stretched from one end of our small yard to the other. Nothing moved. Even the trees stood reverent, their branches extended in silent prayer toward the night sky.

"There," Cassie whispered over my shoulder. "By the fence."

I squinted at the shape huddled in the grass in the glow from the living room window. "Elise?"

She rose to her feet, her legs as shaky as a fawn's. She still wore the denim shorts and white tee I'd seen her in earlier at the studio. But she looked stricken. On the ground next to her, I spotted a brown paper bag with a familiar logo.

"What are you doing here?" Cassie sounded more annoyed than confused. "You're in our backyard."

"Hey, go easy on her," I said. "She's limping."

Elise hopped toward us, favoring her right foot. I let her lean against me, as I helped her into one of our lounge chairs.

Meanwhile, Cassie retrieved the bag, dropping it unceremoniously beside her.

"I think I reinjured it." Elise rubbed her ankle. "I stopped to grab a quick bite at Cosmic Cantina down the street. But, on my walk back, I had this eerie feeling. Like someone was following me. Someone or some*thing*."

I flashed Cassie a worried glance. We'd heard the rumors about Shaun DeMarco, flying his drones at all hours, usually in the vicinity of a beautiful woman.

"I heard a noise, so I ducked behind your gate. I'm so sorry. I feel awful for ruining your night. First, the video mix-up. Now, this."

"It's alright. You didn't ruin anything. Right, Cass?" I waited in vain for my wife to chime in. Then, unable to take the awkward silence, I added, "Did you see anyone?"

Elise shook her head. "Not really. I panicked and ran. It sounds strange, but I heard a whirring noise. Like a swarm of bees."

"Bees? In the middle of the night?" Now that Cassie had finally spoken, I wished she hadn't, and I hoped Elise didn't catch the dismissive lilt of her voice, the skeptical curl of her lip. It didn't seem fair, her taking out her frustrations on poor Elise.

"Honestly, I may have imagined the whole thing. Just worked myself up for no reason. It's different living here in the city. My last nanny gig was in Half Moon Bay. You can imagine it's been a bit of a culture shock."

I nodded, trying to reassure her. "We'd all like to believe that Noe Valley is one of the safest neighborhoods in San Francisco, but you shouldn't walk alone at night. Even here. Do you want me to call the police? Or drive you to the station? You can make a report, in case it happens again."

"No, the cops would probably laugh me out of there. And you're right. I should have known better. The prettiest houses hide the darkest secrets." Elise reached for the Cosmic Cantina bag and struggled to stand. She grabbed ahold of my forearm, giving me an apologetic smile. "But I had a craving for the Machos Nachos that I couldn't resist."

"Been there." A laugh slipped out before I could stop it. I'd pay for it later. "For a bite of those I'd brave any evil."

"So true. I swear I put on five pounds since I discovered that place."

Cassie let out a huff of a breath and retreated toward the house. "I'm glad you're okay, Elise. Now, if you'll excuse me, I'm going to check on Abby. I have an early-morning client meeting."

"She's exhausted." I offered a half-assed explanation, after Cassie disappeared inside. Mostly for my own benefit. Cassie never behaved rudely. "Her work's been pretty overwhelming lately."

"I totally understand. I'm so embarrassed." She hid her face behind her hand, peeping at me from between her fingers. "*Seriously.* Mortified."

"No need to be. Now, let me grab some shoes and drive you back to the Hamiltons'."

"That's not necessary. I've already caused enough trouble." Gripping the stair railing, Elise hopped down and started across the yard, still limping a bit. I followed her, the grass cool against my bare feet.

"I insist. You need to stay off that ankle."

"But won't Cassie be angry? I mean, angrier than she is already."

"Of course not. Look, she's had a rough day. But I can't let you walk back like this. Cassie wouldn't expect me to. In fact, I'm pretty sure she'll be furious if I *don't* drive you."

"Alright." Elise relented, snaking one arm around my shoulders and bracing her weight against me. As she leaned in, her hair brushed against my face, and I caught a whiff of her apple shampoo.

"At least let me repay you, Theo. I know exactly what you want, and I'm prepared to give it to you."

My throat tightened. Keeping my eyes straight ahead, I moved us toward the doorway and tried to quiet my heartbeat. I wondered if Elise could see it throbbing against my neck. For a moment, I let myself imagine what I would do if there was no Cassie, no Abby. No commitments or responsibilities.

But then, Elise shook the paper bag and grinned.

"My Machos Nachos. With extra jalapeños."

Like a criminal, I slipped in between the sheets, careful not to wake my sleeping wife. She lay on her side, facing the baby monitor, cocooned in the covers. I listened to her steady breathing until slowly, slowly, my eyelids grew heavy. Maybe I could fall sleep after all, despite the guilt writhing in my stomach. Even though I'd done nothing wrong. Nothing I could name, anyway. I'd only driven Elise the few blocks to the Hamiltons' and watched her walk inside. I'd even refused her goddamned delicious nachos. Still, I felt like a cliché. Like dear old Dad, sneaking around with women half his age.

Suddenly, Cassie flipped onto her back and sighed. She looked undeniably beautiful, with her hair spilling around her on the pillow and the soft moonlight casting her in a gauzy glow and silvering her cheekbones. I wanted to take her in my arms, but I knew she wouldn't allow it.

"I can't believe you fell for her act."

"What are you talking about?"

"Really, Theo?" She turned her head to me, rolled her eyes right in my face. "Something chases her into *our* yard? She hurts her stupid ankle again? It's been almost two months since she allegedly sprained it."

"What if it was that creep, Shaun, with one of his drones? She said it sounded like a swarm of bees." Elise had seemed genuinely terrified. "Besides, what's the point of her lying? What's her endgame?"

Cassie groaned, all throaty and frustrated. I felt my body respond to the sound.

"Are you that blind?" she asked. "*You*. You are her endgame."

"Me?" I tried to sound clueless. As if Danny hadn't told me the same.

"Don't play dumb. She likes you." When Cassie propped herself up on her elbow, the thin strap of her camisole fell from her shoulder, leaving it bare. "She wanted you to rescue her. Which you did. For all we know, she was peeping into our window trying to catch a glimpse of you in your boxer briefs."

"You do realize this is your friend we're talking about, right? She seems lonely."

"She *was* my friend. A very long time ago. I hardly know her now, and neither do you. But I do know that she's lying."

"And how do you know that?"

Cassie shook her head at me, like I'd missed the bright red sign branding Elise a liar. "Because tonight she grabbed her right ankle. But the last time, when she showed up unannounced, it was the left. She can't keep her stories straight."

"Hmm. I guess you're right." I tucked a strand of hair behind her ear and ran my hand down her arm, resting it on her hip. "Are you jealous?"

"I'm not jealous. I just—"

"C'mon, Cass. Not even a little?" I nudged her, teasing.

"Alright, maybe a tiny bit. You've been spending so much time with her. Her *and* Abby together. It's like I'm a third wheel in my own marriage."

"Is it weird to say I get jealous of Martin Stone? Monopolizing my brilliant wife in her sexy power suits. Sitting across from her in meetings, probably fantasizing about having his way with her on his big fancy desk while I change diapers and watch *The Wiggles*."

Cassie giggled and scooted closer to me. I let myself get lost in her. I could think about Elise and her white lie tomorrow. "He does have a big desk. Really big."

"Oh, he does, does he? I can't compete with that."

"You're right. There's no competition." She gave my chest a playful shove, pushing me back to the bed, and stretched her leg across my waist to straddle me. "You had me at *The Wiggles*."

FIFTEEN

Elise didn't show up to the playground the next morning, so I sipped my coffee at my bench, making silly faces at Abby, until Alexandra wiggled her fingers at me and called me out for being a loner.

"Where's your friend?" Her lips pursed together like she had a bad taste in her mouth. Nearby, Parker sat on a blanket in the grass, tossing his oversized Legos at the ducks. She let that kid get away with anything.

"Don't know."

"How mysterious."

"I suppose. She's probably just busy taking care of the twins. That is her job, you know."

When Alex flipped her hair over her shoulder, I prepared myself. It meant she'd gotten serious about stealing my attention. "I heard the Diddling Droid asked her out."

I didn't need to ask who she meant. Alex had assigned Shaun DeMarco's distasteful nickname over a year ago when he'd commented with a fire emoji on one of her Instagram posts. In his defense, she'd asked for feedback, captioning the photo,

Hot or Not? And her legs had looked damn good in that short leather skirt.

"If he did, she didn't mention it."

"You know what else I heard? She said 'yes.'" She leaned in closer, conspiratorially, and found an excuse to touch my forearm. "I think she's one of *those* girls. You know the type. The ones who take the nanny gig as a cover for hunting a rich husband."

"Well, Shaun's loaded, so good for her." No surer way to get under her skin than to underreact to her pot stirring.

Predictably, Alex rolled her eyes. "You should tell her to be careful. That man spends way too much time with those drones. He's probably already married to a sexbot."

"A sexbot? Sheesh, Alex. Leave the guy alone. Besides, Elise is a grown woman. She can take care of herself."

Alex shrugged it off like she hadn't been the one to mention it in the first place. "Does your wife know how much time you two have been spending together?"

"I don't keep secrets from Cass." I peeked into the stroller at Abby, happily chewing on her toe. I wished she'd get fussy. It would give me a clean out. I already felt bad enough about last night, without Alex piling on.

Fortunately for me, demon spawn Parker came to the rescue. He hovered over the edge of the blanket, pulling up carpet grass by the fistfuls. I pointed over her shoulder, grimacing at his mud-stained cheeks. "Do you care if he eats dirt?"

"It's a good thing you're so damn cute." Abby lay half-dressed on the changing table, smiling up at me. "Because that diaper was nuclear-level bad. *Seriously*. Are you trying to kill me?"

She giggled when I poked her belly.

"Hello?" Cassie's voice carried up the stairs. "Anybody home?"

I checked my watch. Checked it again. Sure enough. Four o'clock on a random Wednesday. "Hey. Is everything okay?" I asked.

Holding her heels in her hand, Cassie scowled from the doorway. An obvious no.

"You're home early again."

"Not by choice." She flinched at the harshness of her own words. A hazard of being a lawyer, I suppose. "That came out wrong. It's been a weird day."

"Nothing I did, I hope."

She tucked herself beneath my arm, pulling me tight to her. "I got ambushed. Elise showed up, Hamilton twins in tow, at Mastro's in the middle of my lunch with the MetaTech CEO. I didn't want to be rude, so I invited her to dinner tonight. I had no choice."

I planted a kiss on the side of her head and turned my attention back to Abby, pulling up her leopard print pants and sitting her up on the table. "I feel like this is my fault. Elise mentioned surprising you at work. I told her it was a bad idea, but I should've warned you."

"It's going to be so awkward. Especially after last night."

"I'm sure it'll be fine. Just pretend it didn't happen. And whatever you do, don't order the nachos."

"Daddy is such a silly goose." Cassie plucked Abby from the table and held her close, spinning around with her. "We're eating here. With you. Elise insisted. She didn't want you to feel left out."

I recognized a landmine when I saw one. I expertly tiptoed around it. "What time?"

"Six o'clock. Plenty of time to feed this munchkin and order takeout."

"Sure." I tidied up the changing table, purposefully

avoiding her eyes. I didn't want to give away the surprise. "I left something for you in your office."

"A present?"

"Uh, maybe. I was cleaning out some stuff at the studio today and found it. I don't think you've seen it before."

"Now I'm intrigued."

Cassie disappeared with Abby, and I waited, barely taking a breath. I almost called out to her, told her never mind. After all, Elise had been the one to mention it. And it suddenly whacked me upside the head how different they were. God, I'd been stupid, thinking Cass would like it.

"How did I not know about this?" Cassie held the *Hard Rocker* issue in one hand, while she bounced Abby on her hip. I couldn't read her.

"I thought you might enjoy seeing my six-pack again. It's been a while since I had the body of a rock star."

She hadn't yet mentioned the Post-it I'd stuck to the cover. Gazing pointedly at my midsection, she cocked her head at me and teased, "Yeah, you've really let yourself go."

"So, you like it, then? I wasn't sure you would."

"You haven't posted it online anywhere, have you? You know Mr. Stone is old-fashioned. He would have a fit if the law firm was associated with anything like that."

"Like what, exactly?" I hadn't expected her to bring up her boss. It stung like the worst kind of insult. Like she'd just pronounced me not good enough for her. "I'm not biting the head off a goddamned chicken."

With a heavy sigh, Cassie set Abby in her bouncer. She held up the magazine, jamming her finger against the photograph of me and my guitar. "You're practically naked. And talking about lacy underwear."

"It was years ago, Cass. No, I didn't post it online. I'm not even online. I gave it to you, *my wife*. Because I thought you'd get a kick out of it. I guess I had some stupid fantasy that you'd be proud of me. That you'd think it was hot."

I turned away, embarrassed, cursing myself because I should've known better. Cassie caught me by the arm before I fled.

"I'm sorry," she whispered. "It *is* hot. You just surprised me, is all. And yes, to your note. Later, though. Knowing Elise, she'll show up early, right in the middle of my... um... *guitar strumming*."

Cassie had called it perfectly. Elise showed up early, halfway through Abby's bath. While I fished my daughter from the tub and dressed her in her pajamas, our guest settled in on a barstool, sharing a bottle of wine and a cheese plate with her old friend. I strained to hear them, relieved at the sounds of light, airy laughter.

Carting Abby in my arms, I padded down the stairs to join them.

"You two sound like you're having fun." The relief in my voice was palpable.

"Elise was just telling me that she met Danny." Cassie gave me a teasing smile. "And that he was every bit as charming I remember."

"Well, you know Danny. He never met a woman he didn't like."

Laughing, Cassie said, "Except me."

Elise shook her head. "I'm sure that's not true. You all must still be close, right?"

"Not exactly. Danny was Theo's first wife. He thinks I broke up the band and their marriage, and he still hasn't gotten over it."

Abby squirmed in my arms, probably sensing my discomfort. Danny had been the one friend I could rely on. The one who let me talk shit about my dad and his escapades. The one who never expected me to be anything other than me.

"Friendships are funny, aren't they? You can be this close one minute." Elise wound her fingers together, then widened her hands apart. There was a distant sadness in her eyes. "And this far apart the next. It was always like that with the three of us. Right, Cass?"

My wife nodded, sipping her wine.

"May I hold her?" Elise asked, when Abby reached for her.

I nodded. But she'd intended the question for Cassie.

"Of course," Cassie said. "I'll get a photo of the two of you together. I want Abby to remember you."

She snagged her cellphone from the counter and snapped a photo of Abby perched on Elise's knee. Abby giggled as she bounced her up and down.

"Are you going somewhere?" I asked Elise, hoping like hell that Cass wasn't being rude, wishing her away.

Cassie answered for her. "Elise wants to get a record deal. She's going to be the next big thing. She certainly won't be the Hamiltons' nanny forever."

The two friends clinked glasses. Elise grinned. "And thank God for that."

AFTER

CASSIE

SIXTEEN

I positioned myself in front of Shaun DeMarco, eclipsing his view of the studio behind me. Shoulders hunched, thighs clenched, he made himself small on the leather sofa. Despite what I'd told him the day before, I had been the one to meet him at the door while my husband waited behind the drum set in the corner of the room. Theo had promised to keep his mouth shut and his hands to himself. He couldn't afford another criminal charge or another headline. I would do the dirty work.

"Well, I showed up like you asked me to. On New Year's Eve, no less. So, let's get this over with." Shaun peered around me, eyeing Theo. He aimed for boldness but the crack in his voice gave him away. "You wanted to apologize?"

"Not yet," I told him, stepping closer. "I have a few questions for you first."

Shaun shook like a leaf. And I felt like an ogre, standing over him. Which was to say that I felt exactly like my father. Sergeant Maines had always maintained the upper hand—at home, at work, and everywhere in between. He never asked a question when he didn't already know the answer. His answer was the right one, the only one.

"That wasn't part of the deal." Shaun got to his feet but didn't go anywhere. He reminded me of my mother, bound to my father by her invisible chains. Always free to leave but never leaving.

"Remember our agreement." I waved the flash drive in his face. "*This* for your cooperation. Theo is innocent, and I have a feeling you didn't tell the cops everything."

He hadn't yet looked away from my hand. I closed my fingers around the drive and concealed it in my pocket.

"You promised you'd get rid of that if I came."

"And I will. When we're done here." I pointed to the sofa, knowing he'd return to it. He could no sooner walk out than I could. I had Abby to think of. "Unless you have something else to hide."

Under the heat of my glare, Shaun withered like a sunburned weed. It didn't feel like a fair fight. "Something *else*?"

"Aside from your penchant for videoing women without their consent. That's invasion of privacy. But you already know that, don't you? It's not your first rodeo."

His sigh reeked of defeat. But he mounted a half-hearted protest. "I don't know what you're talking about."

"Oh, I think you do." I bided my time, knowing that the investigator from Stone and Faber had given me more than enough intel to make Shaun look as reprehensible as Theo. Mr. Stone was right. Everybody's closet has a skeleton. "Does the name Lacey McConnell ring a bell?"

Shaun blinked at me, startled.

"What about Freda Ortega? Jennifer Chen?"

I could feel Theo watching me, his eyes on my back, and I reveled in his attention. He never got to see me work. Never witnessed me dismantle an opposing corporate counsel or pick apart a contract with surgical precision. I wondered if this version of me scared him. Impressed him. Turned him on. He didn't know what I'd uncovered or that I planned to use it like a knife's blade pressed to Shaun's throat.

"You were fired from Player One for stalking and sexual harassment. Apparently, you founded Generation Gamer because no one else would hire you. Nobody wants to work with a pervert, Shaun."

"That's a lie. I quit that dead-end job at Player One. I was their most talented programmer. Ask anyone there. They were lucky to have me. After I left, they started those rumors to ruin me. They couldn't stand my success. They wanted to bring me down the only way they could."

"These weren't rumors. I saw your HR file myself. I made a copy of it. Hiding a camera in the women's bathroom, taking upskirt photos during staff meetings. For a smart guy like you, it's so uninspired. I clearly overestimated you."

Shaun had begun to sweat. The stains crept out from his armpits, darkening his gray polo. "How do you know about all that? Those files are confidential."

"So, it is true, then?"

"It wasn't as bad as they made it seem. Just a few pics. It was harmless fun. Nobody got hurt."

A part of me pitied Shaun for the way I'd ambushed him. I understood shame better than anyone. I knew how much effort it took to keep the past buried. Hidden from others but mostly from yourself. Still, I pushed harder because I could. Because I had no choice. "What about the intern you followed home? Was that harmless?"

"We lived in the same neighborhood," Shaun insisted, as if he realized he'd admitted too much already. "What does this have to do with your husband pummeling me in my own garage?"

I followed his gaze over my shoulder. Theo's face looked pained. But then, he'd asked for this, demanded it even. We needed an alternate suspect. He wanted it to be Shaun. He couldn't jerk on my leash now.

"Well, I'm starting to believe Theo had a good reason. It sounds like you were due for a pummeling."

Shaun sat back on the sofa, suddenly looking smug. His eyes kept wandering back to Theo, to the drum set, to the shelf where his *Starbound* statuette once stood, empty now except for that sad stuffed teddy bear.

"Self-preservation," he said, smirking. "That's why Theo hit me. He didn't want anyone to know what I saw. Especially you."

"What did you see?" I prompted. "Go on, you can tell me. Theo and I don't have secrets. Not anymore."

Shaun laughed. A single dry note. I felt uncomfortable watching him bask in his newfound power.

"We all know that's not true."

"Then, come on. Let's hear it."

"Don't," Theo said. It jarred me, hearing him speak. I spun around to find him standing behind me, his eyes boring into mine.

"Don't." This time it sounded like a plea directed at me, not Shaun. "Please, don't."

I shook my head at my husband, meaning, it's too late. Meaning, I need to know. Meaning, what else have you lied about, you bastard? He backed away from me, afraid, and I understood then that whatever Shaun had seen could be the end of me. I did what any reasonable attorney would do when faced with a no-win situation. I played offense.

"Theo already told me you threatened him with drone footage of him and Elise. I watched every second of it. I understand that they were friendly. That she had a crush. Big deal. It's not the end of the world."

"A *crush*?" Another bitter laugh followed. "It was more than that. When Theo was around, she wouldn't give me the time of day. And yeah, I got a ton of footage of them hanging out at the park. But that's not why your husband rearranged my face."

"Why then?" I wanted to shake Shaun, to hear his teeth rattle in his head like the snare of a drum. Even if my anger was misdirected.

Behind me, Theo took a breath and let it out, long and unsteady.

"Because I saw them together outside the restaurant on the night she died. Elise ran up to him, and they kissed in the rain. Not two minutes later, he walked into Serafina, soaked like a street rat, and sat down at your table. He put that same mouth on yours. I saw the whole damn thing. I witnessed his dirty little secret. That's why he hit me."

The floor under my feet felt unsteady, and I willed myself to remain upright. "Bullshit. You just happened to be at the restaurant? That's a little too convenient."

"Ask your husband."

"I'm asking *you*."

"And I'm telling you the truth. I went for a drink and a bite to eat at that little dive bar next door, planning to walk back home. Then, it started raining again. I was standing beneath the awning, waiting for an Uber, when Theo's taxi pulled up. Elise must've followed him there. I saw what I saw. I have no reason to lie."

"As far as I can tell, you have *every* reason to lie. You were at Serafina. You probably stole Theo's phone and sent that text message, luring Elise to the studio. You knew she had a thing for Theo, that she'd come if he called."

"C'mon, man. Are you really going to let your wife make a fool of herself?"

Anger rose like vomit in my throat. I reared back—my hand took on a life of its own—and slapped Shaun hard across the face. So hard my hand stung. It didn't satisfy me. It only worsened my misery. Now I was no better than my husband. No better than my father.

"*Shit*." Shaun's eyes watered. "No wonder you haven't left him yet. You're just as fucking crazy as him. Do whatever you want with that flash drive. Tell the cops all about me. Just remember, I've got information too."

I caught Theo in my periphery, stalking toward the front door. He flung it open, held it there. "Get out. Now."

"Hey, you're the one who invited—"

"Get out before I remind you exactly how crazy I am."

Swimming through the murk of my devastation, I found my way to the sofa and sat there, not trusting myself to do anything else. The door swung shut.

"Turn it off," I told Theo, gesturing to the recording deck he'd switched on minutes before Shaun arrived. "Delete it. All of it."

How ironic that I'd hoped to catch Shaun in a lie. To force him to admit to his sins. But all I'd done was gather more evidence of my husband's infidelity, his guilt. His endless stream of half-truths and misdirection. It weighed heavy now on my shoulders. Too heavy to ignore. The burden of it burst the dam inside me, my tears flowing freely through the cracks. I couldn't remember ever weeping like this, not even when my mother died.

Theo did what I asked of him, moving silently through the studio, a ghost passing between the walls. Finally, he came to me. He dropped to his knees, laid his head in my lap. I couldn't bring myself to touch him.

"What he said isn't true. That's not how it happened." he said. "*She* kissed *me*."

Theo packed a bag while I waited downstairs with his mother. I stood in the corner of the living room, frozen like a shell-shocked soldier. Abby toddled around me with her baby doll in one hand and my cellphone in the other. I couldn't deal with a tantrum. Not now. So, I'd locked the screen and relented.

"Are you sure this is necessary?" Gloria whispered to me. "This is the worst time of his life. The time a wife should be there for her husband. Instead, you've taken off your wedding ring and you're throwing him out in the street."

"He'll be fine. He has a place to stay." Theo had agreed to move into Gloria's house. I couldn't stomach him sleeping here, not even on the sofa. I refused to become my mother, putting up with anything just to have a warm body next to her. Theo had admitted to the one transgression I couldn't forgive. He'd kissed her. *Her*, of all people. Even if he insisted she'd been the aggressor. That he'd pushed her away. Every time I imagined that kiss, fresh tears burned my eyes. I thought I'd have run out by now.

"But it doesn't seem right, dear." Gloria made a show of peeking through the curtains, though the last of the reporters had pulled up anchor yesterday. "The media will get wind of this. They'll turn up back on your doorstep. Worse, they'll use it against him."

I started moving again, tidying up the living room, straightening the throw pillows. Wiping the dust from the baseboards. Anything to shut off my brain that kept circling and circling like water round a drain. "He kissed another woman, Gloria. How am I supposed to forget about that?"

Silently, I added, *I'm not you.* Shortly after we met, Theo had filled me in on his father, Freddie "Fast Fingers" Copeland. Known for his wicked guitar solos, Freddie had suffered a fatal heart attack at age seventy, leaving a long line of groupies—and his wife—in mourning. After we were married, Theo shared the rest of the sordid story of his father's mid-coital myocardial infarction. Freddie's heart stopped beating in a hotel in Vegas on top of a twenty-something bleach blonde from Idaho.

"These things happen," she said. "I know you're hurt, and rightfully so, but he told you that he didn't initiate it. Can't you give him the benefit of the doubt? You are still defending him, aren't you? Or have you changed your mind about that too?"

I wished she hadn't asked me that. Because I didn't know the answer. It felt impossible to say yes, but saying no would leave it all up to fate. Fate and Stanley Riggles. I preferred to have my husband's life in *my* hands. Abby depended on me.

"Well?" Gloria wouldn't be denied.

Fortunately, Theo appeared at the top of the stairs with a duffel bag in hand. He plodded down the steps, landing in the foyer just as my cell rang.

Abby squealed, putting the phone to her ear. She followed up a high-pitched *hi* with a string of gibberish. Which didn't sound so different than most of my work conversations.

"Come here, Abby." I chased after her. She could move surprisingly fast on those chunky little legs. Of course, the moment I took it from her, her face melted into a puddle of disappointment. The tears followed, and my heart sank.

"Hello," I managed, practically shouting over her screaming. Theo dropped his bag and bent down to soothe her. Pushing down a pang of tenderness, I walked away to find a quiet spot at the back of the house.

"Is this Cassandra Copeland?" The woman's voice sounded smooth, practiced. "Defense counsel for Theo Copeland?"

The universe wouldn't stop poking me. Digging its finger into my open wound. "Yes, this is Cassandra."

"Oh, good. I hoped I would reach you. District Attorney Callaghan would like to arrange a meeting at your convenience. There are some additional discovery materials to hand over."

"More discovery? From where?"

"Apparently, detectives located pertinent items at the Hamiltons' guesthouse where Ms. Sterling was staying. I'm sure Mr. Callaghan will be happy to answer any questions you may have."

I made my way back toward the living room, both relieved

and annoyed to find that Theo had worked his magic with Abby, quieting her tears. I feared I'd be useless without him, exposed as an impostor.

"Is this afternoon too soon?" I asked. "I assume the office will be closed tomorrow for the holiday."

"Mr. Callaghan said the sooner the better. How's three o'clock?"

"Perfect." I already dreaded it. If Callaghan couldn't wait for me to see the new evidence they'd uncovered, I felt certain I'd spend the rest of my life trying to unsee it.

SEVENTEEN

Despite the pit in my stomach, I took the tiniest bit of pleasure in walking into Edward Callaghan's dumpy downtown office in my suede Prada pumps. No shiny marble floors, no commissioned artwork. A sad view of another nondescript multilevel office building. I reminded myself that Callaghan's salary would just about cover Stone and Faber's coffee budget. After this morning, I had to take my victories where I could. Though I'd drowned my eyes with drops and spackled them with concealer, they still felt raw and puffy.

"Right this way, Ms. Copeland." I followed the administrative assistant down the carpeted hallway toward the corner office. At least Callaghan had scored himself the biggest shoebox in the row with a window overlooking a Mexican restaurant and a graffitied travel trailer.

When I opened the door, I noticed the banker's box right away. It sat on the seat next to the one meant for me. From behind his desk, Callaghan looked me up and down and nodded, slightly amused. Surely, he could tell I'd been crying. But I took solace in my power suit, the perfectly coiffed bun at the back of my neck. In the face of his winning record, my armor gave me strength. I could do this.

"Ms. Copeland, thank you for coming on such short notice."

"Of course."

"Please have a seat."

I didn't sit. Because screw him and his frat boy smugness. "That won't be necessary. I assume this box is for me. I'll just take it and be on my way."

"Suit yourself." Steepling his fingers, he sat back and watched me take the box by its handles. The weight of it surprised me, but I didn't let it show.

"Aren't you curious?" he asked.

I shrugged at him, making my best attempt to cast off my fears like a coat. "Should I be?"

There it was again. That insufferable smirk. I'd seen it a hundred times. From the front row pricks in law school. From the old, white men at Stone and Faber who didn't think a woman could be tough. They didn't realize what it was like to be a woman in a man's world. To work twice as hard for half the recognition. To be called a bitch instead of hailed a hero. They didn't realize what I would do to win.

"Have you talked to your husband about a plea deal? I'd be willing to consider a voluntary manslaughter charge. It carries a maximum sentence of eleven years. It sure as hell beats twenty-five to life."

"Plead guilty to murder? That's not an option. Not for an innocent man. Are you worried that your winning record is in jeopardy?" The box strained my arms while I stood there. I'd be damned if I set it down.

"C'mon, Ms. Copeland. We both know you're out of your depth here. You won't do your husband any favors taking this to trial. The evidence against him, well... it's overwhelming. Open and shut, really. I couldn't have scripted a better case."

"That's because it *is* scripted. Scripted by you, scripted by the cops. From the moment they sent Officer Pettigrew to knock on our door, they'd decided Theo was guilty. They haven't considered any other suspects."

He fixed his beady shark eyes on the box and willed me to give in. To admit how heavy it had become. "We go where the evidence leads, and unfortunately for Theo, it's a straight line. Heck, it's a neon arrow."

I stared right back at him without flinching. "What about Shaun DeMarco? He was obsessed with Elise and has a history of sexual harassment, if anybody had bothered to look."

"The man Theo assaulted? As far as I can tell, he was just another victim of your husband's rage." He pointed to the box then. "Would you like to set that down?"

I shook my head and gripped it tighter to me. I'd sooner lose feeling in my arms than show weakness on his turf. I certainly wouldn't ask for his help. Not with the box. Not with the trial either. Men like him only respected strength.

"I know this must be difficult for you to accept, Ms. Copeland. I can't imagine how you must be feeling. Finding out that your spouse had an affair. Then bashed in his mistress's head, all in the name of keeping secrets. That kind of thing will make you question yourself, question your judgment. But let me assure you. You're not the first intelligent woman to fall for a guy like this. You won't be the last. You can take comfort in that."

"The only thing I take comfort in is knowing your perfect record is about to be broken by a corporate law attorney. You don't scare me, Mr. Callaghan. I won't be bullied into making your job easier for you." I gritted my teeth into a smile and braced the box against my hip, making it look effortless. "I'll find my own way out."

.   .   .

I couldn't go straight home. Gloria would be there, waiting. She would insist on opening the box with me, telling me she had the right to see it. Theo was her son, after all. Wouldn't I feel the same about Abby? Backed into a corner, I wouldn't say no to her. We'd open it together—this mountain of evidence I'd carted back alone—and she would find some excuse for it, some excuse for Theo, like she always did. The same way she'd excused all of Freddie's indiscretions.

I drove to the studio instead, lugging the box to the room in the back. I wanted to face this alone.

The lid came off easily, and I tossed it aside. I flipped through the photographs of the guesthouse, seeing traces of the Elise I'd once known. The carefree butterfly who flitted between Jessica and me. Her bed, unmade. Her dresser, cluttered. Piles of her clothing strewn about like the aftermath of a small hurricane. Her guitar stood, solemn, in its case near the door, never to be strummed by her fingers again. My eyes welled with sorrow when I imagined her mother carting it back to Buttonwillow.

I studied the last photograph—a close-up of her desk. One of the items drew me in. A hospital bracelet, its band snipped through. It was dated December 24, with Elise's name and a logo I recognized. Days before the murder, Elise had been hospitalized at Buttonwillow General. I set the photo to the side, separate from the others.

Beneath the photographs, I found a single page on official letterhead inventorying the evidence.

Item 1: Photocopy of Hard Rocker magazine, June 2017 issue

I gaped at the page in front of me, a half-naked Theo smiling back with his guitar strategically positioned over his crotch. The first time I'd seen the spread, this past August, Theo had left it for me in my home office with a flirty note that read, *Want to strum my guitar?* Why did Elise have a copy?

With no one to ask, I laid the pages aside, already feeling uneasy.

Items 2–10: Photocopies of news clippings and Internet articles

My heart sped up as I flipped through the collection. I felt vindicated, seeing it there in black and white. The articles read like a timeline of our lives together: the wedding announcement in the *San Francisco Chronicle* that Gloria had insisted on, though we'd already done the deed at the Little White Chapel; the gossip magazine speculation about our rushed nuptials; Abby's birth announcement nine months later; the "Where Are They Now" feature in *People*, chronicling Theo's rise and fall; and last, a print screen of Stone and Faber's website boasting their newest, youngest female partner. Elise despised me, envied me. She wanted my life.

The rest of the discovery had been packaged into a large binder.

Items 11–102: Photocopies of Poems to Elise Sterling

I turned to the first poem, dated August 15. It had no signature but I recognized the handwriting. The scrap of paper too. It came from a flowery stationery set Gloria had gifted me for making partner. I'd stashed it in the bedroom closet, pronouncing her clueless about corporate law. The poem took my breath away.

> The day I saw you, girl, you breathed life
>   into me.
> I used to muddle through. But now I'm free.

> Can't take my eyes off you. No matter how I try.
> If you'll have me, I'm yours. Till the day I die.
> There's only one way to describe what you've
>   done. You cast a spell on me, and it's my
>   heart you won.
> You bewitched me, girl. You bewitched me, girl.

I read it twice more, once aloud, before I realized. Before I remembered. Theo standing behind me in the mirror months ago, whispering against my hair. *In a word, bewitching*, he'd said. He'd taken the word meant for me and given it to her.

A flash of white-hot heat burned beneath my ribs and boiled my blood. I searched the poems, flipping as fast as my fingers would go. Phrases leapt up off the pages, assaulting my eyes.

> So beautiful it hurts.
> Understand me like no one else.
> Need you.
> Want you.
> Would do anything to hold you.

I sobbed through the Latent Print Examination Report, the examiner's conclusions blurring at the center of the page. Only two sets of prints had been found on the poems. They belonged to Elise Sterling and Theo Copeland. Even Theo's cellphone records didn't help his case. The studio, the restaurant, and our quiet little neighborhood block all pinged off the same cell tower. The phone had dropped off the grid at 2:25 a.m. and never resurfaced.

With a pained howl, I hurled the entire notebook against the wall and stood there until my hands stopped shaking. Then, I tossed it all back inside the box and closed it up. I shoved the lid on tight, fearing I'd just buried my marriage in that coffin.

I drove straight to Gloria's house, barely registering the ten-minute route. No matter how much I'd doubted Theo, no matter how many times I'd suspected his betrayal, I'd always been able to lie to myself. To take solace in the way he looked at me, the way he touched me. The way he loved both of us, me and Abby. But the kiss—*he'd admitted it!* And now the poems too. It couldn't be denied.

I dropped the box on the No Place Like Home mat and rang the bell. Before he answered, I fled the scene like a common criminal. Head down, ashamed. Because I couldn't explain it away anymore. Elise had stolen someone I loved. Again.

The moment I closed the front door, my mother-in-law called to me from the kitchen. "We're in here. You're just in time for dessert."

Uncertain I could manage another colossal failure, I forced myself to follow the sound of her voice. To smile at her like I hadn't just lost everything. Well, not *everything*. Because I still had Abby, with her cattail brown eyes and her little laugh that buoyed me to the surface, no matter how deep I sank. I pressed a kiss against her hair, inhaling the sweet smell of her.

"Are you okay?" Gloria spooned a dollop of yogurt into a bowl. "You look a little pale."

I answered her with a nod, hoping she wouldn't push it. "I'll finish feeding her."

"You don't have to, dear. We've already got a rhythm going. Don't we, Abby?" Abby grinned, flashing her baby teeth and holding her plastic spoon like a scepter.

Snatching the bowl from Gloria's grasp, I left her no choice. I placed it at the center of Abby's tray table and nodded at my mother-in-law. "I've got it from here."

Abby spooned a hefty bite and brought it to her lips.

Inwardly, I cheered. Maybe she'd go easy on me, make me look good—or at least, not bad—in front of her grandmother. But her nose wrinkled and she spit up, unable to hide her disgust.

"She likes it with the strawberries," Gloria said. "That's Theo's trick. Hasn't he told you?"

I swallowed a lump. I wanted to yell at her for no good reason other than the obvious. She'd given birth to him. "Right. Strawberries. Of course."

"I'll get them. I cut some up this morning."

I wiped Abby's face while we waited for the miracle berries. Gloria mixed them in and returned the bowl to Abby's tray.

"So, what did that prosecutor have to say?" she asked.

Abby watched me, as I mimed taking a bite. Then, she smacked the spoon against the surface of the yogurt, laughing as she sent up a spray onto her bib.

"He wants to offer Theo a deal."

"A deal? What kind of deal?"

Another smack of the spoon, and Abby squealed with joy, testing me. Gloria's eyes bored into me, and I had no doubt she'd begun chronicling my maternal shortcomings. "Well, for starters, he'd have to admit to a charge of voluntary manslaughter. He'll go to prison. For a long time."

Gloria shook her head at me, as if I'd made the decision to send Theo away. "That's completely unacceptable. What would Abby do without her father?"

"She'd have me. Obviously."

I turned my attention back to my daughter. Feeling desperate to prove my worth, I directed the spoon toward her mouth. She squirmed in her high chair and moved her head away until I surrendered. I could draft a sound legal contract in my sleep, but feeding Abby left me looking like a total amateur.

"Right, but..."

"But what?"

"It's just that you're so busy with your career. Who would be here day-to-day?"

"I would. With your help, of course."

"Don't be silly. You need your job. It's who you are. Some women are mothers. Some women are lawyers." Gloria maneuvered around to the side of the high chair and got Abby's attention. Opening her own mouth wide as a pike, the spoon disappeared inside. Abby's eyes widened.

"And some are both."

"It's easy to do two things, dear. But not many people can do both things well." She loaded another bite onto the spoon, and Abby grabbed for it. I wished she'd fling it. I imagined the yogurt dripping down Gloria's face. Instead, Abby put the spoon in her mouth, gobbling it up like it had been prepared by a Michelin-starred chef.

"Anyway, what does Theo think about this deal?" Gloria asked, grinning at Abby. It wasn't a competition but it felt like one. I always came in second place.

"I haven't told him yet." Then, to hurt her, I said, "You may think I'm a lousy mom, but I'm a damn good attorney, and I love your son. I'll get him out of this. But you need to accept the truth like I have. Theo's guilty. He had an affair with Elise. Then, he killed her. There's no doubt in my mind."

Gloria looked even more horrified than I'd hoped. But in a pinch, she swept her face clean and kept her focus on Abby, showering her with praise for taking another bite. "Why would he do such a thing?"

I channeled all my anger into an apathetic shrug. "You're such a great mother, I thought you would know."

Theo wouldn't stop calling. I could've set the phone to silent, but I wanted to hear it ringing. It gave me comfort to punish him. To withhold myself. He couldn't sleep. I couldn't either.

Every time I thought of him and that kiss and those poems, my throat ached like a raw sore. I blamed him, too, for the document I'd e-signed that afternoon, making my leave of absence from Stone and Faber official. Everything I'd worked so hard for, gone with one click of the mouse. To add insult to injury, the document had arrived with a personal note from Mr. Stone himself, reminding me to maintain confidentiality regarding all aspects of the MetaTech merger, which really meant I agreed to keep all the firm's dirty little secrets.

Finally, I stabbed at the answer button on the screen of my cellphone just to listen to Theo's breath catch.

"I don't have anything to say to you right now."

"Then, why'd you answer?" His bone-tiredness was audible through the phone. He sounded even more exhausted than that fever-dream of a week when we'd first brought Abby home from the hospital. Nestled in our cocoon of domesticity— just the three of us—it might have been the best week of my life.

"Good question. I'll just hang—"

"No!" His voice came out in a gust before he started again, softer this time. "No. Please don't hang up. You don't have to say a word. Just listen."

"To what? More of your lies?" With the phone pressed to my ear, I turned onto my shoulder to face the empty side of the bed next to me. I'd never felt more forsaken. "You wrote her love poems, Theo. You called her bewitching."

Theo let out a wounded groan. "It's not what you think, I swear to God. They're songs, Cass. Bits of songs we were writing together. If anything, they were about you."

"Right. I'm sure they were." I'd never been that girl. Insecure, jealous, paranoid. Theo had done this. He'd turned me into a nutcase.

"And what about that ridiculous *Hard Rocker* magazine?" I buried my head into my pillow, but it smelled of Theo. Of course it did. Feeling defeated, I flipped onto my back again. "Did you give Elise a copy too?"

"'Ridiculous'?" It figured he would home in on the most insignificant word I'd uttered. "If I remember correctly, you said it was hot."

"Yeah, objectively speaking."

"Well, we had sex afterward, so..."

"Because I thought you needed it. I thought you felt insecure about your body or something."

"So, it was pity sex?"

"Of course not." I shook my head at the ridiculousness of the argument. That stupid magazine was the least of Theo's sins. "I don't want to fight. I don't have the energy for it."

"But you think I'm lying about Elise? You think I slept with her. You think I *killed* her."

The answer scratched up my throat like steel wool, but I still couldn't say it. Not to him.

"That's what you told my mom."

"I'm scared, Theo. I agree with the DA. The evidence is overwhelming. He wants you to take a deal."

"Mom told me. Eleven years." I heard his voice break. "Abby will almost be a teenager by then. She'll have had a dozen birthdays without me. Christmases. First days of school."

"I know."

"But what if the jury finds me guilty? Twenty-five to life, Cass. That means I may never get out. Abby will graduate high school. Go to college. Get married. You'll move on too. All while I'm stuck inside a cage, spinning like a hamster on a wheel going nowhere."

"What are you saying?"

"Maybe I should take the deal."

Abby shifted in her sleep, catching my eye on the monitor. Her innocence squeezed my heart in a vise. I wondered what she'd think of me in five years. In ten. Would she understand I'd done what I had to do? That unlike my own mother, I hadn't just baked homemade pizza and stuck my head in the sand while the world crumbled around me.

"Do you still trust me?" I asked.

"You're the only one I trust, babe. It kills me to know you can't say the same."

"If you trust me, then let me do my job." I fisted the sheet, trying to keep the quiver from my voice. "We take the case to trial. We emphasize your alibi. *Me*. We present Shaun as an alternate suspect."

"I should testify. The jury will want to hear it in my own words. You know, I do have some experience being center stage."

He wanted me to laugh. I scoffed instead. "You will not take the stand under any circumstances. They'll twist your words. They'll crucify you."

For what seemed like forever, we both remained quiet. Our new reality slowly settling like the ground after an earthquake.

"How's Abby?" Theo asked. "Did dinner go okay?"

I curled up in a ball, disgusted with him for being gone. Disgusted with myself for sending him away. He didn't mean it to hurt me but it ripped through my guts anyway, fierce as a tiger's claws. Lying there, bitterly alone, eviscerated, all I could manage was, "You didn't tell me about the strawberries."

After Theo had hung up the phone, I dialed Edward Callaghan's office. I waited out the seven shrill rings before the line went to voicemail. I needed to say it now before I lost my nerve, before I changed my mind.

"It's Cassandra Copeland," I said, my husband's last name weighty as a stone in my mouth. I had to turn away from the baby monitor, Abby's peaceful face too much to bear. "I presented your offer to Theo. Like I told you, I know my husband. He's not interested in anything less than a *not guilty* verdict. We'll see you in court."

AUGUST

FOUR MONTHS BEFORE THE MURDER

Theo

EIGHTEEN

I plopped Abby into the sandbox with the Hamilton twins and made my way to the bench. My bench, of course. But I'd deemed Elise worthy of sharing, so I didn't mind when she beat me there, claiming it for the both of us. Especially since the other mothers kept their distance so they could gossip about us. Let them talk. At least I wouldn't have to hear about Parker's potty-training disaster or the latest trends in baby footwear.

"I have something for you." Elise handed me a leather-bound notebook, the cover softened with age. "Open it."

I unfastened the wraparound and laid it on my lap, unopened. "What is it?"

Her cheeks flushed, and I started to squirm, wondering how right Cassie had been. I hoped like hell Elise hadn't written me a love letter. Or worse, a whole book of them.

"Hey, you might want to..." I drew Elise's attention to Xavier, who'd started scooping sand onto Elliot's head. Not to be outdone by his brother, Elliot tossed it right back at him, starting an all-out sand fight.

Elise let out a world-weary sigh. "Just look at it. I'll be right back."

As she strode over to the twins, the other mothers watched me. By the time I'd psyched myself up to peek inside, Elise returned, wiping her sandy hands on her jeans.

"You're so lucky you have a girl. Those boys are hell on wheels."

I smiled at Abby, off in her corner of the box, babbling happily at the leaves she'd arranged on the sand. "Amen to that."

"So..." Elise briefly rested her hand on my thigh. Though I didn't look up, I imagined Alexandra taking a mental photograph. "Now that I can hold my own on the guitar, I wanted to show you the songs I've been working on. Most of them are unfinished. But I think I've got a good start."

I flipped through the handwritten pages, pausing to read a few lines here and there. Elise had mentioned songwriting, but I'd never imagined this. She'd filled the entire notebook.

"I'm impressed. Some of these lines are actually really good."

"*Ouch*. You sound surprised."

"I didn't mean it that way. It's just that a lot of folks believe they can write. Usually, the ones who think that can't write for shit."

Elise laughed under her breath. "Well, you write beautifully. That song you wrote about moving on after heartbreak, it got me through some tough nights."

"'Secrets The Stars Know'?"

"Yes! I love that line that goes, 'How can we ever explain the choices we've made...'"

I sang the rest. "'Not choices after all... but already written in sand...'"

"'By a sacred hand.'" Elise finished the verse and hummed a few bars. It felt damn good to sing one of my songs again. Even on a random Monday, on a bench, in the playground in Stroller Valley.

I turned the pages of Elise's notebook until I'd arrived at the end. "'Jess's Song'? Is that—"

"Jessica. She and I started writing it senior year before she died. It was meant to be a silly friendship song for the three of us, but then it turned into something more. Something bigger. Like a tribute, I guess. Cassie was the one who inspired me to finish the lyrics."

"Will you sing a little for me?"

"'You're like sunshine on a rainy day. You take all my cares away...'" Her voice caught in her throat.

"It's catchy," I said, hoping to ward off her tears. Alex would have a field day if Elise started crying on my shoulder. "And sweet."

"That's exactly what Cassie said."

"You showed it to her?"

Elise sniffled and nodded. "Remember when I came over for dinner last month? You went to check on Abby."

"Oh, yeah." I'd returned to the two of them crying over their plates of chicken marsala, a palpable tension in the air. Cassie had brushed it off. *Too much reminiscing*, she'd told me later. "I wondered what that was all about."

"I figured she would've told you. She said she'd always wanted me to finish it. That I should show it to you. That maybe you could help me with the music."

I couldn't imagine Cassie saying all that. I'd only been gone a few minutes to soothe a fussy Abby. But Elise looked so pained, so hopeful. "Tell me if I'm out of line for asking. Do you know why Jessica killed herself? I mean, was she depressed, or..."

Just then, a bird swooped in from above us, nearly grazing my head. I yelped like I'd been bitten.

"What the hell was that thing?" I craned my neck toward the sky, the creature a safe distance from us now.

"A black bird. An angry one, by the looks of it."

The bird circled back, staying high above us. But the kids had spotted it now. Abby gazed up from the sandbox, pointing her chubby little finger up to the sky. Next to her, the twins bounced up and down on the grass, unable to contain their excitement. "Bird!" they shouted. Like it was the best damn thing they'd ever seen.

The bird hovered above the playground, flapping its wings strangely and producing a high-pitched whirring. When I spotted Shaun DeMarco lingering on the sidewalk, with a drone remote controller in his hands, I realized.

"That's not a bird."

Elise puzzled. "It's not?"

"It's a drone. *Look.*" Shaun gave me a wave, his cheeks reddening the moment Elise glanced in his direction. Briefly, he took his eyes off the controls. "He's showing off. For you."

Abby let out a screech as the bird plunged from the sky toward the sandbox and crash-landed in the grass. Its wings fluttered and sputtered like a dying thing. Parker and the twins toddled over, kneeling beside the drone-bird. Abby tried to follow but her legs weren't steady yet, and she dropped onto her butt in the sand.

"Be careful," Shaun called out, jogging toward us. "That's a five-hundred-dollar piece of technology. Don't break it."

"They're just kids," I muttered to Elise. But she'd already joined the mothers who'd left the safety of their huddle to investigate. The playground hadn't seen this much excitement since Parker peed on the slide.

Shaun sidled up to Elise. He fiddled with his glasses, then stuffed his hands in his pockets. "It's cool, huh?"

When Elise nodded, his face lit up like a neon sign. "It looks just like a bird. Theo thought—"

"You almost hit me with that thing." I had nothing against the guy, but I'd started to understand why Alex didn't like him.

For a childless bachelor, he seemed to be a regular at the playground.

Shaun shrugged. "I was just screwing around."

"Cut him some slack. I'm sure he didn't mean any harm by it," Alexandra piped up, a wicked grin stretching her cheeks. When she had the group's attention, she stage-whispered, "That drone is probably the only way he can get a good look down his girlfriend's shirt. You are his girlfriend, right, Elise?"

"No," Elise managed, withering. Alex could wilt anyone's soul without trying. And right now, she was definitely trying. I wouldn't fall into her trap. Elise could defend herself.

"I couldn't hear you." Alex leaned toward her, cupping a hand around her ear. "Was that a 'yes'? I wonder what other kinds of toys Shaun likes."

Screw it. I had to say something. "Back off, Alex. There are kids here."

"Oh, I'm just teasing. Don't be such a stick-in-the-mud, Theo."

Disgusted, I turned away from Alex and helped Abby to her feet, guiding her over to the downed drone. She held onto both my hands and peered over the twins' shoulders, transfixed by the robot bird.

"I've got one that looks like a dragon," Shaun said. "And another little stealth one that looks like a bumblebee. It's so quiet you probably wouldn't even notice if it flew right past you."

"Big bird." Parker reached for the drone's tail, just as Shaun resumed the controls, righting it to its metal feet.

"Step back, please. Don't touch it." Any parent worth their salt would recognize that as a clear invitation. Practically a dare.

Parker's eyes glinted with mischief. He plucked the drone from the ground and held it up to his mother, shouting, "Big bird fly!" just before he launched it into the air.

Horrified, Shaun dropped the controller and scurried after

his motorized pet which had landed nearby. He fell onto his knees in the grass and cradled it in his hand, the misshapen tail hanging limply. "He broke it."

I walked over to him with Abby in tow. "No offense, man. But what did you think would happen? Kids are like drunk rock stars. Demanding. Messy. You sure as hell can't trust them with your valuables."

Shaun's mouth pinched tight. He seemed to be on the verge of tears. "Yeah, well. That little shit is going to pay for it."

"Right. He can work it off washing dishes. Hey, maybe he can mow your lawn this weekend."

The mothers laughed. Elise did too. But Shaun remained stone-faced.

"What's your problem with me, Theo?"

"No problem. But you can't blame Parker for what happened."

"Who should I blame then?"

"Well, to be honest, a playground isn't really the place for an expensive drone. It wouldn't have crashed in the first place if you weren't so busy gawking at Elise. So, I'd say you should probably blame yourself."

"*Gawking?* I wasn't gawking."

"Sure, buddy." Now, we had everyone's attention. Theo and Shaun on center stage. I wanted nothing less, but the way that guy looked at me rubbed me the wrong way. "From where I was sitting, it sure looked a lot like gawking."

"Are you jealous?" he asked, taking a step toward me.

Instinctively, I backed away, cradling Abby's head to my chest. When Elise appeared beside me, I ignored her worried face and deposited Abby in her outstretched arms.

"Jealous? Of you and Elise? What's there to be jealous of?"

Shaun wagged his finger between himself and Elise. "We went on a date."

"Good for you. I'm married, so why would I care?"

"Well, from where I was sitting..." Shaun mimicked my voice, making me sound like a pompous ass, "it sure didn't look like you were married."

My clenched fists throbbed. I hadn't thrown a punch since our last night on tour, when Danny got plastered and made out on the bus with the concert promoter's girlfriend. The guy spotted a hickey on her neck and came back with a bat, ready to give new meaning to our name, Sluggers. So, I'd decked the guy. Not out of anger but loyalty. Because that's what friends do. Danny still owed me for that one.

"Theo." I felt a tug on my shirtsleeve and turned to find Elise standing there, holding my daughter. "Just let it go. It's not worth it."

"You sure about that? Cause this guy is a punk."

A push from behind jostled me forward. I spun around.

"Who's the punk now?" Shaun tossed his glasses onto the grass and raised his lanky arms in an awkward fighting stance. When he came closer, I shoved him back, feeling the impact of my palms against his slim shoulders. He rattled like a bag of bones. I wanted to do it again.

In the ensuing stalemate, a tense silence gripped the playground. Even Parker zipped his lips. His eyes mirrored his mother's, darting between Shaun and me. A taut cord seemed to connect us. When I moved one way, Shaun followed. When I advanced, he retreated.

"*Dada.*" It took me a second to process, to realize. That voice belonged to Abby. My Abby.

"*Dada,*" she repeated, squirming in Elise's arms.

I sobered up quick, swallowing my anger in one thick gulp. Abby had just spoken her first word.

On the walk back from the park, I could barely look Elise in the eyes. I'd gone off the rails for no good reason. If I'd socked

Shaun in the mouth, he most certainly would've called the cops. I'd almost gotten myself arrested, which I'd sworn would never happen again. Thankfully, I'd convinced my crazy ex, Amelia, to drop the charges. You spend one night in jail, and it's one night too many.

"I can't believe you went on a date with him. I thought Alex was just blowing smoke." Elise and I stopped our strollers side by side at the crosswalk. "Not that it's any of my business, but he's not right for you."

Though I busied myself fixing Abby's shoe, I could feel Elise's smile. "It wasn't really a date. He invited me to the construction site of the new Generation Gamer headquarters downtown. It's a work in progress, but he's got a great view from the top floor. Anyway, he's all alone in that big house. He needs companionship. And so do I."

"I'm sure he does. But that doesn't mean you have to be the one to give it to him. You should be—"

"I'll be careful."

"How do you know what I was going to say?"

The light turned, and we started across the street. "Because that's what I would tell a friend. A good friend."

Hearing her say "friend" so convincingly brought a sense of relief. Not that I needed convincing. But I couldn't have Elise believing Shaun's nonsense. I had no reason to be jealous.

"So are you going to tell Cassie?" she asked.

"About Shaun? I don't think so. It would just wind her up. Besides, there's nothing to tell. I barely pushed him."

"I meant about Abby. Her first word. I remember you telling me you were worried about it."

Guilt lashed me with its sharp tongue. Me and my big mouth. "It's kind of a big deal. So, I should probably mention it."

Elise shrugged. "Yeah. Cassie will be bummed though."

"You think?" Of course, I knew she would be.

"There's a good chance Abby will say 'mama' next. You should practice it with her. I know Cassie would be over the moon to hear her say that first. Especially after the walking thing. At the very least, I'm sure she'd want to be there to witness it."

"I'll think about it." But it felt slimy, lying to my wife, even if it would make her happier in the end. "If *you* think about losing Shaun's number."

I expected her to laugh but she gripped my arm instead, regret darkening her eyes. "I'm sorry I was in the middle of it all. I ruined your day, and I only gave Alexandra more ammunition."

"Hey, we got to hang out and talk music. It wasn't a total bust."

When we reached Diamond Street, Elise reached into the storage bag on the back of her stroller and withdrew her notebook. "Take this with you. Jot your ideas down, and we can compare notes at my next lesson. Who knows, maybe we'll write a Grammy winner. Same time as usual?"

Something niggled at the back of my brain, as Elise gave Abby an exaggerated wave. I'd nearly made it home when I realized. I'd never agreed to write a song with her. The poor girl hadn't lied. She was just as lonely as Shaun.

THE DOWNTOWN STAR

"Marriage on the Rocks! Alleged Murderer, Theo Copeland, Kicked Out by Attorney Wife!"

Disgraced Sluggers' frontman, Theo Copeland, was dealt another blow this week, when his wife, Cassandra, was photographed for a second time without her wedding ring. Sources close to the couple told *The Downtown Star* that they are living separately, though his wife has not yet withdrawn from her role as his defense attorney. According to the Stone and Faber website, Copeland's wife was named a partner at the corporate law firm earlier this year and has overseen a number of large acquisitions in the technology and consumer goods sector, the most recent of which totaled $16.5 billion. Despite her talents in the corporate arena, Mrs. Copeland has never practiced criminal law, leading some legal scholars to question the soundness of her decision. Copeland's former attorney, Stanley Riggles, described it this way: "A corporate lawyer defending a murderer is no different than an orthopedic surgeon performing an angioplasty. They say love is blind. In this case, it's also imprudent."

Stone and Faber refused to comment on the case against Copeland but issued the following statement: "Citing personal matters, Cassandra Copeland took a voluntary leave of absence from the firm and is currently not affiliated with Stone and Faber. We will evaluate her return to the partnership when the matter in which she is currently engaged has been formally adjudicated. Our thoughts and prayers go out to the family of Elise Sterling. The firm has made a $100,000 donation to the San Francisco Women's Shelter in Elise's memory."

AFTER

CASSIE

NINETEEN

I sank onto the sofa and gaped at the woman on the television screen and the news ticker running beneath her. I wanted to look away, to turn it off. To chuck it across the room like a drunk rock star. But instead I pressed record and upped the volume, grateful Gloria had taken Abby to the park.

Entertainment Now had found Amelia Ford. Or, more likely, she'd found them. After tracking her down online, I had sent her no fewer than a dozen emails over the past few days and received no reply. Amelia worked as a physical therapist at a retirement community in Los Angeles and had put her looks to use, serving as an extra in a few Hollywood movies. Her liquid blue eyes and honey-blonde hair left me convinced Theo had a type. Yet, somehow, he'd picked me. I catalogued all the ways I looked nothing like her. Worse, Amelia reminded me of Elise. That wouldn't play well in the court of public opinion.

"Were you surprised, Ms. Ford, when you learned of the charges against your former lover?"

I shook my head, disgusted. *Lover?* A college fling, at best, to hear Theo tell it. *"To be honest, no. Theo and I dated off and*

*on for almost a year in college. At first, he was the sweetest guy
I'd ever met, a real charmer. I never would've guessed he was
sleeping with my roommate too. After I found out he'd cheated,
he acted differently for a while. Mean and cold. It seemed that he
blamed me for what he'd done. Eventually, he came crawling
back, and shortly before the incident, we reconciled."*

I scrambled for the remote, replaying Amelia's last few
sentences, certain I'd misheard her. *Off and on. Almost a year.
Sleeping with my roommate.* Every word cut to the bone, and I
found myself with a plier's grip on my own hand, working that
web of skin until I cried out in pain.

*"I'm sure our viewers are wondering why you would agree to
get back together, after what he'd done?"*

Amelia twisted her mouth, her red lips screwed up into a
crooked bow of regret. *"Two reasons. I was only nineteen, and
Theo was the hot lead singer in a band. Stupid, I know."*

"Had he ever been violent with you?"

*"Not until that day. But sometimes, he could be emotionally
abusive. Manipulative. He always knew what to say and when to
say it. I could never tell when he was lying. We'd gotten back
together a week before my birthday party at the sorority house,
and he'd promised me that he was done being unfaithful. He
seemed genuinely apologetic. He even cried. And he offered to
play at my party to make it up to me."*

As I listened to the television, the rest of my world seemed
to fall away. It was only me and Amelia and the sound of my
battered heart thudding in my chest.

"So, what happened that night?"

*"Well, a friend of mine spotted him in the hallway making
out with a freshman. I'll admit I'd been drinking, which
certainly didn't help the situation. Naturally, I was upset and
asked him to leave, but he insisted on playing. He accused me of
making the whole thing up. And when that girl got on the stage*

and started grinding on him, something in me just snapped. The moment the song stopped, I confronted her, and we ended up in a fight. Theo stepped in between us. He told me I was being crazy. That I was just jealous of her. I grabbed his precious guitar and wouldn't let go. After his drummer failed to pry my hands off it, Theo let go on purpose. It smacked me across the face, giving me a split lip."

"But the charges were dropped, correct?"

"I couldn't go through with it. As ridiculous as it sounds, I thought I loved him. And I felt so guilty, like it was my fault. Especially after his mother called me and begged me to change my story. And I did. Because I liked her. At the time, I honestly believed I might marry this guy."

"Wow. That's quite a story. What happened between you and Theo afterward? You obviously never got married."

Outside, I heard the approach of the Range Rover, the steady grind of the garage door, but I didn't move from the sofa. I couldn't. In a hundred years, they might have found me still sitting there, fixed like the lamp in the corner.

"And thank God for that. I feel so sorry for his wife. Can you imagine a man so manipulative that he can convince his own wife to defend him for killing his mistress? It's a really sad situation. As for me and Theo, my parents convinced me to end it a few weeks later. At their suggestion, I transferred to another school to finish my degree. I never heard from him again until I saw him on my TV screen in that singing competition. I thought about coming forward then, but I'm a private person. Honestly, I hoped he'd changed."

He *did* change. I wanted to shout it at the screen. Marriage changed him. Fatherhood too. But how much? He was still a liar and a cheat. He could still talk his way out of anything. And Amelia felt sorry for me. She pitied me. She viewed my life with Theo as a bullet she'd been lucky to dodge. A bullet that had hit me square in the heart.

"*How did you hear about the murder?*"

"*My mom called me. She'd seen it on the news. It's been a whirlwind ever since the police report leaked to the media. I had no choice but to speak up. I wanted to tell my story. My family and I have already been the target of scrutiny by his fans. I've been called all sorts of names online. I've even gotten a few death threats. But it's been worth it, if I can help one woman avoid what I went through. And I want Cassandra Copeland to know that she's not alone.*"

"*My goodness. You're so brave sharing your story with our viewers. I have to ask one last question. Do you think Theo is capable of murder?*"

Amelia worked the camera with her face, meandering a winding path to deliver a one-word answer. It seemed that she spoke only to me. I already knew what she would say. "*Yes. Yes, I do.*"

"Mama!" Abby appeared in the hallway, shouting the moment she saw me and tottering toward the sofa with her baby doll in her hand. Her gleeful voice broke the spell that held me motionless, and I quickly clicked the remote, sending my husband's ex-girlfriend into oblivion.

I swept her up in my arms and held her tight to me. Abby had given me a chance at motherhood. A chance to be better, to do better. I wouldn't let her down.

Abby finally nodded off for a much-needed nap. Her sleep had become restless with Theo gone, her mood as edgy as mine. After brushing a kiss against her forehead, I padded down the stairs to find Gloria. The moment I saw her, relaxing on our sofa with one of *my* mystery novels—the ones I never had time to read—my anger bubbled back to the surface and spewed right out.

"What really what happened with Amelia Ford? When Theo and I spoke, he made himself seem like a victim."

She scoffed. "You must've watched that ridiculous program. It's a travesty, the sort of smut they allow on network television."

"You saw it?"

"My son called me while we were at the park. He was in bad shape. I can't say I blame him with that hussy making up a story about him. Some women will do anything for a quick buck."

I sank into the sofa beside her, realizing that Theo had a mother just like mine. Hell-bent on lying to herself and everyone around her. I'd lived through eighteen years of that bullshit, and I wouldn't stomach it anymore. "Is that what you told yourself about Freddie, too? You enabled his father. And now it seems as if you're enabling Theo. Don't you ever get angry about what Freddie did to you?"

"My husband loved me in his own way. Those women meant nothing to him. I was the one he came home to."

"Because no one else would've put up with that. You deserved better, and so did your son."

Gloria smacked the book down onto the coffee table, startling me. Her lips pinched tight together, as if she held something back. Her carefully curated façade threatened to crack under the heat of it. I understood her better than she knew. "Careful, Cassie. You don't want to turn me into an enemy, especially if you lose this case for Theo. Grandparents win custody all the time when a parent is—"

A knock at the door interrupted her.

"Go on. Say it. I dare you to tell me what a bad mother I am. I dare you to cast the first stone from your house of glass."

Blood rushing to her cheeks, she shook her head and fled the room. I heard the thumps of her footsteps up the stairs.

The knock came again, beckoning me. I expected to see Theo on the porch, with a hangdog look on his face, ready to convince me that Amelia Ford had it all wrong. We'd agreed to meet up that afternoon to talk strategy. Right now, our best bet —our only bet—was to hang on for dear life to our alternate suspect theory. Once Callaghan put Shaun on the stand, I would load my weapon. Ready. Aim. Fire. Stone and Faber's investigatory firm had provided plenty of ammo.

A pit opened in my gut when I peered out the window. My alternate suspect waited there, as if I'd conjured him myself. I opened the door and forced a smile, trying to be pleasant, just in case SFTV had decided to camp out on the sidewalk again.

Shaun grinned back at me, then sauntered into the hallway. His cocky demeanor unnerved me. It meant he knew something I didn't, and I wasn't sure I could stand any more surprises. Over the last few weeks, my little boat had been thoroughly rocked and had capsized. I could barely keep myself afloat.

"I need to talk to you." He peered down the hallway. "Are we alone?"

"My mother-in-law's upstairs, but she won't bother us. Theo's probably on his way, though."

"This won't take long."

He followed me into the living room, lingering by the window, before he took a seat. "You know, I've never been inside your house, Cassandra. It's so homey. The fireplace. The hardwood floors. The fresh flowers on the island countertop. It's like something out of a lifestyle magazine. Not what you'd expect for the home of a murderer. But I suppose that's what they mean when they say you shouldn't judge a book by its cover."

"What do you want, Shaun?" I stayed on my feet. I didn't trust him.

"Alright, alright. I'll get to the point." He gestured to the television. "I assume you saw it. *Entertainment Now.* Amelia Ford. It's not looking good for you or your hubby."

"It doesn't matter what that woman says. Her testimony

won't be admissible at trial, and frankly, I don't find her credible. She's getting paid for her story. She's got an angle."

He cackled at me. "Doesn't everyone?"

"Yeah. So, what's yours?"

I steeled myself for another revelation about my husband. Some other way he'd managed to leave me looking like a fool. "You're handling the MetaTech merger, correct? MetaTech and Player One?"

"I can't talk about that, Shaun. It's confidential." I didn't know whether to feel relieved or terrified. "I'm on a leave of absence from the firm. So, I'm not handling much of anything right now. Except..." I held out my hands, "this mess."

"And what a mess it is. You know, my company is the third largest in the gaming industry. We were on MetaTech's radar long before Player One. Our coders are superior. Our tech is better. Our graphics are more realistic. Our CEO... well..." Shaun puffed up like a blowfish.

"I thought you were about to get to the point."

"I need you to squash that deal."

"What?"

"Kill it. Tank it. Whatever it takes. Then, Generation Gamer is next in line for a massive payday."

Stunned, I stared at him. This guy had some nerve. "I just told you, Shaun. I'm on a leave of absence. Not to mention that what you're asking is highly unethical. I could lose my job."

"Understood. But hear me out. I haven't even told you about the upside. It's the deal of a lifetime. If you do this little thing for me, I won't tell the cops that I saw your husband swapping spit with the dead girl. Hell, I'll even get them to drop the assault charges. I'll make him sound like a goddamned angel on the stand. Whatever you want."

"What about the drone footage? I assume you want that back too."

"Keep it. Consider it a show of good faith." Shaun shrugged

at the skeptical lift of my brows. "Think about it, Cassie. I'm throwing you a lifeline."

Just then, a key rattled in the door. It yawned open, and Theo appeared in the hallway. He went from zero to fighting mad as soon as he laid eyes on our visitor.

"What the hell are you doing here?"

Shaun raised his hands in surrender and backed away, slinking toward the exit. "I was just on my way out."

Theo watched through the window, seething, until Shaun disappeared down the block.

"What was that all about?" he asked.

I thought of Mr. Stone. The way he'd dismissed those emails I'd found. The way he'd dismissed *me*. "Blackmail," I answered.

Theo nursed a beer at the kitchen counter while we reviewed a list of potential blood spatter experts. Turns out, if you have enough money to offer, you can find a PhD or an MD or an MD-PhD to say just about anything, including that the blood droplet on the studio wall couldn't be cast off from a fatal blow. It was too round and too perfect. No blood, no crime.

"I think we should go with Dr. Lippman," I said. "He's got the right credentials, and he's been a defense expert in several murder trials. With a three for four record of acquittal."

From across the counter, Theo studied me in silence.

"Well?" I asked, finally.

"Yeah, sure. Whatever you think, Cass."

With a definitive nod, I began gathering the papers I'd spread out before us. I wanted to be done with this, done with him. I needed a hot shower and one of my mother-in-law's Valium, stat. Gloria always kept an emergency bottle in her purse. And today certainly qualified as an emergency.

Theo drained the last of his beer and set the bottle in the

sink. I could tell he had something on his mind. "I'm impressed. You're really *not* going to ask me about it, are you?"

"Ask you about what?" I cocked my head, goading him to say it.

"*Entertainment Now.*"

I kept moving, neatly tucking the documents inside my briefcase. Tossing Theo's empty bottle in the trash. Wiping down the counter with a dishtowel. "It's irrelevant. She won't be testifying anyway. We need to focus on the issues that matter to your case. Nothing else."

"I wanted to call you right after. To explain."

"But you called your mother instead."

"She told you?"

I shrugged. "Don't worry, she still thinks you walk on water."

"Cass, I was an asshole back then. I didn't want you to know that guy. Not ever. The one who acted like the world owed him something. The chip off the old block. I cheated on Amelia. What she said was true. But I didn't let go of that guitar on purpose. I would never hurt a woman. It slipped out of my hands, just like I told you."

When I saw the earnestness in Theo's gaze, I dropped my own to the bottom of the stainless-steel sink, preferring its icy gray to the warm blue of my husband's eyes. The sink had never lied to me. The sink had never kissed my friend. The sink had never driven a stake through my heart and convinced me otherwise.

I glanced up, only briefly, to point to myself. "Attorney, remember? Nothing more."

"Right. I deserve that."

Ushering Theo toward the door, I asked, "Hey, can you watch Abby tomorrow? I need to take a trip, and I'd rather she stayed with you."

"Of course." He slipped on his old leather jacket that fit him like a glove. He'd worn it on stage the night we met, and I knew exactly how buttery soft it had felt beneath my fingers the first time we kissed. I couldn't even look at him without being blind-sided by a memory. "Where are you going? Should I come with you?"

"No, this is one trip I have to take alone."

TWENTY

Buttonwillow General Hospital rose up from the wheatfields on the outskirts of town. When I'd lived there, the massive structure had stood alone. But in the years since, Buttonwillow had grown to meet it. Exit 257 now boasted a Walmart, a gas station, and a Starbucks. I stopped for a cup of coffee to chase the cobwebs from my head, Gloria's Valium still blurring my edges. At least I'd gotten a solid six hours of sleep last night before Abby awakened early, bawling her eyes out. I'd shooed my mother-in-law away and held her until we both drifted off in the rocking chair.

I parked in the lot and headed toward the hospital entrance, trying to ward off the bad memories. Twenty miles outside of Buttonwillow, they began to circle my brain, dark and hungry as vultures. They swooped in when I least expected them. Like the moment I felt the warm blast of air inside the hospital lobby and smelled the bitter antiseptic scent of sickness. The last time I'd walked through those doors, Jessica was still alive, even if a machine was breathing for her. Elise and I had come together to visit her. Clasping hands outside the ICU, we didn't let go until we'd returned to the car and collapsed against each other in tears, finally admitting it to ourselves. We'd just told our closest friend goodbye. The following day, Jessica's parents removed her from life support.

I approached the nurses' station, sending up a prayer that the nurse on duty wouldn't be a former classmate of mine. I hoped to get in and out as quick as I could, to not to be recognized at all, which was no small feat in a town like Buttonwillow, where everybody knew your secrets. It didn't help that Theo's face had made the front page of the *Chronicle* again.

Former Girlfriend of Sluggers' Frontman, Murder Suspect Comes Forward Alleging Abuse.

"Cassie Maines?" The voice came from behind me. Hearing that name, my old name, tied a knot in my stomach. There was never any doubt about me taking the Copeland surname. If only the past could be changed that easily. Reluctantly, I turned around to face the silver-haired woman barreling toward me with her arms extended.

"Deidre? I didn't—" In the middle of her tight embrace, another memory assaulted me. The three of us, climbing Deidre's tree to secure her runaway cat, Cheddar. Deidre lived next door to the Sterlings for a while before her husband died, and she moved in with her oldest son. "I didn't realize you were still working here."

"Only three days a week. But it's about damn time I retire altogether." She took a step back to give me a once-over, while I searched her eyes for a sign that she hated me. "So, what brings you back home?"

I cringed at her polite curiosity. Her *not* knowing felt worse somehow. I'd rather she yelled at me, called me a horrible person for defending my husband. *That* I could handle.

"You don't have to tell me anything. I'm being nosy is all.

It's just that I haven't seen you around here since your mama's funeral. And even then, you hardly stuck around."

"You're right. I haven't been back. Work has been so busy. And I have a daughter now." I thought it best not to mention a husband. If Deidre really didn't know, I'd rather keep it that way.

Deidre nodded. "Abby, right? Elise always kept us up to date about your successes. That girl was so proud of you. Good friends are hard to find. And a friend that knows you like that, that's priceless."

I blinked back at her, trying to steady myself from the shock of my daughter's name in her mouth. The memory vultures struck again, taking me on a vicious nosedive. On my seventeenth birthday, Elise and Jessica had pooled their money to buy me a handheld camcorder. *Let's make our own blockbuster movies this summer*, they'd written on the card. I couldn't tell Deidre that the memories had knocked the wind out of me. That Elise had been obsessed. So, I swiftly changed the subject.

"I was hoping to take a peek at my father's medical records. Since he suffered a heart attack at a relatively young age, my doctor suggested that the records might be useful for preventative purposes. Could you help me with that?"

"I'd love to help, Cassie. But, according to our policy, you would have to submit your request in writing to our records department. They would need to double-check that we have your power of attorney on file. Are you in town for long?"

Too long, I thought, already imagining the sheer joy of putting this place in my rearview. "What if I just look at the records? I can take a few notes. I don't need to print anything." I felt like a teenager again, standing in Deidre's doorway that same summer, with my knee busted. Jessica and Elise had dared me to jump the curb at the end of the cul-de-sac on my bicycle, while they filmed the whole debacle.

"I'll have to supervise you." She waved me to a computer

near the front desk and typed in her password. A few more clicks and my father's medical chart appeared on the screen. Mickey Maines in black and white. "And you'll need to be quick. My shift ends in fifteen minutes."

The scrape of the chair against the hard tile sent a chill up my spine. I felt Deidre's eyes on me as I scanned the pages, making a few notes in the tablet I'd brought with me. No different than Theo's dad, mine had died doing what he loved best. He'd been mid-interrogation of a robbery suspect when he clutched his chest and fell to the floor. Years of French fries, cigarettes, and pent-up rage had finally caught up to him. At the time, I expected my mother to be grateful, relieved. Instead, she hardly got out of bed. I clicked on the final entry in his chart. The emergency room physician had declared him DOA. Dead on arrival.

"All done." I stood up and secured the tablet in my purse. "Do you want to grab a cup of coffee at the Starbucks? I'd love to catch up."

A cloud crossed Deidre's face, but when she flashed me a smile, I felt certain I'd imagined it. "I'd love to. Let me grab my jacket."

The moment she disappeared into the office behind the nurses' station, I darted toward the wall. Checking both ways —*all clear*—I pulled the fire alarm, sending a blaring wail down the hallway. Then, I tucked myself into the nearest restroom and waited for my heartbeat to settle.

After the panicked voices in the hallway subsided, I slipped out and returned to the computer, the screen still open on my father's chart. I stabbed at the keys with clumsy fingers, typing another patient name into the search field. The last record in her chart was dated December 24. *Jackpot.*

Patient reports difficulty breathing, lightheadedness following a disagreement with her mother. Mother drove patient to ER, reports that she has been stressed lately about a romantic relationship. Heartrate elevated upon admission. Visible signs of anxiety, including psychomotor agitation. Patient reported a history of panic attacks, starting at age seventeen, following suicide of close friend. Was previously prescribed Xanax, as needed. Mother confirms patient suffers from anxiety and depression which have previously interfered with daily life. During discussion with physician, patient perseverated on relationship with married rock star. Possible grandiose delusions. Patient encouraged to seek mental health treatment upon discharge.

I snapped a photo of the treatment note and rushed back to the bathroom to wait for the all-clear. I hoped Deidre would head home without me, assuming I'd been lost in the shuffle. When I heard the door creak open, I drew my legs up onto the toilet seat and held my breath. A pair of white clogs advanced toward the first empty stall, then the second, before stopping in front of the only closed door.

"I know you're in there, Cassie. You're as bad at hiding as you were as a little girl, always so shy, ducking behind your mama."

"I wasn't hiding." The crack in my voice insisted otherwise.

"Did you get what you were looking for?" Deidre asked.

"My dad's records, you mean?"

"We both know you didn't come here for that."

I unlatched the door and pushed it open, finding her leaning against the wall with tears in her eyes. "Why didn't you stop me?"

"Because I wanted you to see it. You needed to understand how mixed-up Elise had become, thanks to your husband. That night, when June brought her to the ER, she was a wreck. A lovesick wreck. Your mama would turn over in her grave if she knew what you'd let him get away with. She would've never put up with that nonsense from your father. He would've been out on his ass."

Out of habit, I started to agree with her. To guard the secret I'd buried in the dustiest corner of my heart. But then, it struck me. I didn't need to protect them anymore. "Actually, my mother put up with a lot. Did you know that I stitched her arm once, after my father threw a broken beer bottle at her? Or that she only wore long sleeves because she had to hide her bruises? Or that she called the cops on him once, and he locked her in the bedroom for a week? Did you know that, no matter what hell he put her through, she took him back every goddamned time?"

Deidre swallowed hard, shook her head. "If that's true, I had no idea."

I pushed past her, stopping at the door. My lungs squeezed shut. I couldn't wait to breathe the cold air, to drive back to San Francisco with the windows down. "Did you see Elise after she came to the ER?"

"She checked herself out, packed her stuff, and left. I think she was upset with her mother for not being more supportive. June thought she should quit that nanny gig and stay here for a while. She didn't want her going back and seeing your husband again."

"He didn't kill her." I didn't sound convincing enough. Deidre's mouth drooped. She pitied me too. Just like Amelia Ford.

"At least go talk to June before you leave. You owe her that much."

I parked a block away from the white colonial with the wraparound porch and the blue shutters. My own personal house of horrors. I'd been so anxious to get rid of it, I'd sold it for peanuts to the first buyer—a newlywed couple from Sacramento—two weeks after my mother's death. Now, a little girl played in the driveway, riding circles on her bicycle. Behind her, the first-floor windows glowed with warm yellow light. It looked like a happy place.

I let my eyes drift to the house next door. It was the reason I'd come here, ignoring every impulse to floor it in the other direction and never look back.

Mark and Kathy Sanders still lived here. Mark had retired three years ago, shuttering Sanders Construction. Kathy still worked as a first-grade teacher at Buttonwillow Elementary and volunteered at the animal shelter. Jessica's older sister, Brandy, had graduated from UC Berkeley and taught art history at a community college in LA. I knew everything about them. I looked them up at least once a year. I needed confirmation, proof of life. Evidence that Jessica's death hadn't destroyed them entirely. That some part of them carried on.

I waited there, while the sun sank toward the horizon. For what, I didn't know. But the moment I caught a glimpse of a silhouette in the window, guilt hollowed me out, and I couldn't get away fast enough.

SEPTEMBER

THREE MONTHS BEFORE THE MURDER

Theo

TWENTY-ONE

Abby spoke her *second* first word from her high chair while I smeared cream cheese on a wheat bagel for Cassie. She stood in the doorway, glancing at her watch. Mr. Stone expected her in the office for a client meeting in forty-five minutes. She'd already reminded me twice.

"*Mama.*"

Plain as day. I couldn't have planned it better. Cassie squealed with excitement, dropping her briefcase to smother Abby's face with kisses.

"Her first word! I can't believe it." Cassie dabbed at her own cheeks with a dishtowel, then leaned in to squeeze Abby's. "Your mama's not such a screw-up after all, is she? *No.* Your mama is your favorite."

I cleared my throat and gave her the pointed look I'd practiced with Elise. *Envious surprise*, we called it.

"You're not jealous, are you?" Cassie asked. "I mean, *you* are obviously her favorite. But at least I'm not completely out of the running."

"She loves us both, Cass." I passed my wife her bagel and stirred the bowl of warm oatmeal on the counter, taking a small test bite. "And you especially. How could she not? You're the best mom a kid could ask for. Taking names and kicking asses by day, changing diapers and powdering them by night."

Cassie's laugh—pure joy—made my deception all worth it. But after she polished off half the bagel in a few bites and tossed the other half in the trash, I started to worry. The hopeful excitement on her face scared me a little.

"Do you think I should try to feed her before I leave? Maybe this is some kind of breakthrough."

"Uh... what about your client meeting? Won't you be late?"

Taking the spoon from my hand, Cassie shrugged. "My daughter has spoken. She wants her mama. Mr. Stone will just have to wait."

Thirty minutes and one outfit change later, Cassie trudged down the stairs like a wounded soldier. Abby watched her from the blanket on the living room floor, her baby doll firmly in her grasp. I willed my daughter to say it again, to call for her mother. That would ease the sting of another failed breakfast. Cass had finally given up, surrendering the bowl to me and walking away teary-eyed, with nothing to show but a stain on her blouse.

"I missed a spot." She pointed glumly at the dishwasher, where the oatmeal dribbled down the stainless steel.

"It's okay. I'll get it. You're already late." I reached down to unlock the slider on the cabinet beneath the sink and retrieved a soft towel and bottle of cleaner.

"No. I want to do it. It'll make me feel better. I have to be good for something around here."

The way she said it, I knew better than to argue. I only had myself to blame. I'd brought this on myself, my punishment for deceiving her. I had to take it like a man.

Cassie gathered the supplies from my hands and waved me away. "Go play with Abby. I got this."

I retreated from the kitchen like a scolded dog, tail between my legs. Abby gazed up at me from the floor, reaching her little hands out toward me. I bent down to pick her up, already feeling better. My daughter wanted me. *She* needed me.

"*Dada.*" I gaped at her like I had the very first time. Though she'd uttered it since the studio, it still felt like a miracle.

"Seriously?" Cassie emerged in the hallway, the soft towel in her hand. She shook her head and laughed. But it came with an edge she couldn't hide. "What a little stinker. I guess she didn't want you to feel left out."

"I guess not." I stood there on eggshells, grinning like an idiot, until my phone buzzed. I glanced at the text, even more uncertain now, then tucked it back in my pocket.

"Who's that?"

"Elise." It went down like a lead balloon. "She's coming over with the twins. She'll be here any minute."

"I thought you two always meet at the studio for her lesson. On her day off."

"Usually we do. But she suggested we stay here today and let the kids play together. Kill two birds, you know."

"When were you going to tell me?"

"I'm telling you right now. Hell, I'm just finding out myself."

Cassie cocked her head like she didn't believe me. "So, you didn't know? You weren't trying to get rid of me, reminding me of how late I am? You're wearing your sexy jeans."

"My *what*? You are late, by the way. And no, I didn't know. Does it matter?"

She spun away from me, heading for the kitchen, and I followed, flinching as she tossed the balled-up towel at the counter. It landed on the floor in a heap. "What do you think?"

"Well, judging by how you're acting, it must." I approached

her with caution. Lowering my voice, I tried to soothe both of us. It would only be worse if Elise saw us like this. Cassie would never forgive her for that. "Look, I'm sorry. She just sprung this on me. I'll text her back and tell her no."

Cassie released a breath. She smoothed her hair, straightened her skirt, and retrieved the briefcase by the door. "It's fine. She's got a crush. That's what I get for marrying a dreamboat."

"You're upset. You don't have to joke about it."

"I'm not upset. Abby said 'mama'. How could I be upset about that?" She closed the distance between us and offered me a chaste kiss on the cheek. I took what I could get, grateful when she stopped halfway down the walk. I thought she might apologize. "But if our daughter's next word is 'Elise', I'm drawing the line."

"Oh, gosh. Theo, I feel awful." Elise made herself comfortable on our sofa. Kicked her sandals off, tucked her bare feet beneath her. Abby played quietly on her blanket, while the twins sat side by side on the floor, fixated on Peppa Pig marching across the television screen. "I keep doing all the wrong things."

"It's not you. It was a roller coaster of a morning. Still, we should probably meet at the studio from now on." I took the spot beside her and opened my guitar case. I strummed a few chords, laughing as Abby waved her arms in her own goofy dance.

"Of course. I'd never want to give Cassie the wrong idea."

"I think she's feeling left out. Like you're taking her place with Abby, or something. This whole eating issue has really gotten under her skin." I'd already said too much, giving Elise the play-by-play of our morning, but I couldn't help myself. I needed to talk to someone. Someone who'd been on the planet longer than fourteen months.

"Knowing Cassie, she's putting way too much pressure on

herself. Kids can sense that kind of thing. Plus, she's always had a hang-up about being the odd one out. She got jealous of me and Jess all the time."

I wanted to pump her for more intel but I kept my lips zipped, trying to do right by Cassie. "So, speaking of, I took a look at 'Jess's Song' over the weekend. I think I've got the melody down."

"Really? Will you play it for me?"

By the time I reached the first chorus, Elise began to cry. I adjusted the volume on the TV to mask her crying and pointed her to the kitchen. Abby started to follow us, toddling along the best she could.

"Was it that bad?" I teased.

Elise grabbed a paper towel from the rack and wiped her eyes. "Theo, it was perfect. Just the way I'd always imagined it would sound. You have to teach it to me so we can play it for Cassie."

I hesitated. These days I didn't know what would set Cassie off. Her dead best friend seemed like a real sore spot. Understandably. "I don't know, Elise. It might not be the best time."

"Oh, c'mon. Jess's birthday is next month. It would be such a sweet tribute. Cass will love it. Like I said, she's the one who told me to finish the lyrics."

"Alright. But promise me you won't spring it on her."

"I wouldn't dream of it." Elise winked a teary eye at me, then slashed an X across her heart. "Hey, do you still have my notebook? There's another song I want to show you."

"It's upstairs."

I glanced around for Abby. She'd stopped in the hallway, absentmindedly dangling her doll by the braid and babbling to herself.

"Will you keep an eye on Abby? She gets into everything now that she's on the move."

Elise nodded. "I'll check on the twins too. When they get this quiet, it scares me."

I headed up the staircase and into our bedroom, my mind still stuck on Elise's plan. My wife seemed intent on leaving Jessica in the past but Elise kept resurrecting her. The whole thing made me nervous. I needed to talk to Cass, to get the real scoop on what happened to her friend. But that felt impossible right now, with us teetering on the brink of a massive argument. Like a volcano, Cassie's heat bubbled beneath the surface. But when she exploded, she left a mark.

Notebook in hand, I paused for a moment in the mirror. *Sexy jeans?* These days, I'd do well to find a pair Abby hadn't spit up on.

When Elise screamed, I knew right away. *Abby*. "Oh my God! Theo!"

I shot out of the room and raced down the stairs, so scared I could barely think straight. Like I'd blown into the microphone of my brain. All white noise. "What is it? Where are you?"

"In here."

I rounded the corner into the kitchen, and the room went fuzzy. Only one image burned clear and bright. My daughter, sitting on the floor in front of the cabinet beneath the sink. Its door, open. The child lock, undone. She squeezed the colorful dishwasher pod in her hand and aimed it for her mouth.

"No!" Elise grabbed it from her, and Abby began to cry.

"Did she put it in her mouth?" I asked. But already, I saw the answer. My daughter's lips and fingers were sticky with blue fluid. Another pod lay discarded on the floor, broken and seeping.

"I don't know. I only took my eyes off her for one second."

I picked Abby up and ran for the door, leaving Elise frozen behind me.

Halfway to the emergency room, it hit me like an ice pick to the throat. Cassie must have forgotten to lock the cabinet.

.   .   .

I stood over the stark metal crib, where Abby lay, restless. She clung to the cold, clanky bars, the bed a far cry from the comfy wooden one in her room. Though her bloodwork came back fine, my heart still flopped around in my chest like a fish out of water. She would have to spend the night here under observation. She had a small Band-Aid on the crook of her elbow.

Cassie flung open the door, out of breath and red-faced. Her eyes cut from the chair in the corner to the crib and back again. Elise looked pained. Like she wanted to disappear. She'd just arrived herself, after dropping the boys at home with their mother.

"What's she doing here?" Cassie asked.

"Really?" I glared at her through the haze of my exhaustion. Panic like that really takes it out of you. "That's your first question? What about your daughter?"

"She's fine, Theo. I can see that with my own eyes." Cassie sidled up to the crib, smoothing our daughter's hair with a trembling hand. "Thank God."

"Yeah, she *is* fine. Thanks to Elise. If she hadn't spotted Abby when she did, she would've eaten that thing. It looks just like candy. I told you we shouldn't buy those."

Cassie turned toward me, scowling over my shoulder at Elise. "How did she get in the cabinet in the first place?"

"You left it open," I said. "You forgot to tighten the safety latch."

"I-I... I swear I locked it. Why didn't you double-check it? You knew I was out of it this morning. I had that big meeting, and then Abby's first word and the whole breakfast debacle. And now..." Cassie's voice cracked. "You're blaming me for this."

I wanted to take my wife in my arms. To hold her, reassure her. Tell her that my blood didn't burn with rage. That I hadn't imagined what I'd do to her if Abby died. But I could barely look at her.

Elise cleared her throat. "It was an accident, you two. Neither one of you is at fault. If anybody should take the blame, it's me. Theo asked me to watch Abby when he went upstairs. I should've never let her out of my sight. But Xavier started crying, and I... I feel terrible. That's why I came here. To make sure she was okay. I see now that was a mistake. I'll go."

My wife waited in silence until Elise had disappeared out the door and down the long, sterile hallway. Then she returned to the crib and leaned over our daughter. I watched her sob. I did nothing to comfort her.

Finally, she took a raw breath. "I don't know what I'd do if I lost her, Theo. I don't know what I'd do if I lost *you*. But when I saw Elise here with you, it felt like I already had."

"Well, sometimes I feel like I'm losing you too."

Cassie extended her hand to me, pleading, and I took it. I couldn't *not*. She laced her fingers into mine and tugged me toward her. I surrendered to it.

After a moment, she said, "I don't want you seeing her anymore outside the studio."

I stepped away, and the anger flooded back, familiar as an old friend. "What?"

"I'm serious, Theo. I don't trust her in our home. I don't trust her around Abby. And I certainly don't trust her around you."

"Don't you think you're being paranoid? She hasn't done anything wrong."

Cassie walked to the door. She poked her head out, looked both ways, and shut it. "I know her. She's unstable. She's dangerous."

I laughed a little to cover the queasy feeling inside.

"Do you know how many jobs she's had in the last fifteen years? How many different cities she's lived in?"

"No," I admitted, oddly embarrassed by how little Elise had shared with me about her life after high school. The last fifteen years, a blank space.

"It's a lot, Theo. Tampa, Baltimore, Kansas City, Houston, just to name a few. She's been a cashier, a dog groomer, a waitress. A delivery driver. She even dressed up as a princess for kids' birthday parties for a while."

"So, she's indecisive. She's trying to find her way. We can't judge her for that. How do you know all this stuff anyway? I thought you two hadn't been in touch."

Cassie cocked her head at me. "Stone and Faber has an investigation firm on the payroll. I made a few calls."

"You're unbelievable. What did you think you would uncover?"

"And that's not all." She steamrolled right over my question. "She's been in and out of therapy, on and off psych meds. She got fired from her last nanny gig in LA, after she put cat feces in a little girl's backpack at school."

I stared at my wife in disbelief. "*What*? That's insane. Elise loves kids. There's not a mean bone in her body."

"Oh, really. What about a psycho bone?" The sharp glint in Cassie's eyes scared me, and I steeled myself for a blow. "I didn't want to say anything, but Elise is the reason Jessica's dead."

THE SAN FRANCISCO CHRONICLE

"Trial Set to Begin in the Murder of Noe Valley Nanny"
by Elaine Yu

Opening statements are scheduled to begin on Monday morning in the highly anticipated murder trial of Sluggers' frontman, Theo Copeland. Copeland is alleged to have bludgeoned to death Elise Sterling, who worked as a nanny in family-friendly Noe Valley, the neighborhood affectionately dubbed "Stroller Valley." It is believed that Copeland and Sterling were involved in an affair prior to her death.

Though several trial analysts have called the case a "slam dunk" for the prosecution, Copeland's attorney and wife, Cassandra, issued a statement on Friday, reaffirming her husband's innocence. "The District Attorney offered my client a favorable plea deal, which we promptly rejected. Theo is innocent of this crime, and he will not admit otherwise simply to further DA Callaghan's win record. The prosecution's case is circumstantial at best, and I fully intend to vindicate my husband."

AFTER

CASSIE

TWENTY-TWO

I laid Abby in her crib, watching her nestle against her blanket. It seemed monumental, this moment. I tried to soak it in. The last four weeks had passed in a heartbeat, with Theo at his mother's, and his mother here with me. In a strange way, it felt like practice. But I couldn't let myself think that. Not yet.

"Thanks for letting me come over for dinner tonight." Theo stood behind me, his warmth radiating. He wanted to touch me. I could sense it. Though he held back, I tensed anyway.

"You can't stay."

"I know." His longing travelled up my spine, stiffening my shoulders. He wouldn't make me feel bad for him. "So, tomorrow..."

"Let's not talk about it anymore. It'll be here soon enough." I turned but didn't look at him. It hurt to see how he'd changed. He'd lost weight, let his hair and beard get shaggy. The jury needed to see an innocent man. Fresh-faced and strong.

"Cass, I want you to know how grateful I am to have you in my corner. I can never repay you for this."

I shrugged it off as if it meant nothing. Stooped to pick up Abby's toys. Really, the last few weeks had been an ordeal, the hardest of my life. The late nights and early mornings. The crime scene photos I couldn't get out of my head. The salacious headlines that greeted me every morning on my web browser. The money I'd coughed up from my savings for Dr. Lippman, the blood spatter expert. "You don't have to repay me. You're Abby's father. You're my husband."

"I haven't been a very good one."

"Please, Theo. Not tonight. I can't handle it."

"Just let me say this one thing. Then I'll shut up. I'll get out of your hair, I promise."

I barely nodded. Tossed Abby's clothes in the hamper. Kept moving.

"I've realized a lot in the past few weeks being apart. I hid a lot of things from you. I thought I was making the right decision, doing right by you, protecting you. I see now that I got myself into this mess. Both of us, actually. If the jury gives me a second chance, I hope you will too."

"Can we put this conversation on hold until after? I need to stay focused. I know you want an answer but—"

"It's fine. You need time. I understand." Theo started to leave but lingered in the doorway. "Shaun hasn't bothered you again, has he?"

"I told him to get lost the last time he called. We won't be held hostage."

In truth, I hadn't heard from him since he'd shown up uninvited at the firm two weeks ago, demanding to speak with me. The receptionist had phoned me on my cell and put him on the line. *Is dissuading a witness grounds for disbarment?* he'd asked, smugly. *Maybe Mr. Stone could tell me.* Paralyzed with fear, I'd hung up on him. My partnership at the firm, already hanging by the thinnest thread. I'd waited for the email all afternoon, the notice of my termination with preju-dice. But nothing came. Shaun continued to watch me, though. I knew it. His drone had followed me on my last neighborhood walk with Abby, zipping away when I turned and gave it the finger.

"Good. I'm glad to hear you say it. Are you sure you don't want me to read through your opening statement? You could even do a practice run if you want. Like the old days."

I almost cracked a smile, remembering Theo playing the part of the corporate asshole I'd been tasked to depose in my first case as junior partner. "It'll only make me more anxious. We both need sleep. And you..." I let myself touch his chin— this one small allowance—trying to memorize the scratchy feel of his stubble under my fingers for what might be the last time. "You really need to shave this scruff."

He made a face, stepping back into the nursery to peer in the mirror. "I feel like I'm getting ready for the finale of *Starbound*. Is that weird?"

"No. Well, maybe a little. But the jury *will* be watching you. The judge too. Tomorrow, you'll be on center stage again in the most important performance of your life."

"Then I guess you're right. I better look damn good."

With Theo gone, I made my way downstairs and into the kitchen, legal pad in hand. I poured myself a brimming glass of wine and heated a plate of Gloria's leftover casserole. I'd refused to eat at dinner, intent on watching Theo with Abby. How she lit up every time she saw him. Watching my daughter gobble up her mac and cheese, I'd felt like an impostor. A pretend mother. Like it should be me, not Theo, sent away from here. Like Abby might be better off without me. But then, she'd offered me a spoonful—*Mama, eat*—and my doubts flitted away like little dark butterflies. Still, I knew they'd be back.

Taking a sip from my glass, I studied the blank pad. I picked up my pen and set it down again. Picked it up. Set it down.

Elise's face kept surfacing on the page. I couldn't stop thinking of her. Of December twenty-second, the day I'd taken off work. The day Shaun's drone had followed at my heels. Theo didn't know I'd planned a stop at the studio along my jogging route to satisfy my curiosity. Or that I'd seen Elise put a shiny red box in his hand for Abby. Inside it, a pair of colorful wooden maracas I'd tossed in the trash that same night in a fit of anger. Not because I didn't want Abby to have them. I wanted to give her the world. But those maracas represented all my shortcomings. All the ways that Elise was better than me. They reminded me of her and the past I'd tried to escape. I couldn't have them in my house.

Downing the rest of the glass in one long gulp, I held my pen like a weapon. The words bubbled up in my brain, ready to be written. To be unleashed. At the top of the page, I scrawled, *Opening Statement.*

The knocking roused me, sending a jolt straight through my wine-fogged brain. I'd fallen asleep at the counter, my face pressed against the legal pad. A small spot of drool had dribbled onto the page, spoiling the ink. With a groan, I straightened myself, put the glass in the sink, and shuffled to the door, just as the knocking came again.

"Cassie?" Gloria stood at the top of the staircase, her robe cinched at her waist. She sounded worried. "Who is it, dear? It's late."

I took a quick glance out the window and cringed. When I turned back, I gave her my best smile. "It's okay. It's one of Theo's old friends. I'll talk to him."

After Gloria retreated to her bedroom, I flung open the door, taking satisfaction in Danny's startled expression. At least I'd sobered him up a little. But the open beer bottle in his hand gave him away. I scowled at it.

"What are you doing here?" I asked. "Theo's staying at his mother's house right now."

Danny rolled his red-rimmed eyes. "Hello to you too. And I'm well aware of that. I just left there. I came to see you."

"Oh." I wished I'd never answered. I contemplated shutting the door in his face, but I knew Danny. He wouldn't leave quietly. "Well, it's late, and you're drunk. Did you drive here?"

"I'm not that drunk." He took a lazy swig from the bottle, a smile spreading across his face. "You gonna call the cops on me?"

As I peered behind him, searching for the beat-up Camaro he used to drive, he laughed. "Chill, Cassie. I walked. It's not like it's far. I'm crashing with Theo tonight. And before you ask, no, he didn't send me. He fell asleep hours ago. He has no idea I'm here."

"Which is why again?"

"Because your husband should be here with you. In his house."

"Did he tell you why he's not? I assume you've seen the headlines."

"Yeah, and it's all bullshit." Danny shook his head at me like a disapproving father. Like *my* father. I recoiled from him, pushing the door shut. He caught it with his hand. "Theo didn't cheat on you."

My whole body throbbed with anger. Still, I found myself stuck there. I couldn't walk away from that. From that small seed of hope that wouldn't die no matter how many times Theo poisoned it. "Oh, really. How do you know that?"

"The guy is crazy about you. He hangs on your every word. He quit the band for you. He gave up on his dreams."

"Please. Not that Yoko Ono crap again." Half-open, the door stood between us. I reached for it, ready to put myself out of misery. "Besides, I'm sure you've seen the Amelia Ford interview. You were his friend back then. You know exactly what he's capable of. So, don't tell me I'm overreacting."

Danny wedged the toe of his boot against the door and left us stalemated again. "C'mon, he was nineteen years old. I'm sure you made your share of mistakes at that age. Unless—oh, wait, I forgot—you're perfect."

My one irredeemable mistake loomed so impossibly large that it had threatened to eclipse everything. Even after I'd fled Buttonwillow, it shadowed my heart in cold shades of gray. Work, marriage, motherhood. These were the spots of brightness that allowed my life to bloom.

"Theo's changed since then. He's a grown-up now. A hell of a lot more mature than me. And he's loyal as they come. Elise was into him, sure. She didn't hide it. But for some reason, he only has eyes for you. It's a real mystery."

He gave me a once-over and shrugged. Took another pull from his bottle. "I'm still trying to figure it out."

"Danny, I'm tired. Tomorrow's a big day. Not that it's any of your business, but Theo lied to me so many times I lost count. I saw the way they were together. He wrote her love poems, for God's sake. I won't be one of those women who goes around wearing blinders. Where there's smoke, there's fire. I have nothing else to say."

"Alright." He stepped back from the door, and I waited for him to go. To leave me to another sleepless night. But he raised his eyes to mine, cold as marbles. "So, you've never lied to him?"

"Not like that."

"What about the contract with Soul Patch?"

"What about it?"

"I've got a friend who works at the label now. He told me the contract was solid."

"The contract was crap. Theo knew it. They were trying to take advantage of him."

Danny nodded through his obvious disbelief. "You should show him the contract though. He said he never saw it."

"He told me that he didn't want to look at it. He wanted me to handle it. So I did." My voice came out hard as nails. "Look, I appreciate you supporting Theo, but the best thing you can do for him is to let me get some sleep. I have to be on my game in the morning."

His face softened a little. "You believe him then? You don't think he killed Elise?"

"I'm defending him, aren't I?"

"That's not what I asked. Attorneys defend scumbags all the time, right? People in your profession don't really have a moral compass."

I moved onto the porch and gently closed the door behind me. "Right now, I don't believe much of anything that comes out of Theo's mouth. But I do know my husband isn't capable of murder." Every time I said it, it sounded better. Good practice for tomorrow, when the jury would be weighing my words. As Theo's attorney. As his wife.

I stepped into Danny's space, smelling the alcohol and cheap cologne wafting from his pores. "I also know that you skimmed money from the band's merchandise sales during the tour. I kept my mouth shut, because Theo loves you like a brother. But if you come by here again talking about *my* moral compass, I'll make sure Theo understands exactly how crooked yours is."

Danny stared at me. He didn't deny it. "I hope you're as good an attorney as Theo thinks you are."

As he slunk off to lick his wounds, I watched him through the window. He tossed his beer bottle on the front yard, kicked the garbage can. I whispered to him through the door, "I'm better."

TWENTY-THREE

I tucked my cellphone into my briefcase, taking in the gravity of the text message on my screen. All morning, I managed to stay calm. I'd showered, dressed, flat-ironed my hair. Opened my sock drawer and unceremoniously slipped back on the wedding band I'd tucked inside it. Driven here and parked in the garage. Pushed open the heavy courtroom doors and walked in without a tremble. But now, it all felt too real, especially with Theo fidgeting next to me and the jury filing in to my right. A wave of panic rose in my chest and threatened to sweep me out to sea. I breathed through it.

Two things I know about opening statements, Mr. Stone had texted. *One, tell a story. Two, don't be boring. Boredom is the kiss of death. You'll lose the case before it's even begun.*

I had to tell that story to twelve strangers. The five men and seven women taking their seats in the jury box. Most were married. Half had children of their own. One—a tall, dark-skinned woman who always wore a scarf looped around her slim neck—had admitted her husband's infidelity during voir dire, but I only got so many vetoes. Scarf Woman had her advantages. She worked at a lab. She'd be methodical, scientific, in her examination of the evidence. She wouldn't be swayed by emotion.

Theo leaned toward me, covering his mouth with a legal pad, and whispered, "I'm so nervous."

He looked it too. He'd chosen the Zegna suit, though his mother had bought him two others. It hung loose; his shoulders slim as wire hangers. His cheekbones, sharp as blades. As if he'd sucked in a sudden breath and never released it. I wanted to comfort him. I wanted him to suffer. In the end, I did nothing but nod and wait for Judge Macy to begin.

No matter what I'd told Theo, this was *my* performance. My opening statement would set the tone. Like the first song in a big show. It had to be perfectly pitched, right on key. I took a quick glance over my shoulder and found Gloria seated in the front row, her hands folded so tightly in her lap they seemed knitted together. She'd insisted on being here—as a mother, I couldn't blame her—so I'd found a sitter for Abby. It had never been harder to leave her than this morning, knowing that I held the fate of our little family in my hands.

A face, horrifyingly familiar, caught my eye from the other side of the aisle, and I bit my lip to avoid a gasp. Though I hadn't seen her in fifteen years—not since Jessica's funeral—I could still conjure the sound of her voice, feel the warmth of her arms around me, comforting me in all the ways my own mother couldn't. June Sterling levelled me with the same steely blues she'd given her daughter. Deidre's voice echoed in my head. *At least go talk to June before you leave. You owe her that much.* I wished I could run away like I always did. I found myself grateful when the judge spoke, breaking the spell.

"Good morning, ladies and gentlemen. We're going to start with the opening statements made by the lawyers in this case. I'd like to remind you that these statements are not evidence and should not be considered as such..."

Half of me listened to Judge Macy. The other half travelled far from there. To the night Theo and I first met at the company retreat. My brain numb on tequila, I'd stumbled my way toward the stage, where a shirtless Theo shimmered like a god. I'd already shattered the first of my rules—no more than one drink at company events. It seemed necessary, since hours before Mr. Faber had called me into his office and told me I wouldn't make partner. Not yet. *We're a firm with family values, Cassandra. We like our partners to be settled. Homes, not apartments. Children, not pets. Spouses, not one-night stands.* As I'd watched Theo belt out the lyrics to a song about his broken heart, I'd decided right then to break rule two. Never sleep with a man who's not marriage material.

"Mr. Callaghan, you may begin your opening statement." Judge Macy's announcement dragged me back to the present. To Callaghan, in his suit that fit him like a glove. With his gleaming white teeth and his slicked-back hair, he looked like a winner.

"Ladies and gentlemen of the jury, I'd like to direct your attention to the screen." When an oversized photograph of Elise appeared, a sudden sob escaped from the gallery behind me. I wanted to turn and find the source—it must have come from June—but I stared straight ahead, unblinking. "Meet Elise Sterling. Elise was a beautiful young woman in the prime of her life. Only thirty-three years old. A talented songwriter. A beloved nanny. A cherished daughter and friend."

His expression somber, Callaghan stepped from behind the podium and toward the jury box. It turned out robot-lawyer could emote better than I'd expected.

"In the early-morning hours of December twenty-seventh, Elise was brutally murdered, bludgeoned to death with a blunt object, dragged across the wet pavement, and left in the dumpster like a sack of trash."

Callaghan stood next to the box, shaking his head along

with the jurors. Not one minute in and already, they'd joined his team.

"Now, ladies and gentlemen, turn your eyes to the defendant, Theo Copeland. You may already think you know him. You may have seen him perform on a television show years ago, or even attended one of his concerts. Sure, he's handsome, talented. He has a nice smile."

Callaghan commanded their attention like a politician, humble but self-assured. Directed their eyes like a magician. All of them swiveling at once toward my husband, who shifted uncomfortably at my side, his chair screeching against the floor as he moved. As I turned to him, he smiled. A small, jittery smile, uncertain as a bridegroom at the altar. But the jury wouldn't see it that way.

"It's true, isn't it? He looks like the all-American man. But he keeps another part of himself hidden. In fact, he hides it so well even his own wife doesn't want to admit it. She's here sitting next to him, defending him. The *real* Theo Copeland is a liar. He's been unfaithful to his wife. He's been dishonest with the police. The *real* Theo Copeland is violent. In fact, he has a history of domestic violence. The evidence will show that Theo began an affair with Elise months ago, a woman who just happened to be his wife's childhood friend. But Elise wanted more from Theo, more than he intended to give. She wanted him to tell his wife. Theo only wanted what was good for Theo. And Elise stood in the way."

Callaghan's words had bite. They sank their teeth into me with piercing precision. *Theo only wanted what was good for Theo.* The prosecutor wasn't wrong about that.

"After sharing an anniversary dinner with his wife, Theo arranged to meet Elise at the studio where they spent their time. He summoned her with a text message from his phone and lay in wait for her to arrive. Theo beat Elise about the head with his *Starbound* statuette, leaving her virtually unrecognizable. Then, he lugged her body outside in the rain and left her there, cold and alone, in a dumpster for a homeless person to find."

I felt sick, picturing it all. The room swayed slightly. Like we were on a boat. Like the boat was sinking. Callaghan remained a sturdy, seaworthy captain, sauntering toward the defense table. I heard Theo's heart beating. Or was it my own?

"Don't be fooled by that smile, ladies and gentlemen. This man is a performer. He knows how to put on a show. We will show you the real Theo Copeland."

I expected him to pound the table. To shout. I would have preferred it even. Instead, he hung his head and fled from Theo and me in disgust, waiting for the perfect moment to raise his eyes to the jury, to deliver his final blow.

"And the real Theo Copeland is a cold-blooded killer."

TWENTY-FOUR

Judge Macy gestured into the empty space in front of me. "Defense counsel, the floor is yours."

"Thank you, Your Honor." My voice reverberated in the echo chamber of the courtroom, confident and practiced. But my mind felt gauzy at the edges. Slippery. Like I might blurt something out without meaning to. Something I couldn't take back.

"Ladies and gentlemen of the jury, Theo Copeland is my husband."

I moved from behind the table and faced the jurors. It was easier to look at them than at Theo. These complete strangers whose only task was judgment.

"Together, we share a home in Noe Valley and an eighteen-month-old daughter, Abby. I know him better than anyone. I'm here to tell you that he's not perfect. Who is? We've both made mistakes in our marriage. Mistakes that led us down a path that ended here, with Theo on trial for a murder he didn't commit. I was too focused on my career. I relied on him to do the lion's share of the work with our daughter. I didn't give him the attention or support he needed. Our relationship suffered, and he found comfort in another woman. A friend."

I took a small breath. No one would see it, but I needed it to quiet the roar of my heart.

"Is my husband guilty of having an affair with the victim? Yes."

The gasps came from all around me, mouths hanging open like dark caves. Whispers slithering out until the whole courtroom pulsed with a ferocious energy. But June didn't gasp. She didn't even blink. Whatever I said now couldn't touch her. She'd already lived through the worst. I understood that better than anyone. Some things there's no coming back from. It's a whole new world, a terrible world, and you can only go forward. Make the best of what you have left.

"Mr. Callaghan would prefer to end the trial right now. He wants you to believe that if Theo is guilty of having an affair, of being an imperfect husband, that he is also guilty of the murder of Elise Sterling. But I know the twelve of you are much smarter than that. Think of your own relationships, the pitfalls, the twists and turns, the unforgivable mistakes we've all made. No marriage is perfect. No husband, no wife. But imperfection, no matter how severe, is a far cry from murder."

Every word of it resonated, right down to my core. I held the jury, rapt, in the palm of my hand. Their eyes followed me as I walked toward Theo and placed my hand on his shoulder. He felt more breakable than ever.

"My husband did not kill Elise Sterling. I know that because that night, he lay next to me all night. He never left our home. His cellphone, from which the mysterious text message was reportedly sent, still hasn't been recovered. The prosecutor didn't tell you that. Because he knows the police never considered any other suspects. You won't make the same mistake. You won't destroy my husband's life without having all the facts. You'll hear about Shaun DeMarco, the man who was so obsessed with Elise that he amassed hours of drone footage of her every movement. When she rebuffed his advances to spend time with Theo instead, he couldn't cope. He stalked her. He lured her to the studio, with the intention of getting his revenge on both of them."

Tell a story. Don't be boring. I added my own advice to the list, keeping my gaze on the jury box, unafraid. *Make it personal. Make them believe in you.*

"I stand before you today putting my personal and professional life on the line. I am risking everything to defend my husband. As an officer of the court, I would never testify to a lie. As a wife, I would never allow a murderer in my bed. And most importantly, as a mother, I would never permit a 'cold-blooded killer'—as Mr. Callaghan has erroneously labelled him—to raise my daughter."

When I returned to my seat, I looked straight ahead, though I could hear the push and pull of Theo's ragged breathing. The scratching of his pen on the legal pad. He shoved it over to me.

Affair? WTF was that?

I scribbled quickly, slid it back to him.

Trust me. We have to give them something. They'll never believe you're THAT innocent.

You should've asked me! My life is on the line here too.

I'd expected this, but still. The intensity of his indignation surprised me. The way it wafted from his pores. It annoyed me, too, the depth of his denial. I'd done what needed doing, exactly like I always did. It hadn't been easy to stand up there with all those eyes on me. To lay my soul bare and admit I'd been made to look a fool.

"Mr. Callaghan, you may call your first witness."

I moved the pad away from Theo and flipped to a clean page. I needed to focus now. His tantrum could wait.

"Thank you, Your Honor. The state would like to call Detective Frank Kincaid to the stand."

One hour in, I felt like a war-weary soldier. But Detective Kincaid looked fresh as a daisy with his starched white shirt and freshly shaven skin. Seemingly, he could do this all day, recounting the crime scene as casually as reading his grocery list. He and Callaghan exchanged question and answer in a perfectly choreographed dance, one that would end with both their fingers predictably pointed at Theo.

"So, when you arrived at Mr. Copeland's studio, what did you observe?"

"The responding officers immediately took us to the body. It was inside the trash dumpster at the back of the lot. We didn't know the cause of death at that time, but I saw significant injuries to the victim's head, consistent with blunt force trauma."

"Your Honor, I would like to enter Exhibit A: Crime Scene Photos into evidence." With a click, Callaghan refreshed the screen adjacent to the jury box, and several images appeared. At the center of the grouping of photographs, an overhead view of the dumpster, where Elise's body was splayed alongside a heap of garbage. Matted with blood, her hair clung to her face. Her limbs contorted unnaturally. She looked nothing like the woman I remembered, bubbly and vibrant. Full of life.

Though I'd tried to prepare Theo for this very moment, he'd flatly refused to look at the photographs that had been part of the discovery. Now, seeing them for the first time, he dropped his head into his hands and wept. I offered him a tissue from the box on the table to hide the depth of my bitterness. Underneath it all, I felt like a fool. How could I envy her, lying there with her head smashed like a dropped egg?

"Did you notice anything else at the scene, Detective?"

"Drag marks. The pavement was still wet from the rain the night prior, so they were easy to spot. They led directly from the back door of Mr. Copeland's studio to the dumpster."

"In your experience as a twenty-year veteran of the Homicide Unit, did you form a theory about what caused those marks?"

"I did. The victim was likely dragged on a tarp or blanket and placed inside the bin, using the smaller access door on the right side. It would've been easier than lifting her body over the lip of the dumpster."

Callaghan nodded. "Was there evidence to confirm your theory?"

"We found blood traces on the metal lip of the side door consistent with the victim's. While we weren't able to locate the medium on which the victim was dragged, I suspect the murderer laid down the cover prior to the victim's arrival to ensure an easy clean-up. It would explain why we found so little blood evidence inside the studio itself. The neighborhood garbage pick-up occurred shortly after our arrival on scene, and the cover probably ended up in a bin nearby, only to be dumped in the landfill."

I couldn't let this continue unchecked. I had a job to do. "Objection. Speculation. There's no way the detective could know all of that. Unless he wants to name himself as an alternate suspect."

Judge Macy dipped her chin and gave me a warning glance. "Overruled."

Undeterred by my objection—a mere fly to be swatted—Callaghan continued. "Did you find any other evidence inside the dumpster?"

"We located the victim's driver's license and cellular telephone inside the pocket of her denim jeans and made a positive identification."

"What did you do next, Detective?"

Detective Kincaid put on his reading glasses to consult the pocket notepad he'd brought with him. Calm and conscientious, he made the ideal witness. My father was cut from the same cloth. When he told my mother no one would believe he abused her, she didn't doubt him. That once, when she'd called 911 from the kitchen phone, my father met his buddies at the door and assured them it was an accidental dial. Cops like him could get away with murder.

"My partner and I identified the owner of the studio—Theo Copeland—and sent patrol officers to his home nearby so we could gain entry into the building to search for additional evidence. Once Mr. Copeland allowed us access, I observed a small amount of blood spatter on the wall. A short time later, we obtained a search warrant and administered Bluestar Forensic, a blood visualizing agent, that revealed additional areas of blood evidence, including the object we identified as the murder weapon."

"And what object was that?"

"A gold-plated statuette, owned by the defendant."

"Your Honor, I would like to draw the jury's attention to the third photograph on the screen." The jurors studied the close-up of the statuette, as did I, half expecting the damn thing to be covered with bits of bones and gristle. To spot blonde hairs wound around the base of the gold-plated microphone. The day Theo moved his memorabilia into the studio, I'd watched with pride as he set it on the shelf. I'd marveled at my husband's talent. How lucky I was.

"And now to the podium. To the statuette police found in the defendant's possession."

Callaghan reached into a box beneath the defense table, like a magician pulling a rabbit from his hat. He thunked it down, letting the hollow thump testify for him. One of the female jurors openly grimaced.

"Did you find any fingerprints on the murder weapon?"

"There was only one set of discernible prints on the statue."

"To whom did they belong, Detective?"

"Theo Copeland."

The direct examination plodded on, workmanlike, with Callaghan painstakingly chipping away—one question at a time—whittling Theo's dignity down to a nub. My husband distracted himself with the legal pad, which he'd reclaimed after Callaghan flashed Exhibit C on the screen. The infamous cell-phone message from Theo's number: *Meet me at The Spot ASAP. I want to talk about our future.* Three of the female jurors had gasped. One male shook his head in disapproval. Scarf Woman loosened the loop around her neck like she couldn't breathe. And Theo had reached for the pad like a life preserver, doodling his way through the next thirty minutes of damning testimony.

"When you searched the victim's residence, what did you observe?"

The pen between Theo's fingers came to a halt in the middle of a housetop, the windows beneath it shaded with a heavy hand.

"We found evidence that suggested Ms. Sterling was very interested in Mr. Copeland and his wife. She had collected photographs and news articles about them. We also discovered handwritten notes from Mr. Copeland to Ms. Sterling."

As Exhibit D materialized before us, Theo resumed his drawing. His pen strokes, jagged and dark.

"What was the content of those notes, Detective?"

Kincaid paused. His eyes flitted over to me and away, back to the jury box. "I'd call them love poems."

I wished he wouldn't call them that. *Love* poems. Lust, I could bear. But love, Theo *loving* her, I still couldn't stomach it, let alone understand it. I wondered if I would survive this after all. If it was possible to die from heartbreak.

"Love poems, I see. Would it be fair to say that the evidence indicated a close personal relationship between the defendant and the victim?"

"Yes, that's correct. We spoke to several witnesses who confirmed they were indeed close, spending hours together at the playground and the defendant's studio, where he taught her to play the guitar."

"Did Elise pay for any of those sessions?"

"Not by check or credit card, per the bank statements we reviewed. If she paid him at all, it would've been in cash."

"And other clients of the defendant's? Did they pay for his services?"

"One hundred dollars per hour, as listed on Mr. Copeland's website."

Callaghan planted the slimy seed—the smarmy idea that Elise paid Theo with sex. Then he stood back, quiet, and let it sprout. Riveted, the jurors leaned at the edges of their seats, waiting for the next revelation. I found myself doing the same. My breath so shallow, my chest grew tight.

"It makes you wonder what they were doing in that studio... if there were ever any guitar lessons going on at all. Doesn't it?"

Theo's wince nudged me into action. "Objection! Inflammatory."

Before Judge Macy could respond, Callaghan uttered, "Withdrawn," and sauntered back to the table. As if he hadn't just driven a stake into my heart. "No further questions, Your Honor."

"Your witness, Ms. Copeland."

I stood and walked to the podium. The courtroom was eerily still, like a snow globe on a mantel. Still unsettled myself, I intended to give it a good shake. This I could control. This I could manage. The rest of it—love poems and murder weapons and dead best friends—whirled like a blizzard around me.

"Good morning, Detective." I gave him my corporate smile. The one Theo had once deemed politely cutthroat. The way a shark might greet a pair of legs, flapping in the open water. "You said that the forensic evidence showed that Ms. Sterling had been bludgeoned to death. Correct?"

"That's right. Bludgeoned with your husband's—I mean, Mr. Copeland's—statuette. CSI discovered traces of brain matter in the crevices of the object."

I pushed through my revulsion. I couldn't afford to think too much. "Is it common in cases of blunt force trauma for the scene to be fairly bloody?"

"Well, it's hard to say." He gave the jury a hapless shrug. "Nothing about murder is common. Every case is unique."

"Of course. But, isn't it true that if the murder was committed in the studio, as you suggested—the brutal beating of the victim about the head with a bronze statue—we would expect to see more than mere droplets of blood left behind?"

"As I said—"

"It's a yes or no question, Detective."

"I suppose that in most cases of blunt force trauma, we do see a significant amount of blood at the scene. Often, perpetrators make attempts to clean blood evidence, as was the case—"

"So that's a yes," I interrupted, directing my words to the jury box. "Isn't it also possible that the drops of blood could've resulted from an accident, since the victim spent a considerable amount of time at the studio?"

"It's possible, but the evidence—"

"And the victim could've been murdered at another location and placed in the dumpster, correct?"

"Correct." Detective Kincaid sighed. My rapid-fire questions had worn him down. I relished the thought of Callaghan's disgust when he heard his client agreeing with me.

"And someone else could have gained access to the studio, right? The police report noted that the bathroom windows had a broken latch."

"True. They could have."

"Even the drag marks themselves can't be directly linked to my husband, right? You said yourself that it was garbage day. Might someone have been moving a large bag of trash?"

"I suppose they might've been, however—"

"Forgive me, Detective, but it sounds as if you're not really certain of anything."

As I expected, Callaghan nearly pulled a muscle springing up from his seat. He kept his outrage in check though, maintaining his emotionless tone. "Your Honor, is the defense testifying or does she have an actual question? I know she's not used to the courtroom, but..."

Judge Macy extended her hand, silencing him. "That's enough, Counselor. Ms. Copeland, do you have a question for the witness?"

"Of course. Just a few more questions, Your Honor. Did anyone *see* the victim entering the studio that evening?"

"Not to my knowledge."

"And what about my client? Did any witnesses come forward to tell you they saw him near or at the studio around that time?"

"No, but it was the early-morning hours. And we do have—"

"Thank you, Detective. No need to elaborate. You testified earlier that you sent an officer to retrieve Mr. Copeland from his home. Did he allow you inside the studio when you requested entry, even though you had not yet obtained a search warrant?"

"He did."

"Did he answer all of your questions?"

"Yes, until you intervened."

"During your questioning of Mr. Copeland and myself,

were you informed that Mr. Copeland's cellular telephone had gone missing during the night? That it might have been lost or stolen?"

"Yes."

"Did you follow up on that? Make any attempt to find the cellphone?"

"We conducted a thorough search of the studio and his home, and we contacted the restaurant where Mr. Copeland claimed to have last had the phone in his possession. We didn't find it."

"So, the cellphone is still missing? It could be anywhere?"

"That's correct."

"I imagine that, given your years of experience, you looked Mr. Copeland over for injuries, possible signs of a struggle. Were there any cuts or bruises on his body that morning? Any injuries at all?"

"None that I saw."

"What about bloody clothing? Did you find anything like that at the studio or the house?"

"We did not."

"Last question." I slowed my pace, waiting for the jury to catch up. "You spoke at length about the many steps you took to gather evidence against Theo Copeland. But did you ever once consider that he might be innocent?"

"My job is to conduct a thorough investigation, to follow all leads. As for guilt or innocence, that's the job of the jury."

"A *thorough* investigation. Would you agree that part of a thorough investigation is to rule out other potential suspects?"

"I would."

"So tell me, Detective, did you identify any alternate suspects in this case?"

"We did not."

I parted my lips slightly, widened my eyes. I aimed my shocked face at the jury. "Not a single one?"

"Asked and answered," Callaghan said.

"Withdrawn." I mimicked Callaghan's prior casual dismissal. He needed a taste of his own medicine, and I needed a reminder I could do this on my own, just as well as him. I could go toe to toe with any man and come out on top. "Nothing further, Your Honor."

OCTOBER

TWO MONTHS BEFORE THE MURDER

Theo

TWENTY-FIVE

Six weeks after Abby's accident, I still woke up in a cold sweat some nights, with my heart thrashing against my rib cage with wild abandon. The same way Danny jammed out on the drums. I would spring out of bed and dart down the stairs, expecting to see my daughter's limp body lying on the kitchen floor. Her little face, pale and cold. Cassie forgave Elise's carelessness, just like I'd forgiven hers. But I couldn't forgive my own. Because I *should've* checked the latch. I *should've* been there, watching her. Not looking for a stupid notebook in my sexy jeans.

Shaking off my shame, I settled Abby into the baby swing, while Elise filled me in on the juicy bits of neighborhood gossip she'd overheard on her coffee run to Clipper's. *Parker Fairchild's acceptance at La Petite Academy had been rescinded. The Hamiltons were seeing a couples therapist. Shaun DeMarco had hired a personal trainer to turn him into a beefcake.*

"A beefcake?"

Elise chuckled, glancing over to check on the twins while they played in the grass nearby. "I kid you not. His exact words. He probably showed the guy your picture."

"Ha-ha." I gave Abby another push on the baby swing and prodded my finger into my own midsection. "Even with my daily jogs, I'm probably more cake than beef these days."

"Don't be so hard on yourself. How can anyone say no to cake? Well, except Caroline Hamilton. To her, cake is the devil's manna." She shrugged. "You know, she yelled at me for drinking a Coke in front of them. It's part and parcel for this nanny gig, I suppose."

I let her flirty compliment slide. Because what else could I do? Tell her to stop being so damn nice? Probably. That's what a better man would've done. But I relished Elise's little ego strokes. Especially now, with Cassie head down in the Meta-Tech merger. It had been weeks since she'd seen my body in anything less than sweats and a ratty T-shirt, much less appreciated it. A gut punch of guilt made me spit out the question I'd been holding in for weeks.

"Speaking of, have you always worked as a nanny?"

Her eyes sank to her sneakers, and I felt like a jackass for asking. "I've done a little bit of everything," she said. "Whatever it takes to pay the bills. Besides my music—which wouldn't pay anybody's bills—I can't seem to find *the thing*, you know? The thing that makes you want to keep doing it for the next thirty years of your life. Plus, it's hard to get axed for playing the guitar."

"I can't imagine you getting fired." I pushed Abby again, sending her higher than she expected, and she squealed.

"You'd be surprised."

"Your last job?"

"Did someone tell you?" She glanced over at the mothers, huddled like a pack of she-wolves near the sandbox. "I should've known the word would get out eventually. Especially with Alexandra's big mouth. Parents talk, apparently, even from LA."

"What happened?" I slowed Abby to a stop.

"It's really embarrassing. Promise me you won't think less of me."

I plucked Abby from the swing and sat down in the grass with her near the twins. Elise joined me there. "Hey, in college, I got fired for drag racing in a guy's Porsche. I rear-ended a mini-van. I was the valet."

Elise guffawed, drawing the attention of the pack. "I don't feel so bad then. At least I had good intentions. One of the little boys I nannied for started getting teased about his weight at school. Third graders can be so vicious. They called him a gorilla and put rotten bananas in his backpack. So, I returned the favor."

I raised my eyebrows, less shocked by the story than the fact that Cassie's intel checked out. It still unnerved me that she'd sent the Stone and Faber goon squad to investigate her friend.

"It was only a little cat poop from Fancy's litter box."

Just then, Elliot and Xavier started their daily game of tug-of-war, scrapping like drunken frat boys. They had two of every toy, so it made no logical sense. When Elise returned with the coveted plastic dinosaur in her hand, leaving the boys dumb-founded, she added, "I regret nothing."

"Damn, girl. I know better than to mess with you."

She smiled, shrugged. "So, I've been practicing. I have 'Jess's Song' down. I'm working on the other song too. 'Bewitched'. It's so romantic. Cassie's a lucky lady."

"Can you tell her that? She's been working non-stop these past few weeks. We're..." I searched for the right word, knowing that I'd already said too much. That Cassie would rip my throat out if she knew I'd confided in Elise.

"Like ships passing in the night?"

"Yeah. Except she's an ocean liner and I'm the dinghy capsizing in her wake."

As Abby slowed down again, Elise walked to the front of the swing and made a show of putting the dinosaur in her tiny outstretched hand. "See, boys, that's what happens when you can't play nicely. You can't play at all."

Moments later, Abby tossed the dinosaur into the air. When it landed in the grass near their feet, neither twin gave it a second glance. Elise and I exchanged a look, and we both laughed. Already, I felt lighter.

"It sounds like Cassie needs a reminder of what she's been missing," Elise said. "What if we did something fun tonight to surprise her?"

"Such as?"

"How about an impromptu concert? You know, get the band back together. Maybe you could invite Danny."

"*Danny?*" I checked my watch and plucked Abby from the swing. I'd made plans to meet my mom at the house, and if I showed up late, she'd give me that hangdog look. The one she'd perfected on my father over a lifetime of missed dinners and lipsticked collars. The one that said she deserved more from a Copeland man, even if she didn't expect it.

"Yeah. Danny Hendrix. Your drummer. Remember him?" Elise followed me back to the bench, watching me buckle Abby into her stroller.

"Wait a minute. Are you into him?"

"That's what you think?" Elise ducked her head beneath the canopy of the stroller and screwed up her face at Abby. "Your daddy is a bonehead."

Then she raised her bright eyes to mine. "I only mentioned Danny because I thought Cassie might enjoying seeing the two of you play again. I was hoping it would make her feel better, put a smile on her face."

"I thought you knew that those two don't get along. The last time they were in the same room together, they hardly spoke."

"Oh, c'mon. What if we played her 'Bewitched'? She would adore it."

I knew Cassie better than that. She wasn't the grand gesture kind of gal. She'd always seen right through all that smoke and mirrors BS. It was one of my favorite things about her. "I'll think—"

I stopped short at the sight of Alexandra barreling toward us. Her Bugaboo, aimed for Elise like a kamikaze missile. Parker shouted with glee as his ride skidded to a stop, inches from Elise and the twins. Alex huffed out a breath.

"You have some nerve showing up here." Her hiss sent a spray of spittle into the air.

Elise stepped back, out of firing range. "What are you talking about?"

"As if you don't know what you've done." Her eyes dropped to Parker, who'd busied himself taking off his tiny designer boots and tossing them onto the sidewalk. "You sneaky bitch."

"Hey. Enough." With my own stroller in tow, I stepped in between them like a good soldier, caught in the crossfire. Alexandra angled around me, still shooting darts. As I moved to block her, she ran smack into my chest.

"Do you know what she did?" Alex asked, on the verge of tears. "She made sweet little Parker seem like the next school shooter. And to Dr. Gupta, no less. Do you even know who his wife is?"

I shrugged. "It can't be that bad."

"*Felicia Gupta.* Director of La Petite Academy. Which, thanks to Elise, Parker will no longer be attending. His future is ruined. Without a solid preschool education, he'll never get into Stratford. Without a Stratford diploma, an Ivy League is out of the question. How's he going to become a top-ranked heart surgeon like his daddy with a degree from a state school?"

Parker had discarded both of his boots by now and worked his way out of his stretchy pants. The kid was half-naked and chewing on the arm of his teddy bear, not getting scrubbed up for an angioplasty. "Do you think you might be overreacting just a bit?" I asked.

Alex glared at me. A "no," then. She collected Parker's clothing, tossing it into the stroller. He threw it right back, but his mother had already trained her steely gaze on Elise. Beneath her icy surface, I imagined her blood boiling. "Nobody messes with my kids. You better watch your back."

Alex stormed off, leaving the booties and pants strewn like casualties of war. Elise let out a breath.

"What was that all about?" I asked.

"I messed up. Remember last week, when Parker bit Xavier in the sandbox, and I had to take him to the ER? I may have overshared about Parker's behavior problems. I had no idea who the doctor was, much less who he was married to. Alex is going to hate me forever now. Who knows what she'll do?"

I didn't have it in me to tell her that ship had sailed the moment she walked into the playground, with her long legs and doe eyes. Younger and prettier than Alex, she didn't stand a chance.

"C'mon, don't worry about it. She's all bark and no..." I grimaced. "Well, you know what I mean."

With Abby finally asleep, I collapsed onto the sofa and surveyed the mess. The toys strewn on the floor that I'd undoubtedly trip over on my way to bed. An orange stain on my sweats from Abby's afternoon popsicle. The stack of laundry I'd planned to fold while watching the Giants game. So much for that. I needed a glass of wine and a long nap. When I checked the time, I felt even more pathetic. Barely eight o'clock. And still no sign of my wife.

In the week following Abby's emergency room visit, Cassie had seemed more determined than ever to make it home by dinner time. But gradually, she resumed her hectic schedule, returning well after I'd put Abby down. I couldn't deny that some days I felt like a single parent. Overworked and underappreciated. With no soft place to fall.

I sank into the cushions and laid my head back. Just five minutes, then I'd pick my sorry ass up and make this place look like the respectable dwelling of Theo the House Husband.

My eyes flicked open at the sound of voices outside the front door. I sat up too fast, trying to make sense of it. But my thoughts came slow in my woozy head. Like I'd just pulled an all-nighter with the band. I glanced at the clock, shocked to see that only fifteen minutes had passed.

"No, he didn't mention it." I recognized Cassie first, heard the harsh clip in her tone. I sprang to my feet and headed toward the sound.

"He probably wanted to surprise you." *Shit.* Elise. What the hell was she doing here? Then, it came flooding back. Our conversation at the park. I hadn't told her yes. But I hadn't said no, either.

"Maybe. But it's odd he didn't say anything. I can't promise I'll be very good company. It's been a long week." Her key turned in the lock. "It does sound like fun though."

"Hmph. I didn't realize fun was a part of your vocabulary, Cassie." *Double shit.* Elise invited Danny. "But I'm relieved to hear you say it. Do you know how much trouble it was to lug this damn portable drum kit down here?"

When the door opened, I gave a tentative wave and tried to act casual. To go along with it. But I could see how tired Cassie looked. Even the perfect bun at the base of her neck had come undone. I already knew the commotion would wake up Abby. Thirty minutes of rocking her—until my arms went numb—gone to waste.

"Oh, wow." Cassie continued her bitter exchange with Danny. She dropped her briefcase by the coatrack and ducked my eyes. "You brought a drum kit. To a house with a sleeping toddler. Brilliant."

Elise stepped inside, carrying her guitar. She gave me a guileless smile. Like I'd been in on it the whole time. I hoped my wife hadn't caught that. "It was my idea, Cassie. A bad one at that. You're right. We don't need the drums."

Danny huffed.

Everyone waited for me to react. Everyone but Cassie, who'd already brushed past me and fled up the stairs, making even the soft sounds of her stockinged feet on the steps sound indignant. When she reached the top, she flashed a smile and tossed a "be right back" over her shoulder. It didn't fool me.

As soon as she disappeared from view, I turned to the two of them. "I thought I told you I'd think about it."

"Hey, don't blame me, man." With a wiseass grin, Danny clapped me on the shoulder and set the drum kit in the corner. "I'm just here for the show. And the beer. You've got beer, right?"

Elise hung her head. "I know you said you'd think about it, Theo. But you would've come up with some lame excuse. Besides, what's there to consider?"

"Nothing, now that you've ambushed me in my living room with my smartass drummer."

Danny shrugged like he couldn't be bothered. "Or wine. Hard liquor. Hell, I'll drink whatever you've got. I think we could all stand to take the edge off."

"Cassie seems okay with it though. Right?"

"Trust me, Elise. Cassie can fake it with the best of them." I ignored Danny's snide grin. "This isn't a good surprise. Let's just play the one song. Then you two can leave me to take my comeuppance in peace."

"If it's that big of a deal, we'll leave right now. We can do it another time."

Cassie emerged, wearing jeans and one of my old Sluggers tees. She loosened her hair, letting it fall in soft waves at her shoulders. She was playing along then. I had to admit, so far, she'd handled it better than I'd expected. Which could only mean she was angrier than I feared. "It's fine," she said. "I'm fine. *Everything* is fine. My only request is that we take this little shindig to the deck so we don't wake up Abby. Sound good?"

"That sounds great." Elise's smile broadened.

"One song," I hissed at her, dousing her enthusiasm, as we followed my wife into the kitchen. She'd already selected a bottle of red wine from the rack. She worked out the cork, while I took four glasses from the cabinet and laid them before her, a peace offering.

"I had no idea," I whispered.

She gave no sign whether she heard me. Just poured the wine and took a long drink from her glass, draining half of it in the first swallow.

"Shall we?" She waved a hand down the hallway toward the back door. Elise went first, with Danny a few steps behind her. No doubt checking out her ass. I hung back, hoping to get Cassie alone for a minute. But she kept moving away from me.

After directing me to the baby monitor on the coffee table—"Grab it, would you? And an extra bottle of wine"—she headed outside, leaving me alone. I cursed Elise, cursed myself. Danny too. He'd only made it worse showing up here in enemy territory. *One song*, I reminded myself. How bad could it be? Cassie loved my music. She loved me. She would love the song we wrote.

I walked toward the glow of the porchlight, visible through the back door window. The closer I came, the more I dreaded opening it.

"Who wants more wine?" I asked, disturbed by my own

insincerity. I watched the night career ahead like a runaway train and stood on the tracks, powerless to stop it.

"Cassie's working on a big merger," I said, eager to flatter her. She'd been quiet so far, nodding politely along with Danny's story about getting fired from his latest temp gig. Laughing in all the right places, a grin fixed to her face. "Two major gaming companies."

"It's really not that interesting, honey." She wrinkled her nose at me, finally cracking that plastic smile. "Don't bore them with it."

"*Boring*? No way. Your life is so glamorous." Elise sure knew how to lay it on thick. I couldn't tell if she meant it. "Client meetings and power lunches. It sounds like a TV show."

"Well, I certainly wish there was a fast-forward button that would get me through the next few months. This deal is driving me bonkers. I can't say too much, but these tech guys can be ruthless. And their people skills, *jeez*. You'd think they're all still living in their mothers' basements."

"Ooh. Sounds juicy. I wonder if Shaun knows anything about it. I'll have to ask him."

"*Shaun DeMarco*? Please, don't. I shouldn't have mentioned it. But I can't help feeling like my boss is testing me. It's my first big deal as partner. I hope I don't blow it."

"You? Blow it? Never." Elise took a delicate sip of her wine, watching my wife over the brim. "You're so poised, Cass. So together. I can't imagine you won't totally kill it."

Cassie's cheeks reddened, and she busied herself filling up her glass. I beckoned her over and pulled her onto my lap. "I agree. You're a total badass."

"Get a room." Danny gave my chair a good-natured shove.

"You two are really sweet," Elise mooned. "I wish I had

someone special like that. Who knew everything about me—all my deep, dark secrets—and loved me in spite of it all."

Danny guffawed. "I ain't tellin' anybody all my secrets. I don't care how hot she is."

Cassie lingered for a moment, then hoisted herself up off me and returned to her chair. I wished she'd stayed close. To reassure me this night hadn't been a total debacle. "It's getting late," she said. "Is this song going to happen or not?"

"Of course it is!" Elise jumped up and clinked the side of her glass with her finger, drawing our eyes to her. Even after downing a few glasses of red, she stepped solidly into the halo of light at the center of the deck like a seasoned performer. Her guitar waited against the wooden railing. I couldn't look away from her.

"Today is a special day for Cassie and me. Usually, I spend it balled up in bed with a pint of ice cream, watching reruns of *The Bachelor*. But this year, I'm so lucky. I get to spend it with Cassie, the only other person who can understand what I've been through. What we've both been through. The one person in the world who knows exactly what this day means. The devastation it caused."

Cassie looked stricken. Danny, just as confused as me. The silence between us yawned, deep as a grave.

"As you know, today is Jessica's birthday," Elise spoke only to Cassie now. "Theo and I wanted to play you the song I wrote for her. You inspired me to finish it. I hope you'll hear it and think of Jess, always and forever."

With that, Elise retrieved the guitar and beckoned me over. I glanced in Cassie's direction, hoping for some kind of sign. She tucked her arms across her chest like a shield. Without words, I tried to tell her what I couldn't say aloud. That this wasn't my plan. That I had no fucking clue. That I wanted to toss the guitar over the railing and pretend tonight never happened. That I'd written a song for her.

I took my position beside Elise and began to play. Cassie only listened with half her heart, I could tell. She didn't cry or smile or hum along. She kept her gaze on the baby monitor, where Abby slept snug as a bug. When we finished, she clapped like one of those toy monkeys. Mechanical, unfeeling.

Then, she stood. "If you'll excuse me, I'm feeling tired. I have an early morning."

"Cass, wait."

"It's okay, Theo. You stay. Have fun with your friends."

She took the monitor with her when she returned to the house, closing the door softly behind her. I couldn't see her anymore, but I imagined her anyway. Her spine, straight as a rod. Stiff upper lip. Until she collapsed upstairs, sobbing. I *knew* my wife.

Danny took a swig straight from the bottle. "Who the hell is Jessica?"

"Sorry to cut this short, but you two should probably go."

On the brink of tears herself, Elise dropped into a deck chair. She let out a shaky sigh. "I don't understand. I thought she would love it. She and Jess were so close."

"She felt ambushed, Elise. I don't blame her. It wasn't cool, you showing up here like that. Then playing that song. That's not what we talked about."

"Damn, man. Go easy on her." Danny set his hand on Elise's back, rubbing slow circles. The guy had no shame. "It's not her fault your wife's a—"

"Hey. Careful."

"He's right, Danny. I made a mistake. I just wanted so badly to reconnect with Cassie. It's been really hard for me these past fifteen years. I can't help thinking that if Jess was here, everything would be different. I would be different."

"I get it. But Cassie isn't like you. I know the three of you were close friends in high school, and I'm sure she was devastated about Jessica back then. For whatever reason, though, she's moved on. Maybe you should try to move on too."

Hoping they'd take a hint, I gathered the glasses, tossing the dregs of wine onto the grass, and started toward the house. Danny got to his feet too and collected the near-empty bottles. I could count on him to have my back, even if he acted like an ass. "Alright, buddy. You owe me a drink for this. Some of the expensive shit." To Elise, he added, "I'll wait for you out front."

I stopped at the door and turned to Elise. She hadn't budged from the chair. I shrugged off a strange thought that she didn't intend to leave. That she would stay there forever if I let her, waiting on our back porch like a stray cat. "I have to be honest with you about something. It's awkward, but..."

She huffed out the saddest laugh I'd ever heard. "So was tonight."

"Cassie told me everything. About Jessica's suicide, I mean."

Elise cocked her head at me. "She *did*?"

"Yeah. She did." I waited for her to offer an explanation. I certainly deserved one. Instead, she drew her lips together in a tight bow. "Honestly, I wasn't sure whether to believe it."

"That's understandable," she said, finally. "It is pretty hard to believe."

"But after the stunt you pulled tonight, I know Cassie was telling the truth. It makes sense that you can't move on. You must harbor a lot of guilt."

Elise sat up straight. Like I'd pressed an electric finger to her back. "Wait. What did she tell you exactly?"

"That you sent that video to the administration. To Stanford. The one that got Jessica's admission rescinded. She said she's been covering for you for years." I watched her eyes drift up to the second story. To the light in our bedroom window. "You know it wasn't your fault, right? No matter what you did. Jessica made her own choices."

"Did Cassie say that too?"

"No, but I'm sure she would, if you asked her. She doesn't blame you. She just wants you to get the help you need. I do too." I held out my hand to Elise, and she stood. "Let's go inside."

"Okay." But her knees buckled beneath her and she stumbled forward, landing in my arms. Her cheek pressed against my chest. "I don't feel so good. I didn't eat much today. I probably shouldn't have had that second glass on an empty stomach."

I guided her inside, trying to keep a respectable space between our bodies. Elise, though, latched onto my waist, fisting my T-shirt in her fingers. Her knuckles brushed against my bare skin. Once, twice. It seemed deliberate. But when I glanced down at her, the distress on her face told me otherwise.

Danny sat at the kitchen counter, polishing off the last of the bottle of red. He took in the scene the same way I would have, his eyes lingering on Elise's hand at my side. Still, I couldn't help but feel a tiny bit bad for her.

"She's a little woozy," I said.

"Clearly."

I jerked my head toward the pantry and tried to free myself from her tentacle grip. "I'll get you some crackers or—"

"It's okay. I've caused enough trouble. I'll just call an Uber."

Danny perked up, giving me a salacious wink over her head. "Why don't we share a car? I'll make sure you get home safe."

Elise gazed up at me. "I'm not a bad person, Theo."

"I know. Nobody said otherwise."

"I didn't send that video. I need you to believe me."

And I needed her to let go of me before Cassie appeared in the foyer and saw her fingertips creeping further beneath my tee. "Okay, I believe you."

Finally, she dropped her arm to her side. But the places

where she'd touched me burned hot as a fever. I felt guilty. Like I'd asked for it, wanted it. Like Cassie would be able to tell.

After Elise wandered out onto the porch to await their ride, Danny retrieved his drum kit. He shook his head at me.

"I don't know what the hell just happened, but this is a lot worse than I thought. This is a goddamned catastrophe. You're not just fucked, dude. You're fucked with a capital F."

AFTER

CASSIE

TWENTY-SIX

After dispatching Detective Kincaid from the witness stand, Judge Macy ordered an hour-long recess for lunch. The jurors filed out of the courtroom, already distracted by thoughts of turkey on rye. How nice it would be to walk out those doors and into the bone cold of January. To be free of this place and its heavy burdens for sixty whole minutes. Even Callaghan had it good. Win or lose, his life would go on, unmarred. At the courthouse café, he would enjoy his overpriced salad and make small talk with the girl behind the counter. Meanwhile, I'd be here with the sad sandwich I'd packed and a husband-sized boulder on my shoulders.

Theo mumbled, "I'll see you in there." Without another word to me, he took the legal pad and headed out the side door into the bowels of the courthouse, where we'd planned to eat lunch together in the small attorney–client conference room.

I gathered my notes and sat there for a moment, imagining my own lunch break. Watching the minute hand crawl with Theo giving me the silent treatment. Like I'd been the one to blow up our marriage.

"How could you do this, Cassie?" June appeared in front of

me, bitter as a lemon. And suddenly, I wanted nothing more than to be trapped in that airless room with my husband and a soggy PB&J.

"If you'll excuse me..." I skirted out from behind the table but June followed me, intent on being heard.

"Elise loved you like a sister. You were always so close. I thought she was lucky to have a friend like you, staying in touch all these years. It hasn't been easy for her, after what happened with the three of you. After Jessica."

"*All these years?*" She'd knocked me out of kilter with that, but I didn't want to make a scene. How could I argue with the mother of a dead girl? I hovered by the side door, hoping to make a quick escape. It was worse than I'd imagined, standing face to face with her. "I'm sorry, June. I can't imagine what you're going through. But Theo didn't hurt your daughter. Destroying his life won't bring her back. Elise wouldn't want this. Now, please—"

"Elise would have wanted you to have the decency to speak to me when you came to Buttonwillow. To ask me yourself about her problems, instead of sneaking around. She wanted to make you happy, to be a part of your life. When you found her that nanny job and asked her to relocate, she thought it would be like old times. She'd been going through a bit of a rough patch, but she honestly believed things would get better with you in her life. You and Theo. He took advantage of her innocence, her naivete."

I found myself gaping at her, unable to speak. She filled the silence with a scornful laugh, the soul-scraping kind that made me doubt myself. Made me feel like the crazy one.

"Now she's dead. My daughter is *dead*. And her best friend is defending her killer."

"I don't know what you're talking about. I hadn't been in touch with Elise since high school. I had no idea she was moving to San Francisco until she showed up in my kitchen with a sprained ankle."

"But she went to your wedding. She sent me a photo of you in your dress."

"No one attended our wedding, not even Theo's mother. We eloped. The only picture of me came from some rogue employee at the Little White Chapel who sold it to a gossip rag."

Theo had bought every copy of *The Downtown Star*—the headline, *Former Sluggers' Frontman's Shotgun Wedding*—from the grocery store down the street and tossed them down the garbage chute. But I didn't mind the photo, even with its unflattering angle of me in my off-the-rack dress. It clung to my midsection, fueling the rumors. It was proof, documented right there for the entire world to see. Theo belonged to me, and I to him. We belonged to each other. We had a baby on the way.

"Are you saying my own daughter lied to me?"

"Of course not." Though I had no other explanation to offer. "There's no easy way to say this, June, but I think Elise might have been a little jealous over the way things turned out for me. Marrying Theo. Making partner at my firm. Having Abby. I know she went through a hard time after Jessica died. You realize she blamed herself."

June's bottom lip trembled, and I watched her tuck it beneath her teeth, trying to keep herself from crying. "I imagine you both did. It was a tragedy. But she didn't send the video to the dean. She would've never done something like that. She knew how much Jessica wanted to go to Stanford. Everyone did. The three of you had such big plans."

"I know." I patted her hand. It felt as fragile as a bird's wing. "I probably shouldn't ask you this, but..."

"Go ahead. Spit it out."

"What did Elise tell you about Theo? According to the note

I read at the hospital, you were worried about her coming back here."

"Are you sure you want to know? You still have to represent him."

It wasn't a matter of want. I felt it down in my bones. An ache to unknot the twisted thread of truth, to follow it wherever it went. No matter how ugly. "I *need* to know."

"He told her he felt lonely. He confided in her about how much you worked. How absent you were. Elise thought you took him for granted. Abby too."

"I see. And she had feelings for him?"

June raised her eyes to mine. Elise's eyes. Watery with sorrow and regret. For a moment, I forgot Elise was gone. I forgot about the way her eyes looked, after. Disappeared in a face so swollen and bloodied, I couldn't look at it without feeling sick.

"She thought he deserved better."

"*Her*? He wanted *her*?" I regretted my venom but only because it hardened June against me. She shook her head in disgust.

"Shouldn't you be asking your husband these questions?"

"I already have."

"Well then." She seemed pleased with my answer. As if I'd confirmed her opinion of me. I waited for her to pronounce judgment. To tell me what I already knew. "What did he say?"

I didn't answer. I wouldn't give her the satisfaction.

"There's your problem, isn't it? You don't trust him. Does he even know what happened back then? What you girls did?" She took my silence as an answer. "I figured as much. A relationship without trust is a sandcastle, Cassie. It may look pretty in the sunshine, but it won't last the night."

She left me standing there at the side door, white-knuckling my briefcase. I caught my reflection in the small window. No one would know the weak little girl I used to be. I couldn't let

June get under my skin. I needed to stay strong. To hold my head high. My daughter depended on me to get us out of this mess. And the only way out was through.

I couldn't find Theo anywhere. In the dismal conference room, I sat alone, picking at my lunch and replaying the past. Revisiting all my mistakes, reliving all my failures.

Disgusted with myself, I tossed the remnants of my sandwich in the trash and gathered all my broken pieces, tucking them back where they belonged, hidden from the world. With a breath, I pushed open the door and walked back toward the courtroom. I waited just outside and peered through the small window at Theo. He sat at the defense table, staring blankly at the empty jury box.

"Ms. Copeland, I need to speak with you." Callaghan's voice came from behind me. I wondered how long he'd been standing there. How pathetic I looked. Like I couldn't muster the courage to enter.

I steeled myself and turned to face him. But his hands drew my attention instead. He extended them toward me, a thick folder in his grasp.

"Here," he said. "Take this. You'll need it."

"What is it?" The size of it unnerved me.

"The results of the forensic analysis of your husband's laptop. We've got Janice Binnetti, the IT expert, on deck as our next witness."

"This must be at least three hundred pages. You can't expect me to review this right now?"

"Well, you've got ten minutes. You're a fast reader, right?" The way Callaghan shrugged at me, I wanted to slap the smug look right off his face. "You could always ask the judge for a recess. Either way, I think you'll be very interested in what the witness has to say. On a personal level, I mean."

"I look forward to it." Somehow, I spat that out with a straight face before I fled into the courtroom and took my seat beside Theo. He didn't even look at me. Aside from the bailiff stanchioned in the corner, we were completely alone.

"Where were you?" I dropped the folder onto the table with a pointed *thwap*. A part of me wanted to scour every page of it right then and there, searching for whatever truth it could offer me. Another part, to set it on fire and watch it burn.

"After that stunt you pulled with your opening statement, I needed some alone time."

"That *stunt* was for your benefit, remember?"

Theo finally cut his eyes to me, slicing me like a blade. "I find that hard to believe."

The doors swung open behind us, inviting the gallery inside, but I couldn't stop myself from biting back. "You find *that* hard to believe. That's rich."

Theo shushed me and reached for the folder. Regarding it with suspicion, he opened it to the table of contents on the first page. I decided I'd rather not know. Once, my mother told me that it's better if you don't see it coming. That the anticipation hurts more than the blow ever could.

Judge Macy ascended her throne, surveying the room with a stone face. "Mr. Callaghan, please call your next witness."

"The State calls Lead Forensic Information Technology Specialist, Janice Binnetti."

Dread gripped me with cold fingers, as I watched her shuffle to the witness stand and take the oath. She wore a flowered peasant blouse and shoes with thick rubber soles. She reminded me of a librarian or a grocery store clerk. Someone sitting on a bench in a park feeding the birds. A woman no one would remember. Except me. I would remember her for the rest of my life. The sinking feeling in my gut assured me of that.

"Ms. Binnetti, please explain to the jury your role in this case."

Janice cleared her throat, peering at the jury over the black rims of her glasses. "For the last ten years, I've worked as a supervisor in the Computer Forensics Division of the crime lab. My team examines various kinds of IT evidence, including computer and video footage."

"Did you examine any video footage of the night in question?"

"We did. The Circle Cove apartment complex had an operational street-facing camera, which captured a figure walking up Diamond Street at approximately 1 a.m."

A satisfied smile played on Callaghan's lips while he addressed the judge. "Your Honor, I'd like to enter the video footage into evidence."

The jurors leaned forward, squinting at the fuzzy image on the screen, obscured by the darkness and the merciless beat of the rain against the camera lens. I could almost feel the whip of the wind on my face as I watched the figure move against it, plodding toward a destination unseen.

"What can you tell us about the footage?"

"The original image quality was quite poor due to the outside conditions, specifically the time of day and the rainy weather. As you can see, the subject's face is hidden beneath the hood of the jacket. By using video enhancement, including lighting improvement and sharpening, we were able to reduce blurring and shadow. Our analysis revealed that the subject wore a dark-colored raincoat with a brand insignia on the upper left chest."

"Why is that important?"

"Well, it's consistent with the raincoat officers removed from Mr. Copeland's home on Diamond Street several days after the murder. The coat is a men's size large."

"Is this Mr. Copeland's jacket?"

"It is. You can see they are quite similar."

On the screen, a photo of Theo's raincoat was displayed

adjacent to the video's frozen frame. The jackets were a close match. My mind travelled back to the small puddle of water beneath the coat rack. The *drip, drip, drip* of rainwater from the sleeve. Next to me, Theo made a noise, half-growl, half-sigh. I wondered how much he could take.

"Yes, very similar. Thank you, Ms. Binnetti." The jury nodded along with him. So congenial, so disarming. I'd underestimated Callaghan's likeability. "Your team also analyzed the defendant's laptop, which was removed from his home during that same search, correct?"

"That's correct. We confiscated a Dell XPS 13 laptop, which the defendant identified as belonging solely to him. A thorough analysis was completed by our computer forensics team and provided to detectives within the last twenty-four hours."

"I'm not much of a tech expert, Ms. Binnetti. Can you explain for the jury in laymen's terms what sort of information your team reviewed?"

"We examined the defendant's files contained on the hard drive of the laptop, as well as any files that were uploaded to his Cloud account. We also conducted a full examination of his search history."

"Did your examination uncover anything of significance to this case?"

"I believe so, yes." She paused for a moment. Too long. I wanted her to get to the point, no matter how sharp. "First, we found photographs of Ms. Sterling on the defendant's computer."

"How would you characterize those photographs, Ms. Binnetti?"

"In a word, *salacious*." Janice grimaced, as one of the offending images flashed onto the screen. I pretended to look but let my eyes glaze instead, allowing the lacy red bra to blur into a blood spot. The same bra I'd discovered stuffed between our couch cushions months ago. Another crack in my heart, and I slipped right through into the icy water. My blood went cold.

"Those are the ones," she said. As if Elise's plump breasts and pouty lips had left any room for doubt.

"And second," Callaghan prompted.

"Approximately four weeks prior to the murder of Ms. Sterling, the defendant conducted an Internet search which may be of interest to the jury."

Theo lowered his pen and leaned forward, jaw clenched. I willed him to look me in the eyes. But he'd locked in on Janice. My chest tightened. My lungs squeezed shut. I should've objected long ago. I'd had no time to review the evidence, no time to brace myself. Too late now; I was a drowning woman, desperate for air. The sound of my breathing rushed through my ears like waves crashing against the rocks. I swam toward Callaghan's voice, deep and distorted, at the surface.

"In those four weeks leading up to the brutal murder of Ms. Sterling, what did Mr. Copeland search for?"

Janice paused to take a sip of water, the entire courtroom resting in the palm of her pale hand. I saw her now—the real Janice—beneath her cloak of invisibility. This woman was no librarian, no grocery store clerk. Callaghan's hired assassin, she was about to deliver a kill shot to Theo's head. I was merely collateral damage.

"'How to get rid of a woman.'"

Red-faced, Theo jumped to his feet, upending his chair. "That's not what I meant!"

"Sit down." I tugged at his hand, his skin fever-hot beneath my fingers. He yanked it from my grasp, still frothing.

"I didn't kill her!" Every word landed like a cymbal crash in the pin-drop quiet of the courtroom. Words that felt meant for me. "You have to believe me. She sent me those photos. I didn't ask for them. She left the bra in the couch. She wanted you to find it."

"Listen to your attorney, Mr. Copeland. Sit down or I will find you in contempt of court."

Theo slumped into his chair, rumpled and sweaty. Like he'd just finished a show. He reached for the pen, uncapped it. Held it there, strangled in his palm. For a heartbeat, I feared him and what he might do. The thought unspooled like a movie reel, playing in my mind. The sharp tip of the pen driven into my neck. The spurt of blood onto the table. The gurgling sound of my own death.

Instead, Theo jerked the legal pad from under my elbow. He ripped off the page of notes, revealing a clean slate. His pen strokes marred it, violent as a blade on skin.

Do something.

TWENTY-SEVEN

Gloria turned off the television news and patted Theo on the knee. I let her comfort him because I couldn't. Not after what I'd heard today from June. He'd confided in Elise, shown her the cracks in our marriage. A betrayal even worse than those tawdry pictures. Worse than her bra in our sofa. Worse than screwing her. "It wasn't as bad as they made it seem, honey."

"Mom, don't blow smoke up my ass. They called the evidence 'damning'. They said I had an 'outburst'."

"Well, you did yell at a witness." I couldn't help but rub salt in the wound. Besides, he didn't need his mother coddling him. He needed to face facts.

Gloria gave me one of her looks. The familiar kind of disapproval I'd been fielding since day one as a Copeland. Little did she know, after living with my father, her looks bounced right off me like rubber bullets. They stung but didn't penetrate the surface. "At least there were no cameras in the courtroom, dear. No one can blame you for showing emotion. You're in the fight of your life."

Abby stirred on the baby monitor. Moments later, she began to wail, sending a ripple of guilt through me. Before I kicked

Theo out of the house, she'd been sleeping through the night. Now, she refused bedtime altogether and woke up crying the way she had as a baby. Full-throttle screaming. Like she couldn't bear being here without him. And every time I failed to quiet her tears, all my doubts rushed in again. I felt useless, inept. What if I was no different than my mother? Or worse, *him*. The man who'd taught me that love should leave a mark.

"I'll get her," Theo said.

I nodded but trailed him up the stairs anyway, leaving Gloria alone. From the doorway, I watched him pick Abby up and rock her against his chest. It still left me awed, how he could soothe her with his touch. After she'd settled in his arms, he laid her back in her crib and turned to me.

"She's regressing. All this uncertainty, the instability, it's not good for her. She needs me here."

Couldn't he see that I needed him too? I always had.

"Please, Cass." The tremor in his voice nearly broke me, and I almost caved in. Until I remembered the pity in June's eyes. *How absent you were.* "I know I should try to think positively, but the way this trial is going, I may not see my daughter for a long time. Years. Decades. Don't rob me of these last days just because you're pissed at me."

I followed him out of Abby's nursery and into our bedroom, softly closing the door behind me. I didn't need Gloria eavesdropping on another argument only to throw it back in my face. "I can't believe you have so little faith in me."

"As a parent?"

"As an attorney. You make it sound like it's a done deal. Like we should just give up. I got the IT supervisor to concede that your Google search wasn't all that damning." Janice had admitted that the first few pages of results had nothing to do with murder and everything to do with forcing a crazy woman out of your life. "And I established that those photos had been in your recycle bin for several weeks. That you hadn't opened them since late November. I discredited that video, too. She couldn't explain why they had you going but not coming home. And thousands of people own that same jacket. It means nothing."

Theo gave me no credit. He only shrugged. I'd endured that smarmy picture of Elise's breasts, plastered on the screen for thirty minutes. What did I have to show for it? A lousy shrug. "They have a shit ton of evidence. Even *I* think I look guilty."

"But you're not."

"How can you be so sure?" Theo asked, studying me with genuine confusion. "After all of that?"

"Because I still have faith in the person I fell in love with. The person I married. The person who helped me create our beautiful child."

"*Faith?*" He barked out a dry laugh, his eyes tearing. "You sure have a funny way of showing it. You don't believe me about Elise. No matter how many times I deny it, you still think I slept with her. You told the jury that."

"It was the smart play."

"Maybe. Maybe not. It crushed me, though. You couldn't even tell me the plan." Theo dropped onto the bed, swiping angrily at his cheeks. "So, yeah, to be honest, I lost my faith in you right then. I'm not sure this was a good idea."

"'This'?"

"Letting you defend me. You said yourself you're no trial attorney."

The weight of the entire day crashed down on me, snapping the thin thread that held me together. That kept me from saying things I might regret. "I asked you to stop letting her into our home."

"And I did."

"I told you what she was capable of. What she did to Jess. I knew she would break us. Somehow, some way. Now, look at us. Completely and utterly broken."

"You should know that Elise denied sending that video to Stanford. I asked her about it that night she came over with Danny."

Another night I wished I could burn from my brain, the way you remove a bad tattoo. "Of course she did. What did you expect? She'd never admit to something like that." It irked me that he hadn't taken my word for it. That he believed her over me. Another vicious stab in the back. "Didn't you look through the discovery? She was obsessed with me. With us. She wanted to take my place, and you let her do it."

I hated how desperate I sounded. The way the words whipped out of my mouth like great gusts of wind, threatening to blow us both over. But Theo didn't waver. He just sat there, in the middle of the storm, looking like I felt now. *Empty*.

"Elise didn't take your place. No one ever could. Not in a million years. But..."

"But what?"

"Sometimes, you were so busy. Like Abby and I were an afterthought. It just makes me wonder, Cass. Is this really the life you wanted?"

My cellphone buzzed in my pocket with a call from an unknown number, saving me from Theo's unfair question. How could he ask me that? How would I answer? How could I explain the distance between that first night, tangled in his sheets on the tour bus, and this one, right now? I'd wanted this life. Of course I had. I'd planned it, even, without him knowing. Tossing my little yellow pills in the trash weeks after we met. Though I was no less terrified of being a wife and a mother, I'd imagined it all differently. Wrongly. In rosy hues with soft edges. None of the sharp ones that cut me as a child.

"Hello?"

I waited and listened to the caller take a deep breath. "It's Shaun. Shaun DeMarco. Time's up, Cassie."

I held up a finger to Theo, mouthing, *one minute*, and

retreated to the bathroom, shutting the door behind me. How much could one person endure before they snapped? Gave up completely. Jessica hadn't lasted long under the weight of our mistakes. But then, she hadn't been through what I had. I suppose my father had given me a gift of sorts. Those calluses on my heart, that turtleshell around it, protected me.

"You haven't come through on your end of the bargain. And the District Attorney called me to testify. I'll have no choice but to tell the truth about what I saw that night."

"Well, you know the stakes. I still have the flash drive. It's evidence of your obsession with Elise. I'll use it if necessary."

Shaun's chuckle enraged me. I wished I'd been the one to punch him in the face. The sniveling little coward deserved it.

"Are you asking me to lie on the witness stand, Counselor?"

"Of course not. I would never do that. I'm simply reminding you that actions have consequences. Now, if you don't mind, I'd like to get back to my evening."

"And what a lovely evening it must be. Talk around the neighborhood is that you and Theo are Splitsville. Guess there's trouble in paradise."

"Goodbye, Shaun." My finger descended toward the red X on the screen. I missed the old days, where I could have slammed the receiver down in his ear. Heard that satisfying *click*.

"Wait," he shouted, pulling me back like a yo-yo. "I thought you might say that. Let me give you a little more motivation."

"I already told you. I can't tank the merger. We're talking about my career here. Surely you can understand that. After all this is over, it might be one of the few things I have left."

"But we're not *just* talking about your career, are we?" I could hear Theo pacing outside the door. Down the hall, our daughter slept, thanks to his soothing touch. "I know what happened that night at the studio. I can prove it. Come to my office tomorrow at the noon recess. I'll show you everything."

I hung up fast. Stood in front of the mirror and stared back at myself, wide-eyed. I looked weak, fearful. Exactly like my mother.

Theo pounded on the door, and I jumped. "What are you doing in there? Who were you talking to? Is it about the case?"

I spoke to the thick slab of wood between us. "It was Mr. Stone. There's an issue with the MetaTech merger. He wants me to stop by during the lunch break."

"Really? The nerve of that guy. I hope you told him to fuck off."

"I can't afford to lose my job right now, Theo. If you... If you're not around anymore, it'll be up to me to hold this family together. Surely you understand that."

He answered me with the lonely sound of his footsteps, walking away.

NOVEMBER

ONE MONTH BEFORE THE MURDER

Theo

TWENTY-EIGHT

My wife never took time off. Holidays, weekends, late nights, sick days—Cassie had worked through them all at one point or another. *We have a global clientele*, she'd always say, parroting Mr. Stone's speech to the new partners at their induction dinner. *The law doesn't take vacations.* Once, when she had a nasty stomach flu, she insisted I drive her to the office for a client meeting. She threw up twice on the way there in Abby's disposal diaper bag and rolled her eyes when I asked if she was okay. So, her leaving me in bed at 6 a.m. on the morning after Thanksgiving didn't surprise me. I expected it. But it still got under my skin.

"I'll try to make it home by dinner." She leaned down and pecked my cheek, leaving the scent of her shampoo on my pillow. "I wouldn't want to miss your mom's Thanksgiving leftovers."

"Do you really have to go in today? Doesn't Stone spend Thanksgiving in Hawaii?"

"He does. And yes, I have to go. The MetaTech team is expecting a full debrief on Monday. It's my responsibility."

"I thought we could take Abby down to Union Square. Have a picnic on the lawn. Do some people-watching."

"I can't. You know I can't. Don't make this any more diffi-cult for me."

Before I said something I'd regret—*it doesn't look that diffi-cult*—I turned on my side and settled back in with the baby monitor in view. "We'll save you a plate."

A few minutes later, I heard Cassie slip out the front door. I lay there and closed my eyes, trying to sleep. But my brain kept spinning round and round like a record on a turntable. I couldn't stop thinking about Elise. Since the "Jess's Song" debacle last month, she'd been sulking like a scolded puppy, avoiding me at every turn. She'd even gone so far as to start a conversation with Alexandra. My bench was my own again, but it felt lonely. *I* felt lonely. I blamed myself. Cass, too, to be honest. We'd both overreacted. Not that Cassie would admit it. She'd maintained radio silence about the whole evening.

Screw it. I reached for my phone on the nightstand and tapped out a quick message.

How was Thanksgiving in Buttonwillow? I'd heard her mention a trip back home to one of the playground mothers. The Hamiltons always spent holidays at their Tahoe house.

I stared at the screen, suddenly wanting a take-back. The sun hadn't even come up yet and here I was, texting my wife's ex-best friend. And why? Because I needed a damn bench buddy. Stupid, stupid, stupid.

When the phone buzzed in my hand seconds later, I dropped it onto the bed like a hot coal.

Really lousy. Is Cassie home?

Corporate lawyers don't celebrate Black Friday.

Can you come over?

I sat up. Checked the clock again. Peeked at Abby, still blissful. Typed *Now?* Deleted it. Typed it once more, deleted.
Before I could make up my mind what to do next, she texted
again. Three times, rapid fire.

I need to talk to someone.

To you.

Please.

I tossed off the covers. Abby would be awake soon. I should
tell her no. I should spend the morning alone with my daughter,
fixing her pancakes and watching the shows she loved. I should
find the Christmas decorations, scrub the toilet. Make a casserole from Mom's leftovers. Things a proper house husband
would do on the day after Thanksgiving.

I'll have to bring Abby with me.

My rebellion came with a little zip of excitement.

I'd love to see her. I'm sorry it's been weird lately.

I pulled my shirt over my head and started the shower.

An hour later, Elise met Abby and me at the door of the
Hamiltons' guesthouse in a pair of sleep shorts and a tank top.
Her hair wild and tousled, not a stitch of makeup on her face.
She reminded me of the younger version of herself I'd seen in
that clipping from the Buttonwillow *Gazette*, innocent and
vulnerable.

Behind her, the small living quarters looked a mess. Her

suitcase sat in the middle of the floor, splayed open, clothing strewn from its innards. A lacy red bra and matching underwear lay draped over her desk chair, a set of sky-high heels on the seat.

I swallowed hard, looked away fast. "Did you just get back?"

"Late last night." She peered in at Abby, still strapped in her stroller. "I don't think she remembers me."

"Of course she does. It's Elise," I said to Abby, who smiled back at me, mirroring my enthusiasm. "See. She remembers."

"She probably hates me. You do too, don't you? I've been a shitty friend."

"What?" I took a few steps inside and wheeled Abby toward the sofa. "What are you talking about?"

"I messed up with the song. I shouldn't have done that. I didn't know how to fix it. Cassie told me that you didn't want to see me anymore."

"She *did*? When?"

"The following Monday. I stopped by Stone and Faber to apologize. She accused me of trying to ruin her life. She said you both agreed it would be best if I kept my distance. But then, you texted, and well... I could really use a friend right now. I hope you're not too angry."

Confused, I took a seat on the sofa and unclipped Abby. She reached for me, so I kept her close, like a little grounding rod. Elise tucked herself into the opposite corner.

"It's hard going back home, Theo. I understand why Cassie's avoided it for so long. Everywhere I turn I think of Jess. My mom is no help. She asked me when I'm going to get my life together and start doing something productive. She called me a glorified babysitter. I told her I still want to give this music thing a try. That maybe you and I could pitch some of the songs we wrote together to a producer."

While she spoke, her eyes drifted across the cluttered room

to her guitar and songbook on the bed, surrounded by the notes I recognized as my own. The lyrics I'd jotted on a pad I found stashed in the back of the closet. I figured Cassie wouldn't miss it. "What did she say?"

"She gave me that look. The one you're giving me right now."

I tried to arrange my face into something less skeptical. "I'm not trying to kill your dreams. I know what it's like to get your balloon popped. But I'm not in the music biz anymore, and I don't want to be."

Elise stretched her hand across the sofa, grazing my knee. From my lap, Abby reached back, giggling. "You're so talented, though. Is it because of Cassie? You can tell me the truth. Danny said it's her fault you didn't sign with Soul Patch."

"Danny's just bitter it didn't work out with the band." Something else stirred inside me, pressed its way out. "Honestly though, it *is* partly because of Cassie. She's a partner in a big-time law firm. She needs someone stable. Someone dependable. A family guy. Not a gyrating wannabe who's on the road all the time."

Elise blinked at me, horrified. "Did she say that?"

"She didn't have to. Her boss insinuated it, when he pulled me aside at the first office party she dragged me to." I could still smell the vodka on Martin Stone's breath. "Anyway, we're talking about your future, not mine."

"I want to do this, Theo. For real. I have a decent voice and a lot of great material. Singing makes me feel less alone. It makes me happy." She dropped her eyes. "Is it my looks? Am I not pretty enough?"

I sighed. What the hell could I say to that? "You're beautiful, Elise. Obviously."

"Well, it helps to hear you finally say it. What if *you* managed me? Cassie wouldn't have to know."

"I don't think that's a good idea." Danny heckled me from

the recesses of my mind, pointing out the trouble I'd gotten myself into. I shouldn't have come here. "Actually, I know it's not a good idea. In fact, it's a very bad one."

"You sound just like my mother."

"You told her about me? Managing you, I mean."

Elise's cheeks flushed. "Of course I told her I knew Theo Copeland, Sluggers' frontman. That was the only thing she was excited about. She used to watch *Starbound* every week. But she told me to be careful, since you belong to Cassie."

"That's a strange way to put it."

Her laugh came out strangled. "It's only strange if you don't know Cassie, right?"

"Right." I had no clue what she meant. Only that she expected my agreement. "Hey, I should probably head home. It looks like you've got some unpacking to do, and—"

"It's okay if you like me, Theo. We're just friends. Cassie can't be mad about that."

The hell she can't. "I really do have to run." I stood up, bringing Abby with me, and plunked her back in the stroller. "I'll think about your offer. At the very least, I can give you my former manager's number."

"And you'll help with a demo, right? You'll look at some headshots? Maybe I'll try out for that new singing show on SFTV."

"Uh, yeah. Okay. Sounds great." I sidestepped around her and made a break for the door. Then, I spotted it on her desk. A framed version of the photo I'd seen in the *Gazette*. The three of them, Cassie in the middle, arms wrapped around each other's shoulders. I forced myself to turn around, half expecting Elise to be right behind me. She watched me from the sofa.

"Are you sure you're okay?" I asked. "You know, there's no shame in needing help. My mom saw a therapist for a while after we lost my dad. I can get you her name."

She waved me off with a faint smile that only made me feel worse. "I'm better now. Much better."

Theo the House Husband spent the rest of day doing penance. I cleaned all three toilets. Twice. I made Cassie's favorite left-overs casserole. I even steamed the outfit she'd laid out for Monday, hoping my guilt would disappear like the creases in her silk blouse. I hadn't done anything wrong. But I'd been inside Elise's space. I'd seen her goddamned lingerie. *Red and lacy*. If my wife found out, she would blow a gasket.

I settled in with Abby on the sofa, ready to read from her favorite book. The phone's ringing jarred me. Elise. *Shit*. I let the call go to voicemail. While Abby turned the pages, babbling to herself, I listened to the message.

"Hey, Theo. Thanks for coming over this morning. It was really good to see you again. I've missed our talks. You always manage to make me feel better. I emailed you a couple of pics. Some ideas I had for my first album cover." She sounded uncertain, nervous even. "I know it's just a pie-in-the-sky dream. But maybe someday, right? Anyway, I hope you like them."

My stomach flip-flopped as I hurried to the kitchen to retrieve my laptop from the counter, where I'd left it during my cleaning session rock-out. My Springsteen playlist was still open.

Keeping one eye on Abby, I clicked into my email account. One unread message from e_sterling. Two attached images. *Inspired by you, circa 2017*, she'd typed.

"Jesus Christ." I felt sixteen again, holed up in my room flip-ping through my dad's secret *Playboy* stash.

In the first shot, Elise posed in the lacy red bra and panties, the sky-high heels. She gazed lustfully at the camera. The second image—my *Hard Rocker* cover, recreated by Elise—hit me like a fireball to the groin. I started to sweat.

The front door opened, and my wife materialized in the hallway. "Hey, how are my two favorite turkeys?"

I took one last look at the photo before I willed my body back into submission. Lightning fast, I shut the lid. Later, I would delete the entire email. The pictures too. I swore I would.

Afraid to stand, I gave Cassie a weak wave. "I made a casserole."

It was Cassie beneath me. Cassie's fever-hot skin against mine. Cassie's nails on my back. Cassie's soft moan in my ear. But I saw another woman's face. I saw Elise. I squeezed my eyes shut and thrust into her again and again and again, thinking, *Cassie, Cassie, Cassie*. Still, I couldn't unsee it, and I didn't stop.

Cassie exhaled. I listened to her ragged breathing. "Wow," she managed, finally.

I slumped off of her, disgusted with myself, and rolled onto my back, gaze fixed on the ceiling.

"What's gotten into you, Copeland?"

I laughed a little because she expected it. "You," I said. "I missed you today."

"Apparently." She curled into me, placed her hand flat on my chest. My heart throbbed against it.

I waited for her to fall asleep. Then, I slid out from under her arm and left her there, padding down the stairs toward the kitchen. I knew I had to hurry. Cassie never slept soundly. *Another gift from dear old Dad*, she'd told me once. It hurt hearing that, picturing her as a girl beneath a fluffy pink comforter. Kept awake by the sounds of her father's anger, a wolf just outside her door.

The laptop waited for me there. When I opened it, the screen lit up, beckoning me like a moth to a flame.

I opened the email again and stared into Elise's liquid eyes.

She wanted me. I understood that now. It felt damn good to be wanted. Too good. Like a thousand pairs of eyes fixed on me and screaming their throats raw with my name. Like the stage pulsing beneath me when I sang. *That* good. I'd always wondered about the very first time my dad had strayed. Was this how it started?

My foot knocked against something soft. A quick glance beneath the table and I sighed. Abby's doll. It snatched me from the brink. Whiplashed me right back here, where I belonged. I would not become my father.

Already flooded with relief, I dropped both photos into the recycle bin and opened the search bar, typed: *How to get rid of a woman*.

TWENTY-NINE

The following day, I managed to avoid the playground altogether, thanks to Abby's well-baby checkup. Me and my guilty conscience feigned sleep when Cassie planted a kiss on my cheek and slipped out the door before sunrise. I followed the house-husband playbook to the letter, making silly faces at my daughter while I fed her breakfast; dressing her in her cutest fall sweater; and giving all the right answers at the pediatrician's office. When the doctor asked about Cassie's mealtime struggles, I'd shrugged it off. *She's doing great. They both are. It was just a phase.* Afterward, I'd taken Abby to Pier 39, tourist trap that it was, and ridden with her on the carousel. By the time we arrived home, she'd fallen asleep in her car seat and I had to lug her inside like a little sack of potatoes.

I watched her for a while as she slept. Every precious breath reminded me. I needed to be a good dad, and being a good dad meant being a good husband. I wouldn't have Abby feeling the way I had, listening at the door while my mother cried, with shame curdling my stomach. Because I loved my father desperately. Even with all his faults, I'd never wanted to be rid of him.

A soft knock from downstairs summoned me. Leaving Abby to her nap, I opened the door without thinking.

"Thank God you answered. I thought you'd never speak to me again." Bleary-eyed, Elise shuffled from one foot to the other. Her hair looked tangled; her eyes, puffy. And she might've slept in those clothes.

"Where are the twins?" I asked.

"I requested the day off. I'm a mess, Theo." She hung her head, took a breath. Then, she slowly raised her eyes to mine. Somehow her tears only made them bluer. "I came over to apologize. It was totally inappropriate of me to send you those photos. I don't know what came over me. Can you ever forgive me?"

"Elise..."

"I couldn't go on if I thought you hated me. You're the closest friend I have here. The only friend."

"I don't hate you. You've been a good friend to me too. But..." Elise's vulnerability scared me. I needed to handle her with care.

"But what?" She took a few steps backward, suddenly clumsy on her feet.

"Are you alright?"

She braced herself against the porch railing. "Honestly, no. I feel light-headed. I haven't eaten since yesterday. I couldn't stomach anything. Not after making a fool of myself."

A skeptical frown arranged itself on my face. It felt too familiar, this act. But the sounds of Abby's crying drew me back inside. I couldn't leave Elise on my porch, swooning. "Why don't you come in for a few minutes? I'll get you something to eat."

She barely nodded, leading the way inside. I followed her to the sofa, where she dropped into the cushions like she couldn't bear the weight of herself anymore.

I tended to Abby first, changing her diaper and settling her back in. Then, I hurried into the kitchen and retrieved a banana and a cold bottle of water, anxious to send Elise on her way. But the sight of her tugged at my heart, and I couldn't stop blaming myself for the whole mess. Had I led her on? Been too flirtatious? I was a Copeland, after all. I'd learned from the worst.

"Eat this," I told her, sitting down beside her. "You'll feel better."

"Theo, what you said about me getting help—"

"It's none of my business."

She laid her hand on my arm, softly stroking my skin. "No, you were right. I do need help. It's been wonderful reconnecting with Cassie, but hard too. It's brought up so many memories. I've had trouble sleeping. I'm not acting like myself."

Her fingers slid up to my chest, my neck, my face, before I stopped her, trapping her hand in mine. I placed it back on the sofa and scooted away from her. Right then, I understood my father better than I ever had before. The intoxicating power he must've felt, the heady shot of arousal, every time he seduced a woman who wasn't my mother.

"Like right now, I really want to kiss you," she said. "That's not normal."

My mouth was suddenly bone-dry. It took all my focus to swallow. She licked her lips, leaned in. I knew I could have her any way I wanted. Cassie would never have to know.

I jumped up like a man on fire and zipped to the door, flinging it open. Outside, a little girl pedaled her tricycle down the sidewalk, with her mother walking close behind her. She spotted me and waved, flashing me a smile as infectious as Abby's.

"Elise, you have to go."

"So, it went okay at the doctor?" Cassie nuzzled against me on the sofa, while we flipped through an endless list of movie options. She'd snuck out of work early—which to her meant six o'clock—to come home to us. But I could hardly focus on her. I had my own private movie playing. A double feature of guilt. Because I'd let Elise in the house. I'd let her touch me. I'd pictured her face while I made love to my wife.

"Theo? Are you with me?"

"Uh, yeah. Sorry. Just tired is all. The appointment went great. Abby's growing like a weed. She's in the sixtieth percentile for her age."

"Sixtieth? That sounds low. Do you think it's the feeding thing?"

"Sixtieth is better than average, Cass."

"I know. I just don't want to screw her up." She grabbed a throw pillow from the other side of me and buried her face in it, sighing.

I tugged at her wrists until she relented. Her expression, soft at first, contorted into something hard and unreadable. "What the hell is this?"

Dangling from her hand was a lacy red bra I immediately recognized. My brain fritzed off and on like a power surge. What could I say? How could I explain?

"Is this hers?" Cassie stood up and whipped it at me. "I can't believe you. You had sex with Elise. On our couch. In our house. Was Abby here? Oh *God*."

She fled from the room, stalking down the hallway. I chased after her, arriving just in time for her to shut the door of the guest bathroom in my face. I leaned against it, desperate to touch her. To convince her. I'd done nothing wrong. Somehow, every argument I mounted reminded me of my father.

"It's not what it looks like."

She turned on the faucet to cover the maelstrom of her sobs.

"Nothing happened between us."

"Go away."

"Please let me explain." When she didn't protest, I imagined telling her the truth. That Elise had done this on purpose. That she'd planned it. That she'd wanted Cassie to find the bra, wanted her to doubt me. It sounded unbelievable, even to me. I let myself slide down to the floor, pressed my head against the doorframe. "She came over earlier to show me some outfits for her album cover shoot. She must've forgotten it."

"I should've known." Though I feared what she'd say next, I strained to hear her anyway. Whatever it was, I deserved it. "You're no better than your father."

Later that night, I heard Cassie pad down the stairs to where I lay on the sofa, not sleeping. Sniffling, she curled into the armchair. "Just tell me one thing. How many times?"

"Zero, Cass. It never happened. I swear to you."

We sat in the dark, hurt wedged like a sharp stone between us. "Do you swear on Abby's life?"

Abby had come out with a full head of hair, showing off her lungs. As she screamed, the doctor let me cut the cord that bound her to my wife. In that moment, I made a promise to myself that I would never let them down. "On Abby's life," I echoed. "I swear."

AFTER

CASSIE

THIRTY

I spent the morning intermittently scratching at a rogue spot of oatmeal on my wool skirt. Anything to distract me from the testimony of the coroner, who established Elise's death due to three distinct blows to the head with a blunt object, and the clock which ticked on determinedly toward noon. At least Abby had eaten more than one bite this morning. Granted, it had taken fifteen minutes of willful resistance to get there. With Gloria witnessing the whole scene and relishing my struggles. Maybe I could do this single mom thing after all, if that's how it ended up. I watched Theo from the corner of my eye, feeling guilty for my thoughts. Glad he couldn't read them. I couldn't imagine sitting in his seat, contemplating life in a six-by-eight cell.

With an hour to go before the noon recess, Callaghan summoned his next witness. He glared at Theo when he spoke the name, and I understood that he would show no mercy. A gladiator in a tailored suit, this guy wanted Theo's head on a stake.

Like flowers leaning toward the sun, every head in the courtroom turned to admire Alexandra Fairchild. Even my husband's. Clad in a red sheath dress and nude pumps, she looked out of place in the dowdy courtroom. Her shiny blonde hair swayed behind her like a mane when she sashayed onto the witness stand.

I calmly pressed the heel of my shoe into Theo's toe box, recalling Alexandra's own words to me. *Men can be so simple. So obvious.* I dug in until he winced.

Ogling her isn't helping, I scratched onto the legal pad. Alexandra raised her right hand, vowing to tell the truth. For her, that would be some feat.

Wasn't ogling. Just nervous.

"Good morning, Ms. Fairchild."

Alexandra gave a saccharine simper that made me nervous. "Good morning, Counselor."

"Please explain to the jury how you know the defendant."

I waited for her to look at Theo. The way she always did. Like I was invisible. But she maintained her line of sight, straight at Callaghan. "Theo was a friend. A good friend. We live in the same neighborhood. Our children played in the park together nearly every day."

"You say that he *was* a friend? Why is that?"

"Well, you can imagine with all this business... I haven't seen much of him lately. I'm not sure if I can trust him around my family anymore. I have a young son, and it's important to me that he's exposed to the right kind of role models."

Callaghan nodded. He'd obviously never met Parker. "Did you know the victim, Ms. Fairchild?"

"Not well. We didn't have much in common. She spent most of her time with Theo. But she seemed like a sweet girl."

I risked a quick glance at Theo. He had the same blank face he'd worn after his outburst yesterday.

"What was the nature of Ms. Sterling's relationship with

the defendant?"

"Objection," I called out. I couldn't stop this train, but I could slow it down. And for my own sake, I needed to. It was barreling straight for me, another hit that would pack a wallop. "Calls for speculation."

"Let me rephrase. Did you ever see Ms. Sterling and Mr. Copeland being romantic with each other?"

Alexandra paused for longer than necessary, letting the spotlight linger on her flawless skin. A cruel contrast to my own reflection in the bathroom mirror that morning. The dark circles I'd covered with concealer. The stress breakout on my chin. The dullness in my eyes no amount of makeup could fix.

"I never saw them *in flagrante delicto*, if that's what you're asking. But I saw Elise flirting with Theo a lot. They were always sitting side by side on the park bench. He never asked any of us mothers to join him there. I found it a little curious."

The juror with the scarf looked right at me, then away. Though I couldn't see them and wouldn't dare turn around, I felt the eyes of the gallery burning on me. June's eyes too. Gloria's. Beads of sweat collected at the back of my neck.

"Did Mr. Copeland flirt back?"

A nervous titter from Alexandra. She could certainly play a part. "He's a man, Mr. Callaghan. What do you think?"

"A simple yes or no will suffice, Ms. Fairchild."

"I apologize. I didn't mean to be insulting. The answer is yes. Yes, he flirted back. But Theo was a friendly guy. He never met a stranger."

"Hmm... a friendly guy. I see." Callaghan managed to make a compliment sound downright damning. "So, you've never seen him get angry or aggressive?"

"Well, there was that one time. I think it happened in August. He and Shaun DeMarco, a man from the neighborhood, got into a shouting match, and they pushed each other. I don't recall who started it."

"What were they fighting about?"

"It sounds silly, to be honest. But it started with a drone. My son was playing with it. When it broke, Shaun became irrationally upset. I mean, Parker's just a little boy. Theo accused Shaun of staring at Elise, and Shaun told Theo he was acting jealous."

"The fight was over Ms. Sterling, then?"

"It wasn't really a fight, Counselor. They didn't come to blows. But yes, I suppose Elise was the cause when you get right down to it."

"What happened after they pushed each other?"

"They stood there, exchanging death stares. I was convinced Theo was going to pummel him. Shaun's a bit of a weakling. Not big and strapping like Theo. Then, Abby—that's Theo's daughter—she said her first word. *Dada*. As you can imagine, the whole thing was forgotten."

Dada. Abby's first word. I felt my mouth drop open. A wallop, indeed. Sometimes, the smallest lies hurt the most. But attorneys don't cry. I certainly wouldn't. I dug my fingernails into my palms and dammed off the raging river.

"Ms. Fairchild, I'd like to revisit your initial statement to the jury. You mentioned that the defendant *was* a friend. Past tense. Aside from the charges against him, did something else happen to change the nature of your relationship?"

Theo's breathing grew shallow. He looked like a caged animal, ready to bolt. "Yes, there was something."

"Tell us." Callaghan filled his voice with put-on urgency.

"Theo contacted me last night. He showed up at my house and asked to speak with me outside. Naturally, my husband was suspicious, but I agreed."

"What did Mr. Copeland say to you?"

"Only one thing, really. He begged me not to testify. He said that the case against him was so strong, and I would only make him look bad. Or *worse*, I suppose, given the circumstances. He even brought up his daughter. He said he couldn't bear to leave her. And that I should understand, because I'm a mother. I told him that I had to tell the truth. That I had to set a good example for my son. When I refused to go along with what he asked, he became quite intense."

"Intense?"

"His face turned red, and he cursed at me. He threw up his hands and called me a bitch."

"So, he became verbally aggressive. Did he tell you why he didn't want you to take the stand?"

"He didn't have to tell me. I already knew. There could only be one reason. Several months before Elise moved into the neighborhood, Theo and I shared a moment. An intimate moment. It was a mistake, of course. A one-time lapse in judgment. I feared that if I testified, he would tell my husband everything. But with the subpoena, I had no choice."

"You had no choice," Callaghan repeated. "And what type of intimacy are you referring to, Ms. Hamilton?"

"Physical intimacy, of course."

"No further questions."

With the dam inside me cracking, threatening to break, I did the only thing I could to keep my head above water. "Excuse me, Your Honor, could we have a five-minute recess?"

"On what grounds?" Callaghan could see me struggling. I suppose he had warned me. "Not a personal matter, I hope. Surely Ms. Copeland can keep her roles separate."

"I'm well aware of my role, Counselor. But I'm certain you can appreciate that Ms. Fairchild's testimony comes as a bit of shock. In fact, I suspect you intended that."

"Well, it was only twenty-four hours ago that your client attempted to tamper with my witness. Trust me, I was just as surprised as you were."

"Somehow I doubt that."

Judge Macy cleared her throat, obviously tiring of our

banter. The familiar back and forth calmed me, though, enough that I could breathe again. Theo tried to stand, wavering like a boxer, unsteady on his feet, until I pushed him back into the chair.

"Five minutes, Ms. Copeland. Five minutes."

Theo and I returned to the courtroom together, portraying a united front. Inside, we'd been cracked to the core. I couldn't back down from Alexandra. I couldn't let her win. Though anything less than clawing her eyes out fell short of a victory in my book. I lingered near the jury box, steaming. But when I spoke, I sounded cool and determined.

"Ms. Fairchild, you testified that you shared an intimate moment with my husband. What did you mean by that?"

"You want specifics?"

Nervous laughter bubbled up in the gallery, quickly doused by Judge Macy's glare. I turned to Theo, and he gave a small nod of encouragement. I hoped like hell he hadn't lied about this too. I didn't want to look like an even bigger fool. But he'd seemed earnest back in the conference room, confessing that, after he'd left our house last night, he'd gone to Alexandra in his desperation and asked her not to tell the jury about his run-in with Shaun. He'd insisted there'd been nothing between them. Not once. Not ever. That he had no idea what she meant. He'd also shared something else. A sharp little dagger of information I kept hidden behind my back. I would know when to plunge it through her heart.

"Believe it or not, I do. I want you to be as specific as possible."

"Suit yourself." She looked down at me with contempt, no doubt taking pleasure in painting me as the scorned woman. But she went no further, so I prodded her.

"Did Mr. Copeland kiss you?"

"No, he did not."

"Did he put his arms around you? Embrace you? Hold your hand?"

"No."

"Did the two of you have sexual intercourse?" It hurt to even say it out loud. But I did it. I spoke the words like any others. They were just words, after all.

"Of course not."

I relished having the upper hand for once, especially with a woman like her. The sort who thrived on rubbing my nose in her put-on perfection. "Well then, Ms. Fairchild, you're going to have to explain to the jury what you mean by intimate. Because I, for one, am thoroughly confused."

"Is that a question?"

"It's a request, Ms. Fairchild. Tell the court about this intimate moment, please."

Her cheeks flushed red. Callaghan shuffled his papers, pretending not to be concerned. I'd seen that look before in a dozen men who'd sat across from me at a conference table, negotiating terms. He'd underestimated me. He thought I'd be too afraid to demand the truth. Or maybe, like me, he had no goddamned clue what Alexandra would say next. Either way, I intended to capitalize on his mistake.

"I took my son, Parker, to the playground that evening and set him up in the baby swing, when Mr. Copeland approached me from behind and smacked me on the buttocks. Naturally, I was appalled."

"After he smacked you, what did you do?"

"I—I really can't recall. I think I gasped. I was horrified, shaken to the core."

Theo cleared his throat, drawing my attention. I returned to the defense table, reading the note he'd scrawled on the pad. I took my time before I began again.

"You say you were horrified, Ms. Fairchild. Shaken to the

core. But isn't it true that you smacked him first? That you said, 'Nice ass, Copeland'?"

Alexandra's mouth fell open but nothing came out, until Judge Macy encouraged her. "Answer the question, ma'am."

"Yes, but—"

"*Butt* indeed," I said, prompting a laugh from the jury. When the titters died down, I prepared to fire my last shot over the bow. For once, it didn't matter if I couldn't bake holiday-themed cupcakes or knit booties. If I didn't know every word to the soundtrack of Abby's favorite movie, or even make it home on time to put her to bed. I would be the winner here. The one who cut Alexandra Fairchild off at the knees.

"Isn't it also true that you once threatened Elise yourself? That you told her to watch her back?"

"She put my son's future in jeopardy. Any *good* mother would have done the same. I certainly didn't mean it literally."

"So that's a yes. You *did* threaten the victim. Perhaps that's why you've fabricated a story to make Mr. Copeland look bad."

"Objection, argumentative," Callaghan managed.

"No further questions, Your Honor."

Callaghan waved off the redirect, glowering at Alexandra while she slunk from the courtroom. For a heartbeat, I felt hopeful. As if maybe this would turn out alright. Somehow, someway, I could salvage a happy ending for me and Abby.

"It's nearly twelve o'clock," Judge Macy said. "Let's recess for lunch."

I beelined for the exit, leaving Theo alone to contemplate his fate in the dismal conference room. I swapped my heels for a pair of simple black flats and hoofed the three blocks to the Financial District, where the buildings loomed over the street like giants, obscuring the January gloom. When I spotted the construction site surrounding the Generation Gamer headquarters, reality finally hit me. Shaun would be waiting for me inside. My life was no fairy tale.

THIRTY-ONE

The building rose up ten stories, the bottom floors hidden behind a temporary mesh fence. I approached with caution, giving a quick glance over my shoulder before I slipped behind the barrier. Shaun skulked outside the entrance, his hands hidden in the pockets of his bomber jacket. He looked surprisingly twitchy for someone armed with blackmail material. I sucked in a quick breath to steady my own nerves, still frayed from the go-round with Alexandra. I'd won that battle. But this one loomed large on the horizon. I feared it would be unwinnable.

"You came," he said, letting his eyes slide over me. I wondered how I must look to him. Skittish as a doe in the forest, no doubt. Desperate too, since I'd agree to meet him here. I tried to wipe any trace of emotion from my face, the way I'd always done with my father. I knew how to survive.

"You didn't give me any other options." I gestured to the empty courtyard inside the fence. Piles of dirt and rebar dotted the ruddy landscape, giving it the appearance of a war zone. A fitting spot for an ambush. "Where are all the workers?"

"I told you." He kicked at a stray nail on the sidewalk. "I'm hemorrhaging cash. I put the kibosh on the build for now. We had to correct some issues with the foundation. And that put us way over budget."

"Forgive me if I can't muster much sympathy." I cursed Elise again, certain she'd let it slip to Shaun about the merger. Probably to sabotage me at work. Now that he'd run into trouble, he saw me as his personal cash cow. Fat and ready to take to market. "Let's get this over with. What is it you wanted to show me?"

"We'll need to go up to my office." Reluctantly, I followed him through the unfinished lobby, past the sleek Generation Gamer sign. It lay on its side, waiting to be hung behind the front desk, where a series of security monitors sat idle, their cords still disconnected. It unnerved me, being alone with him. But the alternative—that someone might be watching—was untenable. I couldn't be seen here.

When the elevator arrived, Shaun stepped inside.

"Are you sure you can't just show me down here?" I asked. A little zip of fear travelled up my spine.

"No, I can't. My computer is upstairs. Besides, I thought you'd want some privacy." The door began to close between us. I saw it as my last chance. My last chance to leave. My last chance to stay. Either choice would have consequences.

Shaun's arm shot through the slim opening, and I jumped back, clutching my chest. "I'm not going to hurt you, Cassie. Believe it or not, I'm doing you a favor. A life-changing favor. I could take what I have to the cops. And then where would you be?"

My skin prickled with a cold dread. It crept inside me and nearly made me shiver. "Right. 'What you have.' I'm dying to see it, if 'it' even exists."

"Well, there's only one way to find out."

My choice made, I joined him in the elevator, watching as he stabbed at the button with his finger. *Ten.* We rode in strained silence while I focused on the advancing numbers that appeared on the display.

"You'll like the view from up here," Shaun said, when the doors parted. As if I'd come to meet him voluntarily, just two buddies chatting it up on our lunch break. As if this wasn't a shakedown. I tried to think only of Abby. Of what I had to do to protect her. "I had them install a small balcony."

My eyes followed the marble floors, past Shaun's stream-lined metal desk, to a glass partition that opened to a concrete patio. "It's convenient, I suppose. You can leer at women from your office. Kill two birds. You don't even have to fly your drones anymore."

"That's rich, you know. You judging me." Shaun removed a flash drive from his jeans pocket and held it up, gloating, before he inserted it into the port on his laptop. With a few clicks, he opened a video file and beckoned me over to the leather chair behind the desk.

"More of your drone footage?" I asked.

Shaun stared back at me, issuing a silent challenge. But I met it head-on. Whatever he had to show me, I'd seen worse. I'd cleaned up my own mother's blood, for God's sake. I'd buried my best friend before her high school graduation. I'd stood in front of the world, defending my adulterous husband.

"You may want to sit down for this."

"I'd rather stand." Though my knees already wobbled beneath me. "Just get on with it, already."

"If you say so." The computer screen came to life. On it, a still shot of Theo's studio, empty and dark. The digital stamp in the corner read December 26 at 4 p.m. The afternoon before Elise's murder. Shaun pressed *play*.

"Remember that cuddly teddy bear your husband had on the shelf?"

I nodded, transfixed. Though I could feel Shaun studying me, I couldn't turn away as I waited for Theo's arrival at The

Spot. My voice scratched up my throat, like a dead thing clawing its way out. "Yeah, some kid gave it to him as a thank you gift for his lessons."

"Is that what he told you?" Shaun shook his head at me. The poor, pathetic little wife who believed every lie her husband fed her. I bristled, with the suspicion that I was exactly what he thought I was. "I gave that teddy bear to Elise as a gift. I'll admit I had impure intentions at the time. You already know I'm a voyeur."

"You mean, a pervert? Yeah, I know."

"It's a good thing too. Because that's no ordinary bear. It's equipped with a motion-activated camera I designed myself, and the footage comes straight to my personal laptop. I hoped Elise would put it in her bedroom and give me a private show. But then, lo and behold, she must've gone and regifted the damn thing. To your husband. She had no clue about the camera, of course. Apparently, you and Theo didn't either. To tell you the truth, after she stuck the thing in a drawer, I'd given up on checking it. Until you invited me to The Spot and I saw it sitting there. My golden goose. Even if the cops had given that bear a second look, the camera is so small they never would've spotted it."

I watched the light flick on in the studio, as Theo arrived carrying Abby. Her chunky little legs dangling on either side of his waist. I smiled in spite of my fear.

"Is this the only copy?"

Shaun nodded. "I didn't want this sort of thing on my hard drive, if you know what I mean."

I pondered for a moment, keeping my gaze on the screen. On my husband. My daughter. "How far does the footage go back?"

He frowned at me. Like he didn't understand. Finally, I would know the unknowable. I could see it with my own eyes. The truth of it, not the sordid scenes in my imagination.

"A couple of months," he said. "Elise visited a bunch of times. I watched all of it carefully. Nothing happened between them, if that's what you're wondering. In fact, your husband was nothing short of a true gentleman. He told her to get lost. That he only wanted you."

My mouth dropped a little. Tears stung my eyes. I struggled to regain my bearings, to keep my mouth a thin blank line.

"Trust me, I was as shocked as anyone."

The film played on. Theo laid out a blanket for Abby and sat on the sofa, strumming his guitar while she pretended to put her baby doll to sleep. Elise appeared ten minutes later.

My hands clasped in a death grip in my lap, I leaned in closer, studying them. Like a pair of strangers, yet so familiar to me. I felt strange too, knowing all that happened since. I wanted to stop it, to rewind. To change it all. After a while, Shaun touched my shoulder gently, and I came up for air.

"You can fast-forward if you like."

"You do it," I said.

I hustled back to the courtroom, taking my seat next to Theo. The clock assured me only an hour had passed, but looking at my husband, that seemed impossible. An hour ago, he'd been so far from me, unreachable. Now, I only wanted to take his hand. To comfort him. I made myself a promise, one I'd made a hundred times before. I wouldn't let him slip away again. I would cherish him and the family we'd made together. If we could get through this, surely we could get through anything.

"How'd it go with Stone?" he asked. "Are you okay?"

"I will be." I smiled with my whole heart for the first time in forever and whispered, "I love you."

Theo appeared taken aback, hearing it. How long had it been since I'd said it aloud? Too long. Far too long.

"Ms. Copeland?" I snapped out of my reverie to find Judge

Macy scrutinizing me from the bench, her brows raised with expectation. "I asked if you were ready to proceed."

"Oh, I'm sorry. Yes, Your Honor."

"Very well. Mr. Callaghan, please call your next witness."

After a brief sidebar with his colleague, Callaghan stood. He didn't look nearly as smug as usual. "Permission to approach the bench, Your Honor."

Judge Macy nodded, beckoning us both over.

"We have a problem," Callaghan said. "Our final witness is unavailable to testify this afternoon. I spoke with him on the phone a few minutes ago from the emergency room. He's battling a horrible case of food poisoning. He requested that we postpone until Monday, if defense counsel agrees."

Turning her attention to me, the judge asked, "Well, Ms. Copeland, are you amenable to that? I'm sure the jury wouldn't mind finishing up early on a Friday."

I hid my relief as best I could. Shaun had held up his end of the bargain. "I am. As long as the prosecutor doesn't pull another Alexandra Fairchild. It seems to me that Mr. Callaghan was simply trying to sensationalize in an effort to bolster his case against my client."

"She has a point there, Counselor. I shouldn't have to tell you that you don't put a witness on the stand who you don't trust. I won't allow you to make a mockery of my courtroom."

"Yes, Your Honor. It won't happen again."

As we returned to our respective tables, Callaghan muttered under his breath, "Easiest case I'll ever win. Sensationalize that."

After the judge adjourned the trial for the weekend, I pulled Theo into the conference room. I wanted to talk to him alone, without Gloria sitting in the backseat, hanging on every word.

"So, today didn't turn out half bad." I wasn't thinking of the coroner and his old-fashioned teaching pointer, or the way he'd tapped it against the diagram of the human head while he'd made his morbid pronouncements. *A radiating skull fracture,* he'd said. *No defense wounds. The first blow, the hardest, likely came from behind.* I wasn't thinking of Shaun and his demands. *You've got until Monday morning to make good on your promise.* I was only thinking of how freeing it felt to trust my husband again. Completely.

Theo slumped into one of the hardback chairs and loosened his tie. "Yeah, that's because it was literally half a day, and Alex made a fool of herself. Don't forget that Callaghan's still got one witness to call."

I sat beside him. "It's Shaun."

"I figured as much. Do you think he'll say anything, about the restaurant, I mean? The kiss?"

"I'm not sure. But when it comes to Shaun, we should probably assume the worst." I let myself smile again. "You know, I'm kind of glad you hit him."

"What's gotten into you?" Theo asked. "You seem... different."

"Good different or bad different?"

"Well, you're not yelling at me. So *good,* I guess."

We both laughed, and for a moment, it felt like old times. Before Elise. Before Abby even. When all we needed was each other. "I'm sorry I didn't trust you," I said. "I should have."

"I understand why you didn't. I should've told you about the kiss. And the Internet search. The photos she sent. It all just started to snowball. I should have done so many things differently."

Theo hung his head, but I wouldn't have him feeling guilty. I grazed his cheek with my hand, lifted his chin.

"There's got to be something we can do about Shaun," he said, taking my hand, his callused fingers tender against my own. "What about the drone footage? Can we still leverage that somehow?"

"Maybe. But only guilty people throw stones. I don't want to seem desperate."

"Fuck, Cass." He let go of me, standing up suddenly, like something hot had burned him. "We *are* desperate."

"I know that. *You* know that. But the jury doesn't have to know it. Callaghan messed up with Alex. He got cocky. We scored some points with the jury. We can still win this case. You just have to believe in me."

I reached for my husband, aching to show him that I would fight for him now. *Really* fight for him. When he pulled me close, the knot in my stomach loosened. He understood. Nothing else mattered now but us.

"Did Mr. Stone say something to you at lunch?" he asked, his mouth pressed against my ear. "Should I thank him for this?"

"I just remembered that we're on the same team." I pulled back to look at him. "But Mr. Stone did once quote Norman Mailer to me before I deposed a swindling CEO. 'You don't know a woman until you've met her in court.'"

His eyes crinkled at the corners when he laughed. "I'll second that."

Before I kissed him, I made one last request. "Tell your mom to go back to her place tonight. I want you to come home."

THIRTY-TWO

Theo lay sleeping next to me, his face bisected by the sliver of moonlight through the curtain. I watched the rise and fall of his bare chest. Listened to his breathing, deep and even. He always sounded this way when he had too much to drink.

I turned my head to the monitor to check on Abby and lost my own breath at the sight of her empty crib. Then, I remembered. Theo had softened the blow to his mother by letting Abby spend the night. A win-win, really. Since we'd cracked a bottle of champagne to celebrate his return home. Drank way too much and stayed up way too late, talking and kissing like a hot and heavy high school couple.

I slipped out of bed and dressed quickly in the dark, tugging on my sweats and running shoes. I took only what I needed. It fit in a small bag I clutched at my side like a lifeline. I left my cellphone behind, charging on the nightstand. Theo wouldn't wake up—not for another few hours, at least—but I crept from the bedroom with care. Down the stairs. Out the door, into the cold. I moved like an arrow, swift and purposeful, piercing the wind. Tonight would change everything. I felt triumphant. Nothing could stop me now.

Pulling my hoodie over my head, I followed the course I'd plotted, darting through the dark streets and alleyways of the Financial District until I neared my destination. I spotted the soft yellow light in the tenth-floor window. A homing beacon, it guided me the rest of the way.

I pushed the gate open and ducked inside, making my way into the shadowy interior. I waited in the elevator bay, still breathless from the run. My lungs ached. My chest burned. Sweat dampened my forehead. For a moment, I felt eighteen again. Standing beside Jessica in the heat of the fire she'd set, astonished by what we'd done. Elise was there too. Young and tan and bursting with life, it was impossible to tell one of us from the others. Back then, I had the sense that my life lay out before me like a highway. So many roads, so many choices, whittled down to this road. To Theo and Abby and me. The three of us.

Steeling myself, I pressed the button. *Up*.

Shaun waited for me in his office, slumped in his ergo chair with a half-empty bottle of bourbon. The night air poured in through the open door to the balcony. It chilled me.

"Hi." I sounded like a kid. Looked like one too, shuffling from one foot to the other while he looked me over. "You started the party without me."

"Sorry. I wasn't sure you'd show." His voice was all vowels, soft and wet. I tossed my bag into the corner and walked toward him.

"Did you run here?" he asked.

"I do my best thinking on the run. And I had a lot to mull over."

"I'm sure you did." He poured out a glass and offered it to me. I took it, chugged it down. It went straight to my head. "So, what did you decide?"

"I'll do it. I'll kill the merger. What choice do I have?"

A quick raise of Shaun's eyebrows told me he agreed. I had no choice.

"I have information," I continued. "Something big. It'll be a deal-breaker for Player One when it goes public."

"Well, let's hear it."

I wandered toward the door and let myself out onto the balcony. The lights of San Francisco shone like a million little stars. I'd never heard the city so quiet. "If I tell you, I want an upside. A sweetener. I'm putting it all on the line for this."

Shaun followed me outside, bringing the bottle with him. He set it on the concrete ledge between us and leaned back, crossing his legs in front of him. "No offense. But you don't really have much to bargain with."

"Don't I?" I reached for the bottle and took a long pull. Then, I made my way over to him, running my hand down his chest. He giggled, burped. Giggled again. I let my fingers linger on his belt buckle. He stared at them, then gazed up at me, practically drooling.

"I thought you were batshit crazy about your husband. *Obviously*." He let out another high-pitched laugh that gave away the nerves beneath the alcohol. I wasn't the only one who knew what was riding on this.

I moved closer to him, inhaling the sweet smell of bourbon. "And here I was thinking you were in love with Elise."

He latched onto my wrist and pulled me against him. "I can be flexible."

"So can I." I put my lips on his, and he slipped his pickled tongue into my mouth. My hand snaked into his pocket, searching for the flash drive. When I came up empty, I pulled back, smiling coyly. "As long as I get the video footage from the studio and your promise to convince MetaTech to hire me as corporate counsel after the merger."

He pushed me away, fumbling a bit. "Not so fast," he

slurred. "How do I know you're not bluffing? You haven't given me the intel yet."

"But I will. I'll tell everyone. I'm going to make you a very rich man. Very rich and very powerful." With the bottle in my grasp, I took a few steps back and drank again. Then, I tugged my sweatshirt off, tossing it at him. Goosebumps raised on my arms when the cold breeze bit at the skin not covered by the sheer bra beneath. "First, I want you to watch me. You like to watch, don't you?"

Shaun kept his eyes locked on me. He nodded, his pupils big and black.

"Well, I like to be watched." I swayed my hips to the music in my head, while I shucked off my shoes, loosened the draw-string on my sweats, and shimmied out of them.

"I have emails," I confessed, running my hands over my body while I made a soft moaning sound. "Between newly retired Alex Faber, and Rick Fordham, the CEO of MetaTech. Highly misogynistic emails. He calls Melissa Scott a 'hot piece of ass', among other things. Career-ending stuff. Trust me, it'll go viral."

He let out a low whistle. "The CEO for Player One? *That* Melissa? She's a real ball-buster."

"Exactly." I let down my ponytail and shook out my hair. "Do you want to hear more?"

"I want to *see* more." Shaun wobbled, as he propped himself on the ledge for a better view. "Take it off. Take it all off."

I bit my lower lip seductively and stalked toward him.

DECEMBER 26

THE DAY BEFORE THE MURDER

Theo

THIRTY-THREE

I woke up in an empty bed with a belly full of day-after-Christmas spite. The sound of my wife's laughter travelled in from the nursery. I turned my head to the baby monitor, where I watched Cassie playing with Abby and the push-along doll stroller we'd helped her unwrap yesterday morning. A present from Grandma, it played "Rock-A-Bye Baby" whenever the wheels moved. The kind of gift that kept right on giving. I'd been awake less than five minutes and already my head ached.

I swung my legs off the bed, planting my feet on solid ground, before I reconsidered. Let my wife take the reins for a while. After last night's argument, I certainly didn't feel the need to rescue her. It started with the dishwasher—apparently, the Housekeeping Gods had anointed her The Supreme Loader —and ended in a full-on screaming match that had absolutely nothing to do with glass placement and everything to do with Elise Sterling. Since the bra turned up in the sofa cushions, we'd been arguing constantly, though Cassie kept insisting she believed me.

She had no clue how hard I'd worked for the last month to build a wall between Elise and me. I'd tried to be annoying, to be distant, to be preoccupied. Hell, I'd even tried to be direct, explaining the havoc she'd wreaked. But the more I pushed Elise away, the stronger she came back. Like one of those inflatable Bobo dolls, intent on smacking me right in the face. I couldn't stay mad at her. Not when she batted her eyelashes over those big, blue eyes and told me she'd never intended to come on too strong. That she'd acted out, fearing she was losing my friendship.

Then, she'd shown up uninvited at The Spot with a thoughtful Christmas gift for Abby. Which Cassie had regarded like a poison apple and promptly stuffed into the trash. Good thing I'd left that teddy bear at the studio. *Because you're such a softie*, Elise had told me months ago, giving my arm a squeeze before I could wriggle away. And because I *was* such a goddamned softie, I'd agreed to meet her this afternoon —one last time—to help her choose a few songs for her first demo.

With a groan, I ran a hand through my hair and padded down the hallway. Abby greeted me at the nursey door with an excited "Dada, look," while she drove the pink stroller straight into the wall.

Cassie winced, then turned to me, her face darkening. "Happy anniversary," she said, flatly.

I steered Abby away from the wall. She toddled past me, picking up speed on the hardwood. Cassie rested her hands on her hips.

"What's that look for?" she asked.

"You *know* what. The way you said it. Like I just killed your puppy."

"I didn't say it like that. But it's hard to be in the mood to celebrate, when it feels like we're falling apart."

To hear her say it out loud, with our daughter's musical stroller singing in the background, shook me to the core. Cassie wasn't a quitter. But she sounded on the verge of giving up on us. "You don't want to go to Serafina tonight, then?" I called her bluff.

"Great. That sounds about right. We'll spend our anniversary bickering and eating leftovers. And listening to that damn thing."

Abby reached the end of the hall, and the music stopped for one blissful moment. Though the instant it got quiet and left me with my thoughts, I wanted it to play again.

"What is that supposed to mean?"

"Do you know how long it's been since you've taken me out to dinner?"

"Whose fault is that?"

My wife flashed a bright smile over my shoulder. I glanced back to see Abby coming this way, carrying her baby doll by the arm. The stroller, abandoned behind her.

"I blame Elise," Cassie said, through gritted teeth. "Ever since she rode into town on her high horse, we've been out of kilter. She's constantly showing up at the studio. Showing up at our house. Leaving her lingerie in our couch cushions. Now, she's giving our daughter gifts. She can't stop ogling you. It's purposeful, Theo. She's trying to come between us. Like she did with me and Jessica."

"Are we really doing this now? With Abby right here?"

Cassie cocked her head at me. She'd been the one to insist. No arguments in front of Abby. Well, to hell with it.

"Fine, then. I don't understand what's up with you lately. You've never been the jealous type. Back in my Sluggers days, women slingshotted their panties onstage and begged me to sign their tits. You didn't seem to have a problem with that."

"I told you. This is different. *Elise* is different. She showed up here and inserted herself into our lives. I think you like it. She's beautiful. She's into music. And she's fucking obsessed with you."

Abby toddled in between us. Her little face, contorted in distress.

"'Obsessed'? Really?"

"She's not me. You like that too, don't you? Go on. Admit it. You're bored with me. You're tired of the same old, same old. You don't want me anymore."

At that, Abby sat on the floor and began to wail. Neither of us did a damn thing about it.

"I hardly see you. How could I be bored? If you want to talk about obsession, you seem pretty fixated on your supposed best friend. I don't get it. Why do you hate her so much? What happened between you two? The real story. Why won't you tell me, Cass? Are you going to make me drive to Buttonwillow and start asking questions?"

"*Former* best friend." She plucked our daughter off the ground, smoothing her hair and shushing her. But even her soothing sounds felt like an attack. "You scared Abby," she said, cradling her against her chest.

Crushed, I reached for them both, but she turned away and retreated into the nursery. "That's not fair, Cass. We both scared her."

Cassie sat in the rocker with Abby in her lap, her eyes fixed on the wall, like she'd gone somewhere else. She still hadn't answered my questions. I leaned against the doorframe, spent, and watched her bare feet push the chair back and forth.

"I'm tired of being in the middle of this," I said, finally. "I thought you trusted me. Why don't I invite Elise over and let you hash things out with her?"

"You'd love that, wouldn't you? Two women fighting over you."

"This is not about me. I know it. You know it. I'm sure Elise knows it too. Whatever this is between you, it needs to end. Now. Before it kills our marriage."

The rocker came to a dead stop. "You've got that right. It needs to end. Today. You're the only one who can end it."

"And what exactly am I ending?"

Abby's head lolled to the side as she drifted off, cocooned in her mother's arms. I had to strain to her Cassie's voice. "Your affair."

I let myself into the studio, carrying Abby in one arm and her baby doll in the other. Most days, I couldn't get enough of our daughter. Her cherub cheeks. Her mom's brown eyes. Right now, I wanted to be alone. But of course, my wife had insisted I let Abby tag along. *She loves it at the studio*, Cassie said, when she'd finally started talking to me again. But I knew the truth. Our daughter was meant to babysit *me*. To make sure I didn't spend the next hour screwing the Hamiltons' hired help on that relic of a sofa.

Like an earworm, I couldn't get Cassie's accusatory refrain out of my head. *Your affair. Your affair. Your affair.* She knew what that word meant to me. The history behind it. She'd wielded it anyway, as deftly as a carving knife, leaving me wounded. I wanted to strike back. At her. At Elise. At both of them.

Elise appeared in the doorway at exactly 4 p.m., carrying her guitar and notebook. She let herself in, waving hello, and leaned down to ruffle Abby's hair.

"Did you like the maracas?" To me, she added, "I hope they haven't been too annoying. I probably should've thought it through a little better."

I forced my rage back into its box and told myself to act normally. "It's okay. My mom got her a singing doll stroller, so..."

Elise laughed, reassuring me I'd been convincing enough. "Now I don't feel so bad."

I did though. I felt awful, knowing that those hand-painted maracas had been granted an unceremonious burial in the nearest landfill. A casualty of this whole damned mess. "Elise, I can't help you with your demo today. We need to have a talk. A serious one."

She flopped onto the sofa with a sigh. "Cassie hated the maracas, didn't she?"

"It's not that." I reconsidered. "It's not *just* that."

"Oh, God. Are you sick? Are you dying?" Her frown deepened with each shake of my head. As if she'd saved the worst guess for last. "Are you getting a divorce?"

"Not if I can help it." I took the spot beside her and looked her in the eyes. I could give her that much, at least. "We have to end our friendship. Like I explained to you before, it's starting to get in the way of things at home."

"I see. Cassie finally staked her claim."

"If you want to put it like that, I suppose she did. But she's right to do it. She doesn't trust either one of us, and I don't want to put you in an awkward position."

Elise didn't wither like I feared. Instead, she rooted both feet firmly to the ground. Her mouth set itself in a rigid line. "That's exactly what my mom said at Christmas Eve dinner. She's concerned that I'm still taking guitar lessons. That I'm writing songs. With you, of all people."

"With me? What's that supposed to mean?"

Elise shrugged one cold shoulder. "I think she's worried you're leading me on. Maybe you have been. You can't deny our flirtation. You let me sit on your bench. Alexandra says you never do that. And you talked to me about music. You complained about Cassie. We wrote songs together. Love songs. You came to my house when I needed you. You told me you wanted to help me. You almost kissed me on the sofa, Theo. You were *this* close. It's all a little confusing."

I caught sight of Abby, stretching her doll's soft arms as far as they would go. Pulling, pulling, and pulling. That's how it felt to be caught between my wife and her former friend. Sooner or later, I was bound to snap. "Listen, Elise. Our relationship is platonic. A friendship. It always has been. I've never given you a reason to think otherwise."

"If you say so."

"I do say so. Do I like you? Yes. Have we bonded over our shared interests? Have I confided in you, maybe too much? Yes, and yes. But I won't let you use me to get back at my wife for some high school drama that happened over a decade ago."

"High school drama?" Her sharp tone drew Abby's attention, and I cringed. "You really are as dumb as you look. It makes sense that Cassie picked you. She always liked to be the smarter one."

Blood boiling, I stood up. "Wow."

My voice came out louder than I expected. But not loud enough. I wanted to knock her over with it. "Is this the real Elise? No wonder Cassie doesn't want you around."

Eyes wide, Elise yelled back at me. "You want to know the truth? Cassie doesn't want me around because—"

I spun away from her, stalking toward the door. "I don't want to hear it. You've already done enough damage. I want you gone."

"Theo, please just hear me out."

I flung it open and pointed into the street, resisting the urge to grab her by the arm. "I want you gone from our lives. Out!"

"Fine. I'll go. But I care about you. I know you care about me too. I'm the one you should be with. And if not, you certainly deserve better than Cassie."

She wanted to touch me, but she didn't. Her hand came halfway to my arm before she dropped it. I wanted to shove her out the door. I needed to be rid of her. But I just waited there like a tin man while she moved past me. A walking symbol of my failures. I watched the back of her head grow smaller and smaller until she disappeared completely from my view.

Only then could I breathe again. I dialed Cassie's cell, my fingers fumbling over the buttons.

She picked up on the first ring. That gave me hope. It fizzed in my stomach like champagne bubbles.

"Hey."

"Hey, yourself," I said, trying to quiet my breath. I could feel my pulse throbbing in my throat. "You didn't cancel our dinner reservation, did you?"

"No. Did you?"

"I would never." I glanced around the studio—my guitar, my trophy—and remembered I was still Theo Copeland, the rock star she fell in love with. It gave me courage. "Elise won't bother us anymore. I promise. Can we start over tonight? Just me and you and a bottle of Dom."

"I'd love that."

I'd finally done something right. "See you tonight."

AFTER

CASSIE

THIRTY-FOUR

I straddled my still-sleeping husband. Ran my lips across his stubble. Paused at his ear to whisper, "Wake up." I couldn't wait any longer, lying here stiff as a mannequin and staring up at the ceiling.

Without opening his eyes, Theo's hands found my hips and held me there. "What time is it?"

"Past ten."

"Really? *Damn*. I'm still groggy. Champagne must be my kryptonite." When he kissed me, he tasted hungover, sour as a dirty dishtowel. But I didn't care. I kissed him back hard and let him take over.

He pinned me to the bed. With a mischievous grin, he peeked beneath the covers. "Were you naked when we went to bed last night?"

"You don't remember?"

He laid his head on my shoulder and groaned. "It's pretty fuzzy. Did we...?"

I shook my head. "You were too drunk. You passed out around midnight. Slept like a log. A snoring log."

"That's pathetic. I hope you'll let me make it up to you."

Already, he'd wriggled out of his boxers, his body warm and solid against my own.

I grinned, pulling his mouth back to mine. "When do we start?"

Thirty minutes later, a freshly showered Theo joined me downstairs for a late breakfast. Not surprisingly, Gloria had no complaints about keeping Abby till lunchtime. For the next few hours, it would be just the two of us again. I could be blissfully present with my husband. I felt like a newlywed.

"Hey, Cass?" Theo began, pouring himself a heaping bowl of cereal. I watched a rogue drip of water travel from his damp hair down his neck. "We need to talk about Shaun."

I stuffed my mouth with a bite of bagel and raised my eyebrows.

"He's testifying on Monday. I know you said not to worry. That we'd figure it out, but I am worried. I can't help it."

I kept chewing. Theo kept talking.

"You haven't mentioned anything about the merger. About what he asked of you. But I know what you're thinking, and I won't have you put your career on the line for me. You've already sacrificed too much. With the negative publicity. The leave of absence. I'm sure Stone will hold this whole mess against you. He never liked me anyway."

Finally, I swallowed, then shook my head at him. "You realize you just had an entire conversation without me, right?"

He poured the milk and pulled up a stool next to me at the counter. "In my defense, you had a bagel in your mouth."

I nudged him with my elbow and met his eyes. "Listen, I can't tell you not to worry. My advice is to let your attorney handle it. Whatever Shaun has to say on the stand, it won't be a shock to the jury. Thanks to me, they already think you had an affair."

"You did it, didn't you? You killed the merger. Is that why he didn't show up yesterday?"

"I didn't do anything."

I could tell he didn't believe me. "Jeez, Cass. Why didn't you tell me? This involves me too, you know? If you don't have a job, who's going to support Abby when I'm..."

"C'mon." With an arm around his shoulder, I tried to comfort him. But he stood up, shrugging me off, and stalked into the hallway. "What happened to being optimistic? To handling this the right way? I've changed my mind about you testifying. I think you should tell the jury your side of the story. There's a good chance they'll believe you."

Theo's fists clenched at his sides. The muscles in his back tensed. When he spun around, his eyes shone with a rare flash of anger. I thought he might punch something. Me, even. "Are you delusional? I'm going to prison." Then, softening, he added, "Maybe I deserve to."

"Theo, that's ridiculous. Why would you say that?"

He slumped over the counter, hanging his head. "Because I let her kiss me. I saw her coming toward me. After everything she'd done, I should've known what would happen. I just let her do it. Hell, I was so pissed at you that I even enjoyed it a little. Like, 'I'll show her. I'll do the one thing she keeps accusing me of. I'll kiss this hot girl.' On our fucking anniversary, for Christ's sake. I'm no better than my father."

I sat there and watched his cereal get soggy. Watched him pour it down the sink and talk to the drain.

"I love you, Cassie. So much. You and Abby are everything to me, and I ruined it. Now, your career is in jeopardy too. I won't stand for it. Please let me talk to Shaun. Let me try to make it right."

I could have told him no. Reminded him of a little law called witness tampering, that he'd already broken more than once. I had too, for that matter. But the way he looked at me, I couldn't deny him what he wanted. "I'm coming with you."

I waited for Theo in the passenger seat of the Range Rover while he approached Shaun's front door. I gazed up at the house, finding no signs of life, and beyond to the wispy clouds that smeared the gray sky. Tucking my feet against the dash, I turned on the radio to search for a song to distract myself, to drown out my worries.

Theo rang the bell, then knocked his fist against the door. He waited for a beat before peering into the nearest window. Like an actor in a silent film, he turned to me and shrugged. Returning the gesture, I waved him back.

"He's not home," Theo told me, as he climbed inside to find me humming along with a pop song. Looking at Shaun's empty house, the lightness of the melody sounded out of place. "I didn't hear a peep."

"Maybe he's hiding out. He certainly won't be happy to see us."

"What if we stop by his new office downtown? He might've had an early-morning meeting."

"On a Saturday?"

Theo dropped his chin, giving me a snide look. He had a point. I'd spent far too many Saturdays at work. But that was all going to change now.

"Alright, fair enough."

He needed no further encouragement to put the car in drive. I laid my hand on his knee, pretending we had another destination. Baker Beach, perhaps. I could dip my toes in the ice-cold water and take in the view of the Golden Gate. I made a mental note to bring Abby there in the summer to watch the dogs play in the surf. If I focused hard enough, I could feel the mist from the splashing pups. I could hear her giggle.

"Earth to Cass." Theo squeezed my hand, bringing me back to the here and now. To the neutral palette of the Financial District. To the tall gray buildings that blended so seamlessly I could hardly tell where one ended and the other began.

"Oh, sorry. I spaced for a minute, daydreaming about Abby. Don't you think she'll be missing us? I don't want to put your mom out. Maybe we should head back."

"Abby's fine. Mom too. Besides, we'll be home in thirty minutes. Forty-five tops." He flashed me a reassuring smile that briefly settled my stomach. "Can you look up the address?"

"Take a right on California." Spotting the familiar green of the mesh fence, I pointed up ahead. "It's that one."

A siren rang out from behind us. Theo slammed the brakes, throwing me forward. I followed his wide-eyed stare to the sidewalk, where a small crowd had gathered. A cop car zipped past, lights flashing, and double-parked in front of the Generation Gamer headquarters.

"What the hell?" Theo muttered. From a distance, another siren called. Its desperate wail growing closer and louder the longer we waited. So loud, it demanded action.

"Let me out." I suddenly needed the fresh air on my face. "I'll find out what's going on. Stay in the car."

I cracked the door and stepped out onto the asphalt. The sounds of panicked conversation flitted past me like a flock of wild birds. But I headed straight toward the onlookers. A woman with shaky hands stood at the periphery, holding a small white dog in her arms. The leash dangled freely at her side.

"Do you know what happened here?" I asked her.

"Bitsy got away from me." The dog squirmed in her tight grip. One of its paws, sticky red, had stained the woman's T-shirt. "She found him over there. Behind the fence."

"Found who?"

"I don't know. A man. A dead man." She raised her eyes to the sky, where the ten-story building loomed over us. It cast a long shadow. "The poor guy. They said he owned the building. He must've jumped."

I clutched my chest. I could feel my heart beneath my hand, pounding like a metronome. Predictable, steady. "How awful."

She nodded, burying her face in Bitsy's fur. I moved away from her and walked back to the car. I wanted to run, but I forced myself to take slow, measured steps. To open the door calmly.

"What happened?" Theo asked.

I couldn't look at him. "Just drive. You can't be seen here."

A block away, Theo pulled over and turned to me. "Tell me. Whatever it is."

The whole night looped through my head before I answered him. The slap of my sneakers on the pavement. The lurch of the elevator ride. The way Shaun's lip curled when he watched me dance for him. The warm cocoon of Theo's body next to mine.

"Shaun's dead."

DECEMBER 26

THE DAY BEFORE THE MURDER

Theo

THIRTY-FIVE

I exited the taxi, shielding my head from the spitting rain. After a fat drop splatted onto my cheek and another landed on my leather coat, I cursed myself for leaving my rain jacket behind. As I wiped my face, I caught of glimpse of my wife through the foggy restaurant window. Her dark hair hung loose over her shoulders, catching the candlelight. I was transported right back to the Little White Chapel, standing at the end of the aisle waiting for her to choose me. To promise forever. Only two years, but it seemed a lifetime. Marriage was like that, I understood. Some days flitted past like gulls above the ocean. Others dragged you down beneath the surface and threatened to anchor you there. You did what you had to, to keep yourselves above water. You did what you must. Even my mother's unshakable devotion made more sense now.

I had a sudden need to see my wife. To lay eyes on her. To make her understand we were in this together. I headed for the door with anticipation.

"Theo!"

The sound of my name jarred me out of my reverie. By the time I turned around, Elise closed the distance between us. Her face was wet. Rain or tears, I couldn't tell. She wiped a mascara track on her sleeve, leaving it sullied.

"Cassie sent the video to Stanford." She blurted it out too fast for me to stop her. "She couldn't stand it when Jess and I got close. She didn't want us to be there together without her. She wanted Jess to herself. I thought you should know."

"I figured as much."

"You... you did?"

"I know my wife, Elise."

"It was a setup. A dare. Cassie knew Jess would do it. We'd been pulling pranks all summer. But this one, it went too far. And Jess was eighteen. She took the rap." A gust of wind blew her closer to me. She put a hand on my chest to steady herself, leaned in to whisper. "Silas Gentry. Look it up. I can't forget it. I can't move on."

Her eyes landed over my shoulder on the windowpane. "I hate her. But I want to be her too. Do you know how miserable that is?"

The rain fell harder, but I didn't feel the sting. I focused on the blue of Elise's eyes, a fixed point to stop my mind from spinning away from me. She gazed back at me, holding me with the weight of her stare.

Unlike my racing thoughts, the scene unspooled slowly. One frame at a time, like an old-fashioned camera reel. She reached her fingers behind my neck and into my hair. Rose to her tiptoes. Drew me in. Her mouth collided against mine, the only warmth in the cold December gray.

Instinctively, I pulled back. I gaped at her, shocked at what she'd done. What I'd allowed her to do. But mostly, at all she'd revealed to me.

"Why are you telling me this now?" I asked, breathless.

"Because she's dangerous. She always has been. She'll do anything to get what she wants. Anything to win."

I couldn't see my wife anymore through the hazy pane. But

I imagined her and the way she'd light up, like she did the first night she saw me on the stage. She'd wanted me in a way no other woman ever had.

I nodded at Elise. "I know."

AFTER

CASSIE

THIRTY-SIX

Abby sat in the bathtub, splashing, without a care in the world. I emptied a cup of soapy water down her back, and she squealed. "You look like a little fish," I told her. "A guppy."

Adorably, she parroted my words in her toddler voice, bringing a glimmer of sunshine to the dark horror of the day. Theo chuckled from the doorway, watching us. I wished I could see our little family through Abby's eyes. What would she say about this night ten years from now? Would she recall the unease that clouded her mother's face, the tension in her father's jaw, the same way I did? My own childhood memories stuck to me, as unshakable as my shadow.

I watched the water swirl down the drain while I replayed the last eight hours. On the drive home, Theo had spiraled, driving too fast. *What if it wasn't a suicide? I'll be the prime suspect, Cass.* But the moment we'd retrieved Abby from her grandmother's house, he plastered on a stupid grin. Like Shaun's dead body had never existed. Meanwhile, I'd been obsessively monitoring the SFTV Twitter feed for news.

"I'll dry." Theo grabbed the fluffy towel on the toilet seat.

He scooped Abby up and wrapped her tight, planting a kiss on her forehead.

I followed them into the nursery and made myself busy. With my husband holding back a river, the dam would burst soon enough. I had to steel myself or get swept out to sea.

Theo dropped into the rocker and laid Abby against his chest. I stood there, admiring them. I tried to pretend it was any other night. But when the knock came at the front door, I was the one who flinched.

I hurried to the window and peeked around the curtain. "It's the cops," I said. "The detectives. Kincaid and Mason."

"Shit. I told you." Theo kept his voice surprisingly steady, depositing a sleep-heavy Abby into her crib. "If they try to pin this on me..."

"It's going to be fine. As far as they know, we weren't downtown this morning. So, if this is about Shaun, act surprised."

"Well, what the hell else would they be doing here? They're homicide detectives."

"That doesn't mean anything." I made a settling motion with my hands to calm us both. Before I headed downstairs, I took a quick glance at myself in the bathroom mirror, tugging my hair into a messy ponytail. I felt unusually satisfied with my frumpiness. In my lounge pants and stretched-out tee, I looked like someone's mother.

I caught Detective Kincaid mid-knock, with his fist raised and ready to summon us once more. His partner waited behind him. She offered an apologetic smile and stepped up to the threshold.

"Good evening, Cassandra. We're sorry to bother you so late. Is your husband home?"

I nodded, feeling the sudden warmth of Theo's body behind me.

"Present and accounted for." His joke fell flat. I hoped he wouldn't keep trying too hard. The less we said, the better.

I opened the door and invited them in, gesturing toward the living room. "Please, have a seat. We were just putting our daughter to bed."

"I remember those days fondly. Now that they're over." Mason gave me a nudge. "We don't want to interrupt your evening. We only need a few minutes of your time."

Her partner wasted none of it. He didn't even sit down before reaching into his pocket and laying a clear plastic evidence bag on our coffee table. It drew me in like a magnet.

"Is that...?" I dropped onto the sofa, still gaping. I could feel Kincaid's eyes on me.

"My cellphone." Theo finished my thought, with a bewildered shake of his head. "Where did you find it?"

"That's exactly why we're here." Kincaid stayed on his feet, lording it over the rest of us. It made me nervous how much he reminded me of my father. I half expected him to pummel something just for the hell of it. "Shaun DeMarco was found dead this morning outside his office building in the Financial District. All signs point to suicide."

"'All signs'?" I wondered aloud. "What signs?"

"Well..." Mason began, shutting her mouth when Kincaid cleared his throat pointedly.

"We can't get into that right now. It's an ongoing investigation. But we can tell you that officers discovered your husband's phone next to Mr. DeMarco's laptop up on the tenth floor."

"So, he had it all this time?" Theo asked. "Cassie was right. That asshole set me up." He paused for a moment, rethinking. "May he rest in peace, of course."

Kincaid still hadn't moved. He'd positioned himself directly across from Theo. His feet had grown roots there. "Let's not go jumping to any conclusions just yet, Mr. Copeland. We'll know more after we have a close look at all the evidence."

"Can I have my phone back?"

"Eventually. After we dust for prints down at the lab."

Kincaid finally budged. But the way he perched across from us, like a bird of prey on the arm of the love seat, I found myself wishing he'd stayed put. "Just for curiosity's sake, where were you two last night?"

"Here at home," Theo answered before me. "Celebrating."

I grimaced.

"'Celebrating'? Interesting choice of words. Aren't you still on trial for murder?"

Just then, Abby began to cry. She had my impeccable timing. "Theo, why you don't check on her? I'll finish up with the detectives."

I stood, and Detective Mason followed. Her smug partner remained posted up there, eyeballing Theo as he scurried up the staircase.

"Sure is convenient. DeMarco turning up dead the way he did."

"I'm not sure what you mean. He's the last of a dozen prosecutorial witnesses. As you're aware, we have our work cut out for us."

Kincaid gave a noncommittal grunt and strutted past me and out the door. Like my father, he left a wake of disapproval behind him.

"Don't let him get to you," Mason said. "He's just pissed he got the wrong guy." She must've read the confusion on my face, because she added, "DeMarco typed out a note."

"A suicide note?"

"More like a confession."

Well after midnight, Theo rolled onto his side to face me. Neither one of us could sleep. In thirty-six hours, we would be seated in the District Attorney's office, reviewing the new evidence and making our case for the dismissal of all the charges. Callaghan had begrudgingly agreed to meet me early on Monday morning. As I saw it, he didn't have much choice. His case was circling the drain, and he knew it.

"It's like I'm dreaming," Theo whispered. I could feel the kiss of his breath on my cheek. "Or I just woke up from a nightmare. I don't know what to think or how to feel. Is it wrong that I'm relieved?"

I knew his body as well as my own, and I found him easily in the dark. I laid a finger on his lips.

"You're innocent." I spoke out loud, my voice clear and bright. "And now, we have proof. That's all that matters."

He grabbed my hand and laced his fingers through mine. "Elise is still dead. Shaun too. It's not *all* that matters."

I moved closer to him, nuzzling against his neck, until there was no space between us. No way to tell where I ended and he began. "It's all that matters to me."

DECEMBER 27

THE DAY OF THE MURDER

Theo

THIRTY-SEVEN

I stumbled up the front steps, holding onto Cassie to keep my feet going in the right direction. They seemed to have a mind of their own. Three glasses of champagne and two fingers of Scotch. That's what it took to put me under the table these days. Fucking lightweight.

Abby's sitter met us at the door. I leaned against the wall and tried to hold it together while Cassie doled out a wad of cash and said good night. We'd figured on a late night. Too late for Mom to stay up with Abby. And thank God for that. I wouldn't have wanted my mother to see me in this state.

"We should probably get you to bed," she whispered.

"I'm sorry. I drank way too much." It probably sounded different coming off my drunken tongue, like Abby's gibberish, because Cassie scrunched her face at me.

"Okay, champ. Whatever you say."

I shucked off my shoes and sprawled out on top of the covers, trying to snag Cassie's waist and pull her down with me. I wanted to be close to her. To make up for what I'd done wrong.

"Be right back," she promised. "I'll get you some water."

A name bobbed to the surface of my brain. It floated like a fishing stopper, knocking around up there and giving me a headache. With great effort, I secured my cellphone from my pocket and opened the browser.

My clumsy fingers mashed against the keys. I typed, erased. Typed again. Drunk googling was clearly not my forte.

Finally, I found it. A headline in the Buttonwillow *Gazette*. I squinted at the small print, the letters swimming.

LOCAL TEEN IMPLICATED IN DEATH OF ELDERLY MAN

Police say that they have detained an eighteen-year-old Button-willow female related to the death of seventy-three-year-old Silas Gentry. On the morning of March 13, Gentry was found burned to death in his vehicle. Investigators believe that he was heavily intoxicated and had passed out in the backseat prior to it being set on fire in what detectives called a "prank gone wrong." The case remained unsolved until video evidence materialized, implicating the suspect and her unidentified juvenile companions, who apparently recorded the suspect setting the fire.

"Cassie?" There was no answer. I stabbed at the screen until the article disappeared. Until my phone grew heavy in my hand. "I still love you," I heard myself say. Or maybe I only thought it. Either way, I dropped like an anchor into a deep, soundless nothing.

AFTER
CASSIE

THIRTY-EIGHT

District Attorney Callaghan peered at Theo and me over his steepled fingers. The man had an impeccable poker face. But the dark circles beneath his eyes were a dead giveaway. So was the *San Francisco Chronicle* stuffed into the trashcan at his desk. The headline: *Gaming Executive Found Dead in Apparent Suicide, Sources Say Note was a Confession to Murder*. Still, Callaghan looked at us without blinking.

"Have you reconsidered my plea offer, Mr. Copeland?"

"Let's cut the BS, Ed." It was impossible not to gloat. I'd even worn my victory suit. The navy Carolina Herrera I'd splurged on with my first partner-level bonus. It had grown tight in the midsection since Abby's birth, but the stress of the last few months had whittled my waist back into shape. "We both know your case is shot to hell. You were wrong about my husband. In fact, I think you owe him an apology."

Callaghan had the nerve to scoff at me. But Theo spoke up before I could tell the DA exactly what I thought of him and his boring striped tie and his perfectly positioned desk chair that forced his guests to gaze upon both of his framed diplomas. He reminded me of most of my male colleagues at

Stone and Faber. They thought they'd win simply by showing up.

"It's okay, Cass. He's just doing his job."

"Thank you, Mr. Copeland. It's a shock to find out that you're the reasonable one. I always thought corporate lawyers were a bit more couth."

I offered a tight-lipped smile. "My husband is just too nice to tell you to fuck off. I don't want to state the obvious. But Shaun DeMarco confessed to Ms. Sterling's murder. Theo's cellphone was found in his possession. I expect you'll agree to dismiss all charges."

"That's fairly presumptuous, isn't it?"

"You tell me. Were any fingerprints found on the cellphone? Or the laptop, where the police discovered the letter?"

Callaghan nodded.

"Shaun's fingerprints, correct?"

Another nod. This one, even less enthusiastic.

"Anyone else's prints?"

"His were the only ones CSI could make out on the laptop. And on the cell, only his and your client's, of course."

"And was there even a shred of evidence to suggest this was anything but a suicide?"

He said nothing, which was all the answer I needed. "Exactly. So, as I was saying, you can't expect to proceed with your case against Theo. There's no way forward." I locked eyes with him. "Now, I'd like to read the confession."

Callaghan slid a single sheet of paper across his desk. I leaned forward, scanning the page. No need to read it, I knew every word by heart.

To Whoever Finds This:

I need to get this off my chest. It's been a long time coming, and I don't want anybody else to take the fall. Not even Theo, as much as I can't stand that asshole. The moment I saw Elise in the park, I fell hard. I've never had much luck with the ladies, but she noticed me. I confided in her about my financial problems, and she let me cry on her shoulder. We went out a few times, and I got my hopes up. I thought she'd be different than those other Noe Valley bitches turning up their noses at me.

The truth is that I landed squarely in the friend zone. I never had a chance. Elise was obsessed with Theo. When he came around, she wouldn't give me the time of day. She didn't seem to care that he was married with a kid. I got so jealous, it consumed me. I started to follow her with my drone. It gave me the chance to see her, even if I couldn't be close to her. Pathetic, I know. But, I liked to pretend that it was just her and me in our own little world.

On the evening of December 26, I watched Elise kiss Theo outside a restaurant in the rain... just like a cheesy movie. I wanted that so bad that I couldn't take it. When Theo left her and went to have dinner with his wife, I watched Elise break down. I saw my chance and I took it. I offered her my umbrella but she brushed me off. She had the nerve to get angry with me. To tell me we'd never be together. Suddenly, my whole life felt like a great big nothing. I'd never have the normal things other people had. I'd always be alone. I wanted to punish them for that. Her and Theo.

The idea came to me so suddenly, and once I'd thought it, I couldn't unthink it. It had to be done. Early that morning, I texted Elise, pretending to be Theo. I knew she'd take the bait. She would've done anything for him. I wore my winter gloves to let myself into the studio through the bathroom window. I laid down a tarp I found in the closet to catch the blood. Then, I waited in the dark for her to arrive. It was raining so hard that night, I started to wonder if she'd come at all. But there she was, bursting through the door, soaked to the bone. If I

*couldn't have her, no one could. I came up from behind her,
with the statuette in my hand. I hit her once, hard, on her
perfect little head, and she went down. She wasn't dead yet. I
heard her moaning. I told her I loved her. That I always
would. And then, I hit her again.*

*I didn't expect to get away with it. Even after the cops
arrested Theo, I thought someone would figure it out. I
couldn't sleep. I couldn't concentrate at work. I kept thinking
about the ripples of what I'd done. Cassie and her little girl
don't deserve that. I can't let them suffer for Theo's mistakes.
Or for mine.*

*Wherever I'm going, I hope Elise will be there waiting for
me. I hope she can forgive me.*

Shaun

I waited while Theo finished reading. His face contorted
obscenely, before he sprang up from his seat and reached for
Callaghan's trashcan. Gagging, he doubled over, leaving
Monday morning's breakfast on the newspaper's front page.
"I'm sorry," he muttered, without lifting his head. "I drank too
much last night."

I hurried to him, crouching at his side. "Are you okay?"

"It's just a lot to process."

Callaghan didn't even have the decency to shut his mouth.
"Pretty convenient, I'd say. That's one helluva detailed suicide
note."

"Are you suggesting someone else wrote it?" I rubbed
Theo's back, hoping he could hold it together. We'd nearly
made it to the end of a long and winding road. The finish line
was in sight.

"I won't rule it out. It's certainly a possibility."

"A possibility with no basis in fact. You've got no prints. No
murder weapon. No reason to believe that anything else

happened here except a guilty man putting an end to his guilt the only way he knew how."

"In *your* opinion. In mine, your husband still looks guilty."

Theo let out a rush of breath. As if he'd just been sucker-punched. He stood up and retreated to the other side of the room.

"Be reasonable about this, Ed. I don't like to lose any more than you do. But a dismissal isn't an acquittal. It won't count against your perfect record. Besides, what's the alternative? After I play the drone footage, present Theo's cellphone, and ask Detective Mason to read Shaun's note aloud, it won't matter what you think. There's no way a jury would find my husband guilty beyond a reasonable doubt. Even this corporate attorney knows that much."

Callaghan directed his attention to the file folder on his desk. He reminded me of Abby, pretending to ignore me every time I held a spoon to her mouth. "Thank you, Counsel. I'll take it under advisement."

Theo and I sat in the courtroom, listening to the gallery file in behind us. The news of Shaun's death had travelled as fast as a fire. I could feel the heat at my back. Each whisper like a tiny spark, ready to ignite.

"What if Callaghan doesn't drop the charges?" Theo whispered. "What then?"

"Then, I'll call my first witness, exactly like I said I would, and blow his case sky-high." I squeezed his hand beneath the table. "Trust me, he doesn't want to be embarrassed."

I risked a glance over my shoulder. June stared back at me. Neither of us looked away. When the bailiff called the court to order, she gave a small, sad shake of her head. As if she could see past my armor down to the dark heart of me. I wanted to run to her, to shake her. To tell her she didn't understand. She broke first, dropping her gaze to her hands, and relief washed me clean. I'd done nothing I regretted.

I focused on the here and now. The solemn jury filed in and took their positions. Scarf Woman, with a loop of red around her neck, met my eyes. I would never see her again after today. I felt certain of it.

"Mr. Callaghan, is your next witness present and ready to testify?" Judge Macy asked.

A shot of adrenaline hit my bloodstream. The rest of our lives hinged on the next few minutes. Theo's foot tapped steadily beneath the table.

"No, Your Honor. As you may already be aware, my last witness, Shaun DeMarco, is no longer available to testify. Apparently, he took his own life over the weekend."

Hearing it out loud hit harder than I expected. A chorus of gasps, and the whisper-sparks caught fire again, sending a murmur through the crowd.

"Quiet, please." Judge Macy doused the flames with a quick rap of her gavel. "I'm sorry to hear that, Mr. Callaghan. How would you like to proceed?"

"I have no other witnesses to call, Your Honor. The prosecution rests."

With that, the spotlight shifted to Theo. To me. I didn't shrink. I stood up, welcoming the attention, as Judge Macy addressed me. "Ms. Copeland, are you prepared to call your first witness?"

I relished the weight of Callaghan's stare. "Your Honor, based on the evidence provided by the District Attorney and the events surrounding the death of Mr. DeMarco, of which Mr. Callaghan is fully aware, I move that all charges against my client be dismissed."

The fire raged now. There was no putting it out, even when the judge pounded her gavel again. I felt eighteen again. In awe of my own power.

"Mr. Callaghan? How do you respond?"

The flames licked up Callaghan's tailored trousers. He looked pained. "Your Honor, it is my firm belief that Mr. Copeland is guilty of this crime."

He scowled at Theo. But the fire kept burning all around us. He couldn't stop it, even if he tried.

"However, based on the new evidence that's come to light, the People are unable to proceed at this time."

Obliterated, Callaghan disappeared into the smoke. Only Judge Macy remained, clear and bright behind her desk. An angel of mercy. "The Court hereby grants the defense motion to dismiss. Court is now in recess."

A hundred lifetimes passed in the length of her pause. The fire simmered, burned itself out. Then, "Mr. Copeland, you are free to go."

I let Gloria bake a cake in our kitchen. I let her set the table with the bone china she'd gifted us for our wedding. I even let her sit next to Abby's high chair, doling out the chicken I'd cut up for her, and didn't roll my eyes one bit at her snide comments.

Halfway through dinner, she raised her glass to her son. "I never doubted you, sweetie. I'm just so relieved this is all over."

"Thanks to Cassie," Theo said. "She's the real hero here."

Gloria withheld her agreement. I wouldn't forgive her that. She had no idea what I'd been through. What it took to get to this table, to this moment. The four of us together like nothing had gone wrong. Like my own mother, she'd been a passive observer in her life. Not me. I wouldn't be anyone's doormat.

Theo squeezed my hand. "Give me one second. I need to grab something."

He returned with a small jewelry box. I opened it, fighting back tears. He had repaired the chain on my locket. I snapped it open. Two faces smiled back at me. Theo. Abby. My entire world. "Will you put it on?" I asked.

Sweeping my hair to the side, he slipped it around my neck and kissed my cheek. I caught Gloria watching with something like envy.

"Here's to you," I said to my husband, as we clinked beer bottles. "You're an innocent man."

DECEMBER 27

THE DAY OF THE MURDER

Cassie

THIRTY-NINE

Three girls, thick as thieves, ran through the grass. Heat nipped at their backs, as the flames chased them. The smell of burning flesh raked my nose, and my eyes darted open. The dream again. Always different, always the same. The three of us. The fire. Silas, burning.

I pushed up out of the rocking chair, cursing myself for closing my eyes. For letting myself sleep tonight, even for a moment. I had work to do. I didn't dare touch Abby, for fear of waking her. But I stood over her crib, counting her breaths, and leaned down to inhale the milky smell of her skin. I could've left her with Gloria for the night, but a baby is a convenient alibi. What mother would leave a seventeen-month-old with her drunk husband in the middle of a pouring rainstorm?

With my daughter lost in a dream, I padded to the bedroom. Theo lay on top of the covers like a lump, his snoring audible from the doorway. I walked over to him, nudged his leg. Nothing. That's what a smidge of Gloria's Valium in a champagne glass will do. My hands clad in my winter gloves, I plucked his cell from beneath his hand and tucked it into my own. Later, I would power it off, drop it in a plastic baggie, and bury it with a trowel under the rose bush in the backyard.

Watching him sleep, I felt a sudden pang of affection for him. But I packed it away. It wouldn't help me do what needed doing. Punishment. Retribution. Annihilation.

Instead, I relived the moment I decided to frame my husband. I let it fill me to the brim with rage. I would need every last drop of it to see me through. After he'd called me from the studio, his voice catching in his throat, I dared to hope. I'd stepped into my backless black dress and let my hair down. Dotted my wrists with perfume. When I opened the door to leave, Elise waited on the stoop. *You tell him or I will*, she said, not for the first time. But the way she held my eyes, I could tell she meant it. *He should know who you really are, even if he doesn't want* you *anymore.*

The microwave clock read 12:45 a.m. when I slipped my gloved hands through the arms of Theo's camouflage raincoat, pulled the hood over my head, and opened the door.

I moved as fast as I could through the ghost town of Stroller Valley. The driving rain was the perfect cover. I liked the way it pounded its tiny fists against me, provoking me. Washing me clean. It gave me a place to focus my mind. I didn't have to think about what came next. How unpleasant it might be. How necessary.

I arrived at the studio shortly before 1 a.m. and let myself in through the bathroom window I'd left unlatched. Palming Theo's cell, I composed a new text message to Elise. Short and to the point, it would draw her here. Like a fox to a trap.

Workmanlike, I moved through the studio in the dark, with only the light from the street to illuminate the space. I covered my clothing with a garbage bag, shed my shoes and left them in the storage room. Unlocked the front door. Laid down the tarp a few feet from it. Secreted myself in the corner, holding Theo's statuette in my hands. Waited, waited.

When I saw her, smiling beneath the awning, my body thrummed with dread. With anticipation too. I imagined what she must be thinking. She pictured Theo inside, ready to take her in his arms. To carefully undress her, discarding her wet clothes in a pile. To make her his own. To steal him from me, sneakily, the same way she'd done with Jessica.

Elise placed her hand on the knob, and the door yawned open.

After, when my heartbeat slowed to a steady drumbeat, I stood over her body, watching her the same way I'd gazed down at Abby. It didn't bother me as much as I feared. She hardly looked herself anymore. With the rage emptied from my cup, I felt hollow. Like the wind would blow right through me. Fleeting thoughts flapped across my mind like wild birds. I couldn't catch them. They didn't stay, didn't land.

I simply followed my plan, dragging Elise to the back door and out to the dumpster, where I hoisted her through the bottom hatch. The rain had stopped, and the air felt clean. Like a new beginning. The guilt came then. I reminded myself that she couldn't smell the days-old garbage. That its slimy feel against her skin wouldn't disturb her now.

Returning to the studio, I wiped the statuette with paper towels until the blood stopped soaking through them. I stripped off the garbage bags and loaded all my trash and my blood-soaked gloves into the tarp, which I planned to toss into a garbage bin on the way home. I took a different route, all back alleys. I couldn't afford to be seen now.

In the scalding hot shower, I let myself cry. I scrubbed my skin raw. Theo slept right through it. But not Abby. She greeted me with open eyes, all-knowing. I nuzzled her cheek with my finger and whispered to her softly until she drifted off again.

"Sleep tight, sweet girl. It's you and me now."

EPILOGUE

SIX MONTHS LATER

I let myself in the house and dropped my briefcase by the door. Already, I heard Abby in the kitchen. Her bare feet padded against the floor. When she rounded the corner, her eyes brightened. She let out a squeal of delight, confirming I'd made the right decision. Since I'd left Stone and Faber to work at a boutique firm in the city, I always made it home by dinner time. I took vacation. I slept in weekends when Abby allowed it. I managed date nights with Theo and had even purchased him a brand-new studio space with the generous severance package Mr. Stone used to buy my silence. Those emails leaked anyway. The merger fell through. But I had nothing to do with it. Cross my heart.

"Mama. Up." I hoisted her in my arms and carried her toward the sound of Theo's voice. I studied him from the doorway. My husband. Hunched over the counter and cutting up strawberries, singing under his breath. He arranged them in a face on Abby's plate. The whole scene warmed me like the sun. I had a real family. Not the kind of toxic waste dump I'd grown up in.

When Theo spotted me there, he set the knife in the sink

and levelled me with a look. I surrendered Abby to her booster seat and deposited her snack in front of her, ignoring her willful pout. After a moment, she started eating. It still felt like a victory every time a morsel I offered disappeared into her mouth.

"I know what you did, Cassie."

The solid ground dropped out from beneath me, sending me into a free fall. Stomach in my throat, it all flashed back to me. I scoured my memory. Where had I gone wrong? The teddy bear footage from that night crunched down the garbage disposal before Theo woke up. Shaun's lifeless fingers carefully pressed against Theo's phone. His death ruled a suicide. The bear itself I'd quietly donated to Goodwill. I'd even told Theo about Silas, confessing how jealous I'd been of my two best friends. How I'd emailed the footage from a dummy address the next morning, before I realized the extent of what we'd done. How getting Elise and me out of trouble was the only thing my father ever did for me.

Theo couldn't know how close I'd come to destroying him. How wrong I'd been about him. How I should've trusted him all along, with my heart, with my secret. He didn't know the mistakes I'd made. And he never would. Except—

"*I know.*"

He reached behind him and slapped a sheaf of paper onto the island counter. I almost laughed with relief.

"You lied to me about the contract with Soul Patch. I was looking for Abby's baby book, and I found a copy in the garage. Danny was spot on. It *was* a sweet deal."

Tears sprang to my eyes, and I squeezed them out. "You're right. I'm so sorry. I wasn't truthful about the terms they offered. I was six months pregnant, and I couldn't imagine raising a baby with you gone. Touring. It was selfish of me. Hypocritical too. God knows, I asked too much of you so many times."

"I can't believe you tanked my career, Cass. And worse, you've been dishonest with me about it all this time."

I wiped my face and dared to look at him. "I know. It's unforgivable. But I'm not the same person anymore. Not after what we've been through."

"What if I wanted to get the band back together? What would you say then?"

My chest tightened like a vise, but I managed to speak. "If that's what you need to be happy, I'm in full support. You're talented, Theo. You're a literal rock star. I've always known it."

A smile cracked his face, crinkled his eyes. Lit him up from within. I waited for him to tell me the life we built was over. That I was about to lose him again to his own ambition. "What makes me happy—what I *need* to be happy—is right here in this room. I'm disappointed that you lied to me, but the Sluggers ship has sailed. I just wanted to hear what you'd say. That you'd support me, no matter what."

"Oh." The tension rushed from my body like a ghost passing through it. I walked to Theo's outstretched arms and collapsed against him. *Pure bliss.* Until I spotted a plate of cookies over his shoulder, wrapped in cellophane. A note attached read:

Thanks for lending me your muscles!

Lila

"Who's Lila?" I asked, pulling back to look up at Theo. He dropped his arms, leaving me cold.

"Our new neighbor. She and her daughter just moved into Shaun's old house. I helped her carry some boxes yesterday." He turned toward the counter and lifted the wrapping to remove a single cookie. He held it out to me, offering a bite. "She sells these online apparently. They're delicious."

I took a nibble. The chocolate melted on my tongue. "Not bad."

"Abby loves them."

I resisted an eyeroll and wrapped my fingers around his bicep instead, giving it a playful squeeze. My wedding band shimmered in the light. "I hope Lila knows these muscles belong to me. If she comes near them, I'll have to kill her."

I winked at my husband so he could be absolutely sure I was only kidding.

A LETTER FROM ELLERY KANE

Want to keep up to date with my latest releases? Sign up here! We promise never to share your email with anyone else, we'll only contact you when there's a new book available, and you can unsubscribe at any time.

www.bookouture.com/ellery-kane

Thank you for reading *The Good Wife*! With so many amazing books out there, I am honored you chose to add mine to your library.

One of my favorite parts about being an author is connecting with readers like you. You can get in touch with me through any of the social media outlets below, including my website and Goodreads page. Also, if you wouldn't mind leaving a review or recommending *The Good Wife* to your favorite readers, I would really appreciate it! Reviews and word-of-mouth recommendations are essential, because they help readers like you discover my books.

Thank you again for selecting *The Good Wife*! I look forward to bringing you many more thrills, chills, and sleepless nights.

www.ellerykane.com

facebook.com/TheLegacyBooks

twitter.com/ellerykane

ACKNOWLEDGMENTS

I found my inspiration for *The Good Wife* after watching the intense thriller *High Crimes*, starring Ashley Judd and Morgan Freeman, which tells the tale of an attorney who defends her husband in military court, after he is accused of war crimes. The story of *The Good Wife* was born from a single *what if*: what if a wife defended her husband in the murder trial of his supposed mistress? What would motivate her to stand beside him? And would her support have any ulterior motives? As with all my novels, I try to create characters who are equal parts hero and villain, and I hope you'll agree that both Cassie and Theo fit the bill.

I owe a tremendous debt of gratitude to you, my avid readers, for joining me on my writing adventure. Hearing that my words have impacted you is a little bit of magic, and knowing that my stories have a special place in your heart makes it all worthwhile. A special thanks to Ellery's Entourage, whose members go above and beyond in supporting my work!

I am fortunate to have a fabulous team of family, friends, and work colleagues who have always been there to support and encourage me on this journey. Though my mom is no longer with me, she gifted me her love for writing, and I know she's cheering me on even though I can't see her. Thanks, too, to my dad, who's never been a reader but thinks I'm brilliant anyway.

To Gar, my special someone and partner in crime, thank you for patching all my plot holes without complaint; for helping me craft *The Good Wife*'s many courtroom scenes and letting me pretend that I'm a lawyer; for cheering me on when I need it most; and for championing my dreams as much (and sometimes more) than I do. I know you don't believe me, but I couldn't do any of this without you.

I have been unbelievably fortunate to be matched with an amazing editor, Helen Jenner, and a fantastic publisher, Bookouture, who truly value their authors and work tirelessly for our success. It's been a pleasure to team up with Helen and the entire Bookouture family, including Kim, Noelle, Jess, and Sarah, who have worked so hard to spread the word about my books.

Lastly, I have always drawn inspiration for my writing from my day job as a forensic psychologist. We all have a space inside us that we keep hidden from the world, a space we protect at all costs. So many people have allowed me a glimpse inside theirs—dark deeds, memories best unrecalled, pain that cracks from the inside out—without expectation of anything in return. I couldn't have written a single word without them.

Made in the USA
Las Vegas, NV
20 October 2022

57808583R00219